MAKING MY WAY TO HARLEM

A Novel About the Harlem Renaissance

Inquiries should be addressed to:
Pairee Publications
3363 East Commerce Street
Suite 12
San Antonio, Texas 78220
www.paireepublications.com

ISBN 978-1-7371818-5-9

Interior Design by TWA Solutions and Services

Cover Design by Avista Products

Printed in the United States

To my children, Theresa, Keith, David, and Carrie.

To my grandchildren, Jason, Scottie, Britteney, Jordan, Daniel, Alana, and Amaya, and my greatgrandchildren, Sanaa, Kingston, Makhai, Luscious, Jayce, and Mila.

Acknowledgments

My primary acknowledgment is to God, who has blessed me with the ability to write.

I must also acknowledge the inordinate amount of historical literature I read to prepare for writing this novel. I must acknowledge all the students who were in my class on the Novelists of the Harlem Renaissance at the University of Texas at San Antonio, who encouraged me to keep reading and writing until I finished my desire to write on this subject.

I extend a special thank you and acknowledgment to my cousin, Elliott Williams, Jr., who took time for a couple of weeks to accompany me on my visits to Harlem so I could become familiar with the streets and businesses featured in this story. I had to visit Harlem on two different occasions to become comfortable writing about a place where I did not live. At the time, Elliott lived in New York and was familiar with the Harlem community.

I also want to acknowledge Jessica Tilles of TWA Solutions, my outstanding editor and interior designer, and Carl Booker of Avista Products who did the front cover.

Finally, as always, I gladly acknowledge my wife, Venetta Williams, who is my support and strength behind every one of these endeavors I have undertaken over the years.

MAKING MY WAY TO HARLEM

A Novel About the Harlem Renaissance

Frederick Williams

Pairee Publications LLC
San Antonio, Texas

Foreword

by Danny Glover
Academy Award Recipient of the
Jean Hersholt Humanitarian Award
Recipient of the NAACP Image Award

Novelist Frederick Williams has brought to life on the pages of his historical novel, *Making My Way To Harlem,* the majesty of that grandeur period in our cultural history known as the Harlem Renaissance. Within the pages of this novel, you will meet Langston Hughes, Countee Cullen, Dr. W. E. B. Du Bois, Zora Neale Hurston, Jessie Fauset, A. Philip Randolph, James Weldon Johnson, Alain Locke, and many other artists who made this period so fantastic. You will walk down 135th Street and Lenox Avenue to the famous 135th Street Library, where Regina Anderson held poetry readings and intellectual conversations among the literary elite of the community.

Williams does not just concentrate on the artistic community. He takes you to the other side of Harlem, where the majority of the people reside. You visit a rent party and a tenement apartment, places where people struggle to survive. He introduces you to Casper Holstein, the most successful banker for numbers in Harlem. You will also visit the famous

Harlem nightlife with stops at the Cotton Club, Connie's Inn, and the Sugar Cane Club. There are also scenes at the Amsterdam Theater in Lower Manhattan with the Ziegfeld Follies.

This story is told through three characters who make their way to Harlem from different parts of the country and for different reasons: Sam Arthur, a field hand in Gaffney, South Carolina, who leaves the South because of an altercation with a white man; Nina Jackson, a young high school graduate from St. Louis, Missouri, leaves right after graduation and goes to Harlem because she wants to dance with Florence Mills; and finally Marcus Williams, a reporter with the *Chicago Defender*, whose editor, Robert Abbott, sends him to Harlem to cover the artistic explosion taking place in the community known as the Negro Capital.

Making My Way To Harlem is the first historical novel about the Harlem Renaissance since Richard Bruce Nugent's *Gentleman Jigger* written in 1930 and Wallace Thurman's *Infants of the Spring* written in 1932. Nugent and Thurman were part of the Bohemian writers who defied the conventional style of writing. Williams has scenes with both Nugent and Thurman in his novel.

For readers who love history and enjoy being entertained with a good story, this has to be on your reading list.

PROLOGUE

Gaffney, South Carolina
June 1925

SAM ARTHUR STARED UP AT the sun beating down on him and the other ten Black men chopping weeds in the cotton field right off the main road in Gaffney, South Carolina. Sam, a twenty-three-year-old, dark-skinned man, with muscles rippling through a thin work shirt, stopped chopping and pulled a large rag out of the pocket of his overalls. He wiped the sweat streaming down his face and into his eyes. Just after two o'clock in the afternoon, he still had another half-row of weeds to chop before the end of the day. The scorching June sun had turned him jet-black as it had done to the other men in the field.

He stared over at Jethroe in the next row, and it looked to him that his best friend could hardly make it. They'd already been in the field for six hours and they still had four more hours to go.

"Hey, boy, you all right?" Sam Arthur shouted to Jethroe.

"Got no choice but to make it. Ol' man Shackleford, he'd fire us if we act like we want to stop. Hell, and I need the money. Ain't much, but I sure need it."

"I guess you do." Sam Arthur smiled. "Got all them kids to feed, you ain't got no choice."

"Hey, boy, you ain't far behind." Jethroe chortled. "You 'bout to get married and good as that woman of yours look,

1

she gonna be havin' babies every year. Won't be long you be done caught up with me and Emma."

"Watch your mouth, boy. I know how good my woman look. Don't need no field hand like you tellin' me."

"What you think you is, a house nigguh?"

"There you go. Ain't nobody said nothin' 'bout no house nigguhs. I'm too black to be a house nigguh."

"You got that right." Jethroe laughed, then paused for a moment before he changed the subject. 'What you doin' this evenin'? Old Luther's in town and gonna be over at the club, playin' the blues all night long."

"Don't know. Got to check with Willa Mae. See what she want to do."

An older Black man in the row on the other side of Sam Arthur shouted, "You boys stop all that talking and get back to work. You get us all in trouble if that white man come out here and see we ain't working."

"Old man, shut up!" Jethroe yelled. "You always worryin' 'bout what that man gon' say. Ain't nobody worried 'bout him. We gets the work done and that's all that counts."

"Boy, you young and stupid!" The old man straightened up and glared over at Jethroe. "This ain't no place for talk. Save that for later."

"He right, Jethroe." Sam Arthur bent over, resumed chopping the weeds around the cotton, and continued without looking up. "Man see us out here talking and he'll think we got too much idle time and find a way to beat us out our pay."

Jethroe refused to be deterred. He raised the volume in his voice. "Man, I hear them nigguhs up north be doin' it. They ain't pickin' no goddamn cotton. They dressin' real sharp and sure don't take no shit off white folks."

The old man now stood straight up and stopped chopping. "Boy, you ain't heard nothin' but a whole lot of talk. Ain't nowhere in this world that nigguhs ain't got to take a whole lot of shit off white folks."

Sam Arthur also stopped chopping, "Where you hear that from, Jethroe?"

"Ms. Dana, over at the Pig Feet shack, got a brother who works on the trains. I was over there the other night, and he was tellin' all the boys how he go up to New York once a month and say they even got nigguh cops up there."

"Ain't no way you believe a darkie gonna carry a gun around white folks." The old man smirked. "Boy, you'll believe anything."

"He ain't got no reason to lie to me, old man. What you think, all Black folks living fucked up lives like we do?"

"Come on now, Jethroe, we ain't got it that bad." Sam Arthur again pulled the rag out of his pocket and wiped his face. "We ain't no slaves. We can up and leave this place when we get ready."

Jethroe glared over at Sam Arthur. "Man, what you talkin' 'bout, we ain't slaves? Only difference between us and our grandparents is that they don't have no papers on us. But we work our asses off for 'bout nothin' and we don't even own a damn thing. And that motherfuckuh can fuck with your woman whenever he wants to."

Sam Arthur cringed.

"Yeah, you freeze up, boy, 'cause you know damn well what I'm talkin' 'bout. Everybody know Luke Shackleford got his eyes for Willa Mae."

"Don't give a damn what that white boy got eyes for, just as long as he don't try nothin'." Sam Arthur went back to chopping the weeds.

"You better pray to God he don't decide he want to do somethin' 'bout it. He'll kill you just to get to her."

Sam Arthur stopped again and looked up. "That's what he'll have to do, 'cause I sure gonna kill him," Sam Arthur snarled. "Ain't no slavery times when white man could just take a Black woman, no matter what the Black man felt. Them days is gone."

"Maybe up in New York they gone, but you know damn well they ain't gone down here. Ain't I right, old man?" Jethroe looked in the old man's direction, who still stood upright, listening to the conversation.

The old man stared up at the sun for a moment and then over at Sam Arthur. "He's right. They got all the guns, and they got all the money, so they can do whatever they want to do, no matter what. The bastards can cheat you out your pay, they can run you off the land, and they sure as hell can take your woman and kill you if you don't like it. Ain't much changed, except we can leave out of here if we want to."

"Maybe Willa Mae and me will leave after we get married and just head up north. That way I won't have to worry 'bout Luke Shackleford." Sam Arthur bent down and went back to work. He spotted old man Shackleford on top of his stallion, riding up from the rear of the field.

Sam Arthur sat with his large right arm around Willa Mae's neck, sipping on a bourbon drink brewed in the back of Ms. Sadie's Blues Club located right on the outskirts of town on the Black side of the railroad tracks. Jethroe and Emma sat on the other side of the table cuddled up. The club's exterior was an old wooden structure, while the interior had space for twenty wooden tables, each with four wooden chairs, lined up against the inner walls, leaving the wood plank floor in the center open for dancing. A string of lightbulbs, hanging from a lowered wire from the ceiling, lit up the club. At the back end of the club was a bar area with chairs. On the right side of the bar, there was an elderly Black man with short gray hair on the sides of his head and a bald patch in the center. He was seated on a stool, playing a guitar.

In his raspy voice, the man sang while plucking on the guitar.

"Hard time here and everywhere you go.
Times is harder than ever been befoh."

Jethroe smiled over at Sam Arthur. "Times sure gettin' bad for the Negro down here since them men come back from the war and actin' like they supposed to be equal to the white man."

"Ain't supposed to be equal, is equal." Sam Arthur took his arm from around Willa Mae's neck and leaned forward. "Negro got to start standin' up for himself the way they do it up north."

"We ain't got the same rights they got up there." Jethroe took a sip from his paper cup.

Emma leaned forward. "No, no, none of that talk in here. Y'all leave that talk for the fields. We gonna enjoy ourselves this evening and not worry 'bout that man."

Jethroe leaned back and put his arm around Emma. "You right, baby. You right."

"And the people they all drifting from door to door.
Can't find no heaven, I don't care where you go."

Sam Arthur pulled Willa Mae in close to him and kissed her on the cheek. "I don't know what that old man singin' 'bout, 'cause I got my heaven rights here. Ain't that right, baby?"

Willa Mae snuggled in closer to Sam Arthur and laid her head on his shoulder.

"Well, you hear me singing; my lonesome song,
These hard times can last us just so long."

The old man ended his song, got up, and walked over to the bar and sat down.

Jethroe looked at Sam Arthur. "You ready for another drink?"

"No, I got to get Willa Mae home 'fore midnight, and it's already after eleven."

Willa Mae smiled. "That's alright, baby. Go ahead. I'll be alright."

Sam Arthur smiled. "With that permission, I guess I will have another."

"You got it." Jethroe got up and headed across the dance floor to the bar.

Instantly, the door to the club swung open. A white man dressed in a suit, wearing gloves and holding a riding stick in one hand, looked around and spotted Sam Arthur and Willa Mae.

With his back to the man, Sam Arthur didn't see him enter the club, but Emma did, and a frightened expression spread across her face as she sat straight up in the chair. The rest of the men and women in the club who saw him enter also sat straight up.

Jethroe, standing at the bar, saw the man come in. "Oh hell," he scowled and hurried back to the table. "Sam, behind you!"

Willa Mae raised up from Sam Arthur, who looked behind him just as the man swung the riding stick back, bringing it forward, aiming to strike him. Sam Arthur jumped up from the seat, and just as the stick came down, he grabbed it and yanked it out of the man's hand.

The man stood there, looking at Sam Arthur, and then looked over at Willa Mae.

"Told you, boy, to stay away from this woman. Told you I'd fire you if you didn't."

Jethroe got between Sam Arthur and the man. "Mr. Shackleford, sir, you can't come in here like this. Please, sir, please don't do this."

Sam Arthur pushed Jethroe to the side. "Don't beg that peckerwood for nothin'." He moved in closer to young Shackleford. "Me and Willa Mae 'bout to be married, and I'll kill you if you come around tryin' to mess with her or any of these women."

Jethroe grabbed Sam Arthur by the arm, trying to pull him away. "Sam, man, come on. You cain't threaten to kill that man. We all works for his daddy." He then moved in closer to young Shackleford. "Mr. Shackleford, please, sir, he don't mean all this talk."

Young Shackleford again looked at Willa Mae, who looked away. He ignored Jethroe and moved closer to Sam Arthur. "Boy, you fired. Get your ass off my property by morning."

Sadie, a large Negro woman behind the bar, finally came around with a shotgun in her hand. "I don't want no trouble in my club, but ain't gonna be no shootin' and killin' in here lest I'm doing it." Sadie stood next to young Shackleford. "Boy, I know your daddy and know he'd be spitting mad about you coming in my club and causing this trouble. So why don't you just go on home, and you all work this mess out somewhere else?"

Young Shackleford looked one more time at Willa Mae, who still looked away. He then looked at Jethroe. "If you let him stay at your place then you fired, too. You got too many kids and wife to take care of to stick up for him." He turned his gaze on Sam Arthur. "Be gone in the morning or the sheriff will be there to put you off." He snatched his riding stick out of Sam Arthur's hand, turned, and stormed out of the club.

Silence reigned as no one knew exactly what to say. Finally, Sadie broke that silence. "Boy, you got to get out of here tonight and I mean you got to get out fast."

Stunned by what had just happened, Sam Arthur first looked over at Willa Mae and then at Jethroe. "I ain't got nowhere I can go. Can't stay here at nobody's place."

Sadie shook her head. "No, no, you don't understand. You got to get out this town and this state. In the morning, them white folks gon' come for you. You can't challenge no white man in this town and think you can stay here."

Willa Mae finally jumped up and grabbed Sam Arthur by the arm. "I'll go with you. We can leave tonight."

Sam Arthur hugged her and then pushed her away. "No, I can't have you do that."

"How much money you got?" Sadie asked.

"Not much. We get paid on Monday."

"Well, you can forget 'bout that Monday 'cause ain't no way they gonna pay you and you got to be out of here tonight. Don't go back to your place 'cause they might be waiting for you there."

Sadie tucked her big hand inside the top of her dress and pulled out a wad of dollars. She counted a number of bills. She then looked at Jethroe, took the keys to her truck out of her pocket, and handed them to him.

"You got to drive this boy up to Charlotte, North Carolina. There he can get a bus north to anywhere he wants to go."

She handed Sam Arthur the money. "This enough money to get you all the way to New York if that's where you want to go. Understand plenty Black folk make their way up there into that Harlem area where there's so many of us they'll never find you there."

Willa Mae threw her arms around Sam Arthur, grasping him tightly. "No, baby, you can't leave. We supposed to get married. You can't do this."

Emma got up, hurried over to Willa Mae, pulled her away from Sam Arthur, and hugged her. "It'll be all right. He just gonna find a new place for you all and you can join him after this all is over."

Still obviously stunned, Sam Arthur tucked the money in his pocket, turned, and looked at Willa Mae. "Baby, soon as I get to the Harlem, I'll get you up there and we can get married. I ain't ever gonna lose you, not never."

Pulling away from Emma and rushing back to Sam Arthur, Willa Mae hugged him. "You promise you gon' come back and get me?"

Sam Arthur stared at Jethroe and then kissed Willa Mae. "Yes, baby, I'll be back to get you. I promise you, baby."

"You got to go, boy," Sadie scowled. "Them peckerwoods might try to come back in here and if they do, I'll have to shoot 'em 'cause I ain't gon' let them take you. I ain't ready to die and ain't ready to go to jail. So, get going. Don't worry 'bout this girl. We'll watch after her."

Jethroe tugged at Sam Arthur's arm. "Let's go. I got to get up there and back case them white folks come to my house. And we got to do it before old man Shackleford finds out what happened and puts the police on us."

Jethroe pulled Sam Arthur toward the exit. He kept looking at Willa Mae. "I ain't gon' lose you, baby. I ain't. You'll hear from me soon as I get to Harlem. I ain't gon' lose you."

They exited the club, ran around the back to the truck, got in, and drove off down the road.

⚜

St. Louis, Missouri
June 1925

THE PACKED AUDITORIUM OF PROUD, well-dressed men and women sat looking up at the fifty students standing on stage at Booker T. Washington High School. Principal Woodrow Jones, a tall, slim, Black man, also stylishly attired and wearing horn-rimmed glasses, strolled up to the podium at the front of the stage.

"Good evening to you, proud parents, friends, and relatives of these fifty young men and women who will graduate from high school this evening. This is a very important day for Booker T. Washington because today these young folks will walk across this stage and receive their high school diplomas, placing them in a very select category of our race."

Standing in the first row at the end, beautiful fair-skinned Nina Jackson grabbed the young boy's hand standing next to her. Claude Lee squeezed her hand, smiled, and then released it. They had been together since elementary school and claimed they someday would spend their lives together. But Claude, who had received a full scholarship to Howard University in Washington, DC, would attend college with plans to become a lawyer, then return to St. Louis and they would be married.

Earlier in the day, while they were alone at Nina's home, he asked her to promise to stay put in St. Louis until he graduated. She refused to make that promise because she had plans of her own. Standing next to him, she grabbed his hand as a gesture of making up. He held her hand only for a short time, then released it. She knew he was still upset with her, but she had plans of her own.

"I'd like to ask both Nina Jackson and Claude Lee to step forward." Principal Jones turned and looked back at the two. "Nina was our school queen and Claude, the most outstanding student with straight 'A's' for three straight years."

The two strolled up to the podium and stood next to Principal Jones. "Do you young folks have anything you'd like to say? This is your time to shine."

Claude stepped up to the podium. "I love Booker T. Washington High School and it will always have a special place in my heart. And, of course, I am so thankful to my mother and father, who are out there in the audience, for the wonderful opportunities they have given me over the years. I look forward to leaving here for Howard University and then on to law school and coming back home to practice law. Thank you." He stepped back.

Nina slowly stepped up to the podium. "I also am thankful for what Booker T. Washington High School has done for me and thankful to my mama, who couldn't make it here this evening, but gave me a wonderful childhood and now almost an adult life. Many of you have attended my dance performances here at the school, so now I plan to take my talents, hopefully, to Harlem, New York, and make a career as a dancer, just as Florence Mills and Josephine Baker have done. Thank you."

After a brief applause for the two, Principal Jones now stood at the podium. "Now it is time for all of these young people to get their diplomas and so, as I call your name, please come forward."

Strung along the wall of the school's gymnasium were banners reading "Congratulations to the Graduates of Booker T. Washington." Strings of balloons extended from the ceiling. White tablecloths covered tables lined along the walls as a five-piece band played lively music, creating a joyful atmosphere. Many of the graduating students gathered at the center of the floor and started dancing, celebrating their special day.

Claude and Nina sat pensively and quietly next to each other at a table close to the band. Nina wanted to dance, and Claude couldn't dance, so she didn't press the issue. She also knew he was still upset with her announcement of her plans to move to New York. She loved Claude, but she also loved dancing just as much. Many nights she lay in bed, imagining herself dancing in the musical *Shuffle Along*. She smiled as Principal Jones strolled up to the table and sat in one of the empty chairs.

"You two enjoying yourselves?"

"Yes, sir," Claude said.

Those are the first words he's spoken since we arrived at the prom over an hour ago, Nina thought. "Yes, sir, we certainly are."

Principal Jones looked directly at Claude. "I understand you have a work permit and you'll be doing chores for Dr. Woodson in the History Department at Howard. You are certainly fortunate because Dr. Woodson is one of our outstanding scholars on Negro history."

"Yes, sir. I've made up my mind to do my bachelor's degree in history and then, of course, go on to law school right there."

"Based on your excellent work here at Booker T. Washington, you will represent the school quite well and we'll all be proud of you."

He turned his chair, facing Nina. "And, young lady, that was the first I heard of you wanting to go to New York, and specifically Harlem. When did all this come about?"

"I been reading about what's happening in Harlem with all the dances and the musicals. I read about it in the *Crisis Magazine* in the school library." Nina was nervous, not knowing where the principal planned to go with his questioning.

"I'm certainly pleased to know at least one student is reading the *Crisis*. It is the very best and most important magazine about what is happening in Negro America, but do you know anyone living in Harlem, and how do you plan to support yourself until you get a job dancing?"

"I've saved over one hundred dollars for the past year, working odd jobs at Stanley Grocery Store on the corner of our apartment building. I don't know nobody there, but I'll contact a lady by the name of Ethel Nance. She's the secretary for a Mr. Charles Johnson, editor of the other magazine you have in the library."

"*Opportunity Magazine.*"

"Yes, sir, that's it. They say she helps people who come to Harlem. Even let them stay at her apartment until they get on their feet. I have her address and everything."

"I know Mr. Johnson and will contact him for you before you leave. But are you sure this is something you really want to do? Harlem, New York, is a big place and can be a lonely place."

Nina looked over at Claude, who stared at her. She loved him, but he had made his decision to pursue his career away from her and she had the same right to decide about her future.

"Mr. Jones, you know, sir, that I have been dancing all my life. I used to come to the school when I was in elementary school and dance at Christmastime and danced many times here at the school. Is there any doubt this is what I want to do?"

"With that kind of determination, I guess not." Principal Jones now turned his chair, so his attention was on the two young high school graduates. "The two of you have been the pride of our high school for the three years you've been in attendance. Nina, you are one of the prettiest and most talented young girls to ever attend this school and Claude, you are one of the brightest boys. But something else very unique about the two of you is that you've been close since you got here. I think it was taken for granted that you would marry and start a family right here in St. Louis." He paused momentarily and looked at Claude and then at Nina. "Are those plans ending with each of you going in different directions now that you've graduated?"

"No, not at all," Claude said, with no hesitation. He looked at Nina. "We've been together since elementary school and nothing's going to come between us. Isn't that right, Nina?"

"Yes, yes, definitely."

"In fact, I'll be in Washington, DC, and she'll be close by in New York, so I can visit her on weekends and sometimes she can come down to DC."

Principal Jones gave Nina a hard look and then stood up. "Well, you two enjoy yourselves while you are still here, and both make sure you come and see me before you leave town." He walked over to another table.

Nina watched as he walked away.

The band leader turned and faced the students. "Okay, this is our last song for the night. So, grab the one you are with and get in your last dance." He turned, and the band played.

Nina grabbed Claude's hand and pulled him up from his chair. "Come on, we're gonna dance."

Claude reluctantly got up as she dragged him to the dance floor. "But I can't dance."

"Don't matter, just follow my steps because we're going to dance. This will probably be our first and only dance for a very long time."

✕◌✕

Chicago, Illinois
June 1925

MARCUS WILLIAMS STUMBLED INTO THE office of Robert Abbott, the owner and publisher of the *Chicago Defender*. Marcus's problem, as he plunked down into a chair in front of Abbott's desk, was that he suffered from a slight hangover from last night when he attended the jazz concert of Louis Armstrong, a young trumpeter who had just arrived in Chicago from New Orleans. Abbott always assigned Marcus to cover new entertainers just arriving in the city. On occasion, he would overindulge, and last night was one of those times.

Abbott tossed a copy of the *Amsterdam News* on his desk and pointed to the headline in the Harlem, New York, paper. "Just look at that."

Marcus looked at the headline and read it aloud. "Harlem becoming the cultural capital for Negro America." He looked up at Abbott. "What's the problem with that headline? You got something against Harlem?"

"No, no, no. You know better than that. I admire what is happening in Harlem. What I don't like is that the *Amsterdam News* has a prime position in covering that growth."

Marcus adjusted himself in the chair and rubbed his forehead, hoping to relieve some of the throbbing pain.

"You have to get to New York."

"What?" Marcus now sat straight up and leaned forward. Suddenly, the headache became quite insignificant.

"You have to get to New York right away," Abbott repeated, with more authority in his tone. "We can't allow James Anderson to dominate on this story. This is the most important development for Negroes since the Thirteenth Amendment and the *Defender* cannot miss out."

Marcus relaxed in his chair, leaning back, but the persistent headache reminded him it was still there.

"Mr. Abbott, I can't just up and leave Chicago. And for how long?"

"Yes, you can, and for how long the story dominates and is important."

"What do I tell my wife?"

"That she's moving to New York and Harlem, the center of all cultural activity. Helen's a poet and she should love being around Langston Hughes and Countee Cullen." Abbott leaned forward across his desk. "Marcus, you are one of the most talented Negro reporters in this country. Harlem deserves the best writers covering the historical significance of what is happening there."

"Thanks for the compliment, but under these circumstances, I'm not sure it's all that meaningful."

Abbott ignored Marcus's rather sardonic response. "The paper will cover all your moving expenses and I'll up your salary to one hundred dollars a month and, of course, get you a place to live."

Knowing he had no choice other than to quit the job with the most prestigious Negro newspaper, Marcus relaxed back in his chair. "When do you expect me to pull up roots and make this move?"

"As soon as possible. Now go on home and tell Helen the good news. Be ready to move a week from today."

"How about my story on Louis Armstrong? You still want me to write it?"

"Absolutely! Armstrong is the hottest musician with this new jazz music taking over the city."

"I'll have it ready tomorrow if I'm still living after I drop this news on Helen."

"She'll be all right. Mark my word, she'll be overjoyed with the news."

"What?" Helen shrieked, sitting upright on the couch in their brownstone home in the Bronzeville district, with the tenor of her voice rising a couple of decibels. "You can't be serious? Mr. Abbott has no right to ask us to do this. We got friends. I have my church that you refuse to go to and he's asking us to give all this up?"

Sitting in an armchair, Marcus listened pensively. His assumption of how Helen would respond was accurate. She was not upset, but angry.

"And how do you know anything about Harlem to go there and write about it? You haven't even been there."

"I'm a reporter and you know I do read."

"I'm sorry, but I am just not ready to up and move on such short notice." Helen sounded irritated.

Marcus moved to the edge of the armchair, taking Helen's hands in his. "Okay, let's work this out because I cannot pass up this opportunity. Big things are happening in Harlem and I—we have the opportunity to be a part of history."

"What's so important about Harlem? We're doing some exciting things right here in Chicago, and, baby, you're covering them." Helen's tone was much softer.

Marcus squeezed a little tighter. He definitely wanted to take on this challenge, but he didn't want to lose his wife in the process. "I know great things are happening right here and Negroes are making a difference all over the country," he conceded, but he could not give in. New York was where Mr. Abbott wanted him and that was an opportunity he just could not pass up. "But New York is the center for all the great beginnings of a new Negro, and he is going to change the course of history in this country." Marcus got up and sat on the couch next to Helen. "Please, you can't deny me this opportunity. I'll be making history by writing about all the artists making the same history for our race."

"No, I don't want to deny you this opportunity. If I do, you'll never be happy, and, most important, you'll never forgive me."

"Then you'll agree to go?"

"Not right away, Marcus, but I'll come later with the understanding that I can come back home if I just don't fit in."

Marcus leaned back on the couch, threw his hands up, and looked directly at Helen. "Oh, baby, I know you'll love it. You're going to meet all the great poets that are producing great works just like you'll do when you get there."

Helen smiled. "I'll have you know I'm already producing great poetry." She reached over and kissed Marcus on the lips, then leaned back on the couch. "So, when do you plan to leave?"

"Within the next week. Of course, I have to work out all the financing, so you're comfortable while still here. Mr. Abbott's covering all my expenses in New York."

"That's awfully nice of him. Don't you think that's the least he can do?"

Marcus detected a bit of sarcasm in her voice. "Mr. Abbott cares a great deal for us and has our best interest in the decisions he makes. He could have hired someone right in New York, but he chose us—"

"He chose you, Marcus, and I just happen to be an afterthought. But I have agreed to go along with this new and surprising plan for our future. I love you, baby, and want the best for you. If you think this is the best, I'm going along with it."

"I know it's the best, and you'll feel the same way once you join me there."

"Promise me one thing, Marcus. If you, at some point, believe this isn't the best professional move for you and us, you'll agree to come back to Chicago."

"You got it, my promise."

"And you'll be honest about it?"

Marcus placed his right hand over his heart. "I promise."

"Okay, can we now please eat? It's getting late and I need to get some sleep. Tomorrow is going to be a busy day as I prepare for this new life."

I.

Harlem, New York
July 1925

CLUTCHING ONLY A BAG, SAM Arthur walked up the steps of the subway stop at 125th and Lenox Avenue. Standing there in a state of incredulity, he stared at all the Negroes hurrying. It seemed unimaginable to him that there could be this many Negroes in one place at one time. Cars and buses flooded the street, all driven by Negroes. Dumbfounded, he peered at a Negro in a police uniform, blowing his whistle, instructing drivers what they could and could not do. He could hardly believe it. Nothing like this ever happened in Gaffney, South Carolina.

After recovering from his delightful shock, he came back to Earth and knew he had to find his way to the YMCA, where he could get a room. From his pocket, he retrieved a small piece of paper. On it was the address Sadie had scribbled, suggesting that the best place for a newcomer to stay was at the YMCA—800 East 135th Street between Lenox and Seventh Avenue.

"You lost, young fellow?." An elderly Negro man with a balding head and gray hair around the sides stood before him.

"Yes, sir, looking for the YMCA." Sam Arthur was reluctant. Sadie had also told him to be careful who he talked with in Harlem. It was full of hustlers who'd be looking for young boys coming up from the South.

"Looks like you got off the subway one stop too soon. Should've stayed on it up to 135th and got off there." The old man pointed up Lenox Avenue. "Just walk up to 135th, look to your left and you'll see the Y one halfway up from Seventh Avenue."

"Thank you, I appreciate your help," Sam Arthur tipped his head as a gesture of his gratitude to the old man. "I'll be getting on my way." He walked away.

"Hold up, young fellow. You running from the law?"

Sam Arthur stopped abruptly and turned to stare at the old man. "Why you ask me something like that?"

"'Cause so many of you young fellows running up here to find a place to hide from the law down South. Don't matter to me, just wondering."

"I ain't running from nobody. Just decided to make a change and heard this was the best place for a man to make that change."

"I imagine you gonna be looking for some kind of work?"

"I got a little bit of money, but it won't last me too long, so I sure am gonna be out trying to find a way to eat. You got some suggestions, old man?"

"Got the best man for you to meet." The old man pulled out a scratch of paper and took a pencil from behind his ear and wrote Casper Holstein and handed it to Sam Arthur.

Sam Arthur stared at the name as if it was gold. "How do I get in touch with this man?" He knew he would need work, and soon.

"Ask anybody at the Y and they'll be able to tell you. Good luck." The old man walked away.

Sam Arthur watched while the man headed the opposite way on Lenox Avenue. He stared at the name on the scratch paper, then turned and headed up Lenox Avenue. He stepped off the curb into the street and quickly jumped back. A speeding jalopy almost hit him.

A passenger in the jalopy stuck his head out the window and shouted at Sam Arthur. "Hey, nigguh, keep your Southern ass off the street 'fore you get hit."

He ignored the man's comment and continued up Lenox Avenue. Not that he liked being called a nigguh, and back in Gaffney, he would've torn that bastard's head right off. But caution would be his mode of operation until he got to know the land he found himself in. As he kept walking up Lenox Avenue, he made sure not to step off the curb without extreme caution. He'd only been in Harlem for a very short time and already knew he didn't like it. Too much hustle and bustle and antagonistic people. For a moment, Sam Arthur thought maybe he'd rather return home and face up to whatever was going to happen to him.

He reached 135th Street and headed toward the YMCA that stood out conspicuously in the middle of the block. Again, he allowed his thoughts to wander. That night at Ms. Sadie's Blues Club in Gaffney, South Carolina, he had to leave in such a hurry that he didn't bid a proper farewell to Willa Mae because Emma, Jethroe's wife, swiftly took her home. He wasn't sure how he could survive here in this monstrously big city without Willa Mae there with him. Soon as he got settled, he would send for her and guess they'd have to make a life right there. In the meantime, thoughts and visions of her pretty face and smile would have to sustain him. As he walked into the YMCA, he didn't know how long that could last.

He stood in the lobby, looking all around him. It all seemed so gigantic to him. The largest building he'd ever been in was the Gaffney City Building, and it was only one floor. He stared over at the man standing behind a desk, who was looking at him.

"Can I help you?"

Taking that as his cue, Sam Arthur strolled over to the counter. "Yes, sir, I need to rent a room. I just got here from out of town?"

The clerk frowned. "Yes, I can see that. How long you planning on staying here?"

"Don't know for sure. Guess for quite a while. I don't know nobody up here to stay with. This is gonna have to do."

"We could go weekly, and I need the entire week's rent upfront. You got the money?"

Sam Arthur pulled out his wad of money all wrapped up. "How much?"

The clerk stared at the wad of money and a scowl came across his face. "Boy, are you crazy? Don't pull out no wad of money like that right here in public. You don't know who might be watching you and first chance they get, they'll be all over you." The clerk paused, allowing his warning words to sink in with Sam Arthur. "Where you from anyway?"

"Gaffney, South Carolina."

"Well, this ain't South Carolina. It's Harlem now, so put that wad of money away."

Sam Arthur pulled out two ten-dollar bills and stuck the rest of the money back in his pocket. He placed the money on the counter.

The clerk snatched up the money, turned, and grabbed a key from a key rack behind him. Then turned and handed the key to Sam Arthur. "Room 315 on the third floor. Twenty dollars gets you two weeks' rent. You might have to share your room with someone else according to how crowded I get. There are two beds in there, so you don't have to share no bed." The clerk chuckled. "Bathroom is at the end of the hall. Be sure to flush the toilet when you finish using it. Any questions?"

Sam Arthur stuffed the key in his pocket and pulled out the scratch of paper the man at the subway had given him. He looked at the name scribbled on the paper.

"Yes, sir, do you know where I can find a Mr. Casper Hol—"

"Casper Holstein," the clerk snapped back before Sam Arthur finished saying the man's name. "Where'd you get his name?"

"Man back at the train place told me he could help me find a job. I got to find a job so I can get my girlfriend up here and we can get married."

"Mr. Holstein got an office on 136th, one block over and down a half block. A place called the Turf Club is where you'll find him, but not this time of morning. Wait until 'bout nine o'clock this evening and then go up there. He'll be there and get yourself some rest before you go. You're gonna need it. And change out of them raggedy coveralls. You do have a change of clothes, don't you?"

Sam Arthur lifted the bag so the clerk could see it. "Yes, but why I got to go up there so late?"

"You'll find out real soon here in Harlem nothing gets done in the daylight. Life starts after nine at night. Good luck and make sure you change out of them damn clothes. You'll be laughed right out of the club."

Walking out of Grand Central Station into the roar of the streetcars and the rush of the crowd, Nina felt a surge of excitement like she had never experienced before. After a long arduous train ride from St. Louis, she had finally arrived in the city that never slept. Before leaving St. Louis, Principal Jones had told her he attended classes with Charles Johnson at the University of Chicago. He knew that Ethel often allowed artists to crash at her apartment until they got on their feet. He had contacted her through Johnson, and she agreed to let Nina stay there until she found a job and could get out on her own.

Principal Jones's words resonated with Nina as she stood outside Grand Central Station, somewhat taken aback by the enormity of her situation being in New York and knowing no one.

"When you get to New York, don't talk with anyone and when you get outside the train station, make sure you get a checker cab, the black-colored ones, and tell the driver to take you up to Ms. Nance's apartment. You got the address."

Thank God, she thought, it was a checker cab with a Black driver parked at the front of the line. She hurried up to the cab and stuck her head inside.

"Excuse me, sir, I need to get to 582 St. Nicholas in Harlem."

The cab driver quickly got out of the cab, hurried over to her, and grabbed her suitcase.

"Get in." He tossed the suitcases in the trunk.

Nina climbed into the back seat of the cab.

The driver hurried back around and got into the driver's seat. He pulled his cab out into the traffic and headed up Fifth Avenue.

The cab driver glanced at Nina in the rear-view mirror. He did it once and minutes later, did it again. "You're new to New York?"

Remembering Principal Woods' warning, "Don't talk to anybody," Nina turned her head and stared out the window.

"Hey, lady, I don't mean no harm. Just making conversation, but if you are new to the city, you'd better be careful where you go."

Nina smiled and looked at the taxi driver, who had turned his attention back to the traffic. *He called me a lady*, she thought. First time that happened. Back home, she was always a girl and young lady. She was a lady now that she was out on her own. It felt good.

"Yes," she said, now trusting the driver because he had paid her a compliment.

The driver now looked at her through the rear-view mirror. "Well, you're a really pretty lady, and going up into Harlem, you got to be real careful. Not the safest part of the city."

"Thank you, but I understand where I'll be staying is a nicer part of Harlem."

"You right about that. Up there on St. Nicholas Avenue is where the better class of our people live. But don't wander down around this part of town."

Nina again looked out the window. She glanced at the street sign. It read 5th and 125th Street. She would remember the cab driver's advice.

"Where you from?"

"St. Louis."

"Guess it's a lot different than here."

"Yes, it sure is."

The driver pulled up in front of a large brick apartment building. He got out of the cab and got Nina's suitcase out of the trunk.

Nina got out and opened her purse. "How much?"

"Two dollars."

Nina took two dollars out of her purse and handed it to him.

"Don't I get a tip? It's common in New York to give the driver a tip."

She grabbed two coins and handed them to him.

He smirked at the coins but took them. "Good luck, lady." He turned, walked back over to the driver's side of the cab, got in, and drove off.

Nina watched and smiled as the cab headed down St. Nicholas Avenue. That was the second time she'd been called a lady. She picked up her suitcase and walked up the ten cement steps, opened the door, walked up the stairs to the second floor, down the hall, and knocked on the door to Apartment 2B. For the second time, she felt anxiety just as she felt walking out of the train station onto the busy streets of New York. She didn't know what to expect.

The door swung open, and she instantly relaxed as the woman standing there smiled at her.

"You must be Nina?" Without waiting for an answer, Ethel Nance opened the door wider. "Come on in."

Nina strolled into the large living room and waited for Ethel to close the door. She took Nina by the arm. "Come on, girl, we're all in the study." They walked into a room and the first thing Nina saw was a lot of books on shelves along the wall. She had never seen that many books in one room but at the Negro library in St. Louis. Two other women were also in the room, both sitting in overstuffed chairs.

"Nina, this is Regina Anderson, my roommate." She pointed to a light-skinned woman with long straight black hair, small features, and very pretty. "And this is Zora Hurston, who moved up here from Washington, DC. She was a student at Howard University. She is temporarily staying with us, too." She hesitated for a moment and then continued. "Girls, this is Nina, a new arrival in Harlem from St. Louis." She pointed for Nina to take a seat on a small couch.

"From St. Louis, you're a long way from home," Regina said. "What brings you to New York?"

Nina scooted up on the couch. "I want to dance."

Zora and Regina looked at each other, then at Nina. "Do you have an audition set up for some show?" Zora asked.

"No, I don't."

"How old are you?" Regina asked, then looked over at Ethel.

Nina was feeling a little uncomfortable. She wasn't sure what these questions were all about, so she lied. "I'm twenty."

"Okay, girls, that's enough drilling," Ethel said and got up from her chair. "Let me get Nina set up in her room." She looked at Nina.

Nina got up, feeling relieved that Ethel bailed her out of that mess.

However, Regina still had questions. "How long is she going to be with us?"

"Don't know, until she can get settled," Ethel shot back. "Come on, let me show you where you'll be sleeping."

Nina picked up her suitcase and followed Ethel out of the room.

Ethel led her to the back of the very large apartment to a room with the door closed. She opened it. "For the next week, you'll be in Lucretia's room. She's our third roommate, but she had to go home to Georgia to bury her grandmother."

They strolled into the room. "You can sleep here until she gets back and then, unfortunately, you'll be on the couch."

Nina placed her suitcase on the floor next to the bed and quickly turned and looked at Ethel. "Can you help get me to meet with Florence Mills? I heard she is really a good person and likes to help new people when they come to town."

"I don't know. I hear she's rehearsing for a new musical, *Bluebirds,* and is really busy."

With excitement in her voice, Nina asked, "Can you get me an interview with the producers and maybe they'll give me a chance to join the chorus line? I know they'll like me. I been training all my life for this chance. Can you do that for me?"

"I'll see what I can do," Ethel said with some reluctance in her voice.

"I'm a real fast learner and it won't take any time for me to learn the routine." She paused and placed her hand on Ethel's shoulder. "I know I can do it and that's why I came to Harlem."

Ethel hugged her. "I know you can, and I'll make some contacts tomorrow. In the meantime, let's get you something to eat. You must be famished."

Nina smiled. "I've been so excited I haven't even thought about eating."

The two walked back out of the room and into the living room where Regina and Zora sat, still talking.

***

Marcus picked up a copy of the *Messenger* magazine as he sat in the reception area of the magazine's office at 573

Lenox Avenue, waiting to meet with A. Philip Randolph. He'd arrived in New York two days after leaving Chicago. All that time on the train allowed him to think through his plans. He needed a good introduction to the artistic community in Harlem and chose Randolph as the best person to do the job. Robert Abbott, the publisher of the *Chicago Defender* and his boss, had agreed with him.

Marcus admired Randolph immensely because he shared his ideology. He respected him for standing up against the war. Randolph didn't believe young Negroes should go overseas to fight for democracy in white Europe when they couldn't get it in Black America. Leafing through the *Messenger*, Marcus found what he read to be striking. The writing was so powerful; he had to read it twice and practically out loud.

"In politics, the New Negro, unlike the old Negro, cannot be lulled into a false sense of security with political spoils and patronage. The New Negro demands political equality."

"Mr. Williams, Mr. Randolph is ready to talk with you now," said the young man, who looked to be in his early twenties, jolting Marcus out of his concentration on the article.

Marcus folded the magazine and placed it back on the table. He followed the young man into the office. Walking inside, he noticed another man who stood up to greet him, along with Randolph positioned behind his desk.

"Welcome to New York," Randolph said.

"Thank you." Marcus walked up and stood next to the other man.

Randolph gestured for the two men to sit. He also sat and pointed at the other man. "By the way, this is Theophilus Lewis, our excellent theatrical critic here in Harlem."

Marcus reached out and the two men shook hands.

"Yes, welcome to Harlem," Lewis said.

Marcus simply nodded and turned to face Randolph, who then took the lead.

"I want you to know you are privileged to work for a real pioneer in the publishing business for our race. I have admired Robert Abbott for years."

"I recognize the opportunities he's afforded me, not only in this assignment but the ones back in Chicago, also."

"I'm not surprised that he has added what's happening here in Harlem as one of his lead stories," Randolph said.

"What are you looking to write about while you're here?" Lewis asked.

Marcus adjusted his position in the chair now, turning and looking at Lewis. "Harlem and all its intricate parts as the major Negro community in the entire country."

Lewis clasped his hands in his lap. "That's quite an undertaking. There is now over a quarter of a million Negroes here and they are still coming in large numbers from all over the South and even from the islands."

"He'll find his niche after he's been here a while," Randolph interjected.

George Schuyler walked into the room. "But don't get caught up thinking all the Negroes in Harlem are a part of this New Negro Movement."

Marcus looked back and smiled. He recognized Schuyler from years ago when he wrote for the *Pittsburgh Courier*. The three men stood up as Schuyler strolled into the room.

Schuyler looked directly at Marcus. "You must be the reporter Robert Abbott has sent here from Chicago."

"That's right and you are George Schuyler."

"That is also right and you are here to capture that meaning of this great new movement of the so-called New Negro."

Somewhat surprised at Schuyler's sarcasm, Marcus turned away from him and looked at Randolph. This was the first time he heard someone refer to the New Negro Movement sarcastically.

Randolph saw the concerned expression on Marcus's face and directed his comments to Schuyler. "Don't you think that's a rather cynical way to refer to what's happening here?"

"It's all in one's perspective observation," Schuyler shot back.

Lewis chimed in. "Why don't we let Marcus get his feet wet before we offer our own critique of what's happening here?"

Nodding, Schuyler conceded. "Fair enough."

Randolph changed the direction of the discussion "When I talked to Robert, he mentioned he'd rented you an apartment on St. Nicholas. Have you checked in yet?"

"No, I haven't. I came here right from Grand Central Station. My luggage is right out in the reception area."

"I'm just a block up from St. Nicholas," Schuyler joined back in. "If you sit here and converse with these gentlemen for the next half hour while I finish my editorial for this month's magazine, we can share a cab."

"Wonderful, that'll work out fine," Randolph said.

Smiling, Schuyler quipped, "Maybe I can share some more of my cynicism about this New Negro Movement in the cab." He hurried out of the room.

2.

SAM ARTHUR STOOD IN THE hallway on the third floor of the YMCA, waiting for the person occupying the bathroom to come out. He didn't mind standing there. It was far better than what he had left behind in Gaffney, South Carolina, where the bathroom was outside.

The door swung open and a young woman with a towel wrapped around her body stared at him and then hurried down the hall. Sam Arthur found that rather strange. Only men were supposed to stay at the YMCA. But it was Harlem, and he clearly understood he would find a great deal of what happened there strange. He hurried into the bathroom and closed the door.

Having no idea what he was getting himself into, Sam Arthur hurried up Lenox Avenue to 136th Street to 111 West 136th, the address of the Turf Club. All he knew was that this man, Casper Holstein, helped Negroes looking for jobs to find one. At least that's what the old man told him, and he had to follow it up. He couldn't waste any time because the money Sadie had given him would soon run low. He also couldn't waste any time, because he had to get Willa Mae to Harlem, where she would be safe.

He gasped as he walked up the cement steps leading to the large brownstone building and faced two very large Negro men standing at the door. He wondered what they were all about and if they would prevent him from going inside. That wouldn't happen if he had to go through both of them. He was going to see this Mr. Holstein.

Sam Arthur slowly made his way up the steps, measuring the two men who moved closer to each other and blocked his entrance into the building.

"Where the hell you think you're going?" the larger of the two men brusquely asked. "Are you lost?"

Sam Arthur, carrying the slip with Holstein's name on it, looked at it and said, "I'm here to see a Mr. Holstein."

"You are? Who the hell are you and what's your business with Mr. Holstein?"

Sam Arthur didn't scare easily. He moved in closer to the two men. "I need a job and I was told he's the man who can give me work!"

The second man guarding the door took one step toward Sam Arthur. "Boy, you up here from the South?"

Sam Arthur took one step back, giving him sufficient space to get a full blow-off if necessary.

"Nigguh, who you calling 'boy?'" He wasn't going to allow anyone to disrespect him, be it a redneck in South Carolina or this Negro standing in Harlem.

The large man interceded before it got out of hand. The last thing his boss inside wanted was a fight on his front steps, possibly attracting the police.

"Hold up," he said, looking directly at Sam Arthur while pushing the other man back. "Who told you that you could get a job with Mr. Holstein?"

Irritated and ready to fight if that was what it took to get inside, Sam Arthur said, "That's what an old man told me when I got off the bus yesterday."

"Do you have any clue as to what kind of business Mr. Holstein has?"

"No, I don't. I just know I got to get a job 'cause I'm about to run out of money, and I got to get my girlfriend up here from South Carolina before that white boy hurts her."

"You running from the law?"

"Not the law, but the white man's rules."

The second man, having changed his position and backed away from Sam Arthur, spoke up. "This man's got balls. He's willing to take on both of us and he done took on the white man down South. This is the kind of man Mr. Holstein might be able to use."

"He's either got a pair or he's crazy," the larger man said. "Either way, you might be right. Let me check with Mr. Holstein." He turned, opened the door, and disappeared inside.

The second man took a step closer to Sam Arthur and extended his hand. Sam Arthur initially jumped back.

"Don't mean any harm to you, my brother, but our job is to keep Mr. Holstein safe by checking out anyone wanting to see him." He kept his arm extended.

Sam Arthur relaxed and shook the man's hand. The man was no longer a threat.

"I'm kinda wondering what kinda business Mr. Holstein have?"

"If he agrees to see you, I'll let him explain that to you. But I can tell you with your nerve and guts willing to take on both of us, you can make a helluva lot of money with him."

The door swung open, and the man held it and waved to Sam Arthur. "You got it. Come on in. Mr. Holstein will see you now."

Sam Arthur followed the big man inside a vestibule into the foyer. As he followed behind, he stared in amazement at the size of the brownstone. Along the walls hung pictures of racehorses and pictures of Negro jockeys in their riding paraphernalia. They reached the end of the foyer, and the big man opened a door, and they stepped inside.

A well-dressed Negro man, sitting in an executive leather chair behind an enormous oak desk, waved to Sam Arthur and the big man, nodding to the two leather chairs in front of the desk. Feeling somewhat intimidated, something unusual for Sam Arthur, he sat and waited for the man he assumed to be Mr. Holstein to break the silence. It didn't take long.

"You looking for work?"

"I gotta find work and real fast?" Sam Arthur answered and scooted up in his chair.

Holstein leaned forward with his body extended. "Where you from and how long you been here in Harlem?"

"I'm from Gaffney, South Carolina, and I been here for a day."

"You running from the law?"

"No, not from the law, but from a white man that tried to come between me and my woman."

"If it's not the law, then why'd you have to run?"

Sam Arthur hesitated before answering the question. He thought maybe this was some kind of set-up, a trap.

"You got an answer for me?" Holstein insisted. "And what the hell is your name?"

Sam Arthur's instinct pushed him to jump up and hustle out of there, but his reasoning took control. He needed a job.

"My name is Sam Arthur, and you must know the unwritten rules of the South."

"No, I don't," Holstein shot back. "Never been down there. I came straight to New York from the islands. So, explain to me the rules of the South."

Sam Arthur momentarily glanced over at the other man, who remained quiet, and then back at Holstein.

"It's much like it was during slavery. White man want your woman, then he gonna take her and the law protects him." Sam Arthur paused, allowing Holstein to respond. He didn't and Sam Arthur continued. "It gets worse if you works on that man's land. Then you have nothin' that belongs to you, especially not your woman."

"You worked for this man."

"Not him, but his poppa."

"And you fought this man over your woman?"

"I didn't fight him 'cause the others stopped me, but I would've killed that peckerwood."

Holstein looked over at the other man and smiled. He then looked back at Sam Arthur.

"You ever heard of the numbers game?"

"No, can't say that I have."

"You want to make some fast money 'cause I guess you want to get that girl of yours away from that peckerwood."

Sam Arthur was feeling good about the direction the conversation was going. "I sure do. I'll do most anything to get my girl, Willa Mae, up here."

Holstein again looked over at the other man. "Jonas, here, going to help you get started as a numbers runner for me."

Sam Arthur turned and looked at Jonas. "What is numbers runner?"

Jonas did not answer, and Holstein continued, changing the conversation.

"Those the only clothes you got, them overalls and that shirt?"

"Got another pair just like these. I almost had to fight and only had time to grab few clothes I got and get out of there."

"You can't be a numbers runner for me looking like that." Holstein turned his attention to Jonas. "Take him over to Willie's. I'm sure he got some decent slacks and shirts he can fit Sam Arthur with. Tell him I'll cover it. And make sure he gets some decent shoes and socks and even underwear."

Holstein now looked at Sam Arthur. "Jonas is going to work with you for a week and teach you the numbers game and then you going to be out there on your own. And right now, he's going to take you over to the hot man and get you some clothes." Holstein looked over at Jonas and smiled. "I'll get my money back from your first commission. You learn one thing and you learn it fast: don't ever cross me. There will be plenty of opportunities to do that, but don't fall into that trap. Now you all get out of here and get to work."

Sam Arthur got up and followed Jonas out of the room, feeling exhilarated by what had just happened.

Nina took a deep breath as she neared 220 West 135th Street. With her nerves on edge, once in front of the brownstone, she wasn't sure she could climb those seven steps and knock on the large front door. She'd dreamed of this day when she first learned about Florence Mills four years ago, when the entire Negro world raved about her performance in the first all-Negro musical *Shuffle Along*. As much as she possibly could, she followed the great star's career. Now, if she could only conjure up enough nerve to knock on the door, she was about to meet her.

It was Ethel Nance who arranged the meeting. She knew Florence and her reputation to reach out and help other young dancers who made their way to Harlem, some seeking stardom and others just the opportunity to dance in the musical capital of the world. Ethel knew Florence would be responsive to her request, and she was. Now the rest was up to Nina. She had to knock on that door so the beginning of her dream could begin. She finally did.

Instantly, the door swung open, and a man smiled at Nina. "You must be Nina Jackson?" Not waiting for an answer, he motioned for her to come inside.

She hesitated, not expecting to be greeted by a man.

He detected her hesitancy. "I'm Ulysses Thompson, Florence's husband."

Nina allowed her body to relax. "Yes, I am." She walked inside the house.

Ulysses closed the door. "Follow me. Florence is waiting for you in the living room."

Nina followed Ulysses down a hallway, and, with each step, she felt she might fall over. Nervous anxiety again took over. Being a Southern girl, with no experience in the big city and under the bright lights, and only performing at church during Christmas and Easter and on the stage at her high school, her insecurities took over.

Ulysses opened the door to the parlor and Nina stepped inside. What struck her most was just how tiny Florence appeared, sitting at one end of a large couch.

Florence motioned to her. "Hi, Nina. Come and sit next to me."

Nina strolled over and sat next to Florence. Ulysses closed the door and sat in a chair next to the victrola.

Florence smiled warmly at her. "Ethel told me you just got here. Where are you from?"

Her tone was relaxing, and Nina relaxed, too. "I got here a couple days ago. Ms. Nance and her roommates took me in. My home is St. Louis."

"Ethel also told me you were a beautiful young lady, and she was right about that."

"Thank you."

"But can your dancing complement your beauty? If it can, you're in the right city at the right time. This is the Negro's chance to shine, and this is the right city for it." Florence looked over at Ulysses. "Put on Ethel Waters 'Down Home Blues.' It has a nice beat to it."

Ulysses picked up a record, placed it inside the victrola, and instantly Waters' voice filled the room.

Florence looked at Nina. "Can you dance a routine to this rhythm for me?"

Caught off guard, she was not sure what to do. "Right now, right here?"

"Why not? A dancer can dance anywhere and anytime. Come on, you can do it."

Nina got up and took off her shoes and began snapping her fingers to pick up the beat. She moved her body and, using her ingenuity, began a dance routine to the beat of the music.

After a few minutes, Florence glanced over at Ulysses and they both nodded in approval. The four-minute recording ended, and Nina stood, looking at Florence.

"Very good. In fact, outstanding." Florence motioned over to Ulysses, who took the Waters' record off and placed another in the victrola. "But let's change the beat. One of the favorite songs from *Shuffle Along* was 'I'm Just Wild About Harry.' See what you can do to that."

Nina had mixed feelings about the song. She had heard it numerous times when her mother played it on the victrola back in St. Louis, but she was just as little reluctant to dance to a tune made famous by Florence.

"Don't try to imitate me in any way and don't be concerned that I performed it in the musical. Just do your own thing."

Ulysses started the record and Nina went into her routine she had practiced to that song almost every day back home.

Again, Florence smiled and looked over at Ulysses. "That's enough." She then looked at Nina. "You can do that routine better than me. That was wonderful. Come sit with me."

Nina hurried over and sat next to Florence, turned, and faced her.

"Ethel wanted me to recommend you to Les Lewis, who is our producer for *Blackbirds*, scheduled to open right here in Harlem next year if I felt you were good enough to be in our chorus line. I think you are, but there is only one problem. We have no openings." She reached over and took Nina's hand. "But someday, you are going to dance with me in a future show."

"What if she starts at one of the clubs?" Ulysses suggested. "It's good experience."

"No," Florence shot back. "This girl's too young and too innocent for that kind of exposure."

"I'm not suggesting one of them clubs down Jungle Alley, but one of the finer clubs. You got the Cotton Club, Connie's Inn, and Small's Paradise."

"There is no way I'd send her to the Cotton Club or Connie's Inn because they don't allow Negroes in there as customers. Maybe Small's because it is Negro-owned and serves Negroes and whites, but I just don't know about exposing her to the nightclub environment." Florence was not comfortable with her husband's suggestion.

Nina sat there, practically traumatized. The woman she most admired in the entire world sat next to her and held her hand. Besides, she just heard this great entertainer say that someday she would dance with her. What more could she ask for? She wasn't sure about dancing in a nightclub and her mother would be terribly upset. And how about Claude, whom she promised to marry someday? But she was willing to do almost anything if it would get her on the same stage with Florence Mills. She continued listening to the two of them discuss her future.

"She'll need that kind of experience before moving on to the bigger stage," Ulysses suggested. "But we have to consider she just got out of high school less than a month ago."

"If she's gifted, which she is, that doesn't matter. Remember, I got started at age five and was only twenty-one when *Shuffle Along* was launched."

"Florence, you are an exception to the rule. I don't think there's any dancer who could do what you've done."

"Well thank you, darling, but there is always someone, maybe not even born yet, that can be as good as the very best today."

"If you believe she is good enough to get on at Connie's Inn, regardless of the segregation practiced there, she'll be under the training eye of Leonard Harper." Ulysses figured mentioning Leonard Harper, recognized as the best and most creative choreographer in New York, would influence Florence.

Florence moved right up to the edge of the couch, releasing the grip she had on Nina's hand. "Who we going to have watch over this child while she's there?"

"Leonard will."

"You gonna talk to him?"

Ulysses got up, walked over, and sat on the other end of the couch with Nina between the two of them. He twisted his body toward Nina. "Connie's Inn has the most beautiful and fabulous dancers working there. Single and married white men frequent the club because of all those beautiful Negro women."

Nina moved her body in a nervous gesture. When she left St. Louis, she never dreamed that she would be exposed to this kind of conversation. What was worst for her, she didn't know why it was necessary. She didn't plan on getting with some white man or Negro, for that matter. Her commitment to Claude remained strong.

"Reason I'm telling you this is because you're going to have to be strong to the temptation. If you don't think you can do that, then you'd better go on back to St. Louis and don't try to make it here."

His words jolted Nina out of her hesitancy. "I want to dance." She turned and looked directly at Florence, who had remained quiet while Ulysses ran the situation down to her. "And I want to dance with Florence Mills. I'll do what it takes to do that someday."

Ulysses stood up. "All right, I'll arrange an audition for you tomorrow evening with Leonard. I know they have a couple openings. Two of the girls got strung out on drugs and they had to let them go."

Florence also got up and Nina followed her.

"Be on time for your audition and remember that you are dancing there for only one reason, getting to the time when we can dance together," Florence said as they walked out of the room.

Marcus climbed the steps to the entrance of the National Urban League on West 23rd Street, where he was to have his first formal meeting in Harlem with Charles Johnson. Unlike when he first arrived and met with Randolph for the first time, he felt more relaxed with Johnson, a man he knew from Chicago. He met Johnson right after the riot in 1919, when a white mob had killed a young Negro boy. Marcus had just signed on as a reporter with the *Defender*, and Abbott assigned him to cover the work of the interracial commission established to study the causes of the riot.

Johnson was the associate executive secretary for the commission, and Marcus had interviewed him several times and his stories went nationwide. They helped Johnson develop a national reputation on race relations. That led to his appointment as Director of Research and Investigation for the Urban League. In many ways, he owed his position in New York to Marcus and Abbott. That's why he felt very relaxed as he entered the building and Ethel Nance, Johnson's secretary, greeted him.

"Welcome to New York, Marcus. Mr. Johnson is expecting you." Ethel got up and disappeared into an adjoining room.

Marcus sat in a chair next to a table with various copies of *Opportunity Magazine* on display. One particular copy caught his attention. The front page read: "The Debut of the Younger School of Negro Writers, May 1924." He recognized the importance of that volume because of the story on the pages inside. It covered one of the most significant historical events in New York on the evening of March 4, 1924. Some considered it the beginning of a collaborative effort of Negro and white artists to improve the conditions between the races.

Ethel walked back into the reception area. "Marcus, Mr. Johnson is ready to meet with you."

Both men smiled and shook hands as Marcus sat in one of the two chairs in front of Johnson's large oak desk.

Sitting in his high-back leather chair, Johnson leaned forward. "It's been a while."

"It certainly has. My God, we haven't talked since you left Chicago for the big city."

They both laughed.

"Let me assure you, Chicago is quite a city also, and I do miss it."

"We've been following what you've been doing here, and I briefly glanced at the June issue of last year's *Opportunity Magazine*."

"Yes, it was a real breakthrough literary event. It was an introduction of the talented Negro writers to the larger white literary community of New York. We all met at the only downtown club that allows the mixing of the races and talked about how important it is for the white publishing companies to commit to publishing our talented authors."

"You know that's why Mr. Abbott wanted me here. So where do I start?"

"First fact that you need to know is there is no unity among the Negro writers here in Harlem. You have two different driving forces. The young new writers who are determined to write free of any interference from either white or Negro concerns. Then you have Dr. Du Bois, who believes all literature should be for the uplift of the race. And in between those two groups, you have Dr. Alain Locke from Howard University, who seems to be here every weekend and considers himself the godfather of the movement."

"You all were pretty hard on Marcus Garvey, also. Word is that Dr. Du Bois and even James Johnson cooperated with the federal authorities to bring him down. I guess you all had some unity to get rid of him."

Johnson stretched his arms across the desk. "I, too, was not a fan of Garvey. He really was an embarrassment with all his talk about taking us all back to Africa and selling shares to some kind of ship that couldn't sail any further than right out of New York harbor."

"I take it you're not a strong fan of Africa or our return to the homeland?"

"I have nothing against Africa, but why are we going to go back there when they're all trying their best to get over here?"

"You have a point, but maybe we should get them over here so they can experience all the obstacles and problems we face here in the so-called land of the free."

"But we may have found a breakthrough as a way to elevate our people in the eyes of white folks, and the answer is right here in Harlem."

Marcus moved to the edge of the chair. "Do I need to start taking notes?"

Johnson smiled and leaned back in his chair. "No, not yet. There'll be plenty of time for note-taking. But no people are recognized as civilized without producing fine literature. That's what's happening now, and it is going to spread to other cities. Already Chicago, Washington, DC, and Philadelphia are establishing their own renaissance."

"Again, when and where do I start?"

"You have already begun your discussion today with me and I understand you have talked with Randolph. I'd say you're off to a good beginning."

"I understand Langston Hughes just got back from overseas and I certainly look forward to talking with him as well as Countee Cullen."

"You must, they are the new faces in the literary community here and they are leading the way. I am sure you'll have that opportunity. Now I have to get over to the library for a talk with Regina about some future programs, one which I believe will be with Langston."

Marcus got up. "Hopefully, I can meet with you again and in the very near future."

"I'll be here whenever you're ready."

Marcus turned and walked out of the office.

3.

SAM ARTHUR EXHIBITED NOTHING BUT pride as he strutted down Lenox Avenue in his new purple suit, white shirt, and bright red tie. Holstein had kept his word and fronted him the money with the understanding that one of his number runners couldn't persuade people to lay their bet with them with Sam Arthur dressed like a bama. He had to make this work for him, and quickly. No doubt that white boy back in Gaffney was making Willa Mae's life miserable. He had to make some quick money and send for her.

After four hours of nothing but failure, Sam Arthur's exhilaration was waning. He wasn't able to get not one bet as the people he approached told him they placed their numbers with another runner, and he'd better be careful where he worked. These Northern people did not understand fear was something that did not register with him. Nothing could be worse than the rednecks in Gaffney. He thought back on what Sadie had told him just before he left. "Do not contact anyone here because if the authorities found out, that person would be forced to tell them where he was. And by all means, do not plan to return to Gaffney ever." This was advice from a woman he respected, but it was advice he could not live with—he'd need to communicate with Willa Mae, and that was something he'd have to figure out how to do.

The screeching tires of an automobile brought Sam Arthur out of his musing. A Negro policeman jumped out of the vehicle, ran up, and stood in his face.

"Hey, boy, we got word you trying to hustle people for numbers!"

A second white policeman hurried around the vehicle and stood next to Sam Arthur. "Who you working for, boy?" he also shouted. "We know you ain't out here on your own, trying to hustle numbers, so who is your banker?"

Sam Arthur froze up, not knowing how to respond. Jonas hadn't schooled him on what to do or say if stopped by the police.

"I bet this boy's out here hustling on his own, not knowing how this game is played," the Negro officer said.

"Is that it, boy? You out here hustling on your own?" the White officer added. "I guess we'd better run him in."

This was something Sam Arthur couldn't let happen, but he knew there was no way he could fight two policemen.

Just as the Negro policeman grabbed Sam Arthur by the arm, a white Lincoln pulled up behind the police vehicle. Jonas jumped out of the driver's seat, ran around, and opened the back door. Holstein got out and hurried up to the police. He pulled out two twenty-dollar bills and confronted the policemen.

"He's one of mine." He handed each of the policemen a twenty-dollar bill. "I'll take it from here."

The two policemen took the money and released the hold on Sam Arthur, who quickly moved over and stood next to Holstein.

"Put out the word that I got a new runner be working the streets about 125th up to 145th."

"Yes, sir, we got it, Mr. Holstein," the Negro officer responded. "We'll let the other boys know. It's kinda easy to recognize him with that outfit he's wearing."

The two policemen got back in their vehicle and drove off.

Holstein turned to Sam Arthur and pointed to the car. "Get in the backseat with me."

Jonas got in the driver's seat and pulled off.

"Take us to the Sugar Cane Club," Holstein instructed.

Jonas drove down 135th Street, crossed over Seventh Avenue and the farther he drove, the more run-down and dilapidated the surroundings. This was a part of Harlem Sam Arthur hadn't yet seen, and there was nothing glamorous about it.

"I'm going to introduce you to the bouncer at the Sugar Cane Club. It's a good place for you to start. This is where a low life of Negroes hangs out. They can't afford the more expensive clubs and couldn't get in if they could. Clubs like Cotton Club and Connie's Inn is for white folks only and most of them is the white mob." Holstein paused for a moment, took out a cigarette, and offered Sam Arthur one, who turned it down. Holstein lit the cigarette and continued. "You spend time down here and you'll make a lot of money. The numbers is the only way any of these people will ever make any money. They play and they pray."

Jonas pulled up and parked in front of the large brick building. He got out, hurried around the Lincoln, and opened the door for Holstein, who got out. Sam Arthur slid over in the backseat and also got out and closed the door.

The three men walked up to the entrance to the club. A large man inside the building looked out a window and when he saw them, yanked on a chain and the front door to the club opened. Holstein was the first one through the door.

"Big Max, how are things going?" Holstein asked the man who had opened the door.

Max reached out and shook Holstein's hand. "We're hanging in here, Mr. Holstein, and we'll have a packed crowd tonight."

Holstein took Sam Arthur by the arm and moved him to his side. "This boy here is my new runner; going to spend some time in here." He took out a fifty-dollar bill and handed it to Max. "Make sure he's treated right."

Max took the fifty-dollar bill and stuffed it in his pocket. "You got it, Mr. Holstein. He'll be in good hands."

Still gripping Sam Arthur's arm, Holstein walked over to a steep flight of stairs. Jonas followed closely behind.

"Let me show you where you're gonna get your first break and make some money," Holstein said.

They walked down the steep flight of stairs to a basement cramped for space, with twenty wooden tables and wooden chairs. A bandstand was on the far-left side of the basement and the middle of the room was for dancing.

Staring incredulously at the small size of the club, he couldn't imagine any more than fifty people fitting inside.

"Don't look like you could get no more than fifty people in here," Holstein said as if he were reading Sam Arthur's thoughts. "Well, I can guarantee you that tonight this place will be jumping with at least two hundred Negroes out to have a good time."

Sam Arthur extended his right arm and waved it from left to right. "You mean they gonna get two hundred people into this tiny space?"

"They will and you got to be here by at least eleven o'clock. Give 'em all time to get liquored up, feeling happy and I promise you'll be getting a ton of numbers."

"Listen to him," Jonas spoke up. "I started here, and he knows what he's telling you. Work here and hit some churches on Sunday morning and you'll be sending for that gal of yours in no time."

Holstein turned and walked back to the steps. "You are set up with Max and he'll take care of you. Let's get out of here."

The three men walked back up the stairs and out of the club.

Nina felt uncomfortable wearing only a skimpy chorus girl outfit, exposing her long shapely legs and accentuating her full breasts. She sat in front of the mirror, staring at her half-naked body, knowing what her mother would think and explode if she saw her dressed like this. And then there was Claude.

"You are looking beautiful," said a girl also dressed in chorus line garb as she stood right behind Nina. "No doubt you'll be dancing here. No way Mr. Immerman will turn you down even if you can't even keep up with the rhythm. My name is Addie Henderson and welcome to Connie's Inn."

Nina scooted her chair around and looked up at Addie. "I thought I was auditioning with Mr. Harper."

"Oh no, girl, he don't make no decisions. You got to perform in front of Louis Immerman. He's the manager here. Once he says okay, which I know he'll do, he loves you Creole-looking girls, then you'll learn the routine with Mr. Harper."

The dressing room door swung open and a large man hollered from the entrance. "Nina Jackson, out front."

The blaring voice forced Nina to jump.

"Don't be nervous, girl," Addie said. "Remember, you got all they want in a colored girl: big breasts, fine legs, and a pretty face, and you got 'em all."

Nina got up and walked out of the dressing room down a short hallway, and the man directed her onto a small platform stage. She grimaced as a bright spotlight shined on her. She could hardly make out the images of the two men sitting at a table close to the stage. But she knew one was white and the other one was a Negro man.

"My name is Louis Immerman, the manager here at Connie's Inn. Leonard Harper is here with me. We want you to do your best movements to the music of 'Girls, Girls, Girls.' Have you ever heard that music?"

"Yes, sir, my mama got that on a record back home in St. Louis."

"Good, then let's get started." He signaled to a man standing to the left of the stage. The music filled the room and Nina began a routine she had practiced numerous times back home in her room. The more she got into her routine, the more confident she became as she picked up her beat.

"Stop, that's enough," a voice from the back of the club shouted. George Immerman, the owner of Connie's Inn, walked to the front. "You're hired." He turned and looked at Immerman and Harper. "Get this girl ready for this Friday night." He turned and walked to the back of the club.

Nina stood there, looking at Harper.

"Get dressed," Louis instructed. "Leonard will get with you. George wants you in the chorus line by Friday night's show. We got two days to work with you and that doesn't give us a lot of time. No doubt you're a good dancer, but you'd better be a fast learner."

Nina hurried off the stage, excited about what had just happened. She was now a chorus line dancer in Harlem, and it all happened within two weeks. Life was looking up for her.

"What, you got a job dancing at Connie's Inn?" Regina shrieked.

Nina, Regina, and Ethel sat in the living room at the 582 Apartment. They had just got in from work and Nina was already there waiting for them with her exciting news. The excitement was only momentary.

"Is that where Florence sent you?" Ethel asked. "I thought you were talking with her about joining the dance team for *Bluebirds*?"

Nina squirmed nervously in her chair. She didn't expect this kind of response. Did they think she had done something wrong, and did they also think working at Connie's Inn was a bad thing for her?

"She wanted me to dance with her, but there were no openings, but she promised me that someday soon I'll have a chance to dance with her."

"But why did she send you to Connie's Inn, of all places?" Regina asked.

"Well… it was more on the suggestion of her husband."

"Ulysses!" Regina exclaimed.

"Yes, it was him. He said I would get excellent training for the future when I'll be able to dance with Ms. Mills from a man named Leonard Harper. And the experience would prepare me for when I do get that opportunity."

"I don't like it. You're much too young to be hanging out in a nightclub," Ethel said.

"I can take care of myself," Nina blurted out.

Momentarily, Regina and Ethel looked at each other with concerned expressions all over their faces.

"In St. Louis, were you in a mixed environment or only a Negro one?" Regina asked.

"Where I lived was segregated and we hardly ever went around white people. Mama works for a white family, but I never went with her to their home."

"You're about to enter a world where all your customers will be white because they don't allow Negroes in the club but to entertain the downtown crowd who come here for only one reason and that's to let their uptight hair down."

Nina felt compelled to defend her decision. "It's only going to be for a short while. There will be openings with *Bluebird* and Ms. Mills all but assured me that I would fill the opening."

"When do you start?" Regina asked in a tone exuding disgust.

"Friday night." Nina detected the dry tone in Regina's question. "Ms. Regina, I don't want you upset with me but I cant's just sit around and wait. And Ms. Mills told me that training I'd get from Mr. Harper will help me with my progress."

"Let's pray that it is the truth," Ethel said. "You're welcome to stay here with us until you get on your feet. We need to watch over you. I owe that to Mr. Jones, your principal, back in St. Louis. We have to make sure nothing happens to you."

Regina got up. "In the meantime, we have to get back over to the library. Langston Hughes is going to read from his soon-to-be-published poetry." She looked at Nina. "I want you to come with us. You need to see the better side of Harlem."

The basement room at the 135th Street Library was packed when Marcus arrived a little before seven o'clock. Seeing Schuyler sitting in the back row, he strolled back there and took an empty seat next to him.

Schuyler extended his right hand out to Marcus. "I see you've found your way to the real heartbeat of the cultural explosion, and that's right here at the library." The two men shook.

"My second time here. Came here with Charles Johnson a few days ago." He watched as Ethel, Regina, along with a very attractive young girl, walked into the room and took seats in the front row.

"So, you've already met the man who really got this movement started."

"Charles Johnson is one of the reasons I'm here in Harlem." Marcus now watched as Johnson, Dr. W. E. B. Du Bois, and Walter White walked into the room and took seats in the front row. He turned and looked directly at Schuyler. "Langston Hughes has become a pretty important poet if he can get Dr. Du Bois out to hear him recite."

"Don't leave out Walter White," Schuyler added. "He's an up-and-coming important Negro in Harlem."

"Is Walter White a Negro? He looks more like a white man than one of us."

Schuyler smiled. "He is more Negro than a lot of Negroes who look like a Negro."

Marcus chuckled. "That's a play on words."

"That's what I get paid to do."

Marcus turned his attention back to the entrance to the room and watched as Jessie Fauset escorted Langston Hughes inside. He was struck by the fact that Fauset was practically as tall as Langston. This rising star with a very tall growing reputation, Marcus thought, his physical size would be similar.

Fauset stood at the lectern and Hughes next to her. The room went silent, and she broke the silence. "I have been working closely with this young man since the time back in 1921 when he sent the *Crisis Magazine* copies of his poem 'I Have Known Rivers.'" She turned and looked at Langston, smiled and turned back. "He was just a young boy, but an extremely talented boy. Now, three years later, he is about to be published by a major New York publisher." She paused while the crowd lightly applauded.

"He got the publishing deal with Knopf through Carl Van Vechten," Schuyler whispered.

"Who is Van Vechten?" Marcus asked, also in a low tone.

"I'll explain later." Schuyler turned his attention back to Fauset.

"When Langston asked me to introduce him this evening, I was thrilled to accept. So let me now do just that. To some of you who already know him, and to others who are just meeting him, I present to you our own special, talented poet, Langston Hughes."

Langston moved to the front of the podium, placed papers on top, and then looked out at the crowd.

"When I wrote my first published poem that Ms. Fauset referred to, I had just crossed over the Mississippi River and I knew then poetry, the art, and New York is where I belonged. Since that time back in 1921, I have done a lot of traveling but always with Harlem on my mind. I say all that as a preface to telling you all thank you for being here and making my trip here from Washington, DC, so fulfilling."

It was Marcus' turn to whisper. "He doesn't live here in Harlem?"

"No, right now he's living in Washington and has built a close relationship with Dr. Alain Locke. I believe he was trying to get into Howard University, where Dr. Locke teaches philosophy. I am pretty sure Langston is doing work for Dr. Woodson, the eminent historian who is doing a great deal of research on our ancestors in this country."

"I've heard a great deal about Dr. Locke and want to meet him."

"You'll get your chance. He's always here in Harlem on the weekends and I believe is close friends with Charles Johnson."

They returned their attention to Langston, who continued.

"My first book of poetry is set to be released this year, thanks to a very good friend, who actually wrote the introduction to *Weary Blues*, Carl Van Vechten. I was hoping that he would be here tonight but was unable to make it."

"I really need to meet this Van Vechten." Marcus couldn't control himself.

"You'll get that opportunity," Schuyler whispered while keeping his attention focused on Langston. "He's Harlem's own white savior."

"I will now share with you all five of the poems in *Weary Blues* and I will begin with 'I Have Known Rivers.'"

As Marcus listened to Langston recite the poem, his mind wandered. Two new names that seemed to be important caught his interest: Walter White and Carl Van Vechten.

Sam Arthur decided not to wait until eleven o'clock, got to the Sugar Cane Club at eight. He was so excited about the prospect of finally making some money, he just couldn't sit around at the YMCA, waiting until eleven.

Sam Arthur walked up to the door, waited momentarily, and it swung open. He hurried inside and heard the loud beat of the music coming from down below.

"I see you're real anxious to get started making money," Big Max said as he closed the door behind Sam Arthur. "You real early, but that's okay. The joint is full and jumping."

"I had to get out of the cramped room I got at the Y, so I figured I just come on over here early."

"You at the Y?"

"Sure am, since I got here."

"You do well for Mr. Holstein, and you won't be there long."

Sam Arthur looked over at the stairway where the music was coming from and turned back to Big Max. "Sounds like you got a big crowd down there."

"It's packed, and it's only eight-thirty. By eleven there won't even be standing room down there. Get on down there and start making you some money. I'll be down there soon."

Sam Arthur walked down the stairway and when he reached the bottom, he looked on a dance floor full of men and women dancing so close they were practically standing in place and just shuffling their feet with no movement. Walking along the side of the dance floor, he made his way over to the bar and sat on the only empty barstool right at the end. For the first time since he had come to New York, he felt out of place. Sadie's Place back in Gaffney was nothing like this. There was always some room to breathe back there.

These people were like sardines, packed in there so tightly, and unlike Sadie's, there was very little room to even breathe. He looked over to the far corner of the club and smiled as he glanced at the piano player, drummer, and guitarist, all dressed in tuxedos. The woman at the microphone singing wore a tight-fitting dress with all kinds of glistening trinkets.

"You want a drink?" the bartender asked.

Sam Arthur swung around to face the bartender. Before he could answer, Big Max walked up and stood next to him.

"It's on Mr. Holstein's tab," he said to the bartender, then looked at Sam Arthur. "What you drinking and it better be something pretty strong to relax your body. You seems right uptight."

"How am I gonna take numbers in here when I can hardly move around?" he asked Big Max, ignoring the question about a drink.

"The band will be taking a twenty-minute break and the dancers will be at their tables. At least of them got chairs. In that twenty-minute time, you hit the right side of the room. The band will come back out and play for another hour, take another break, and you get to the other side of the room. You do that all night long and you gonna get numbers for half these people and the ones coming later on in the night."

Sam Arthur relaxed as he listened to Big Max explain how to work the club.

"Most of these people are regulars and come in here three to four nights every week. They'll get to know you after a while and know you running for Mr. Holstein, and they trust him that he'll pay if they win. They'll be looking for you."

The music stopped, and the dancers cleared the floor, returning to their tables. Max signaled for the bartender to come back over to them.

"Johnny, this here's Mr. Holstein's new runner; gonna work the club."

"What happened to the runner he had in here before?" Johnny asked.

"Don't know and don't care 'bout that. Ain't none of our business. Our business is to make sure this boy is protected." Big Max placed his large hand on Sam Arthur's shoulder.

"I got it," Johnny said, looking at Sam Arthur. "What you drinking?"

"Shot of bourbon straight up."

The bartender poured the drink and placed it in front of Sam Arthur.

Big Max patted Sam Arthur on his shoulder. "It's only nine o'clock. Relax and have your drink. I'll be back down here when the band takes their next break and I'll introduce you around and make my people here comfortable with you. They'll give you plenty of business tonight."

Sam Arthur watched as a well-dressed man walked across the dance floor and stood next to Big Max.

"Where the hell is Holstein's runner? I got some winning numbers?"

Big Max looked at Sam Arthur. "Looks like you ain't gonna have to wait." He turned and faced the well-dressed man. "This here's the new runner. He can take your bet and your money."

The well-dressed man moved in close to Sam Arthur, who pulled out a small square piece of red-colored paper and a pencil from the inside of his jacket pocket.

The man handed him a dollar. "I dreamt these numbers last night and just been waiting to play them. They's 739."

Sam Arthur wrote the numbers on the slip of paper, of which he gave the man a copy, and placed them in a bag Jonas had given him to place his bets and the money in.

"I'll be looking for you tomorrow night with my winnings." The well-dressed man walked back across the dance floor to his table. He said something to another man at his table and pointed to Sam Arthur. The other man got up and started walking across the dance floor.

Big Max smiled. "That man coming over here to see you. Look like you might not need me after all. Been a couple weeks since a Holstein runner been in here and these Negroes just been waiting."

Sam Arthur took a heavy gulp from his drink and sat straight up as the man approached him.

"You're on your own," Big Max said. "Make that money, 'cause when you do, we all get paid." He again patted Sam Arthur on the shoulder and walked away just as the man reached the bar and stood next to Sam Arthur.

⁂

"There is no doubt, given the content of those five poems Langston recited tonight, that he is challenging the old guard," Schuyler said as he sat at a table across from Marcus at the Craig Restaurant on Eighth Avenue and 135th Street.

"Before leaving Chicago, we heard that there was a difference in writing between these new and younger writers and the old guard like Dr. DuBois."

Schuyler watched as Langston strolled into the restaurant with Fauset, Regina, Ethel, and Nina. They sat at a table next to a window looking out on Eighth Avenue.

"Looks like you just might get a chance to ask Langston himself that question." Schuyler got up and walked over to the table the four had just occupied.

Marcus watched him as he talked with Fauset. After a brief minute, Schuyler waved his arm, inviting Marcus to come over to the table. He got up and hurried over and stood next to Schuyler.

Schuyler looked directly at Regina and Ethel. "I believe the two of you have already met our fine guest from Chicago." They both nodded and Schuyler turned his attention to Langston and Fauset. "To you, Langston and Jessie, allow me to introduce you to Marcus Williams, a reporter from the *Chicago Defender*. He is here doing an in-depth study of the burgeoning cultural arts movement here in Harlem."

They nodded in acknowledgment.

Schuyler continued. "Now, Langston, Marcus has a particular interest in you since you are one of the leading new artists in this new Negro movement."

"Hurry and ask your question," Regina said. "It's been a long day, and we just stopped here for a refreshment, not a long question-and-answer session."

Marcus looked directly at Langston. "Word outside of Harlem is that you younger writers are no longer willing to follow the lead of the older Negro writers and are determined to do your creative work as you see fit. Is that what's happening here?"

Langston concentrated his attention on Marcus. "Sir, we respect the old guard and appreciate all they have done for our race, but we younger writers must write as we see fit, only obligated to our brothers and sisters who are the common folk."

Marcus momentarily looked at Schuyler, who shrugged, then back at Langston. "Who are 'we' besides you?"

Determined not to let this turn into an interview, Regina spoke up. "Mr. Williams, we appreciate your job and, of course, respect Mr. Abbott, but this is not the time."

Detecting this needed a mediator, Schuyler said, "That's a good beginning at least you had an opportunity to chat with one our leading poets."

"Good enough," Regina said. "Now, if you all will excuse us, we'd like to order, eat, and get out of here. It's getting late and tomorrow is a workday for us."

"Certainly," Schuyler replied. He and Marcus turned and walked back over to their table.

By closing time at the Sugar Cane Club, Sam Arthur had a bag full of red slips and money, most being coins from a nickel to fifty cents. He sat at the bar while the crowd started up the stairs. He decided to wait until everyone had left, just in case the ones who hadn't placed a bet still wanted to at the very last minute.

Just as the last person disappeared up the stairs, Big Max came down into the club. He hurried over and stood next to Marcus, looked at the bag on the counter, and then at Marcus.

"From the looks of the bulge in that bag, I believe you did quite well for your first night in here."

Sam Arthur didn't respond to Big Max because he watched as the four band players packed their instruments and headed toward him.

"You the new runner for Mr. Holstein and we got numbers we want to play," the piano player said as the four walked up to Marcus.

"He sure is," Big Max answered. "Hurry up and give him your numbers 'cause we got to close these doors in the next five minutes."

The band players took the red slips from Sam Arthur, wrote their numbers on the slips using their own pencils, and handed them back with their money. Sam Arthur gave them copies. They turned and headed toward the stairs.

"Come on, let's get out of here," Big Max said.

"Yeah, I got to get this money over to Mr. Holstein tonight."

"No problem." Big Max patted Sam Arthur on the back. "Soon as you walk out the door, Jonas will be waiting so let's get out of here."

Sam Arthur and Big Max got up and headed up the stairs.

4.

NINA FELT COMFORTABLE AND AT ease, as she moved her body in sync with the other thirteen chorus girls, dancing to the music beat of "The Charleston." When she first strolled out on the stage with the others and looked out to a packed club of white men and some women, her knees momentarily went weak. She'd never danced in front of white people, and she'd never been half-naked in skimpy attire in front of any group of people. With them being white, made it worse. Once the band struck up a bouncy beat, the girls jumped right into the rehearsed routine, and all her energy became immersed in the dance.

By the third performance at a little after eleven, she felt the eyes of a well-dressed white man concentrated on her. He had worked his way to the table closest to the stage. Early on before the show, Addie had told her that white men would zero in on her and that she definitely should not stare back. She tried her best to follow Addie's advice, but she couldn't help but to look at him. One time she did, and the man smiled at her. Nina quickly looked away. She was relieved when the set ended, and the girls retreated into the dressing room for a half-hour break.

Nina plopped down in the chair, reared her head back, and closed her eyes. She hoped the man didn't take her glancing at him the wrong way.

Addie walked over and sat in the empty chair next to Nina. "Girl, you sure didn't take any time at all for you to get an admirer." She smiled. "That white man looked like he was drooling, looking at you."

Nina opened her eyes and sat straight up. "You noticed him looking at me?"

"Me and every other girl in the chorus line," Addie replied. "We knew it wouldn't take long, but never imagined it would happen your first night in here."

"What's gonna happen?"

"He'll probably tell Mr. Immerman that he would like to buy you a drink. Mr. Immerman will send one of his bouncers with a message to you, and the strong recommendation that you accommodate the man and at the next break in the dancing, you go out there and sit with him."

Nina's eyes widened. "What! I don't want to do that. I've never socialized with a white man, and I have a boyfriend at Howard University who I'm committed to."

"Girl, you don't have to do nothing more than entertain him between shows. That's something understood when you dance in a club like this. And it's something Mr. Immerman insists we do so they'll keep coming back. He's competing with the Cotton Club for the richest and best white business. It's best you go along with it if you want to keep dancing here."

"Maybe nothing will happen, and he'll be gone when we go back out there."

"Maybe he won't be, but if he is, try your best not to look at him."

"I didn't take this job to entertain no men at their table, only on the stage," Nina said with indignation.

"Here, you entertain at both places," Addie retorted. "Get ready because at some point it's going to happen."

At three in the morning, Sam Arthur walked out of the Sugar Cane Club again with a sack full of red slips and money. He hurried over to the Lincoln waiting for him and got in. Instead of driving off, Jonas looked at him.

"You made a good score in there tonight."

"Sure did, and if they didn't have to close at three, could've made a hell of a lot more," Sam Arthur proudly proclaimed.

"I tell you what, it don't have to end tonight."

"What you mean?"

"You ever heard about the rent parties?"

It was late and Sam Arthur was tired. He'd been practically locked in the Sugar Cane Club since eight, but he was still fired up and if he could take more bets, he was ready to go. He adjusted his body toward Jonas.

"No, I ain't heard nothing about that."

It's poor people's party in other people's apartments. But this time, them flats be packed with people."

"Is it like the Sugar Cane where people bet the numbers?"

"It's just like that and them folks been drinking that rotgut gin and be looking for a runner. It's Friday night and most of them don't work in the morning."

Sam Arthur straightened his body. "Let's go. Hell, I can sleep all day until I go back to the club tomorrow night."

"Let's go make some more money." Jonas pulled out onto Fifth Avenue and drove north. He pulled up at a large apartment complex. They got out and as soon as they entered the apartment, Sam Arthur could hear the loud raucous music and smelled the fried chicken and chitterlings coming from the second floor.

At the top of the stairs, the crowd had drifted out of the apartment, and they had to dodge around the couples dancing in the hallway. They reached the entrance to the apartment and Jonas gave the man sitting at the door fifty cents to cover their entry into the party.

Sam Arthur thought he had seen a great deal of what Harlem had to offer right down in the basement of the Sugar Cane Club, but as they fought their way inside the apartment and he viewed all the people dancing, drinking and just standing around the walls, he knew there was so much he did not know about this place.

Jonas worked his way to the back of the room next to the piano player, an extremely large man sweating profusely and beating his feet to the rhythm he was creating. Following closely behind, Sam Arthur noticed it was mostly young-looking women standing next to the walls. There had to be at least five women to every man in the room. Curiously, that got the best of him. He tapped Jonas on the shoulder to get his attention just as he was going to talk to the piano player. Jonas turned and faced him.

Sam Arthur shouted over the music. "All the women in here far outnumber the men. Is this a special women's party?"

Jonas smiled. "All these rent parties are set up for the women. If they can get the women here, they know the men gonna come. Lots of them just got here from the South just like you and they looking for a man." He paused and waved his arm. "Take your pick and you gonna be treated real good tonight."

"Oh no, that ain't for me. I got to save myself for my Willa Mae."

Jonas's smile spread even further across his face. "We'll see how long that's gonna last. You got to stretch them pants unless you queer. And a lot of the men in Harlem are queer."

"What you mean queer?" Sam Arthur asked just as the music ended and the piano player got up and stood next to Jonas.

"Wondering if you was coming through." The piano player looked at Sam Arthur. "Whose this young fellow with you?"

Jonas grabbed Sam Arthur by the arm and pulled him standing right in front of the piano player. "This is Sam Arthur and he's the new runner for Mr. Holstein."

"So, he's the right one?"

"He's the one."

The piano player pulled out fifty cents and held it out to Sam Arthur. "Had a dream that the three numbers 918 were winners and was just waiting for Mr. Holstein's runner to show up."

Sam Arthur took the fifty cents and wrote the numbers on a red slip and gave the piano player his copy with the numbers.

The piano player turned and faced Jonas. "Got to get back to work 'cause these people just raring to dance. Better grab you one of these girls and get you some pleasure." He sat back at the piano and struck up a tune.

5.

MARCUS SAT AT A TABLE at Small's Paradise, one of the few nightclubs owned by a Negro. It was a little after eight in the evening and he had plans to meet Alain Locke with Carl Van Vechten there. Just for introduction purposes, Schuyler also promised to meet them at the club. It was Schuyler who had contacted Locke in Washington, DC, where he had just been dismissed from his professorship at Howard University for leading a student revolt against the administration and told him this reporter from the *Chicago Defender* would like to meet with him. Locke agreed but told Schuyler that he would have to bring Van Vechten with him. Schuyler assured Locke that the reporter would welcome Van Vechten because it would be like killing two birds with one stone. The meeting was set for nine o'clock, but Schuyler agreed to meet Marcus there at eight and brief him on Locke and Van Vechten.

A waiter dressed in a tuxedo and on roller skates skated up to Marcus's table. "Can I get your order?"

Just as he did, Schuyler strolled through the door and hurried over to the table.

"Just in time. I was just going to order."

"Good." Schuyler looked at the waiter. "None of that rotgut stuff you got in the back. Tell your boss George Schuyler wants the real thing." He looked at Marcus. "What you drinking?"

Marcus thought back on the last time he had liquor in Chicago the night he covered the Louis Armstrong concert and how he felt the next morning. "Just any soda will do."

"On the wagon, huh?" Schuyler smiled and looked back at the roller-skating waiter. "You heard him, and a scotch and soda for me."

"You got it." The roller-skating waiter skated back toward the bar area.

Schuyler relaxed back in his chair. "Well, my friend, you are about to meet the Negro godfather and the white godfather of this new literary movement here in Harlem."

Marcus leaned forward. "Why do you refer to them in those terms?"

"It's a long story but the shorter version is last year at the Civic Club dinner organized by Charles Johnson, and really was the stimulus to this so-called literary movement, Johnson conceded the limelight to Alain when he made him the master of ceremonies. In that role, Alain took control and instead of Charles writing the article in the *Survey Graphic* magazine dedicated to that event, it was Alain. Since that time, he has been the go-to guy to introduce Negro authors to Van Vechten, who then gets them to the right publishers to publish their works."

"How did they get so close if Alain lives in Washington, DC?"

"Alain may live in Washington, but he is up here every weekend and sometimes it extends to during the week. Their close relationship might be because they are both homosexuals."

Marcus hesitated before responding. He wanted to get his words right. "That's interesting. Two homosexuals, one Negro and the other white, are responsible for the success of this movement. Can I assume, then, that a number of the artists are also homosexuals?"

"Yeah, probably you can say that."

They paused as the roller-skating waiter skated up to them and placed their drinks on the table. Marcus handed the man the money, and he skated away.

"You sound rather hesitant?"

"I am because many of the artists who might be that way hide it from the public."

"Who are some of the homosexuals?"

"Now you're trying to get me in trouble."

"I don't want to do that, so just tell me the names of the ones who don't hide it and there is no way that should jeopardize your standing in the community."

Once again, Schuyler smiled. "You're good. I see why Robert sent you to do this story."

"Thanks, but I don't need a compliment. I need names."

Schuyler leaned forward in his chair so that no one else could hear. "To start with, the one most open with his homosexuality is a young artist from Washington, DC, Richard Nugent. Unlike some of the others, he is proud of who he is, but others like the young poet, Countee Cullen, and some claim even Langston are homosexuals, but not openly indulging."

The mention of Langston caused Marcus to jerk his head up. "Are you suggesting that Langston Hughes sleeps with men?"

"No one knows for sure, but word got back that last year while he was in Paris, he spent some quality time with Alain, and it was well known that Alain liked the young and innocent-looking young men for his sexual eroticism."

"Are there others that I should know about?"

"It's believed that the poet, Claude McKay, is a homosexual, but he is hardly ever in the country."

While listening to Schuyler, Marcus watched as the two men, one white and the other a rather petite, well-dressed Negro, strolled into the club. In all his years, he had never even carried on a conversation with a known homosexual. As the two men approached his table, he was about to experience just that.

Addie had told Nina that the Saturday night crowd would be the largest. As she and the other girls made their way to the stage, and with some trepidation, she looked out at all the full tables, hoping she didn't see that one man, but saw him at a table close to the stage. He smiled at her, and she looked away.

Right behind her in the line, Addie leaned forward and whispered, "You must have looked at him because I saw him smile. Don't at all look his way. You're inviting problems."

The music began, and the girls went into their routine.

Back in the dressing room after the first show, Nina felt exhausted. Not so much from the dancing but from the strain to not look over at the man who stared at her throughout the entire performance. Every time the dressing room door would open, she looked over to see who was coming in. She just knew it would be Immerman walking through that door to direct her out to the man's table. With all the trepidation building up in her, Nina considered getting dressed and running out of that place. She quickly jettisoned that thought, because to do so would spoil her chances of ever dancing with Florence Mills.

"You feeling all right?" Addie asked, causing Nina to jump. "Girl, you nervous and you got to get over that right now. When we go back out there, it'll affect your performance."

"If they come and get me, I don't know what I'm gonna do." Nina sighed.

"What are you gonna do? You're gonna go out there and ignore that peckerwood's face and do your job."

Nina looked all around her and moved in closer to Addie. "I've never been in the company of no white boy, and I got a boyfriend at Howard University I'm committed to."

With scorn on her face, Addie whispered, "You mean you came to work in a place like this and you still a virgin?"

"I came here to dance with Florence Mills not to get involved with no man. I don't know how to."

"Girl, you done come to the wrong place with all that innocence. And to Harlem, of all places." Addie looked at the other dancers to make sure they weren't trying to listen to their conversation. Convinced they weren't, she continued. "You think all of them white folks come over to Harlem 'cause they like us? Not at all. They come down here to loosen up, let their hair down, and do things here they can't do in their homes. And girl, we are a part of that good times." She paused to let it all register with Nina. "So, if you want to keep your job, you'll go out there and show your fine body, pretty face, and dance for them. And every once in a while, you got to go out there and sit with them and feed their fantasy. That's what this is all about."

The dressing room door swung open, and the bouncer stuck his head inside. "All right ladies, it's show time."

Addie and Nina got up, as did the others.

"Let's go feed their fantasies for another hour, and please do not look his way, even if you have to keep your eyes closed throughout the entire performance."

Sam Arthur sat across from Holstein at his office in the Turf Club. Jonas sat in the chair next to Sam Arthur. Holstein sat in his large leather chair, counting money. A surge of excitement shot through Sam Arthur's entire body, watching Holstein and especially the money. He had never seen that much money in his entire life, and he was responsible for a portion of it. He had done well, given the short time he'd been in the business.

Jonas nudged him and smiled. "You ain't never seen that much money, have you?"

"Can't say I have."

Holstein counted out some tens. Then put the money on top of the desk close to Sam Arthur. "This is your earnings, and I'm throwing in an extra ten for the great job you did, and this is just your first week."

Sam Arthur took the money and stuffed it in his pocket. "Thank you, Mr. Holstein."

Holstein looked directly at Jonas and smiled. "Jonas told me you ain't never done nothing with a woman. You a man virgin. Is that true?"

Nervously Sam Arthur answered. "Yes, sir, that's true. Saving myself for my Willa Mae when I can get her up here and we can get married."

"You got it all wrong," Holstein shot back. "It's the woman that got to stay pure for the man she's going to marry. Ain't natural for a man to wait." He took a ten-dollar bill and handed it to Jonas, then looked at Sam Arthur. "It's still early and you don't have to be at the Sugar Cane for a couple hours. Jonas going to take you to a private room and get you broke in. I can't have no man working for me, walking around all frustrated 'cause he ain't getting none."

Sam Arthur reared back in his chair, determined not to move. "What's he gonna do?"

Holstein and Jonas laughed.

Jonas looked directly at Sam Arthur. "I ain't gonna do nothing to you, so get up and come on. Let's get out of the boss's office. He got another meeting."

Not sure what they had planned for him, Sam Arthur reluctantly got up and followed Jonas out of the office and down the hall.

Jonas opened the door to a room and Sam Arthur followed him but came to an abrupt stop as he looked at a young woman in only her bra and panties sitting on the side of the bed.

Jonas walked over and handed the girl the ten-dollar bill, whispered in her ear, then turned and walked to the entrance to the room where Sam Arthur stood. "Have fun and I'll be back to get you at ten and get you over to the Sugar Cane Club."

"But I don't want—"

Before Sam Arthur could complete his protest, Jonas walked out and closed the door.

Sam Arthur looked at the young girl. It was the first time he'd seen a woman practically naked. He felt excitement building.

The girl stretched her body on the bed, spread her legs, smiled, and waved for Sam Arthur to join her.

"So, you're interested in writing about this new Negro movement," Locke said as he and Van Vechten took the two empty seats at the table with Marcus and Schuyler.

Marcus nodded. "I am, but more important, the man I work for is interested."

"Robert Abbot. He is a good man and doing good things with his newspaper," Locke continued.

"Hold up just one minute, so is the *Pittsburg Courier* doing great reporting," Schuyler spoke up.

"No offense meant," Locke replied. "We know you did good work for them until you transferred over to the *Messenger* and A. Philip Randolph."

"Don't leave out the *Amsterdam News*," Van Vechten spoke up.

"All our newspapers, with the exception of the *Age*, support what's happening here in Harlem," Schuyler said. "But that's not the reason this man is in our city. He wants to write about all the great things happening here."

Locke looked directly at Marcus. "Well, ask away."

Marcus sat straight up in his chair. "I guess we can begin with who is this new Negro coming out of Harlem that we hear so much about?"

"Just think of the old subservient Negro who was beholden to the will of the white man and that is what the new Negro is not. They are the new revolutionary and their revolution will not be with guns and bullets, but with pen and paper," Locke answered.

"Who is the leader of this new Negro?" Marcus asked.

"There are many leaders," Van Vechten added. "Alain is one of them and Charles Johnson also. You need to interview Charles."

Marcus looked directly at Van Vechten. "I have already interviewed him and will again. But how about your role in this movement?"

"I'm not sure I have a role to play," Van Vechten replied.

"To the contrary, aren't you the contact between these young writers and the publishing companies?" Marcus suggested.

"I guess you can say that." Van Vechten leaned forward in his chair. "But what you need to know is there is a national movement among white writers to break from the old stifling Victorian style writing. In this country, our writers are freeing themselves. Just like the new Negroes are breaking the chains of control from the white domination, the white writers are also breaking out of the domination from across the ocean, and that brings Greenwich Village to Harlem. They view the Negro as playing a major role."

Marcus leaned even further across the table. "Can you give me an example?"

Van Vechten did not hesitate. "Yes, definitely. Eugene O'Neil's play, *Emperor Jones,* was a major breakthrough. The Ku Klux Klan threatened to kill Paul Robeson for his part in O'Neil's play, *All God's Chillun Got Wings,* 'cause he touches a white woman."

"I heard about that play. It takes on a taboo subject of miscegenation. That was quite a breakthrough and very courageous of O'Neil to write it."

Locke also moved in closer. "You have to understand that what is happening in Harlem among the Negroes is the same as what has happened in Ireland and Czechoslovakia. There is a new movement among the people of those countries, much like the movement in Harlem."

Marcus turned and looked at Schuyler as if to say, *What is this man talking about?*

Schuyler picked up on his expression. "You have to understand that Alain is more of an internationalist, so his comparisons are quite profound."

"He is also a well-recognized scholar in his field," Van Vechten added.

A smile crossed Locke's face, and he sat up straight, obviously enjoying the accolades.

Marcus added to the praise. "Yes, we in Chicago are very much aware of this man's accomplishments: Phi Beta Kappa from Harvard and the first Negro Rhodes Scholar. That is quite a resume. But what happened at Howard?"

Locke's smile turned to a smirk. "Mr. Williams...it is Williams, isn't it?"

"Just call me Marcus." He detected the cynicism in Locke's questioning of his name.

"Well, Marcus, I took a strong stand for the students. I sided with them in their protest with the administration and they dismissed me from my professorship." Locke leaned halfway across the table. "I would imagine if you took a position contrary to one taken by Mr. Abbott, you would suffer the same outcome."

"You're right, he probably would." Marcus knew he was losing this very arrogant and proud man. He needed to back off.

Schuyler rescued him. "I understand you are writing a book about this movement," he said, looking at Locke.

"Yes, I am. It's a collection of essays with some wonderful drawings, poetry, and short stories from some of the finest young artists in Harlem." Locke's smile had returned. "It is rightfully titled *The New Negro*."

Tired of this man's puffed ego, Marcus shifted the conversation to Van Vechten.

"One of the most important happenings taking place in Harlem, according to Charles Johnson, is the integration of Negro and white artists and the growing interest white publishing companies have in Negro writers. I understand it is due to you, Mr. Van Vechten—"

"No, not Mr. Van Vechten. Please, just Carl."

"The point I was trying to make or better my question to you, Carl, do you consider this a passing fad, or will the relationships have some permanence?"

Van Vechten leaned back in a relaxed position. "I am not the right one to ask that question."

"Who do you suggest I ask, then?"

"They will be at my apartment on Sunday afternoon for hors d'oeuvres and tea." Van Vechten looked at Schuyler. "George, could you accompany Marcus tomorrow afternoon at three?"

"I can do that."

"Then it is done. We will continue this discussion tomorrow afternoon."

Sam Arthur stood there frozen in place, despite the girl's urging him to join her on the bed. No doubt he was excited, but he was also scared. Not of the girl, but of the repercussions from Mr. Holstein if he didn't have sex. He knew that if he made it over to the bed and got next to her, he would find it difficult to control himself and would not be worthy of Willa Mae's affection and love.

The girl finally sat up with her back against the bed backrest. "Okay, what's the problem? You can't get it up? Come over here and I'll help you."

It was best to be honest with his commitment to Willa Mae. He had an erection just looking at the girl in only her bra and panty, but it couldn't be for her. He had to tell her that and hope she'd understand. After all, she had the ten dollars, so why should she care?

"Come on, baby, let me do what I got to 'cause if I don't, Mr. Holstein gonna want his ten dollars back."

Suddenly, Sam Arthur had an idea that might make this work out just fine for both of them. He walked over and sat on the side of the bed.

"I don't mean you no harm," he said, looking at the girl. "But you see, I got my Willa Mae back in South Carolina and I got to stay pure for her."

The young girl broke out laughing. "You mean Mr. Holstein done sent me a virgin to break in? I'll be damned." She sat on the side of the bed next to Sam Arthur. "Well, we got ourselves a situation here. I don't want to give these ten dollars back and you don't want to get fired."

She put her hand on Sam Arthur's knee, and he froze up. "Relax, sweetheart, I'm not gonna force you to do something you don't want to do. Although I have to tell you, it's your loss. I ain't never have no man complain."

Sam Arthur did not remove her hand. "I guess you must think something's different about me. There ain't nothing I'd rather do than lay with you, but you got to understand why I can't, and I sure don't want to get you in no trouble."

The young girl moved in close to Sam Arthur and kissed him on the side of his face, then moved back away from him.

"In my business, I got to admit I ain't never met no man like you."

"I ain't no different from no other man. I got urges, and I sure got one right now and when I walked through that door, seeing you lay there looking all good. But it ain't fair to my Willa Mae when I know she back there saving herself for just me."

"This Willa Mae got to be one lucky woman to have a man like you all nice looking and strong all to herself. I hope she deserves it."

Sam Arthur took a deep breath and released it. "She do, for sure she do."

"So, what do we do with this situation Willa Mae got us in?" She did not wait for an answer. "Jonas will be here in a few minutes to pick you up. You just tell him how much you enjoyed Mary in the bed, and you got my address when you want some more."

Sam Arthur managed a smile. "Your name's Mary. I got a sister back home named Mary. Momma named her after Mary, the mother of Jesus. Was you named after that Mary? She and Momma moved up to Chicago a year ago. I ain't seen them since."

Ignoring Sam Arthur's question, Mary reached over and grabbed a pencil off the small table in the room. "Give me one of your red slips for the numbers."

Sam Arthur handed her the slip. She wrote her address on it and handed it back to him. "Show my home address to Jonas and he'll believe we did something in bed. That way, you keep your job and I'll keep these ten dollars."

"Whatcha gonna do when you leave out of here?" He didn't know why he asked her because there was no reason he should care. But he did.

"I'm gonna go home and feed my baby and get me some dinner."

"You got a baby?"

"Sure do, be three years in October."

Sam Arthur took five dollars of the money Holstein gave him and handed it to her.

She took the money. "Why you doing this?"

"I don't know. I guess I think it's the right thing to do if it helps you not to have to do this. It ain't much. I'd give you more, but I got to save it for my Willa Mae."

"Now I owe you."

Sam Arthur jerked back away from her.

"Not that way, silly." She smiled, took Sam Arthur by the arm, and pulled him back over to her. "You got to let me cook you a meal. I know you probably not eating right, having to be working all the time. That's the least I can do for you."

Sam Arthur relaxed. "You people up here don't know nothing 'bout no good home cooking." He smiled for the first time.

"What you mean, man? My mama and grandma from Georgia and I learned from them when I was only ten. They brought the South up here with them. So, what you say, you gonna let me make it up to you?"

"Yeah, I guess I can do that."

The door swung open, and Jonas walked in and smiled. "Look like you all done hit it off really good."

Mary tightened her hold on Sam Arthur's arm and cuddled close. "We had a good time."

Jonas looked at Sam Arthur. "Now that you got that load off, you ready to go and make some money?"

He lightly kissed Mary on the lips and broke from her embrace. "Thank you, Mary."

"No, thank you and you got my address, so use it."

Sam Arthur followed Jonas out of the room.

6.

A KNOCK ON THE DOOR of the apartment awakened Nina. She was still living with Regina and Ethel, who agreed she could stay with them until she made enough money to get a decent place of her own, or maybe move in with chorus line dancers who had more in common than they did with her. She also had to sleep on the couch since Luella had returned to the apartment. It wasn't the most comfortable, nothing like back home in St. Louis, but getting off work at three in the morning and having danced four sets, she had no problem falling asleep.

That morning she had slept through Regina, Ethel, and Louella leaving out for church, but the knock had awakened her, and she wasn't sure what to do. She knew it couldn't be anyone there to see her. Suddenly, a frightening possibility shot through her. What if that crazy white man had found out where she lived and was right outside the door? If it was him, the door was locked, and he couldn't get in.

Whomever it was, knocked again and much as she didn't want to know, she got up and slipped on a dress she'd worn home last night and creeped over to the door. With extreme trepidation, she stood next to the door.

"None of the women who live here are home," she called out loud enough to be heard on the other side. The reply shocked her.

"It's Claude and I'm here to see Nina. Is she in?"

"Claude! Is that really you, Claude? What are you doing up here, and how did you find me?"

"Yes, it's me and I'll tell you if you open the door and let me in."

Nina swung the door open, and Claude hurried inside and put his arms around her. She did not respond. Claude moved a step back.

"Nina, what's wrong? You act like you're not happy to see me."

Nina needed to relax. "No, it's not that at all. Certainly, I'm happy to see you, but it was so sudden," she tried to explain, but she felt something different. Her life had made such a drastic change since high school and that was just a month ago. Was she moving away from her past and was that a good thing?

"Well, are you going to invite me in?" Claude asked brusquely.

"Yes, but you can't stay long." She waved him inside. "I'm staying with some wonderful ladies, and they haven't given me permission to have company here. When they get back from church, I don't want them to be surprised."

Claude sat on one end of the couch and Nina sat in a chair, but reached over and took his hands in hers.

"How did you find me, Claude?"

"I contacted Principal Woods, and he told me he believed you were staying here, so I took a chance because I had to see you."

Nina deflected. "How is college? Do you like it?"

"Yes, just taking some summer school classes and I love it, but what's going on with you? Are you taking Harlem by storm?"

Nina released her grip on Claude's hands and reared back in the chair. "I'm doing okay, still looking for work as a dancer." She didn't tell Claude where she danced and how she danced.

Claude scooted right to the edge of the couch. "Well, since you haven't been able to dance here, why don't you come to Washington? You'd get a job right away, and you'd love it there. And most important, we'd be together."

Nina sat straight up. "Claude, I appreciate your concern, but there is no way I'm leaving Harlem. You know that."

"What's happening to you, Nina?"

"What do you mean?"

"I don't know. It just seems like you've been here for only a short time, and you've changed. This is not the Nina I know."

A feeling of guilt creeped into Nina. She didn't know why she was reacting to Claude this way. "No, Claude, I haven't changed and I'm sorry. You know I've always wanted to visit Washington and soon as I can raise a little extra money, I'll come down there and visit you."

"You don't have to wait. I have a student work job with Dr. Woodson in history. I can pay your way down there."

Nina didn't expect that response from him, but she felt uncomfortable accepting that offer and forcing her to commit. She wasn't going to leave Harlem, not even for a week, just in case the word came from Florence, and she'd be gone. She also didn't want to hurt Claude any more than she already had with her behavior. Why did this have to happen? Everything was going fine, with the exception of the white man at the club.

"Nina, you heard my offer and I want you to accept it so we can get back on the right track with boyfriend and girlfriend." Claude's tone was much sterner.

"Boyfriend and girlfriend? Don't you think we've outgrown that?"

Claude sprang from the couch and stared down at Nina. "I don't know what's happened to you, but you've changed in the short period of time you've been here, and I don't like it."

Nina got up and faced Claude. "You knew my plans have always been to dance, and that's what I want to do so—"

"So, I guess you no longer have time for me. Evidently, your dancing is more important that our future together." Claude hurried to the door, opened it, and looked back at Nina, who still stood there. "I know I love you, Nina, and I thought you felt the same way about me. Or maybe I was just fooling myself. You never felt the same for me."

Nina wanted to move toward Claude and ask him to understand her drive to dance. She wanted to tell him she really hadn't changed but had become even more driven after meeting with Florence and getting her promise to someday they would dance together. But she couldn't do it and just continued to stand there.

"I will be in Washington at Howard University if you change your mind or, better still, come to your senses. You can reach me in Dr. Carter Woodson's office." Claude walked out.

Marcus followed Schuyler into the plush apartment building on Fifty-fifth Avenue. As they waited for the elevator, he caught up and stood next to Schuyler.

"So, this is where the more affluent New Yorkers live?"

"They are that if nothing else," Schuyler replied.

The elevator opened; they got inside.

"To Mr. Van Vechten's, I assume," the elevator operator said.

He was correct, but Schuyler did not like his assumption. "Why do you assume that's where we are going?"

"Because a number of important Negroes have already went up there," the elevator operator answered.

"Well, we are not important Negroes, but that is where we are going," Schuyler said.

The elevator operator closed the door and started the elevator's motion upward.

"It seems that important Negroes go to Mr. Van Vechten's apartment at least once a week," the elevator operator said.

Neither Schuyler nor Marcus responded to him. Instead, they stood silently, waiting for the elevator to stop on the second floor. It did. The operator opened the door, and they walked out.

The apartment double door swung open, and Van Vechten smiled. "I'm pleased that you made it." He looked at Marcus. "Some very influential people are already here in my drawing room."

The first person Marcus recognized as he walked into the well-decorated room was James Weldon Johnson. Van Vechten took Marcus by the arm and led him over to James Johnson, who smiled as they approached him. Schuyler was right behind them.

"This, Marcus, is James Weldon Johnson, Secretary of the NAACP and all-around talented writer and musician," Van Vechten said.

Marcus reached out and grabbed James Johnson's hand, vigorously shaking it. "I met you once before in Chicago when you spoke at an NAACP event."

"Oh, yes, I thought you looked familiar," James Johnson responded. "You're Robert Abbott's reporter. What brings you to New York?"

Schuyler joined in the conversation. "He's here to write about all you new Negroes that are defining Negro culture."

"I just met Marcus the other night at Small's," Van Vechten said. "And like any good reporter, he started interviewing me."

"I'm sure you could handle all his questions." James Johnson smiled and patted Van Vechten on the shoulder.

"As a matter of fact, there was a question I didn't feel informed to answer, so I invited him to come today and pose the question to you and others driving this new literary movement," Van Vechten responded.

James Johnson looked directly at Marcus. "I'm not sure this is the right place to take on a question that Carl couldn't answer, but I'll give it a shot. What is it you want to ask?"

Marcus did not hesitate. "You all are doing some outstanding things in all aspects of the arts, to include novels, music, and paintings. I don't believe there has ever been anything like it in our race. But do you think it will last and pass on to future Negro artists?"

James Johnson now looked directly at Schuyler. "Quite a question, George. Has he asked that question of you?"

"No, he hasn't," Schuyler replied. "He was saving it for the real movers and shakers in Harlem. That's you and Carl. I do just what Marcus does for a living. That is, I write about what's happening here."

"That's fair," James Johnson concurred, but didn't back off. "So, let's assume that you're doing just what Marcus is doing and you have to answer that question. Is this permanent or will not live any longer than with this generation of younger writers? How would you answer it?"

Schuyler answered with no hesitation. "It will last just as long as white publishers will allow it. You all are trying to define what is nothing more than a disillusioned culture."

Locke, who had just walked into the drawing room, hurried over to join in the conversation. "We are defining our culture as distinct and separate from whites. Something they have prevented us from doing since emancipation, but no longer!"

Marcus noticed Van Vechten smiling. Evidently, he was enjoying the exchange. He thought back to the elevator operator's comment. Van Vechten cherished this opportunity to be an intricate part of what was happening in the Negro world more than in his own world.

"Every race of people must have a literary culture in order to be considered legitimate," James Johnson explained.

His comments snapped Marcus out of his musing. It was his turn to jump back into the conversation. He addressed his remarks to James Johnson. "If that is what's happening here with literature, then I would assume it's a good thing."

It's not only good, but also wonderful," James Johnson replied. "We are on the precipice of a great awakening of a great race of people and to answer your original question, yes, I believe it is permanent and will be just as applicable one-hundred years from now."

"There you have it," Van Vechten said, still with a broad smile. "Now that you've gotten the answer from a strong supporter of what's happening here, can we take a break from the serious talk and get drinks? You know I don't get the bootleg rock gut whiskey. Mine comes straight from Paris."

"That sounds like an excellent idea." Locke smiled. "He does have the best champagne in all of New York."

As they made their way into the next room for libations, Marcus thought what a different story he had to report back to Abbott.

Sam Arthur sat in the back row of Abyssinian Baptist Church, listening to the fiery sermon being delivered by Reverend Adam Clayton Powell, Sr. It had been months since he had attended church, something he did regularly back in Gaffney. The only difference was, back home, he always went with his Willa Mae. She forced him to go, always telling him the man that she married had to be a God-fearing man. And the man whose children she would bear had to be dedicated to the church and the Lord.

He'd asked around at the YMCA and was told Abyssinian was the best in town. Listening to the choir's melodious voices singing one spiritual after another to open the service and the rhythmic delivery of Powell's sermon, he knew Abyssinian was the right decision and once he got Willa Mae up to Harlem and the church, she would feel just like she was back home.

"Praise the Lord. If we have any visitors, will you please stand up and allow us to greet you in the name of our Savior?" Powell called out, having just finished his sermon.

Sam Arthur felt like all eyes were on him. He stood up and couldn't believe one of those pairs of eyes looked just like Mary. But that couldn't be. Women like her didn't go to church. But when she smiled at him, he knew that it was Mary.

"On behalf of the Abyssinian Baptist Church Family, welcome," Powell said.

Sam Arthur paid no attention to him. His eyes and mind were riveted on Mary. A prostitute in the church. Harlem was a different kind of place.

"You can take your seats," Powell instructed.

Sitting in the back, Sam Arthur was one of the first to exit the church. He wasn't sure if he should wait for Mary to come out or just hurry away. He thought back on her invitation to cook a meal for him, but never intended to take her up on it. It was just a little too much temptation, but he could enjoy a good home-cooked meal, having eaten only at restaurants since he arrived in Harlem. But he decided against waiting and started up 138th Street toward Seventh Avenue.

"Sam Arthur," Mary called out. "Sam Arthur, stop."

He stopped, turned, and looked at her, holding the hand of a little boy not more than three years old. She practically ran toward him, dragging the child along with her.

"You never came by," she said, breathing heavily.

His first impression was that she looked different from when he first saw her. "You look different," was all he could think to say.

She chuckled. "I guess so, silly. I have all my clothes on."

"What you doing at church?"

"What you mean? I go to church every Sunday. And I just adore Reverend Powell."

"But with your profession…you know, in all, I didn't—"

"What? You didn't think a working girl could attend church. Well, how about you? You're not in what you would consider a Christian profession."

"Back home I always went to church with my—"

"I know, with your Willa Mae," Mary said with a bit of sarcasm in her voice.

Sam Arthur detected her irritation. "I know I probably mention her too much, but that's because I miss her so much."

Mary put her hand on Sam Arthur's arm. "I know and I told you before she was a very lucky woman to have a man like you. But she'd better hurry up and get up here to Harlem or one of these fast women be done took you away from her."

Sam Arthur smiled. "I just about saved enough money to get out that YMCA and get me an apartment. Then I'm gonna send for her and we gonna get married right here in Harlem."

"That's good and wonderful but in the meantime, you got to eat, and I owe you a meal. Are you ready for it this afternoon?"

That was exactly what Sam Arthur had been avoiding, but now confronted with the invitation, he didn't know how to turn it down.

"I guess I am. I don't have to be at the club until eleven this evening, so why not?"

"Good, I live within walking distance from the church."

They walked back down 138th Street across Lenox Avenue, and as they neared Fifth Avenue, Sam Arthur couldn't help but notice how the neighborhood changed. There were rows of tenement apartments and garbage strewn in the streets. As they turned up Fifth Avenue, the smell of chitterlings and pig feet coming from vendors lined up next to the curb consumed the air. This was a part of Harlem he hadn't seen.

Mary caught the frown across his face. "This ain't the Harlem you used to, is it?"

"Can't say that it is."

They reached 141st Street and Mary walked up to a dilapidated structural building, climbed up the steps, and into the building. Sam Arthur followed close behind. She opened the door and waved him inside. He and the boy followed behind and she closed the door.

Sam Arthur stared at the extremely small space with a tiny living room, kitchen table but no cooking stove, a very small icebox, a cupboard, a couple of chairs, a wood table in the tiny living room, and no bathroom. He could see into the small bedroom with just a bed and a dresser with clothes on top.

"This is where you live?" were the only words he could speak.

"This is not where we live. It's where we stay. No one lives in a place like this. You only stay here, hoping that soon you can find a decent place where you can live and call your home."

Sam Arthur momentarily thought back on times in Gaffney when they would imagine what it would be like to live in a big city like New York. They never imagined it to be like where he was now standing.

Mary opened the small icebox and took out a cut-up chicken. She opened a small cupboard and handed the chicken to Sam Arthur.

"Hold this while I get the potatoes and some greens out the cupboard. I got to go down the hall to cook this. That's where the community stove is."

She reached into the cupboard and took out the potatoes and some greens. "Don't worry, they all good. I bought them this morning before going to church."

She grabbed a tin container and put all the food inside. "You just sit here with my boy while I go down the hall and cook. He'll be quiet."

Mary hurried out of the apartment. The boy went into the bedroom and Sam Arthur sat down in one of the chairs in the living room, still stunned by how Mary was living.

7.

NINA COULD NOT BELIEVE THE headlines in the *Amsterdam News:* "Florence Mills has Left for Europe." She again was alone in the apartment on Monday morning. Regina, Ethel, and Luella had left for work. She could only stare at the newspaper. This couldn't really be happening. Evidently, Florence had forgotten about Nina and her promise that someday they would dance together.

Nina jumped up, threw on her clothes, and rushed out of the apartment. Maybe Ulysses didn't go with her and if he didn't he owed her an explanation. She ran out of the apartment building, determined to get an answer.

She ran practically all the way to 135th Street and to Florence's brownstone. Breathing heavily, she bolted up the steps and banged on the door. After waiting over a minute, Nina raised her fist, prepared to bang again, but the door swung open. She stared at Ulysses.

He waved her to come inside. Instead, she stood her ground.

"Do you want to come in and let me explain?" Ulysses said.

Defiantly Nina shrieked, "No, this will do just fine!"

"Have it your way." Ulysses stepped out onto the porch. "It was a last-minute agreement between the producers and their European contacts. Florence had no choice in the matter. When she got word, they had to leave right away. She was swamped with things she had to do. We're sorry, but we did not intend to mislead you."

"How long will she be gone?" Nina asked, still defiant in her tone.

"She'll be gone for a year. She'll be living in England and Paris."

"A year? Oh, my stars, what am I going to do?" Nina's tone was now more desperate than defiant.

"You have a good job at Connie's Inn and from what I've heard, you're doing quite well."

"But I came here just to dance with Mrs. Mills."

"There are hundreds of young girls just like you who come to Harlem, dreaming of doing the very same thing."

"But she promised me."

"Young lady, you have two choices," Ulysses said, with a much firmer tone. "You can continue to dance at Connie's Inn, or you can return home."

Nina stared at him momentarily, then turned and hurried back down the steps. His suggestion offended her, suggesting it might be time for her to consider going back to St. Louis. There was no way she would admit failure by running back there and that would end her dreams of becoming a dancer on stage other than in a nightclub. With the news about Florence, she lost all incentive to keep dancing at Connie's Inn.

She stood on the corner of 135th and Lenox, unsure what to do. She didn't want to go back to the apartment. The three women were really good to her but would not understand how she felt. She needed to talk with someone much more like her. Addie was the answer. Sometimes after work, they would get the same ride and they always dropped Addie off first. She knew where her fellow dancer lived. She headed up Lenox toward 139th Street, hoping her friend would be home and receptive to her visit and understanding of her grief.

Nina's mind had gone blank, and she ran down the boulevard, paying no attention to the immaculately dressed women making their way to the dress shops and beauty parlors. She ignored the bright sun lighting up the boulevard and creating a beautiful Monday afternoon. Not aware of her surroundings, she recognized the brownstone where Addie lived.

She bolted through the front door and knocked on the first apartment door in the foyer, praying it was Addie's. The door swung open, answering her prayer.

"Nina, what are you doing here?" Addie asked, with a surprised expression across her face.

Without responding to Addie's inquiry, Nina asked, "Can I come in?" in a choked-up voice.

"Certainly." Addie waved Nina inside and closed the door. She pointed to an overstuffed chair. "Sit there and tell me why you're here?"

In an attempt to compose herself, Nina answered with a statement. "Florence Mills left for Europe last night."

"Yes, I know. In fact, everyone in the dancing world knows she left."

"But she promised me that I—"

"Grow up, Nina!" She paused. "I'm sorry, I didn't mean to interrupt you or shout at you, but Nina, you have to realize you're in Harlem."

Nina was now subdued. "What do you mean by that?"

Addie got up from the couch and sat in a chair closer to Nina. "Girl, you are so naïve. I'm sure Florence meant well, but she has to go when her producer tells her it is time to go. She had no choice. It's nothing to do with you. It's just business in the big city."

Tears flowed down Nina's cheek. "I don't know what I'm gonna do."

"Yes, you do. Nina, do you know how fortunate you are? You are beautiful with a shape a lot of women would die for and you're an outstanding dancer." She let her praise register with Nina. "You're going to go into that club tonight and dance your ass off and you're going to do the same tomorrow night and every night like all of us girls do, and hope someday an agent will recognize us, sign us up, and take us out of there. The doors are opening up for Negro dancers who look white enough to dance on a larger stage than at Connie's Inn."

Addie's words of encouragement relaxed Nina, and she stopped crying. "Can I stay here until it's time to go to the club?" She had no idea why she asked Addie, but it just seemed right.

"Yes, you most certainly can. One of the girls living here is moving out and going back home to Louisiana. You're welcome to move in here and be with people more like you. You'll have to pay your part of the rent and—"

"Yes, yes, yes. When can I move in?"

Addie smiled. "As soon as you can get all your belongings over here."

"Tomorrow." Nina practically shouted with joy.

"Okay, good," Addie said, much calmer than Nina. "Now you need to rest and get ready for tonight." She got up, grabbed Nina by her hands, and pulled her up. "Let me show you to the vacant room, but it still has a bed in there."

She led Nina down the hallway to the room.

"It is nothing like we thought it was." Marcus sat in Schuyler's high-back leather chair in his room at the *Messenger* office, talking on the phone to Robert Abbott in Chicago.

"What do you mean? You telling me all the great things that the *Amsterdam News* has been writing about Harlem are not happening?"

"No, I don't mean that at all. There is a great movement taking place, but it is not unified. So far, in just a month, I have identified two distinct schools of thought about what the movement is all about."

"And what are they?"

"It's really a difference in writing from what can be identified as the older group led by Dr. Du Bois and—"

"Have you had a chance to interview the great man? Dr. Du Bois is the most important Negro in America."

"No, not yet, but I will real soon. As I was about to say, the other school of thought is led by a younger generation, probably the most visible is the poet Langston Hughes."

"That's interesting because the *Crisis Magazine* first published young Langston's poetry and Du Bois edits that magazine."

"You're right, he is the editor on paper, but it's Jessie Fauset, his assistant, who has managed to get Langston's poetry published. But that will probably all come to an end when Knopf publishes Hughes' poetry that does not measure up to Du Bois's standards."

"Keep me informed. I have another meeting. Keep up the good work."

Just as they hung up, Theophilus Lewis, accompanied by a young man, walked into the office. "I'm surprised to see you here," he said. "Thought George would be here."

"I was talking to Mr. Abbott." Marcus stood up and looked at the young man with Lewis. What struck him was just how extremely dark and fragile in appearance he looked.

Lewis put his arm around the young man's shoulder. "This young man is a recent arrival to Harlem all the way from the West Coast in Los Angeles."

The young man broke from Lewis's arm and aggressively reached across the desk, grabbed Marcus' hand, and vigorously shook it. "My name is Wallace Thurman," he said, still shaking Marcus' hand. "We have something in common. You write for a Negro newspaper, and I did, too." He released Marcus' hand and stood back next to Lewis.

"What brings you to Harlem?" Marcus asked.

"Same reason I suppose you are here. To be a part of what is happening here in the year 1925. First time in our history in this sick country that we have been able to define a culture about us and for us."

"Wallie is an exceptionally talented writer," Lewis said. "He will be a great addition to our cause."

Marcus looked directly at Thurman. "So, on what side of this cultural dichotomy will you be a part of, the older generation or the young bohemians?"

"I'll tell you what I won't do. I will not use literature as a sociological study of the Negro."

"It's apparent you've been following what's happening here," Marcus said.

"Who hasn't?" Thurman replied. "Harlem, New York, is setting the literary and artistic standard for the rest of Negro America. I tried to emulate what's happening here back in Los Angeles, but it didn't work."

"I can't speak for the rest of the cities, but Chicago is developing quite a number of writers." Marcus felt he must stand up for his home. "And we are definitely ahead of Harlem in many music genres, especially jazz. Just before I came here, I covered an up-and-coming jazz giant—"

"Louis Armstrong," Lewis joined in the conversation. "And he's on his way to Harlem. Going to be at Connie's Inn. The Immerman brothers have to compete with the Cotton Club. Right now, Duke Ellington is performing there, and I understand drawing a lot of the money people from downtown."

Marcus looked back at the entrance to the office as Schuyler walked in. He started walking from behind the desk.

"No, stay put," Schuyler said to Marcus. He walked up and stood next to Lewis. "I heard part of the conversation and let me tell you all what is happening here are two Harlem's. The one for the Negro and the one for rich and important whites, specifically in those two nightclubs."

"That's a story in and of itself," Marcus commented.

"But those artists performing in clubs for whites only will make their way to Negro after-hour clubs and perform even better for the Negroes' late-night parties," Schuyler added.

"I have to say, Harlem is a very interesting place," Thurman said. "I do believe this is the place I should be."

Schuyler had piqued Marcus's interest. "Where are these after-hour joints?"

"Down Jungle Alley there are plenty of them," Schuyler answered. "The most popular one is the Sugar Cane Club, not quite down the Alley but at the beginning of the slum area. It's where the everyday people who work as maids and on the docks go to release all their pent-up anger about how they have to live."

"When is the best time to go?" Marcus' interest was now on this new information and knew this was a part of Harlem he also had to cover.

This time, Lewis spoke up. "That place is busy every night. Sometimes, even the white folks will make it down there after the other clubs have closed and they still want to party."

"This is Monday. Will this be a good time?" Marcus asked.

Schuyler answered. "Like Theophilus just told you, any night is a good night. One thing you have to know is that Harlem parties every night. Besides being the literary and artistic capital of Negro Americans, it is also the party capital of the race."

"Can I get you to go with me?" Marcus asked Schuyler.

Aware the conversation had moved away from Thurman's arrival, Lewis momentarily changed the subject. "I need to get Wallie settled in, so we're going to leave you two to make your plans to party for tonight."

"Sorry for the distraction," Marcus replied. "But George just introduced me to the possibility of an additional story." He stopped and looked at Thurman. "Is it possible that we can talk once you get settled in?"

"It would be my delight to converse with a fellow writer because we will probably be doing the same thing and that is capturing the history of these magical moments in Harlem. I will be in touch with you because the plan is for me to hang out here during the day."

"With that said, we'll bid farewell to you and let George have his office back." Lewis finished and he, with Thurman, walked back out the door.

Again, Marcus started walking from the desk.

"Stay put," Schuyler said. "I got meetings with Mr. Randolph in his office. You need to make any calls, go right ahead. After we finish this evening, we can make a stopover at the Sugar Cane Club, and you can see how real Harlem lives." He walked out of the office.

Sam Arthur sat in his usual spot on a barstool at the bar inside the Sugar Cane Club. It was a little after nine and the club was filling up. The dancers had packed the floor, moving to the rhythm of the music emanating from the band. Many of his usual customers were coming up to him and placing their bets on three numbers they derived or got from the songbook at church yesterday, or any other way they could put numbers together. He was taking bets because it had become second nature to him, but his mind was not there but yesterday at Mary's small living space and the meal she prepared for him. He just couldn't reconcile the two different people in one body. Mary was a completely different person last night than the half-naked prostitute he first met in that room at the Turf Club. Back in Gaffney, he could easily recognize the distinction between the two—a prostitute was not welcome in the Christian community and was not welcome in the church unless she repented and gave up her sinful ways. Here in Harlem, they were the same.

"Looks like you're having a real good night," Big Max said as he walked up to the bar. He looked at the bartender. "A brandy." He turned back to Sam Arthur. "You sure done got a helluva good reputation in here. These people just wait for you to get here to place their bets." Sam Arthur heard Big Max, but his attention was on the two men who walked into the club. He'd been working there practically every night for the past month and had never seen these two in the club before.

"They're not cops," Big Max said. "Cops don't come in here, so you can relax."

Sam Arthur appreciated that bit of information, but that was not his concern. Was it possible that they were private detectives hired by Shackleford back in Gaffney to find him? He was always aware that white man wouldn't be happy until he got revenge for the confrontation at Sadie's that night, forcing him to leave Gaffney.

"Hey," Big Max said, voice rising. "Are you all right?"

Sam Arthur snapped out of his wandering thoughts. "Yeah, yeah." He still closely watched the two men making their way to the other side of the dance floor until they disappeared behind the dancers. If they were there to force him back to Gaffney, they'd have to kill him first. If he went back there, it would be to get his Willa Mae.

"You still worried about them two men?" Big Max tapped Sam Arthur on his shoulder to get his attention off those two men. "Trust me, they ain't the police. They've been paid off not to come in here. Too much money to their bosses for them to come in here."

Big Max's words were reassuring and just in time as the two men rounded the end of the dance floor and walked directly toward him. Before they got to him, a heavy-set woman hurried up to Sam Arthur.

"I got a dime on number 435 'cause that's the time my man got home last night and now he's in the hospital."

Sam Arthur wrote her number on the red slip, gave it to her, and took the dime. The woman walked along the side of the dance floor back to her table.

"You must be a numbers runner," Marcus said, walking up to Sam Arthur.

Sam Arthur faced Marcus with Schuyler standing next to them. Big Max took a gulp from his drink, put it back on the bar counter, and moved in closer to Sam Arthur.

Marcus looked at Big Max and smiled. "No worries."

Big Max relaxed, leaning against the bar counter. "What you looking for?" he asked Marcus.

"What if he wants to play a number?" Schuyler got in the conversation.

Sam Arthur took out a red slip from his jacket pocket. "What's your three numbers?" he asked Marcus.

"501."

"How much?" Sam Arthur asked as he wrote the numbers on the red slip.

Marcus was really not a betting man but wanted to know more about Sam Arthur, who did this for a living. This was another part of Harlem life and just like he had to interview writers and artists on the other side of Harlem, he had to interview this man. But first, he had to win his trust. If having to make this bet was the way to get it done, he would.

"Come on, mister," Big Max said.

Marcus ignored Big Max and looked directly at Sam Arthur. "If I bet a dollar and win, what are my returns?"

"Around about five hundred and fifty dollars."

"But your chances of winning are a thousand to one," Schuyler interjected. "Only people getting rich off this con game are the bankers."

Big Max stood up from leaning against the bar counter. "Come on, man, bet if you're gonna," he said in a strong voice.

Marcus didn't want to alienate the big man. He pulled out a dollar, but before handing the money to Sam Arthur, he asked. "If I win, how can I contact you?"

"If you win, you can meet me down here where you made the bet, and we'll take you to Mr. Holstein and he'll pay you."

"I can use five hundred dollars," Marcus said and handed the money to Sam Arthur.

Sam Arthur handed the red slip to Marcus.

"Now that you've seen the place and even made a contribution to the bank account of one of the richest men in Harlem, we can leave now?" Schuyler said.

Marcus stuffed the red slip into his pocket. "You'll be seeing me here tomorrow night to collect my winnings," he said to Sam Arthur.

"I'll be here."

Marcus and Schuyler walked up the stairs and out of the Sugar Cane Club.

8.

NINA STOOD NEXT TO ADDIE on the dance floor as the music began and she put all her energy into the dance routine. In the time she had danced at Connie's Inn, she never felt as determined as at that moment on stage. They went into a high kick routine from left to right and Nina raised her legs in rhythm with the other dancers. She thought about Addie's words to her earlier in the day. Maybe that person who recruits Black girls out of the club and onto the stage on Broadway was there, and she had to make sure he recognized her. She could no longer depend on Florence. Now she had to depend on some stranger somewhere among the packed crowd watching her dance.

She did her best not to look. He was there as usual, smiling and staring at her. As the first dance routine ended, she stood there with the others, waiting for the music to start again. She looked all around the club at all those well-dressed white men who, before that night, had no meaning to her. She didn't know why, but momentarily, as she swayed, waiting for the music, she thought about Claude and his visit Sunday morning. She didn't know why, nor did she understand her behavior. Maybe she should have taken him up on his offer to move to Washington, and if she knew that on the very next morning, her dreams to dance with Florence Mills would be shattered, she may have agreed to leave Harlem.

Her wandering thoughts ended as the music began and with the other dancers, she moved to the beat of the band.

"Girl, you were really performing," Addie said to Nina as the two sat in chairs in the dressing room. The first set had just ended, and they were resting and waiting to go back out there.

"I feel it. For some reason, I really feel it tonight. Maybe it has something to do with what you told me earlier today."

Addie chuckled. "Well, whatever I said sure has affected you tonight."

Nina scooted her chair closer to Addie. "You think one of them white men looking for Negro girls for Broadway is out there tonight?"

"That's why you out there trying to outperform everybody else?" Addie ignored Nina's question to her.

"No, that's not what I'm trying to do." Nina felt compelled to deny Addie's accusation.

"Don't feel bad." Addie smiled. "We all do it even if we don't know we're doing it."

Addie's smiling relaxed Nina. She didn't want her only friend to be upset with her. She relaxed back in her chair.

"Well, do you think any of them people are out there tonight?"

"I don't know, Nina. But I do know that you must relax and let it come to you. Just don't try too hard. Pretty soon it becomes too obvious."

Nina took Addie's advice and changed the discussion. "I've never asked you, but how long have you been dancing here?"

"Yeah, I noticed that you never asked. But now that you have, I been here a little over a year."

"And you're still here?" Immediately, Nina was sorry she asked.

"I guess you're wondering why I haven't been picked up by one of those kinds of white men."

"I'm sorry, I didn't mean—"

"You didn't mean that evidently, I wasn't light skinned enough to catch their attention."

"But you're so pretty and you dance so well."

"Doesn't matter, not here in Harlem. Color is not only important to white people who come over here to get their kicks. It's important to the dicties right here in Harlem."

Nina leaned forward again in her chair. "What are dicties?"

"They're the upper-crust Negroes who live up on St. Nicholas and 38th and 39th Streets above Seventh Avenue."

The dressing room door swung open and Immerman hurried over to Nina. "You got a request from a very prominent and very good customer to buy you a drink at the end of tonight's show."

Nina's heart practically dropped out of her body. It just couldn't be that one man.

"His name is Larry Madison, and he sits in the front row practically every night since you been dancing here. He wants to meet you. Hang around after the show, spend a half-hour with him. He's a good customer and spends a lot of money because of you and we don't want to lose his business to the Cotton Club." Immerman turned and hurried back out of the dressing room.

Nina couldn't move as she watched Immerman go out the door. She finally looked at Addie with a blank expression. What she feared most had happened.

Addie placed her hand on Nina's shoulder. "You knew it was going to eventually happen. You are too pretty for it not to happen. Now compose yourself, get through the remainder of our dance routines, spend a half hour with him, and I'll be waiting outside for you."

The door swung open. The bouncer stuck his head inside. "All right, ladies, let's go. It's showtime."

Nina got up with the others and started through the door, determined not to look at that man she had been ordered to meet, no matter how much she dreaded the order.

Sam Arthur was doing so well in collecting the bets at the Sugar Cane, he thought maybe he would leave early and get a good night's rest, something he hadn't done since he came to Harlem, and especially since he went to work for Mr. Holstein. He looked up at the clock on the wall behind the band. A little after twelve and the early crowd would leave soon, and the late partiers that didn't have to report to work at seven in the morning would show up.

But if he left early, how would he get the money to Mr. Holstein, because Jonas would not be there to drive him over to the Turf Club until after three? He would have to walk the six blocks at midnight, and that was not a very smart idea. As he stood there, trying to decide what to do, the answer appeared, strolling into the club.

Sam Arthur stared at Mary as she made her way down the stairs and strolled along the other side of the dance floor. She looked stunning in her red dress just below her knee, leaving her shapely legs accentuated by the nylons tightly hugging her bare skin. This was the other Mary who he first met that night at the Turf Club. Not the Mary he saw in church, who called out to him, walking, and holding the hand of a little boy. Not the Mary, who had cooked a meal for him that they both enjoyed eating in her place with only two rooms.

It was now after midnight, and she was in the club, obviously teasing some man who would pay her for a couple of hours at one of the cheap, hourly hotels. He didn't know why, but he couldn't let that happen. He had to stop her.

The band was on a break, so the dance floor was empty. For the first time since working in the club, he left his position at the bar and hurried across the dance floor.

Mary saw him coming and quickly hurried toward the other end of the club. He caught up with her and put his huge hand gently on her shoulder. She turned and faced him.

"I didn't think you'd be in here tonight."

"Why are you doing this?" he asked.

"Because I have a baby boy that likes to eat, and he has a father that doesn't do a damn thing for him."

"I understand that, but how can you go to church yesterday and tonight be out here selling your body in sin?"

Mary took a step closer to Sam Arthur. "And what do you do here? You take money from poor people and know damn well they ain't gonna win nothing."

He didn't want to fight with Mary. He wanted to help her. "How much money will it take for you to go home and not do this?"

"Sam Arthur, I do not want your money! Don't you need it for your precious Willa Mae somewhere down South?"

Sam Arthur knew everyone in the club was looking at them. He couldn't let this go any further. He pulled out a ten-dollar bill and forced it into Mary's hand.

"Don't matter 'bout Willa Mae. Take this and go home. I'll be by tomorrow and we'll talk." He had to take control of the situation. "It looks bad for my business to be standing here arguing with you, but I can't let you do this. Not anymore and tomorrow we'll figure this out."

In a more somber tone, Mary said, "I don't want to do nothing to hurt your business." She lightly kissed Sam Arthur on the side of his face, turned, and walked briskly to the stairs.

Sam Arthur walked back over to his place on the other side of the room. He'd just given away the money he had made for the night. He knew now he would have to stay there and catch the late crowd, and hopefully, they would be in a betting mood and help him earn back the money he had just given away.

Nina reluctantly walked out of the dressing room across the stage and stood at the table where the white man sat. He smiled at her, got up, and pulled out a chair.

"Please sit."

Once she sat on the opposite side of the table, he hurried back over and sat back down.

"I know you've noticed me watching you every time you're on the stage." He waited for a response from Nina but got none. "Let me introduce myself. I am one of your greatest admirers, and believe me, you have a lot of them coming here every night. But my name is Larry Madison." He reached his hand across the table in an effort, obviously, to shake Nina's hand.

Nina sat there, not moving, and did not extend her hand. In all her life, she had never touched a white person. She did not want to encourage this stranger, and shaking his hand, she knew, would send the wrong message. But instantly she recalled Addie's words that first night at her apartment. He might be one of those white men who sought Negro girls to take them to Broadway. Just in case, she didn't want to take a chance. She reached her hand over to his, and he held it tightly for what seemed like a long time. She tried to release the grip, but he made it worse by extending his free hand on top of her hand.

"Relax, Nina. I only want the best for you."

She relaxed her hand inside of his. What did he mean he only wanted the best for her? Was that a hint that he was one of those white men who could get her out of the club and on to better opportunities? Despite him being white and an absolute stranger, she needed to follow his advice and loosen up.

"How did you know my name?" She didn't know what else to say.

Larry smiled. "I know quite a bit about you." He finally released the grip on her hand and signaled for a waiter to come over to his table. "Bring me a brandy and the young lady a glass of your best champagne," he said to the waiter.

"Yes, Mr. Madison." The waiter walked back toward the bar.

Nina leaned forward. "No, I don't drink."

He ignored her comment. "I know you came to Harlem from St. Louis, and you want to dance with Florence Mills, but now you've lost that opportunity, at least for a year." Larry chuckled. "You should see that look on your face. You're probably wondering how this white man knows so much about you. Am I right?"

"Yes."

"When I like someone, I make it my business to know all about them."

The word *like* caused Nina to stiffen.

"No, don't take it the wrong way. Please, you have to relax, Nina, if you want me to help you get where you want to go."

The waiter placed the drinks on the table. Larry gave him a twenty-dollar bill.

"Keep that change."

"Thank you, Mr. Madison," the waiter said, and walked away.

He held his glass up. "To you, Nina, and your future."

She didn't want to drink the champagne, but she did not want to insult this man, who kept telling her he wanted to help her. She held her glass toward him. Nina watched as Larry put his glass to his mouth and drank. She took a small sip of the champagne and frowned.

Larry smiled. "Now it wasn't that bad, was it?"

"No, not really."

"Well, drink up." Larry swallowed the rest of his brandy.

Nina didn't want to drink the rest of the champagne, but she knew Addie was waiting outside the club for her. She figured if she finished the drink, it might bring this to an end. But she didn't want to anger him either, because of the promises he'd subtly made. She took another drink but couldn't finish the rest.

"I know you're anxious to go."

She felt relieved this was coming to an end. But that lasted only momentarily.

"Listen, I've arranged with Mr. Immerman to get you the night off tomorrow. I want to take you to dinner and talk more about your career."

"My career?"

"Have you heard of the Ziegfeld Follies?"

An excited Nina responded, "Yes," and then reality set in.

"But they don't use Negro girls."

Larry practically leaned across the table. "Nina, you don't have to be a Negro."

"What do you mean, I don't have to be a Negro? I am a Negro."

"With your physical features, you have practically white skin, and your straight hair means that you can pass for white, and it happens all the time here in Harlem."

"But—"

"Don't throw away what you have going for you. You are an outstanding dancer and most important, you can be white and get yourself out of here. There is no advantage to being a Negro. And this is no place for a beautiful girl like you."

Immerman approached the table. "Pardon me, and I don't want to break this up; you all seem to be going so well, but we must close our doors."

Nina felt relieved. It was too much coming at her too fast. She was relieved that this would end for now. But there would be no way she could sleep. Tomorrow, if she decided to go, would be the most frightening day or night since she'd been in Harlem.

Immerman turned and walked away.

"I'll have my chauffeur pick you up at seven tomorrow evening. Get prepared because your life is about to change."

He got up and walked toward the exit, leaving Nina still sitting there.

9.

WITHOUT QUESTION, THE INTELLECTUAL GIANT among all the intellects in Harlem was Dr. Du Bois. He was also a man aloof from most people, and it was very difficult to solicit conversation with him. Marcus knew this about Du Bois, but still sought a meeting with him, and Jessie Fauset made that happen. Du Bois agreed to give him one-half hour in his office at the NAACP at exactly seven-thirty that morning.

He was right on time as he walked into the NAACP office at 70 Fifth Avenue in Lower Manhattan, and Fauset was waiting there for him.

"Very good. You're right on time. He is here waiting for you and if you'd been five minutes late, he'd have canceled the meeting."

"There was no way that was going to happen," Marcus said.

"Follow me. He's ready for you."

He followed close behind Fauset down a hall to the back of the office. She stopped at a room with the door open and stepped inside.

"Dr. Du Bois, your first guest is here right on time."

"Bring him in."

Fauset moved aside, and Marcus walked into the office and stood there, waiting for Du Bois to speak first. He knew that was the kind of respect this man demanded. He didn't have to wait long. Fauset closed the door, and he was one-on-one with the most important Negro in America.

"Have a seat."

Marcus sat in one of the two chairs in front of the desk. He pulled out a pad and pencil from his jacket pocket. "You don't mind if I take notes?"

"Young man, you have one-half hour. If I were you, I wouldn't waste any of that time writing. Let's just talk, and you'll remember the most valued parts of our short discussion."

Marcus folded the pad and put it and the pencil back in his jacket pocket.

Du Bois leaned forward. "Your boss is a good friend of mine and that's why I agreed to this meeting. So, ask away."

Marcus scooted up in the chair. "What is it that you would like to achieve with this new Negro movement taking place here in Harlem?"

Du Bois now reared back in his chair. "Why do you think it is new?"

"Well, sir," Marcus began, being cautious on how to respond. Answering a question posed by the intellectual giant of Harlem was no easy task. "I've heard it referred to as a new movement being led by a group of young and energetic writers."

"The only thing new about what is happening here are the new arrivals to the city looking to be discovered as the new Paul Laurence Dunbar."

"If not new Nego movement, how would you identify it?"

"Let me explain so you'll better understand and, most important, you can write about it the correct way." Du Bois got up, walked to a bookshelf, grabbed a few books, tossed them on the desk, and sat back down. "This new Negro in the arts is nothing more than an extension of artists that have gone before them. It is not new because Negro writers have been around for a long time. They just didn't get the same attention that we are getting in Harlem now."

"Why the change and now Harlem artists are getting the attention the earlier ones didn't?"

"Things change with time."

Marcus felt a bit more comfortable after the first ten minutes of discussion, but only had twenty more left. He needed to get right to the most important issue. "Dr. Du Bois, I understand, from talking earlier with others, there is a difference growing between the younger generation of writers and you. How true is that?"

"Have you seen that utterly disgusting movie, *Birth of a Nation*?"

Marcus felt a slight tinge of irritation. Now again, he was asked to answer a question instead of getting an answer. But he had no choice.

"No, I haven't, but I've heard a lot about it and nothing good."

"There is a reason you haven't heard anything good because it is a terribly demeaning depiction of our race."

"What does that have to do with my question, with all due respect, Dr. Du Bois?"

"It has everything to do with it, young man. For the past two hundred and fifty years, those people have done nothing but treat our people as ignorant, oversexed animals unable to fit into their culture. They have, for the past seventy-five years since the end of slavery, put blackface comedy on and laughed at the buffoonery. And they have been so good at it, many of our people believe it is true." Du Bois paused to catch his breath. "What we write should be to uplift the race from the terrible distortion of who we are as a people. And literature that doesn't do that is worthless."

Marcus had ten more minutes. He decided to shift the conversation. "If uplift is what it's all about, wasn't that exactly what Marcus Garvey was attempting to do and you turned against him, as did other Negro leaders?"

"Marcus Garvey was the most dangerous Negro in America. He sold poor Negroes on the idea that they could invest in this ship that would take them back to Africa because America is not their country. He collaborated with the Ku Klux Klan—the terrorist white racist organization responsible for thousands of our people being lynched in the South."

Marcus detected Du Bois's irritation with the question, but he had to pursue it because it made for a good story. Garvey was a part of Harlem, and his confrontation with practically all the Negro leaders deserved coverage.

"However, Dr. Du Bois, he did preach racial uplift. His rallying call was 'Up you mighty people.'"

"Young man, he was a traitor to his people when he rallied around the enemy of the Negro. He was not good for the progress of our people and needed to be stopped, and he was. So do not compare my efforts to uplift with what he was doing."

The door swung open, and Fauset stepped inside the room. "I'm sorry to break up this discussion, but Dr. Du Bois has a meeting at nine and needs to prepare."

Du Bois stood up behind his desk. Marcus also got up.

"Thank you, Dr. Du Bois. I appreciate your time."

"I know you have more questions you'd like to ask and I want to accommodate my friend, Robert Abbott, so get with Ms. Fauset and we can talk again."

Marcus turned and walked back toward the door, smiled at Fauset, and left the room.

⁂

Sam Arthur wasn't sure why he was about to do something that would interfere with his plans to get Willa Mae out of South Carolina and up to Harlem. What he knew at that moment was he had to save Mary from the life of sin that had engulfed her and made her into someone she wasn't.

He slept late, especially when he stayed late at the Sugar Cane Club. Last night was one of those nights. He had to make back the ten dollars he'd given Mary, which he did. With only three hours of sleep, Sam Arthur got up, rushed down the hall, washed up, and got dressed.

He lifted the mattress on the bed and counted out one hundred dollars, hurried out of his room, locked the door, and hurried out of the YMCA. As he walked up Fifth Avenue toward 141st Street, he had second thoughts about what he was about to do. It really wasn't his responsibility to save Mary from the life she had chosen. There were plenty of girls in Harlem in the same financial dilemma who didn't sell their bodies to make ends meet. He just about had enough money to get Willa Mae up there. If he gave Mary this money, it would delay getting the woman he wanted to marry there with him. He could still turn around, go back to the YMCA and not bother with Mary. But he knew if he didn't, he would have to watch her walk into the club and walk out with some man that she cared nothing about and give him her body for money to pay her rent and feed her child. He had the money, and he had the power to prevent that from happening.

Sam Arthur reached 141st Street, turned, and walked up the steps at the tenement apartment. He stopped in front of her place and hesitated before knocking on the door. What if he had really misread this woman, and she was in there with another man? Maybe she didn't have the potential to be a good woman and his efforts and money would be for naught. He didn't want to get caught up in an ugly situation and the best that he could do was to leave her alone.

He turned to walk away when the door swung open. He stared at Mary standing there. Momentarily, neither one of them spoke.

"Sam Arthur, what are you doing here this early in the morning?"

Sam Arthur took one step toward her. "I told you last night that I'd be here this morning."

"I know you did, but this early?"

"We got to work this out," he shot back, with no hesitation. "You can't keep doing what you're doing."

Mary stood there, not moving.

"Are you gonna invite me in or is there someone in there you don't want me to see?"

"Sam Arthur, I get with men out of necessity and not for pleasure. That ended the day my baby's daddy left me stranded to raise that boy with no help from him."

"Well, are you gonna let me in so we can talk about all of this?"

Mary moved aside and waved Sam Arthur into the room. As he walked past her, he glanced into the small bedroom and saw the little boy still asleep in the bed. He sat on one chair and Mary on the other one.

"You leave your son here alone while you go out?"

"Only in the morning when I have to get to the market and buy some food. If he wakes, he knows to stay in the bed until I come back."

"Do you leave him—"

"No, I don't leave him here alone when I'm working. My neighbor watches him and thank God, she doesn't charge me, but I always give her a little something. We girls have to help each other."

Sam Arthur leaned forward in the chair. "I got to help you get out of this terrible situation."

"Why?" Mary's tone was stern.

Sam Arthur used the same stern tone. "What do you mean, why? Look at the way you're living. Isn't that reason enough?"

Mary also leaned forward. "If you help me, I have to pay you 'cause I don't want no handouts. I work to take care of my family. You may not like the work I do, but it's work, and I earn my way. I can't take your help because you won't let me work for it."

Her reasoning caught Sam Arthur not knowing how to respond. He considered what she did sinful, and she considered it just a job. If he gave her one hundred dollars, he would have to engage in sex, and that was something he didn't want to do. Even though he was taking some of the money he saved to get Willa Mae up there, he still would not destroy the sanctity of their love by having sex with another woman. As they sat, just looking at each other, he did not have an answer for this predicament he had created for himself.

Sam Arthur watched the boy run out of the bedroom and over to Mary, who picked him up and settled him down on her lap. Staring at the two of them interact, he was more determined to help Mary. This young innocent boy, who loved his mother, had to be protected from someday knowing this woman he loved violated his relationship with him by what she did at night.

He got up and walked over to Mary. He held out the five twenty-dollar bills. "Okay, you win. Take this money. I'll let you work for it."

Mary didn't reach out and take the money. "Are you sure? What about your Willa Mae?"

"Just don't you worry about that. You want to earn your money, I'll let you do that."

She held her hand out and took the money. "Thank you. You got to be the nicest man I ever knew. Each one of these twenty-dollar bills gets you a date. We can start tonight when you finish at the club. There's a place around the corner from the club that us girls take our dates. Is that good for you?"

"That'll do, but you get that baby what he needs and get something for you. I'll see you tonight."

He reached down and kissed Mary on her forehead and walked out of the place.

Nina strolled out of the apartment and paused at the top step as she looked at the shiny white Lincoln limousine parked at the curb. She was about to enter a world far beyond her comprehension. She thought it wasn't too late. She could go back into her apartment and just forget about this new adventure.

The chauffeur came around the side of the limousine and opened the back door. "Miss Nina Jackson, Mr. Madison is waiting for you at his office. We can't keep him waiting. I assume you are ready?"

It was too late for her to turn back. Nina walked down the steps and got into the plush back seat. The chauffeur closed the door, went around and got into the limousine, and drove off. She relaxed back, closed her eyes, and let her thoughts wander. She feared all this was happening much too fast. Just a few months ago, she was graduating from high school. Now she was going to meet a man who practically promised he could get her on Broadway dancing in the Ziegfeld Follies. This was like a dream to her, but would it stay that way? Was this man on the up and up? As they pulled up in front of a building on Wall Street, she would soon find out.

The chauffeur got out of the limousine, hurried around, and opened the door for Nina. "Mr. Madison is waiting for you in his office."

Nina slowly got out of the limousine and followed the chauffeur into the building up to the tenth floor. Her nerves were on edge as they exited the elevator into an elaborate office. Just as she was admiring the décor and the paintings along the wall, Larry came around the corner, smiling.

"You made it," he greeted her. "Welcome to the other side of Harlem, the real New York side."

Nina struggled with words but managed. "I don't know what to say. I mean, this is far beyond my—"

"Don't say anything right now. Let me get my coat and we'll go to dinner and further discuss your future. You up for that?"

"Yes, I guess so."

She watched Larry as he disappeared back further into the office. She then looked over at the chauffeur, who stood silently near the elevator. While waiting, she thought of her one-bedroom small apartment back in St. Louis, where she had to sleep on the couch in the living room. How she and her mother struggled after her father abandoned them. She briefly thought of Claude and how he showed up at the apartment that Sunday morning and her cold reception. She didn't know why these thoughts shot like speedballs through her mind. But one thought she couldn't reconcile was why she was in this elaborate office building about to have dinner with this very rich white man with plans to move her out of the past and into a new reality.

Marcus was getting a better understanding of the dynamics at work behind the extraordinary development of the Harlem movement. But outside that movement, there was another Harlem. He'd gotten a touch of it when Schuyler took him to the Sugar Cane Club. Much of the coverage in Harlem did not include the Negroes who were not a part of that select group. However, for his work to be inclusive of the entire community, he had to extend his coverage. But first, he had to discuss this with Mr. Abbott.

Sitting in Schuyler's office, he dialed Abbott's home number in Chicago.

"It's after eight and you're still working now. That's dedication," Abbott said.

"What else am I going to do but work? You did interfere with my personal life I had when you—"

"Please spare me. You worked just as hard when you were here. And speaking of personal life, how is Lucille holding up with this temporary separation?"

"I've talked with her a number of times and she's still not happy and still refuses to come to New York."

"Not even a visit?"

"Not even a visit. She's being stubborn. So, I'd better hurry up and complete this assignment or the separation will become a permanent one."

"Is that what this call is all about?"

"Not really. It's about how much bigger this story is all about, much more involved than just about the literary movement and the defining of the culture from that perspective. What's happening here is about the majority of our people, who are not a part of the art movement and are struggling to make it from day to day. I need to include them in this story, and that's the reason for the call."

"Do it as you see fit and we'll weed out what should and shouldn't be in the final story. But just keep in mind our people love to read about success stories. They give them hope and that's what we are all about." Abbott momentarily paused, evidently to allow Marcus to consider the suggestion he had put forth. "If you want to get the other side of the story, then you need to talk with James over at the *Amsterdam News*. We're old friends and I'll call him in the morning and set you up a meeting."

"Wait, I thought the reason I was here was to compete with him for the story of Harlem?"

"That story, my friend, is bigger than just one newspaper covering it. He understands that and will welcome you with open arms. I'll get it done. Just go to his office tomorrow. He'll be expecting you. Now you interrupted me when I was about to sit down to dinner."

"I won't take up any more of your time. I'll be at his office in the morning and talk with you next week."

"You can call me anytime."

"Enjoy your dinner." Marcus hung up the phone and looked up just as Schuyler came running into the office.

"Have you checked your number?"

"What number?"

"The number you played the other night with that number runner at the Sugar Cane Club?"

"Yeah, I got it right here, but I kind of forgot all about it." Marcus looked at the number on the red slip. "501."

"That's it!" Schuyler practically shouted. "That was today's winning number. You just won five hundred dollars."

Marcus stared at the slip and then looked at Schuyler. "Are you sure?"

"Yes, I'm sure, and we need to get over to the Sugar Cane Club and hope that runner is there."

Marcus got up, came around the desk, and followed Schuyler out of the office.

Sam Arthur stood at his usual spot in the Sugar Cane Club, feeling good about what he had done earlier in the day. He didn't particularly like that he had to agree with Mary to get her to take the one hundred dollars. But knowing she wouldn't be on the street, selling her body to support her son was worth the lie. Unfortunately, that money would last maybe a month and she probably would not accept any more money from him because he did not let her earn it her way. He just didn't plan on cheating on Willa Mae.

The music filled the club as five of his regulars hurried over to him, placed their bets, and returned to their tables.

Even though he was sure that Mary wouldn't walk down those stairs in that tight, short red dress, he kept staring over at the stairs. This time, when he did, he watched Marcus and Schuyler walk into the club and head straight for him.

"Hey, big fellow," Schuyler said. "This man here had today's winning number 501."

"I didn't know I had a winner," Sam Arthur responded. "Mr. Holstein keeps all the slips and the money. He's at the Turf Club this time a night, paying off all winners today. You got to go over there and see him."

Marcus turned and looked at Schuyler. "You know where the Turf Club is?"

"I sure do, Lenox and 136th, let's go."

The two men headed back up the stairs.

❈

The chauffeur-driven limousine, with Larry and Nina in the back seat, pulled up in front of Keen's Steakhouse on 36th Street in Lower Manhattan. He got out, hurried around the limousine, and opened the door. Larry got out first, then held his hand out to Nina, who took it and got out.

"Give us two hours," Larry said to the chauffeur. He took Nina by the arm, and they walked into the restaurant.

The interior of the restaurant looked much like that at Connie's Inn, but Nina was looking at it not from the stage as a dancer but as the guest of apparently a very important man. This all seemed so surreal as a tuxedo-wearing host greeted them.

"Good evening, Mr. Madison. And who is this lovely lady with you?"

"A very special friend."

A feeling of importance shot through Nina's entire body. She had been called a lady by a white man in an exclusive Lower Manhattan restaurant. That was the first time, and it made her feel special.

Still holding her arm, Larry followed the host to a table in the corner. The host pulled the chair back for Nina and she sat right across from Larry.

"Your usual drink, Mr. Madison?"

"Yes, and bring my friend a glass of your very best champagne."

Nina did not object. She was so wrapped up in what was happening, she couldn't speak.

"Most certainly, Mr. Madison. I'll get your drinks and get your waiter over here to take your choices for dinner." He turned and walked away.

"What are you thinking?" Larry asked as he took a cigarette out of a pack in lit it.

"I don't know what to think."

"I know this is all new to you, but you can get used to all this if you just give yourself a chance."

"Everyone is white. Are there any Negroes in here?"

Larry chuckled. "No, there are no Negroes in here except as dishwashers in the back. Does that bother you?"

"Mr. Madison, I have never tried to pass for white and I don't feel comfortable doing it now."

"Please, do not call me Mr. Madison. It is simply Larry, and what does this have to do with you being a Negro?"

"I—"

"Nothing, Nina, absolutely nothing. There is no advantage to being a Negro in this town or, for that matter, no other town in this country."

A waiter placed the drinks on the table. "Are you ready to order, Mr. Madison?"

"Yes, bring the best steaks, medium cooked, with a light vegetable for both of us."

The waiter wrote the order and walked away.

Larry leaned forward. "Nina, it's time for you to take a step up in life. Your people are plagued with a color problem, but you don't have to suffer being a part of that race."

"If you feel that way about Negroes, why do you always come to Harlem?" Nina had worked up the nerves to ask.

"It is where white people can go and relax, loosen up. We can let our hair down and do whatever we want, and, of course, meet some of the most beautiful girls in the city, just like you."

His compliment made her nervous. She detected it was more than just helping her to dance on Broadway.

"You said you were going to help me possibly dance with the Ziegfeld Follies?"

"I meant it, but first I needed to introduce you to this world so when you do meet Florenz, you won't be nervous like you are right now."

This really had been too much for Nina to deal with. "I think I need to go home."

"Relax, just enjoy your dinner and I'll have the chauffeur take you home. And we'll do this again. Is that okay with you?"

"Yes, Mr. Larry. Please don't think I don't appreciate all you're doing for me because I do."

"I know you do, and you'll appreciate it even more as you begin to really enjoy this lifestyle over the one you are living now."

※

Jonas escorted Marcus and Schuyler into Holstein's office. They sat in chairs in front of the desk, and Jonas stood off to the side, watching the two visitors' every move. Holstein leaned forward in his high-back leather chair on the other side of the desk.

"I knew I had a winner today," he said. "And I knew soon you would show up. So, which one of you boys is the big winner?"

Marcus leaned forward in his chair. "I'm the man who has the slip." He held up his piece of the red slip.

"And can you believe it's the first time he's ever played the numbers?" Schuyler added.

Holstein leaned further forward, looking directly at Schuyler. "I know you. Don't you write for the *Messenger* and you're friends with all those literary geniuses?"

Schuyler chuckled. "I don't know about being friends, but I do know most of them."

"I just left a meeting earlier today with Charles Johnson. I've committed money for the next book writing contest." He handed Marcus five hundred dollars.

Marcus stuffed the money into his coat pocket. He appreciated the money, but something else occupied him. Here was a man engaged in an illegal operation giving money to a legitimate business to help promote a literary explosion. This had to be another story, but how to approach it with this man was the dilemma. He didn't have to. Schuyler did it for him.

Looking at Marcus, he said, "From the expression on your face, you're surprised that a big-time banker for the numbers would also be a part of this new Negro movement you're covering." Schuyler paused and looked at Holstein while pointing at Marcus. "This man is here from the *Chicago Defender*, covering what's happening in Harlem for the paper."

Holstein stuffed a wad of money back in the desk drawer and leaned forward, looking at Schuyler. "Why would he find that so surprising?"

"Mr. Holstein," Marcus spoke up. "The numbers game is quite prevalent in Chicago, but the men involved in it are not also involved in the community."

"I make no apologies for what I do," Holstein said. "Over the years, I have paid out quite a bit of money to some very happy people. In fact, I just gave you five hundred dollars on a one dollar bet. I'm sure that makes you happy."

"Receiving five hundred dollars isn't money an average man like me comes across, so, yes, it makes me happy and will make my wife very happy when I send it to her."

Schuyler stood up. "All right, I think we're finished here."

Holstein remained seated, ignoring Schuyler. "I don't think I got your name?"

"Marcus Williams."

"Well, Marcus Williams, I am a businessman, just like those white people on Lower Manhattan. They set up the rules to only apply to them and so we had to devise our own rules. I think you'd agree that we all have a right to make money?"

"But Mr. Holstein." Marcus wanted to be respectful because he knew a good story when it came his way. "There is a real important difference—"

"They consider my way illegal because they don't control it. And because they don't control it, they don't know how lucrative it is. Once they find out, believe me, they will invade our money-making game and take it over."

Evidently, no one paid any attention to Schuyler, so he sat back down.

Marcus enjoyed this exchange with Holstein. It opened some new doors for him. He felt more confident. Paying no attention to Schuyler, he continued. "They can close you down when they want to."

Holstein looked over at Jonas and smiled, then back at Marcus. "That will never happen. The authorities from the Harlem precinct from the captain to the cops walking the streets are getting their cut and don't want to lose that. The money they get they use it to take their families on vacations or pay to put their children in private schools or pay their whores. So, everybody benefits, even you, with those five hundred dollars you just stuffed in your pocket."

Schuyler got back up. "Enough gentlemen. It's after ten and we need to get out of here. I still have a story to write for this week's paper."

Marcus followed and got up, as did Holstein. Jonas walked over and opened the door. Holstein looked over at Jonas.

"Who took this winning number?"

"Sam Arthur over at the Sugar Cane Club," Jonas answered.

Holstein turned his attention to Marcus. "I suggest you might want to visit that young man and place another bet with him. He seems to be your lucky charm."

It was Marcus' turn to smile. "I might just do that, Mr. Holstein, but not to place a bet but to get what could be a very interesting story."

Marcus and Schuyler followed Jonas out of the office.

At three in the morning, Sam Arthur waited until the last dancing couple walked up the stairs, packed up his belongings, and was about to leave when one of the band players ran up to him.

"Here is my quarter on number 235," he said, and handed Sam Arthur the money.

He wrote the numbers on the slip, handed a copy to the man, and followed the band player up the stairs. He nodded at Big Max and walked out the steel door and abruptly stopped as Mary stood there smiling at him. She had on that red dress and was looking sexually inviting.

"I didn't come downstairs 'cause I knew it would upset you. So, I waited out here." Mary pointed to a cheap one-hour motel down the street. "I already paid for the room. I usually get it for one hour, but I got it for the whole night, tonight."

Sam Arthur attempted to ignore her words. "Mary, what are you doing here this time a night?" He didn't know why he asked that because he knew why she was there. "And where is your baby? You didn't leave him in that room alone, did you?"

The smile disappeared from Mary's face. "Sam Arthur, don't start with me," she scowled. "You know I owe you, and you agreed to let me work for that money you gave me today. And don't worry about little Henry. I told you when I work at night, my neighbor keeps him." She grabbed Sam Arthur's hand and tried to pull him in the direction of the cheap hotel. "Now, come on Sam Arthur. Don't play with me."

Sam Arthur did not budge. "That's the first time you ever called your son by his name."

Mary ignored his comment and tried to jerk him in the direction she wanted to go. He still did not budge and was too strong for her to force him to move.

"Damn it, you the stubbornest man I ever knew! I ain't ever had to beg no man to have me."

"Now that's what I don't like. I don't want to know nothing about no man."

Again, she ignored his comment. "Is something wrong with you? Is you a queer?"

"Hell no, I ain't no queer. You mean a man can't do nothing good for you just 'cause he want to?"

The two watched as a police patrol car slowed down and then kept moving up Fifth Avenue.

"I told you before I took that hundred dollars that I don't want no handouts. Now you gonna let me earn that money, or do I have to give what's left of it back to you?" She opened her purse and pulled out the money.

Just as she tried to force the money into Sam Arthur's hand, the police car circled back and pulled up to the curb, and the policeman stared at them. She tucked the money back in her purse.

"We got to get off this street or they gonna arrest me. Now come on, you got to go with me."

Sam Arthur looked at the policeman, who continued staring at them. He took Mary's hand and walked toward the hotel. The police car pulled off.

The two walked to the front of the hotel and Sam Arthur stopped right there. He released Mary's hand, turned, and looked directly at her. "Mary, I told you before I can't do this."

The police car had turned around and started back toward them. Mary grabbed his hand and practically pushed him through the open door into the hotel.

"Come on." She kept pushing him down a narrow hallway, stopped in front of a room, and unlocked the door. Mary pushed him inside.

Sam Arthur stood in the small room with only a bed. Mary sat on the side of the bed. He kept standing at the foot of the bed.

"I'm telling you, Mary, I don't want it to be this way in a cheap room." He squeezed the bag with all the money and numbers inside tighter in a nervous gesture.

Mary opened her purse and started taking out the money. Sam Arthur hurried over and sat next to her. He put his large hand on top of hers, preventing her from getting the money out of the purse.

"No. I didn't mean you couldn't work for that money. Just not this way."

Mary stuffed the money back into her purse. "What you talking about, Sam Arthur?"

"The number of people I got giving numbers to me is growing real fast. I got a number of locations I been looking at working. But most of my time is right here at the Sugar Cane Club. Maybe you can help out at those other locations."

"Are you serious? What Mr. Holstein gonna think about that?"

"He don't have to know about it and it will only be a couple hours every day. You know I do have to sleep sometime."

"I ain't never thought about nothing like that, and I don't know no girls doing that."

"There is always a first and if it don't work out, then at least by that time you be earned those hundred dollars."

"Let me think about it." She pulled Sam Arthur down on the bed. "Don't worry. I ain't gon' force you to do nothin'. But I got this room for all night. You got all that money, and you don't need to be out this late at night."

Sam Arthur stretched out on the bed next to Mary. "Ain't no harm in holding you."

Mary tucked in close to Sam Arthur. "Ain't no harm at all."

10.

NINA SAT AT THE KITCHEN table in her new apartment home, sipping a cup of tea. It was a little past eight in the morning and it felt good to be up before noon. Usually, she didn't get to the apartment until after three in the morning. Last night was different. After dinner with Larry, the chauffeur dropped her off a little before ten. When the limousine pulled up to the apartment building, the few men standing outside looked at her as the chauffeur ran around the Lincoln and opened the door for her. She felt important and strolled up the steps and into the building. All that had happened to her in the last forty-eight hours, since she sat at that table in the club with a strange white man who practically promised her the world, was too good to be true. Now she had to return to reality and show up later that night and dance. Would he be there and if not, how would she feel?

"Nina, how'd it go last night?" Addie asked, as she slowly walked into the kitchen and sat on the other side of the table.

"You're up early."

"I am because I knew you would be up. Now tell me how it went last night?"

Nina took another sip from her cup as a way of hesitating to answer Addie. Should she level with her about Larry's encouragement to pass for white, and the amenities she experienced with the limousine and the restaurant had caused her to at least consider it?

"So, what happened?" Addie's tone intensified. "Will you still be dancing at Connie's?"

139

Nina instantly responded. "Why do you ask that?"

Addie gave Nina a hard stare. "I have seen other girls go out on those dates with those men and they never come back to the club. If I happened to run into them again, which most of the time I didn't, they dressed different, walked with a strut, and had a totally different look, the kind that announced they were no longer Negroes. So, what happened on that date?"

"Well, that'll never happen to me," Nina responded, still without answering Addie.

"So, when do you plan to meet with your newfound friend?"

Nina caressed her cup with both hands, lifted it up, and took another sip. "I don't know. We didn't make no plans."

"I'm sure he'll be at the club tonight." She turned and walked back to her bedroom.

⚜

Sam Arthur woke up alone in bed. Mary was gone, and he did not wake up whenever she left. He reached down to the floor and grabbed the money bag. Momentarily, he thought about what he had done, not delivering the slips and money to Mr. Holstein last night, as was required by all the runners. He probably had Jonas and every one of his other henchmen out looking for him. He had to get to the Turf Club before the morning numbers were posted.

He pulled out his pocket watch—only eight o'clock. He had time. He sprang out of bed, out of the room, and out into the street. Holding the bag extremely tight, he ran down Fifth Avenue to 136th Street, pushing through the crowded streets. He ran up the steps of the Turf Club and into Holstein's office. Holstein, sitting at his desk, looked up, and Jonas ran into the office and grabbed Sam Arthur by his arm.

Sam Arthur broke loose from Jonas' hold on him, threw the money bag on the desk, and wrapped his strong arms around Jonas as the two struggled.

"Stop!" Holstein shouted.

Sam Arthur released his grip on Jonas and stepped back. "Both of you sit down."

Both of the men sat in chairs in front of the desk.

Holstein looked at Sam Arthur. "What happened?"

Sam Arthur paused before answering. He didn't want to lie, but he also didn't want to tell this man that he was in a cheap room with a woman he had introduced Sam Arthur to a month ago, with all of his money vulnerable.

Holstein pointed to the money bag and then to Jonas. "Count it and give me all the slips."

Jonas grabbed the bag, opened it, and took out all the money and slips. As he began counting, Holstein again looked at Sam Arthur.

"If any of those slips don't match up with the money, tell me now, and do not lie."

His insinuation angered Sam Arthur, but he had to maintain his composure because he had to keep his job and he knew all the money and slips would match up. But what if Mary had dipped into the money bag while he slept? After all, she was a street hustler. Nervously, he turned and watched Jonas count the money and the slips.

"It all matches up," Jonas finally said as he stuffed the money and the slips back into the bag.

Holstein leaned across the desk toward Sam Arthur. "You get one chance to fuck up," he scowled. "You just had that one chance. Don't let it happen again."

"I won't Mr. Holstein, I won't."

"Make sure." Holstein turned and looked at Jonas. "Now the two of you get out of here and drive Sam Arthur home. I need both of you and can't have you all fighting."

Jonas got up, and Sam Arthur followed him out of the room with a load lifted off him.

✻✻✻

Marcus made his way up the steps and into the building housing the *Amsterdam News* at the corner of Seventh Avenue and 135th Street, for an early afternoon meeting with James Anderson, founder and owner of the newspaper. Much like his boss Abbot, Anderson had started the *Amsterdam News* with only a ten-dollar investment of his own money. He also initially worked out of his home at 65th and Amsterdam Avenue. Again, just like Abbott, his success was because of his hard work and determination. Marcus admired him because of those attributes and was anxious to pick this man's mind about the literary movement in Harlem. Anderson had been there since its beginning and was one of its strongest supporters.

As he strolled into the office, he smiled, looking into the face of Edgar Gray, a fellow journalist he had known for years. They had corresponded on different stories when Gray worked as a reporter for the *Pittsburgh Courier*. Marcus had no idea he had made his way to New York and was now working for Anderson.

"Well, finally, someone I know," Marcus said, extending his hand to Gray.

"Marcus, welcome to Harlem," Gray said as the two men shook hands. "It's been a while."

"That it has. You're now working for Mr. Anderson?"

"Yes, and I'm covering economic and social issues, primarily around Harlem."

"Maybe you're the one I need to talk with."

"That's why I'm here. Mr. Anderson wanted me to be a part of his discussion with you. He's waiting for us in his office."

Marcus followed Gray down a narrow hallway and into an office with the door open.

James Anderson stood up behind his desk as the two men walked up to the front of the desk. "Please have a seat."

Marcus and Gray sat in the chairs in front of the desk and Anderson sat back in his high-back black leather chair.

"So, you're Robert's hotshot reporter he sent to Harlem to compete with the *Amsterdam News* for stories."

His comment caught Marcus by surprise, but a smile from Anderson let him know he was not serious. Still, Marcus felt he had to respond diplomatically.

"Mr. Anderson, we would never attempt to compete with the *Amsterdam News*. We view you as the voice of Harlem."

"That is kind of you to say, but there are other newspapers also trying to figure out just what is happening in Harlem."

"I'm very much aware of the work that Mr. Randolph is doing over at the *Messenger*, and he is kind enough to allow me to work out of his office."

"Phil and I had our differences over this entire thing about socialism, but I think he has not concentrated so much and has George Schuyler over there denying that the movement taking place in Harlem is for real."

Earlier in the day, Marcus had thought about asking Schuyler to join him at this meeting, just as he had done for some others. But listening to Anderson mention Schuyler in not so nice of a way, not doing so, had been the right decision. He really hadn't paid much attention to his new friend and running buddy's writings, but going forward, he would.

"There is also the work that Mr. Thomas Fortune has done over the years with the *New York Age*." Anderson brought Marcus back into the discussion. "But he sold it back in 1909 and has moved on to do work for other newspapers. But there is no doubt he was the early pioneer in the newspaper business here in New York."

"And we must also mention Mrs. Gerri Major of the *Pittsburgh Courier*," Edgar finally spoke up. "She does a column for the *Courier* called 'New York Social.' In fact, it might be someone you might want to talk to. She knows all the ends and outs of what are called the dicties here."

Marcus turned and looked at Edgar. "Dicties? What or who is that?"

Both Anderson and Edgar chuckled. "It is the name given to the upper-crust Negroes who live on Strivers Row," Edgar answered. "And she is very good at it."

"I guess there's a lot I still have to learn about Harlem," Marcus said.

"It is a complicated place," Edgar said. "You haven't even started to deal with the folks from the islands who are here and coming in large numbers."

"And there is a great deal of animosity between those from the islands and the home-grown Negroes right here in Harlem," Anderson added. "And then there are the few Africans who somehow found a way to get over here."

"Marcus Garvey seemed to do quite well, and he was from Jamaica," Marcus said.

Anderson leaned across his desk. "Garvey was the most successful organizer of the poor people in this country. But he got in the way of the so-called leaders and that includes Dr. Du Bois and Phil. They believed him to be a charlatan and nothing but bad could come from his leadership."

"His big mistake was meeting with the head of the Ku Klux Klan," Edgar said. "There was no way he could justify that with the other Negro leaders."

"But he seems to still be strong even though he's locked up in a Federal prison in Atlanta, Georgia," Anderson said.

This was all great information and Marcus would follow up on it, but he needed to get back to his reason for being there. "Can we talk just a minute about the dichotomy that seems to be growing between the older writers and these younger ones, like Hughes?"

"What is it that you would like to know?" Anderson now asked.

"How do you view the differences?"

"The difference is time," Anderson said. "You have the Du Bois crowd and I believe I can put Charles Johnson in that category. They believe our writers should write for a specific purpose and that is to uplift the race. Especially Charles, who is of the opinion that the racial problem can be solved through literature. Du Bois is even more extreme. He believes all writings from Negroes should be essentially propaganda-driven with a message."

"Do you disagree with him?"

Anderson paused, rubbed his forehead, and leaned forward, looking directly at Marcus. "White people have done us a disservice over the years with the kind of filth they put out about our people. And it really came to a head when President Woodrow Wilson had a showing of the movie *Birth of a Nation* in the White House. That was a terrible movie about us and Dr. Du Bois believes that all our writing should be to dispel the myth of white America's perception of our race." Anderson leaned back in his chair. "So, somewhat, I do agree with him."

Edgar leaned forward in his chair. "However, we cannot take away the creative freedom of these young writers. Their works have a place in our culture."

"Do you think they will ever rectify their different approaches and come to some kind of understanding?" Marcus asked.

"That's not the problem," Anderson answered without answering. "The elephant in the room is the white publishing houses. Some of them are now reaching out to our writers, but they do expect the works they published to be acceptable to a white reading audience."

"What are the implications behind that?" Marcus asked.

"The question that must be explored is what kind of literature are white people willing to accept from Negro writers?"

"Why can't we just write for a Negro audience?"

"Because Negroes do not buy the books. Oh, there is a certain class of Negroes that do. The Striver Row crowd and a few others." Anderson again leaned forward. "But a Negro writer cannot survive on what he makes from sales in our community. And the other problem is that we do not have a publishing company to publish our works. We have to depend on white publishers, and they do dictate the terms."

Marcus also leaned forward in his chair. "Will this ever change?"

"Probably not in our lifetime, but on a positive note, we are opening the doors for future Negro writers fifty to sixty years from now," Edgar added. "Maybe by then, we will have a more sophisticated class of Negroes and maybe even a publishing company, so we can control the nature of our works."

"Let's hope that's the case," Anderson said, and got up. "I really have to get out of here and attend another meeting."

Marcus and Edgar also got up.

"Listen, if you're not busy this evening, there is a discussion group meeting at the home of Reverend Cullen and his son Countee, who is one of the most prominent poets in the city, will be there. Would you like to come along?" Edgar suggested.

"Absolutely," Marcus answered enthusiastically.

'Where are you staying?"

"At the apartments on St. Nicholas and 136th Street."

"Be out front at seven o'clock and I'll pick you up."

Anderson walked around his desk and stood next to Marcus and Edgar. "This is good. You'll meet the poet laureate of Harlem, and I believe this very discussion will be carried on tonight at Reverend Cullen's house."

The three men walked out of the office and out of the building.

II.

NINA FOLLOWED ADDIE OUT OF the dressing room and looked over to where Larry usually sat. He was not there, and a tinge of disappointment hit her. The chorus dancers took their usual positions and as the music began, Nina and the others moved to the rhythm and sounds throughout the club. During the routine, she kept looking at the entrance to the club. After forty-five minutes, the music stopped and Nina, with the others, walked off stage back toward the dressing room. Just before going inside, she looked back over her shoulder, and a feeling of excitement shot through her body. She saw him sitting at his usual table.

"He showed up," Nina said, sitting next to Addie in the dressing room.

"You really didn't think he wasn't going to show up?" Addie sarcastically shot back. "They always come back when they have their eyes on one of us. And he definitely has all his attention on you."

Nina appreciated Addie as her only friend since she'd come to Harlem, but often her comments were irritating. What Addie said was true, but it was just the way she said it.

"I really don't know what you're getting at."

"Nina, stop playing naïve. You know what's going on and I got a feeling that you are starting to really enjoy it."

They both looked over at the dressing room door as it swung open and Immerman walked in. He stopped right in front of Nina.

"You have company," he said.

Nina looked at Addie, who had that I-told-you-so look all over her face.

"You need to go out and sit with Mr. Madison," Immerman continued. "He has paid to have you miss the next set."

"I don't want to do that, Mr. Immerman."

"What's that got to do with anything? You work for me, and you'll do what I'll tell you to do."

Addie reached over and placed her hand on Nina's shoulder. "I know why you don't want to because you feel you're abandoning the team. Don't feel that way. We're used to this."

Addie's words relaxed Nina. At that moment, her feelings were running in all different directions. She really wanted to go out there, but didn't want to sit at the table, thinking the girls on stage would look at her with envy or disdain.

"Come on, Nina." Immerman took Nina by the hand, helping her out of the chair. "We don't keep a fine guest like Mr. Madison waiting."

Nina practically glided over to the table where Larry sat. He stood up as she approached, walked over to the other side of the table, and pulled the chair out for her. Nina forced a smile on her face as she sat down. Larry hurried to the other side and sat down.

"It's good to see you again, Nina."

"I don't think this is right."

"What's not right?"

"Me sitting down here while the other girls are on stage working."

"Nina, didn't I tell you last night that if you'll only let me, your life is going to change for the better?"

"Yes, you did, Mr. Larry, and I appreciate what you're doing for me, but—"

"Leave 'but' alone and just let me do this for you." He sipped from his drink. "Don't you know any of those girls up there would trade places with you right now and think nothing of it? Is that what you want me to do?"

She looked at Addie as the dancers strolled onto the stage. She wondered if Addie would do that. The music started and the twelve girls moved to the beat. As they danced, Nina felt their eyes were on her.

Larry snapped his fingers at her. "Nina, are you with me? I asked you if you would like to trade places with one of the other girls and return to the stage?"

Nina forced a smile. "I'm sorry, no, I wouldn't want to trade places."

"Then stop feeling like you are doing something wrong."

The waiter approached the table and placed a glass of champagne on the table in front of Nina.

"Anything else, Mr. Madison?"

"I think we're fine right now, thank you."

The waiter then looked at Nina, smiled, and walked away. She was feeling like a bright spotlight was shining down on her. Just maybe she was better than the Negroes. She had a special gift of light complexion and beauty. Maybe she should use it to her advantage. Instead of looking at Addie and the other dancers, she took a sip and looked at Larry.

"I really didn't get a chance to eat today. Do you think you can get me out of here early so I can eat?"

Larry smiled. "Most certainly. I have already arranged that. And I have a special place to take you to eat and a special person for you to meet." He signaled for Immerman.

Edgar and Marcus walked into the parsonage of the Salem African Methodist Episcopal Church on the corner of 129th Street and Seventh Avenue. Countee Cullen, sporting his Phi Beta Kappa key, hanging from a gold chain around his neck, met them as they made their way into the foyer.

"Welcome to our home," he said in his high-pitched voice. Looking at Edgar, he continued. "You are the excellent journalist with the *Amsterdam News.*"

"Thank you for remembering me." Edgar extended his hand, and the two shook.

Cullen turned his attention to Marcus. "And who is this handsome man with you?"

"Marcus Williams and he's here in Harlem writing a story about us for the *Chicago Defender.*"

"Oh my God, then I'd better be on my best behavior," Cullen said.

Marcus' attention was on another man who walked up and stood next to Cullen and put his arm around the man's shoulder.

"This is my dearest friend, Mr. Harold Jackman," Cullen said. "We've been friends since high school."

"We'd better get back into the study," Jackman said. "Pastor Cullen is ready to get started. This is your special time."

"Yes, you're right. I was on my way back in when these two fine gentlemen came in," Cullen replied.

He led them down a corridor and opened the door to the study, where a dozen people were mingling. Marcus recognized Jessie Fauset and Ethel Nance. He hadn't talked with any of them since that night at Craig's Restaurant. Just as he moved to walk over to them on the other side of the room, an elderly man he assumed to be Reverend Frederick Cullen, Countee's adopted father, tapped on a small podium at the front of the room.

"Listen up, everyone," Reverend Cullen began. "We are here to celebrate Countee's two exceptional accomplishments in this year of 1925. We are celebrating his graduation as a Phi Beta Kappa exceptional student from New York University. And his book of poetry was recently published. Congratulations, son."

While the guests clapped, Countee walked up and hugged his father. He stood at the podium next to him.

"Speech, speech, speech," Marcus joined in with the others.

Jackman walked up to the podium and stood on the other side of Countee.

"I'm not good at making speeches," Countee started. "However, I thank you all for joining me and my family on this special occasion."

Reverend Cullen moved closer to Countee. "Does anyone have any questions for my son?"

Marcus couldn't pass up this opportunity. "Yes, I do."

"And who are you?" Reverend Cullen asked.

Edgar spoke up. "He is here with me, and he is with the *Chicago Defender*, visiting Harlem."

"I would prefer someone from Harlem ask or comment to Countee," Reverend Cullen said. He looked at Jessie and Ethel.

"No, Father," Countee interrupted. "I would like to hear what our visitor has to ask. Go right ahead, Marcus."

Marcus moved a step forward. "Over the past month, I have been here and talked with quite a few people. There has been a difference among the artists as to how you all should portray Negro culture in your works. On which side of this debate do you fall?"

"On neither side. With my poetry, I am not attempting to create a Negro culture. My poetry has no color attached to it."

"You and Langston Hughes are the two most notable Negro poets in Harlem and—"

"No, Marcus, I do not identify as a Negro poet, only as a poet. Now I have a great deal of respect and do, in fact, admire Langston dearly, but our approach to our art is very different."

They were all staring at Marcus. He didn't know if that was a good or bad thing, but whatever it was, he had to continue.

"So then, can I assume you don't buy into the new Negro movement?"

"No, I do not. Of course, as an individual, I am a Negro. But as a poet, I do not recognize my work in any racial category."

Again, Marcus was not quite certain how much further he should pursue this line with Countee, but until they stopped him, he would continue.

"I have read several of your poems, particularly 'Heritage' and 'To Make A Poet Black,' and they both seem to address the race issue."

Reverend Cullen stepped back up next to Countee. "I think that is enough. Let's all retire to the parlor, where we have refreshments."

Marcus turned and looked at Edgar, who shrugged. They followed the others out of the room.

Standing in his usual spot in the basement of the Sugar Cane Club, Sam Arthur felt his nerves on edge. He knew Mary was sure to show up, excited about her possibilities to make money other than by laying on her back. The problem was, he had no idea how to pull this off. He used that angle as a way to get around having sex with her. He got into this mess, trying to remain loyal to Willa Mae, who he knew was back in Gaffney, waiting just for him. He was tempted last night, laying there next to Mary; the first time in his twenty-three years he had slept in the bed with a woman.

The music started, and dancers filled the floor. A heavy-set woman who never danced, but showed up every night, walked along the side of the dance floor up to Sam Arthur. She handed him a dime.

"Put this on Number 488. I dreamt these numbers last night."

Sam Arthur took the dime, wrote the numbers on a slip, and handed her a copy. The heavy-set woman turned and started back toward her table.

Sam Arthur felt her presence and jerked his head toward the stairwell. Mary hurried along the side of the dance floor, and before Sam Arthur could control her movement, she wrapped both arms around him. She squeezed him tightly and then released her hug. She stood there, smiling.

"I'm ready to go to work," she said, elated. "I told all the working girls in the building that I won't be hustling anymore."

Sam Arthur had struggled with his promise to put Mary to work as his helper. He had decided that just was not something he could do, but her excitement standing there was something he couldn't take away from her. If he disappointed

Mary, he would send her right back to hustling. He needed time to figure this out.

"I been thinking about this, and maybe this ain't the right kind of work for a woman."

Mary slugged Sam Arthur on his arm. "What you mean? You promised me last night, Sam Arthur. I never thought you the kind of man to go back on his word."

"I ain't, Mary, I ain't, but I got to work this out. Got to figure out just how to do this."

"Well, I guess while you trying to figure this out, I got to go back to my hustle. I never should have believed you 'cause you just like the rest of them. You just like my baby's daddy."

Her angry words struck deep in Sam Arthur. What he couldn't let happen was for her to look at him in the same way as her baby's daddy.

One of the band players hurried over to Sam Arthur. "I got 655 for a quarter," he said as he handed him the quarter.

Sam Arthur took the money just as Mary walked away. He wrote out the number on the slip and handed the band player his copy. He ran up the stairs and took Mary by the arm before she could get out the door.

"Where you going?"

"Back to work," she answered indignantly.

"No, Mary, don't. Give me some time to figure this out."

"While you're figuring this out, I also got to figure out just what I got to do." She broke from his grip and walked out the door.

⁂

The Lincoln limousine pulled up and stopped in front of the Fifth Avenue Restaurant on East 24th Street in

Manhattan. The chauffeur jumped out, ran around, and opened the passenger's back door. He took Nina by the hand and helped her out. Larry followed. He took her arm and escorted her inside.

The maître d greeted them. "Welcome, Mr. Madison."

"I'm expecting Florenz Ziegfeld. Is he here?"

Nina, with a shocked expression, stopped. "Did you say Ziegfeld?"

Both Larry and the maître d also stopped.

"Is everything all right, Mr. Madison?"

"Yes, it is." Larry nudged Nina to keep her moving forward.

"Mr. Ziegfeld is in the private room in the back, and he is expecting you."

Nina's knees were weak as she managed to keep up with Larry and the maître d who opened the door to a small room with a white linen tablecloth and four chairs.

Florenz Ziegfeld stood up as Larry and Nina walked in. The maître de walked back out, closing the door behind him.

"Larry, my friend, good seeing you again," he said as he extended his hand.

Larry shook it vigorously. "I only bother you when I know it'll be worth your time."

Ziegfeld looked directly at Nina and smiled. "I do believe this will be worth my time."

The Lincoln limousine pulled up in front of a Fifth Avenue apartment building. Larry did not wait for the chauffeur to come around and open the door. He got out and took Nina's hand and helped her out.

Nina stared up at the magnificent apartment building as Larry led her to the front, and a doorman opened the door for them. Still holding her hand, Larry started into the building, but Nina froze in place. He looked at her.

"What's wrong?"

"Where are we going?"

Larry smiled. "Silly girl don't be afraid. Florernz just hired you to be a Ziegfeld girl. You can't continue to live over there in Harlem. Ziegfeld girls are classy girls, not like the dancers at Connie's Inn. You have to play the part."

Nina took one step back. "What do you mean, like the girls over at Connie's Inn? I was one of those girls and still am until I talk with Mr. Immerman."

Larry grabbed her hand and pulled her in close. "You were one of those girls and that's why I took you out of there. You deserve much better than what you can get there. And you don't have to bother telling Immerman, he already knows. Now please allow me to introduce you to two of the girls who are working as Ziegfeld girls and will be your roommates. And for God's sake, don't tell them you are a Negro."

Nina did not feel good about the way Larry constantly told her to reject her race. In doing so, she rejected all eighteen years of her life, including her mother. But walking into this marvelous building with marble floors and low-hanging chandeliers, she couldn't do what she knew was right.

They reached the elevator, stepped inside, and the operator closed the doors. Nina couldn't take her eyes off the numbers indicating the floor. They kept going all the way up to the top floor. The door opened, and Larry again took her hand and led her down the hallway. She did not resist.

He led her into the apartment, and her first thought was that this could not be real. The apartment was exquisite, with gorgeous furniture. She watched as two beautiful girls strolled into the room and smiled at her.

Larry hugged both of them and took control. "Myra and Lucille, please welcome your new roommate and new addition to the Ziegfeld girls. Nina."

Myra hugged Nina. "Welcome!" She moved back and stood next to Lucille, who did not make an effort to hug Nina.

Lucille looked directly at Nina, not smiling any longer. "Where are you from?"

"She's from St. Louis and just recently arrived in New York."

Lucille finally hugged Nina, but quickly moved back away.

"Nina starts her training tomorrow and will move in here right after that."

Nina had remained silent, trying to absorb all that was happening. She was standing in the most amazing apartment far above Harlem down below, and she would now be living there with two white girls, whom she couldn't let know she was really not like them. This was the beginning of an overwhelming challenge.

"I want you girls to make Nina feel like this is home, just like girls before you moved in here made you all feel the same way," Larry continued to control the conversation.

"We will, Larry," Myra spoke up. "We definitely will."

Lucille glared at Larry. "I assume she has gotten the limousine treatment, and all that goes with it?"

Larry's tone changed and became quite stern. "That's none of your business. Now I want no trouble, do you understand?"

Lucille did not respond but kept glaring at Larry.

He glared back at Lucille. "Do you understand?"

"Yes, Larry, I understand," Lucille complied in a soft tone.

"Now that we all understand each other, we can get out of here. Nina has to get her belongings from where she's been staying and will get all moved in tomorrow." Larry's tone was much calmer.

"Oh? Where's she been living?" Lucille asked.

"That's not important." Larry turned and looked at Nina. "Let's go so you can take care of your business and get ready for a new career and new life tomorrow."

Not knowing what to do or what to say, Nina just nodded at her two new roommates and followed Larry out of the apartment.

"You're gonna do what?" Addie shrieked as she ran into Nina's bedroom while she was placing her belongings into a suitcase.

Nina stopped packing and looked at Addie. "Don't worry, I'll cover the rest of this month's rent."

"You know damn well I'm not talking about no rent." Addie sat on the side of the bed. She patted the bed. "Come and sit. We got to talk."

Nina put the clothes she held in her hand in the suitcase and sat.

Addie took Nina's hand in hers. "Nina, you're only eighteen. You have no idea what you're getting yourself into. That's the big leagues over there. The stakes are high, and those white folks don't do nothing for a Negro girl, no matter how beautiful they are, without a payoff for them."

"What are you talking about? Larry has been nothing but nice to me."

"Oh, my God, Nina, that's what I mean. You're so innocent."

Nina snatched her hand out of Addie's grip. "I know what I'm doing," she said, trying to remain calm. She wanted to leave as friends with Addie, but she was going to leave. "Addie, you're the only one who told me when I first started working at Connie's Inn that someday I'd get an opportunity to move on. Well, this is my opportunity."

"But Nina, it might not be the right one. You need to take some time and think this through. Believe me, I am only looking out for you."

"Looking out for me? Ha." Nina felt she had to strike back. "You and any of the other girls would take my place in a second if given the opportunity."

"Is that what your friend Larry told you? I know he did when you were having second thoughts about leaving us last night."

"No, he didn't." Nina lied, knowing that was precisely what he said, and at the very time she was having second thoughts about leaving Connie's Inn. Still, she was not going to let Addie know that.

Addie stood up and looked down at Nina, who was still sitting on the bed. "Yes he did and you're lying because you know I'm right."

Nina got up. "Well, if he did, he was only looking out for my best interest."

Addie took Nina's hands in hers. "Remember when you came over here disappointed because you weren't going to get a chance to dance with Mrs. Mills?"

Nina did not pull her hands back from Addie's grip. "Yes, I remember."

"Well, don't let it happen to you again."

"I won't. I have to finish packing. The limousine will be here to pick me up any minute now."

Addie released the grip on Nina's hands. "Just like I was there for you before, I'll be here for you again." Addie turned and walked back out of the room.

12.

THE YELLOW CAB PULLED UP in front of Marcus' brownstone home. He paid the cab driver and, feeling generous, gave him a five-dollar tip. He had the five hundred dollars he won playing the numbers with that country boy runner at the club. He got out of the cab and walked up the steps to his brownstone, anxious to hold and kiss Helen. It had been a few months since he had been home, and it really felt good to be back, even though it would only be for a couple of days.

Marcus unlocked the front door and stepped inside a dark home. He had been confident that Helen would be there at nine o'clock at night. He turned on the lights, walked to the bedroom, then the kitchen, finally back into the living room, and sat on the couch. Maybe it was a mistake not to call and tell her he was coming home. He wanted to surprise her. Not only with him being there, but with an additional five hundred dollars. Before he left home for Harlem, she would always be there when he got back from one of his late-night assignments. What had changed and why wasn't she there now?

Sitting there, wondering where she might be, he heard the door unlocking and Helen walked in, but abruptly stopped when she saw Marcus sitting on the couch. She stood there, looking at him with a surprised expression. Marcus got up and hurried over and hugged her, but she did not return the hug. He backed up a few steps, putting some space between the two of them.

"I thought you'd be home."

"I had no idea you were coming home, Marcus."

Marcus forced a smile. "Aren't you happy to see me?"

Helen walked past him, putting her purse on the table. She stood there for a moment, then walked over and sat on the couch. Marcus hurried over and sat next to her.

"Helen, what's wrong?"

"You've been gone it seems like a long time doing God knows what and I'm supposed to be happy to see you?"

"Sweetheart, I've been doing my job. So, what do you mean, 'God knows what?'" He reached into his pocket and hesitated. Maybe sharing the five-hundred-dollar surprise right at that moment might create even more problems.

"Marcus, you know I never wanted you to leave Chicago. We were doing quite well, but you felt a stronger commitment to your job than you did to my feelings." She took a deep breath and released it. "Now you suddenly show up and I'm supposed to be excited."

Her chilling words irritated Marcus because she had agreed to what he was doing in Harlem. He never put his job above her. He was doing it for them. He believed his success in covering a historically important cultural phenomenon was her success, too. He had to explain that to her. He scooted closer, and she moved further away.

"Helen, stop! I thought you understood that what I am doing I do for the two of us, not just for me. I thought you knew that our success takes sacrifice and remember, you decided not to come with me."

"I did, Marcus, but I never realized how much I would miss you and how could you do that to me?"

Marcus relaxed on the couch and threw up his arms. "What is it, Helen? If you want me to come home right in the middle of this project, then I will do that. I don't know how well that'll go over with Mr. Abbott, especially after he has invested money into this project."

"And you would resent me for asking you to do that."

What the hell, Marcus thought. He pulled out the money and tossed it between the two of them. Helen touched the money but did not pick it up.

"Marcus, where did you get all of that money?"

"That's not important, but I did win it legally and wanted to surprise you with it." He paused for a moment. "I thought you would be happy to see me and pleasantly surprised with this money that we certainly can use. I guess I was wrong."

She didn't appear to be moved in a positive way by his words.

He picked up the money, stuffed it back in his pocket. "I'm sorry, Helen, I knew you were opposed to me going to Harlem, but I also thought that over time you might change your mind. I guess I was wrong." Marcus got up. "I can find a room for the night downtown."

"Wait, Marcus." Helen also stood up. "You don't have to do that. After all, this is your home. And I have to admit that I have missed you."

"Finally, something pleasant coming from you."

"I'm tired, Marcus, and I want to go to bed. We can talk in the morning."

"I'll sleep in the guest bedroom."

Helen finally smiled. "No, you don't have to do that. After all, the bedroom is also yours. And I have to admit I've missed you in there also."

The two walked back to the bedroom.

Marcus sat across from Robert Abbott in the office of the *Chicago Defender*. He experienced a sense of relief because his evening at home with Helen had gone exceedingly well, exceptionally well, in fact. That morning, she even agreed that she would consider coming to Harlem just for a visit. He was making progress because he was not sure he wanted to come back to Chicago once he finished his assignment. But he wanted Helen there with him. Once she visited and recognized that was where they should be, she would agree to a permanent move there.

"When are you going back?" Abbott asked.

"I'm catching a train this afternoon and will get back there tomorrow morning."

"I'm pleased to know that things are good at home."

"I wasn't sure they would be when I first got home and Helen wasn't there, but it all worked out just fine."

"You need to get your wife up there with you."

"I'm working on it."

Abbott leaned across the desk. "No, you have to do more than just work on it."

Abbott was piquing Marcus' curiosity. What was his interest in Helen getting to Harlem? Did he know something that Marcus didn't? He had to ask.

"What are you driving at?"

"It's not good for a man and wife to be separated for a long period of time."

Marcus had never, in all his years working for Abbott, felt any kind of anger toward him. He felt it coming on, though. He had to confront him.

"Remember, you are the one who forced this separation."

"I know, but I just knew by now Helen would want to join you. I never imagined that she would be so stubborn."

Marcus relaxed as he thought maybe Abbott really was just concerned about their separation and knew nothing specific.

"This morning she told me she would consider coming there for a visit and that is progress."

That was enough. Marcus no longer wanted to discuss his private life. He needed to shift the conversation back to the reason he was at Abbott's office.

"I am discovering some very interesting things about Harlem that their papers do not report in the glowing stories practically every day."

Abbott relaxed in his chair. "That's interesting. What's the angle?"

"The angle is there are two Harlems." Marcus leaned forward in his chair, relieved he had successfully gotten off the subject of his marriage. "There is the artistic Harlem with its writers, artists, and of course the musicians who are changing the landscape of the Negro culture."

"I believe the correct assessment is that they are now creating a culture that has existed but never been articulated before."

Marcus ignored Abbott's correction of his description. He had something much more important to share with him.

"But that artistic group is less than ten percent of the Negroes living there. The other ninety percent know nothing about that cultural revolution occurring all around them."

Now it was Abbott's turn to lean forward. "Are you suggesting that we expand the scope of our interest in covering Harlem?"

"Exactly, and I know where to begin that coverage."

"Do you want to change the focus of our story over to the ninety percent?"

"No, I'm suggesting that we merge the two and give the readers a comprehensive view of Harlem, the good and the bad. Our people are struggling from day to day."

"How long will it take you to complete this expanded assignment?"

"I don't really know until I dive into it."

"Will Helen be all right with this?"

"Yes, she'll be just fine."

"Then let's do it."

Marcus did not want to get back on the subject of Helen. He would make it okay with his wife. He needed to end this conversation, one he had never had with Abbott. It was time to go.

He got up. "I need to get back home and pack."

Abbott got up. "Call me in a week and let me know of your progress. This could be a major breakthrough in covering Harlem. We can consider it the other side of Harlem. I really like it."

"If you have decided to take on an additional assignment that means you will spend more time away from home with no idea when you might return, then I think we should consider a divorce because this is no longer a marriage," Helen calmly said as she and Marcus sat on the couch in the living room of their home.

Marcus instantly thought back on his conversation earlier with Abbott. He knew Helen had been upset when he first arrived home last night, but he felt that was all worked out. Now she was suggesting a divorce if he extended his stay in Harlem. He wasn't sure how to respond. They had been married for five years, and evidently, he didn't know his wife as well as he thought he did.

"Well, Marcus, aren't you going to say something? I need to know, is it our marriage or your precious story?"

Once again, Helen was testing his nerves with this nonsense about a divorce. Somehow, he just couldn't make her understand that all he was doing was for both of them. He had to respond.

"Helen, are you seeing someone else?"

"How dare you!" she shot back with disdain in her response.

"Then why are you doing this? I don't know why you want to do this. I thought we were doing fine this morning when I left to meet with Mr. Abbott."

"That's just my point. Before you left, I had accepted the reality that you were going back, but it would soon end, and you would be coming home. But you came back and now you're telling me as you prepare to leave that your time there would now be much longer."

"Helen, I love you and I want our marriage to work, but I love my work and I want more than anything to complete this assignment. By doing so, I will be a part of history. Fifty years from now, or even a hundred, I will have provided the world with an important part of our history. Don't deny me that opportunity. Please do not do that."

"I love you, too, Marcus, but I want a husband here with me and not gone away for God knows how long."

Marcus got up from the couch. "I have to catch my train. Will you come to New York, and we can work this out?"

Helen also got up. "No, Marcus I will not. And I suggest you let me know what's it going to be and real soon."

Marcus tried to kiss Helen, but she turned her head to the side. He picked up his suitcase and walked out the door.

Harlem

WORKING AS USUAL AT THE Sugar Cane Club, Sam Arthur couldn't get Mary off his mind. It had been a week since their confrontation. She probably hadn't been back because she figured he would stop her from hustling there. Or just maybe she still had enough of the first hundred dollars he gave her so that she did not have to hustle. But when that money ran out, she would be back out on the street, and he couldn't let that happen.

Sam Arthur's problem was he couldn't keep his promise to set Mary up to work with him. He practically felt obligated to keep providing her with money to make her whole again. He had to break the contradiction of Mary going to church on Sunday and selling her body on Monday and every other day of the week. He had to save Mary's soul from damnation.

Suddenly, it occurred to him that he was thinking more about Mary than about Willa Mae. Were his feelings shifting from his love for Willa Mae, whom he knew was pure, to a woman who was far from being pure? Maybe it was a matter of time. It had been two months since he arrived in Harlem and the only woman he had any contact with was Mary. All he had to do was see Willa Mae and he would be back on the right track. Maybe it was time to bring her up to Harlem. He would stay in the club until three, taking as many bets as possible. He would collect his pay tonight from Mr. Holstein and let him know he would be gone for a few days.

❊❊❊

Gaffney, South Carolina

SAM ARTHUR RUSHED OUT OF the segregated section of the Crescent Limited Railroad Train and through the colored section of the Gaffney Train Station. New York had made him into a new man, and it angered him when he had to sit in the front segregated car after they entered the state of Virginia. Once back home, he found himself back in the old dilapidated one-room in the station. Nothing like Grand Central Station in New York, a magnificent structure that allowed him the same freedoms as the whites.

Coming back to Gaffney, Sam Arthur dressed in the old coveralls and shirt he used to wear when working in the fields. He'd preferred to dress up in the suit he wore in Harlem to show the people how well he was prospering up North, but that would have caught the attention of the wrong people. He had to get Willa Mae and be out of there before they found out he was back in Gaffney.

As he walked toward the Negro section, he noticed just how poor everything appeared to him. No bright lights, no traffic, no people out and about, as it was in Harlem. He crossed over the railroad tracks, and it got even worse. He stopped as three stray dogs ran in front of him. The country backwardness of Gaffney was now strange to him.

It seemed to Sam Arthur that he'd been walking for hours, but it had only been a half-hour as he walked up to Willa Mae's small house on a dirt road. The house was dark, no lights were on, and it was nine o'clock. He knocked on the door, and it swung open. He stepped inside and stopped. There was no furniture in the small living room. He hurried over to the two small bedrooms, and they both were empty— no beds and no clothes. He walked back into the living room and stopped in the middle of the floor. He had to figure this out. Why was the house empty, and where was Willa Mae? Sadie would know. He ran out the door and kept running the six dark blocks to Sadie's Blues Club.

Sam Arthur burst through the door and Jethroe's eyes bulged. "Sam Arthur!"

From behind the bar, Sadie looked over at him. "What in God's creation?" she shrieked. "Sam Arthur, what are you doing back here?"

The other men and women in the club looked at him. Jethroe got up from the booth he shared with Emma, ran over to him, and wrapped Sam Arthur in a hug. They broke from the hug and Jethroe frowned.

"Brother man, what are you doing coming back here?" Jethroe asked.

"Yes, that's what I wanna know," Sadie said as she hurried from behind the counter and hugged him. She broke the hug but held his arms with her huge hands.

Sam Arthur pulled away from her, pulled out one hundred dollars from his pocket and handed it to her.

"This the money I owe you, Miss Sadie."

Jethroe stared at the one-hundred-dollar bill. "Where you get that kind of money?"

"Don't matter where I got it, plenty more where that come from."

Sadie moved in closer. "Sam Arthur, I know you didn't come all the way back here just to pay me that money. So why you back here when I told not to ever come back?"

Sam Arthur smiled. "I come to get my Willa Mae and take her up North, but when I went by her house, it was empty. So, I figured she might be here, or you all would know where she is?"

Sadie took a step back and looked at Jethroe. "You tell him."

Sam Arthur jumped right up in Jethroe's face. "Tell me what? Come on Jethroe, tell me what?"

Jethroe pushed Sam Arthur back. "She done up and left out of here. That Shackleford boy got after her so bad and you weren't here and she ain't heard from you, so she and her mama left here a month ago up to Charleston."

"What?" Sam Arthur shouted. "You know where she at in Charleston?"

"Nobody knows," Sadie spoke up. "But I know you can't stay here in Gaffney. That Shackleford boy find out you here, he sure gonna come for you."

"I ain't scared of no honky. I got to find my Willa Mae."

"Boy, you crazy," Sadie scowled. "You done gone up to that Harlem and got all beside yourself. This is South Carolina, and you'd better act like you scared and get the hell out of here."

"She right, Sam Arthur, you got to get out of here tonight," Jethroe added. "Them white folks know everything happens this side of town. Just like Miss Sadie say, this ain't Harlem."

A frustrated Sam Arthur ignored Sadie and Jethroe. He moved past them. "Don't nobody in here know where Willa Mae live in Charleston?"

No one spoke up. Sadie walked up to Sam Arthur, who had moved to the center of the club. "Sam Arthur, stop! I can't let you upset my customers. You got to go."

Sam Arthur walked back to Jethroe and pulled out fifty dollars. "Take this money and go to Charleston and find Willa Mae and tell her to come to Harlem and come to the YMCA, and I'll be there."

Jethroe pulled his hand back away from the money. "I can't do that, Sam Arthur. I got to work."

"Give me the damn money." Sadie walked back next to Sam Arthur. "I know somebody who can do that for you. But they got to get paid."

Sam Arthur pulled out another twenty dollars. "This should cover their fee. The fifty is for Willa Mae to get up to Harlem. And remember, tell him she should come to the YMCA, and sure, it's the one in Harlem."

"Now, Sam Arthur, you got to get out of here," Sadie said in a calmer voice. "Them white folks be coming around here every night checking on us."

"You can stay at my place for the night but got to go in the morning," Jethroe said.

"Good, now you all got to get on out of here," Sadie ordered.

"I owe you for my drinks," Jethroe said.

"Don't worry 'bout them drinks. Just go."

Emma got up, walked next to Jethroe and the three of them walked out of the club and into the night.

13.

"YOU WERE OUTSTANDING TODAY IN rehearsal and that was just the first time," Myra said to Nina as they walked back into the Fifth Avenue apartment.

"But there were so many girls," Nina said.

"That was a small group," Lucille said. "There are two hundred Ziegfeld girls, and every once in a while, we'll all be in the same routine."

"Especially if Flo wants to do something extremely extravagant," Myra added.

Lucille moved in closer to Nina. "Do you have Negro blood?"

Her question caught Nina off guard. She recalled Larry's cautious advice: *by all means, do not let them know you are a Negro.*

She stepped back and glared at Lucille. "What are you talking about? I am not a Negro and I do not have Negro blood." She instantly felt guilty.

Lucille didn't back off. "I'm talking about your shape."

Myra stepped in. "I have to agree with Nina. What are you talking about? She might have a little darker skin tone, but that's about it. And Larry wouldn't bring a Negro to live with us."

"It's her backside. White girls don't have a backside like she got. That's something you see on Negro girls."

"What are you talking about?" Nina said, her voice rising. "You go around looking at Negro girl's butts?"

174

Lucille moved in closer to Nina. "How dare you?"

"Girls, stop it." Myra turned and looked at Lucille. "That's just silly. Why would Nina pass for white and lie to Larry?"

Lucille didn't back down. "There are a lot of light skin Negro girls who pass for white to improve their lifestyle. I mean, I don't blame them. Who would want to be a Negro?"

Nina's anger was so intense she wanted to explode and shout, "Yes, I am a Negro, and I am not ashamed," but her life had improved just as Lucille said. So, she remained quiet.

Myra again came to her defense. "That's enough, Lucille," she said in a stern tone. "Nina gave you her answer, and that's good enough. And let me again remind you that Larry does not deal with the trash in Harlem."

Nina had had enough. She had to bring this to an end. "Myra, would you please show me to my room? I'd like to get settled in and prepare for tomorrow."

"Yes," Myra said. "You're going to love it."

Nina gave Lucille a hard look and followed Myra down the hall.

⁂

The knock at the door awakened Sam Arthur in his bedroom at the YMCA. He had left Gaffney that morning undetected and arrived back in New York after nine at night. He was exhausted when he got back. Not so much from any physical exertion, but more from the emotional disappointment when he arrived at Willa Mae's house, and she was no longer living there. He had considered going to work at the Sugar Cane Club because he had to make back the money he spent trying to find Willa Mae. But the mental exhaustion won out, and he went right to the YMCA, to his room, and fell out on the bed.

He forced himself out of bed, opened the door, and stared into the face of Mary. He quickly situated his body behind the door with his head peeking out at her. He was only wearing his underwear.

"Mary, how'd you know where I was at?"

She just stared at him. "Are you gonna let me in?" She did not wait for an answer. She pushed the door back and walked into the room.

"Mary, I ain't got no clothes on."

Ignoring his comment, she kept walking inside and sat on the bed. "As I recall, you saw me naked and you ain't all the way naked." She laughed. "And I done seen a whole lot of other men with less than what you got on."

Sam Arthur closed the door, no longer concerned with his exposed body. "I don't want to hear no talk 'bout that."

Mary glared up at Sam Arthur as he stood back by the door. "Why you care, Sam Arthur, who I been with? You not interested in getting with me."

Sam Arthur rushed over to the side of the bed and grabbed his pants and slipped them on. Feeling more comfortable, he relaxed.

"Why you come all the way over here this time a morning, and where's Henry?"

"I need some money." She exhaled and started crying.

Sam Arthur sat next to her and put his arms around her. "Don't cry," he said in a soft voice. "I can't stand to see you cry."

She pulled back from his embrace and regained her composure. "Of all the people, you the last one I wanted to come and ask for money, but I ain't got nobody else to go to."

"Why you need money when I just gave you that hundred dollars?"

"I still got part of that left." Mary stood up. "I need money for something else."

Sam Arthur continued to sit. "What you need it for?"

"I can't tell you that, Sam Arthur."

"You want me to give you money and you can't tell me why you need it?"

Very excited, Mary said, "Yes, yes, yes, that's right! Now you going to help me or not?"

"Clam down," Sam Arthur said in a stern voice. "How much you need?"

She calmed down. "At least fifty dollars."

"You telling me you gonna take this money and not insist you work for it?"

Mary sat back on the bed close to Sam Arthur and faced him. "Ever since you gave me that money, I ain't had to hustle nobody. And I feel good about myself 'cause somebody did something for me and just because they care 'bout me and my baby." She took Sam Arthur's hand. "I used to pray that someday I would meet somebody like you. It didn't happen right away, but I didn't give up on God or praying. When you saw me in church, that's why I was there. And God answered my prayer when you showed up that afternoon at the Turf Club."

Sam Arthur didn't quite understand. "What did I do?"

"You treated me like a lady and that felt really good. I was afraid to show that side of me at first, but after being off the streets and having time to think, I'm not afraid anymore."

"If I give you these fifty dollars, does that mean you ain't gonna do that no more?"

"That's why I need the fifty dollars." She broke down and shared part of the reason she needed the money. "I promise I ain't going to do that no more. You got to promise to help me."

Sam Arthur got up. "Let me work tonight and I'll come by your place after closing with the money."

"You sure, Sam Arthur? Don't play with me."

"I ain't never played with you and if these fifty dollars can keep you out the streets hustling, then it will be worth it."

Mary got up and lunged into Sam Arthur's arms and kissed him. "I'll be waiting." She walked to the door, opened it, turned back, and smiled at Sam Arthur, then turned and walked out the door.

Sam Arthur ran his hands across his lips. Her kiss was so soft and captivating, something he had never felt with another woman, not even Willa Mae.

❦

Nina was awestruck by the extravagantly flowing outfit with feathers and silver she wore. She was astonished as she strolled down the winding staircase high above the floor, accentuated by the cross-lighting that created rainbow patterns shining on her body. She stood behind a full orchestra below as it played. And she was stunned, looking out at the large crowd of well-dressed white men who filled the cavernous Roof Theater atop the beautifully structured Amsterdam Theater in lower Manhattan on West 42nd Street between Seventh and Eighth Avenues. For this particular routine, they did not dance but just stood there and allowed the men in the audience to admire their beauty.

After twenty-five minutes of just standing there in a pose for the men, she followed the lead girls down to the bottom of the steps, across the stage, and back to the large dressing room. Ziegfeld followed the girls inside and walked up to Nina.

"The next routine is a high kick routine that you practiced with the girls yesterday. Your rhythm and movement are outstanding. Get with Erté. He has a different fashion for you and the other girls, who will be back out in twenty minutes."

"Yes, sir." She got up and followed the other girls to a different dressing area. As she walked by Lucille, she couldn't help but notice the frown on her face.

Walking into the dressing area, Nina was again awestruck with the many different beautiful outfits hanging on the racks. She sat at one of the dressing stations.

"Your first time back here," one girl said.

Nina smiled. "Yes, this is my first show."

The girl extended her hand. "My name's Sarah and I've been with the Follies for two years."

Nina grasped Sarah's hand, and they shook. "There are so many beautiful dresses in here," was all she could say.

"Erté is the designer. He's from Paris and Flo brought him over here just to design the outfits as he envisioned them for the various settings. He is one of the only designers who's been able to satisfy Flo's taste. I've seen them come and go."

"I guess I should feel privileged 'cause he picked me out of all the girls in the last set to do this one also."

"We all watched you yesterday in rehearsal, and we all knew that you would be with the dance team. This is a very special team, and you definitely have the talent, not to mention the kind of body shape that Flo loves."

"How many girls does he have?"

"We got over two hundred, so for you to move up the ladder so fast as you have is very unusual." Sarah smiled, but then continued, turning her smile into a frown. "But that can be good and bad."

"What do you mean, bad?"

"I mean there are at least a hundred and fifty girls who would give up their bodies to Flo if they could have your place and they are going to know you've done it without having to sleep with him, and they will turn against you."

Sarah's words caused Nina to frown. "What do you mean, sleep with him? He sleeps with the girls?"

"Yes, he does, and if they don't agree, well then, they're usually let go. But most of them do because Flo has such a strong personality and is quite persuasive."

Nina thought back on her conversation with Addie before leaving the apartment when she warned her, in so many words, that this kind of thing happened in this environment. She wanted to ask Sarah if that had happened to her, but held back.

"Oh, don't worry, you are probably way back on the list. He'll first want to really impress you, then make his move."

Nina watched as Erté walked up to her. "You're next. I need to get you fitted for the next set and we only have fifteen minutes. Come with me."

Nina got up, looked at Sarah, and followed Erté to another part of the dressing room, thinking that maybe she was way in over her head and Addie had been right.

***

Marcus got out of the cab in front of the Sugar Cane Club. He had arrived back in Harlem at noon. For the twenty-four hours on the train, he found it difficult to sleep. He couldn't deal with Helen's ultimatum to come home soon or get a divorce. He didn't want to lose his wife, and he didn't want to give up writing this historically relevant story. Marcus' body was tired, and he needed to sleep, but he was excited about his new twist on the story, and sleep could wait. He had to get on it right away.

He hurried down the stairs into the club and saw Sam Arthur standing in his usual spot, surrounded by club-goers placing number bets with him. He figured Sam Arthur could provide him with some names of people he could interview. It was a lower class of people who frequented the club and placed bets with him. The bettors returned to their tables and Marcus energetically strolled up to Sam Arthur, who was busy stuffing slips into a bag.

"I bet you don't remember me?"

Sam Arthur looked up and smiled. "Yeah, I do. You the lucky man who won five hundred dollars."

"That's right. Thanks to you."

"You here to place another bet?"

"No, not really."

"Well, why you here?"

"I'm here to have you help me to write a story."

Sam Arthur frowned. "Do what?"

"Write a story."

"Mister, I don't know nothing 'bout you and I sure don't know nothing 'bout writing no story."

A young man and woman came down the stairs and walked up to Sam Arthur. Marcus stepped back.

"Put ten cents on number 626." The young man gave Sam Arthur the ten cents.

As Marcus observed the two individuals, he pondered whether they might belong to the group of individuals who were unaware of the artistic movement embraced by the writers and painters. He couldn't help himself. He stepped up and stood next to the two.

"Excuse me, can I ask you two a question?"

Sam Arthur gave Marcus a hard look. He handed the man his slip. "Why you want to ask them a question?"

Marcus looked at Sam Arthur. "For a story I'm writing for my newspaper in Chicago."

"We gonna be in a newspaper?" the young girl asked.

"Come on, let's get out of here." The young man grabbed the girl's arm and jerked her forward toward the stairs and hurried up them.

Marcus watched the two run up the stairs. He turned and looked at Sam Arthur. "Are those two regular customers?"

"No, they not regulars but they run down here every once in a while, and place numbers. I think they live somewhere near here. And why you want to ask them a question and what newspaper you say you work for?"

"I'm here in Harlem to write a story about what's happening in the arts, and I write for the *Chicago Defender*, and—"

"You write for the *Chicago Defender*?" Sam Arthur asked with excitement in his voice.

"Yes, I do," Marcus responded, feeling encouraged. If this man had heard of the paper, maybe he would be more willing to help him. "You've heard of the paper?"

"Have I heard of it? Down in South Carolina, we used to get that paper from the Negro Pullman Porters and read about all the good things Negroes doing up there."

Marcus figured he could play on Sam Arthur's ego as he had done before when trying to get sources to work with him.

"That's outstanding because the story I'm writing will be in the paper. And you can be a part of making that happen."

Sam Arthur's enthusiasm waned. "No, I don't know nothing 'bout writing no story."

Marcus knew he was losing him. "You won't be writing the story. I'll do that. All you have to do is introduce me to someone who can provide me the information I need."

"What kind of information?"

The band returned to their places, and the music started. Men and women filled the dance floor.

The music was extremely loud, and Marcus had to raise his voice a couple of levels. "Do you know anything about the writers and painters here in Harlem?"

Sam Arthur also raised his voice. "I don't know nothing about that."

"Do you know where the Negro library is here in Harlem?"

"I don't know nothing 'bout no library?"

It dawned on Marcus that he didn't know this man's name. "What is your name?"

"Sam Arthur."

"My name is Marcus Williams, and I would like to buy you lunch tomorrow if that's possible?"

"Why you want to do that?"

"Because then I can explain to you exactly how you can help me with this story."

Suddenly Sam Arthur thought of Mary. If this man needs someone to help him write his story, Mary would be the best person for the job.

"Can I bring someone along with me who might be better to help you?"

This is progress, Marcus thought. He would probably bring someone who fit the category of the kind of people he was looking to interview because certainly this young man definitely fit in that category.

"Yes, please do."

"Okay, I can do that. Where and when?"

Marcus thought momentarily that he would probably sleep most of the morning and maybe a little into the afternoon, since he hadn't really slept since that night at home in Chicago.

"Let's say one o'clock at Craig's Restaurant. You know where that is located?"

"No, but we can find it."

Marcus smiled and pulled out a one-dollar bill and handed it to Sam Arthur. "Put that dollar on 125. Maybe my luck hasn't run out."

Sam Arthur took the dollar, wrote out the numbers, and handed part of the slip to Marcus. "Maybe it hasn't."

"I'll see you tomorrow at one o'clock and your friend."

Marcus turned and walked up the stairs and out of the club, feeling good about his progress in exploring the other side of Harlem.

Nina was exhausted after performing in four sets. With each set, she sat for Erté to test two to three new and beautiful outfits coordinated with the ambiance in the theater for each set. Ziegfeld changed the décor with each new routine. Since she performed in the final routine, she was one of the last to leave the Roof Top Theater.

She took the elevator down to the first floor of the Amsterdam Theater with five other girls who had performed in the final routine. She'd missed Myra and Lucille. They had gone on before her. The apartment was only a few blocks from the theater, but since this was really her first full night, she felt a little nervous walking there. She was not in familiar territory and when not having to pretend, she was a Negro and knew that created a fear in her.

As she walked out of the theater, she breathed a deep sigh of relief. Larry stood leaning against the Lincoln limousine. He smiled. "Thought you might need a ride home after performing in four of the routines."

She also smiled. "How'd you know how many sets I did?"

"Because I was there for the entire show." Larry opened the door.

Nina got in and Larry slid in next to her. The chauffeur pulled off. Nina laid her head back and closed her eyes.

"I guess I was right. You are quite exhausted."

Nina sat straight up and opened her eyes. "Thank you, Larry. I've never been this exhausted. Never like this over at Connie's Inn."

"It's the pressure. Everything is moving so fast that you never have a chance to relax."

Nina looked at Larry. "I don't think Lucille likes me."

"Lucille doesn't like anyone she perceives as competition, especially someone prettier than her."

"She asked me did I have Negro blood."

"Don't pay any attention to her. She's just probing."

He took Nina's hand, and she did not resist. "Would you like to get something to eat?"

"Oh, please, not tonight. I just want to go to bed and sleep all day tomorrow until it's time to go to the theater."

Larry pulled her over to him and kissed her. She was surprised, and it happened so fast that she didn't have time to resist. When he released her, she sat there, stunned. A rich white man had made a sexual advance, and she did not know how to respond. She felt relieved as the limousine came to a stop in front of the apartment.

Larry did not wait for the chauffeur to come around and open the door. He opened it, stepped out, and held his hand into Nina's. She got out; he pulled her close and kissed her again, and she did not resist. They broke from the embrace.

"I have to go to Paris and I'm leaving in the morning. I'll be gone for the next three weeks." He handed her a piece of paper with a name and number. "This is the number to the chauffeur. The limousine will be available to you all the time I am gone." He kissed her, and again she did not resist.

Larry got back in the limousine and Nina stood there, stunned by what had just happened. She watched as the limousine turned and disappeared out of sight. Momentarily, she thought about Claude, and she never felt that way the few times they had kissed. He was the only person she had kissed, and it was nothing like Larry. Before she had kissed a boy, now it was a man, and it felt good. What felt best is she was becoming a woman. Smiling, she turned and headed up the steps into the apartment.

✴︎✴︎✴︎

Sam Arthur was excited about the prospect of introducing Mary to this man who, out of nowhere, had brought him the ideal way to satisfy her need to work for money. Even though she told him that would no longer be a factor in their relationship, a job working with this newspaper reporter would take care of that situation.

He watched as the last couple made it up the stairs and he followed them up. He hurried past Big Max and out the door. Jonas was sitting in the car waiting for him. He jumped in and handed Jonas the bag. He took it and reached to start the car.

"No, I don't need a ride tonight."

Jonas looked at Sam Arthur and smiled. "All right now, the country boy here done become a city boy. One of them party ladies in the club been stretching your pants."

Sam Arthur didn't respond. He got out of the car and walked up Fifth Avenue. He double stepped up the front steps of Mary's tenement apartment, walked in and knocked on her door. It was less than ten seconds, and the door swung open.

Mary threw her arms around Sam Arthur's neck. "I didn't really believe you were going to show up. Thank you."

He gently pushed her away and walked into the room. "Why you think I wasn't gonna come?"

Mary closed the door. "Because the last time you said you was going to do something for me, it was just to get rid of me and when I showed up believing you was serious, you told me you couldn't do what you promised."

He pulled out the fifty dollars and handed the money to her. "I never let you down when it comes to money."

Mary took the money and again tried to hug Sam Arthur, but he held her at bay. He couldn't keep getting these hugs, feeling her soft body, and not giving in. He still hadn't given up on Willa Mae. He had to remain loyal to her.

"I got something to tell you."

They took seats at the table. "What is it, Sam Arthur?"

Sam Arthur looked in the bedroom and Henry was not there. "Where's the baby?"

"I wasn't sure you was going to show up, so I had to take him to my friend's apartment upstairs, just in case I had to work."

Sam Arthur pounded his fist on the table. Mary jumped straight up.

"You told me you wasn't gonna do that no more." He frowned.

"Believe me, Sam Arthur, I didn't want to, but just in case you was lying to me and didn't show up like you lied to me before, it really wouldn't matter to me, and I swore I'd never trust another Negro man as long as I live."

"But now you satisfied that you could trust me and you ain't gonna go out to the streets no more."

"I promise. Now what is it you wanna tell me?"

Sam Arthur leaned forward, almost across the small table. "I met this man in the club tonight who had placed a bet with me a couple weeks ago and won five hundred dollars."

"What?" Mary adjusted her body in the chair. "He going to give you some of the money?"

"No, he wasn't there for that reason. He's a reporter for a paper out of Chicago who is here for a little while, writing a story on Harlem."

"Why he come all the way from Chicago to write about Harlem?"

"'Cause he wants to write about all the writers and painters that done come to Harlem and evidently it's an important story."

"What's that got to do with us? We ain't no writers and we sure don't fit in with them Negroes up there on St. Nicholas Street."

"Well, what he told me is that he also wants to write about the common folks who ain't a part of that crowd and asked me could I introduce him to some people to interview and I thought about you."

Mary sat straight up in her chair. "Me? What I know about telling him 'bout other folks?"

"You ain't got to tell him 'bout them folks, but just give him some names of folks he can talk to. As a matter of fact, he can start with you."

"What's he asking about?"

"About living in Harlem and how hard a time you got trying to feed you and your baby."

"No, Sam Arthur, I ain't 'bout to get caught up in that kind of thing."

Sam Arthur leaned even further across the table. "Remember, you told me you wanted to work to pay for the money you made doing what you did?"

"What's that got to do with this?"

"This is your chance to work for the first one hundred dollars I gave you and now for the other fifty."

"I had plans to get a job. That's why I asked you for the money."

"You're getting a job?" Sam Arthur smiled.

"I don't have it yet, but I got to train for it."

"What kind of job?"

"I wanted to surprise you when I got all trained. Don't make me tell you now."

"Okay, I won't, if you'll do this one thing for me."

"What is that?"

"This man wants to meet us for lunch tomorrow at one. Agree to go with me and at least hear what he got to say?"

"That's all I got to do?"

"Right now, yes."

"You going to be with me? You ain't going to leave me alone this time, is you?"

Sam Arthur found that interesting coming from a woman who met many strangers in strange rooms. "No, I won't leave you. I'll be with you until he finishes telling us exactly what he wants us or you to do."

"Long as you going to do it and long as I don't have to tell you what I'm training to be right now, okay?"

Sam Arthur got up to leave. "Okay, we straight. I can pick you up here in the morning about ten."

Mary jumped up and in an excited voice said, "Henry ain't going to be here until tomorrow, so just stay the night. You don't have to do nothing. But just stay with me."

Sam Arthur thought it was already four in the morning and he had to go all the way back up Fifth Avenue to 135th Street, so why not? "I can do that."

"Good, I want that."

Without touching each other, the two of them strolled into the bedroom.

14.

MARCUS WALKED INTO THE *MESSENGER'S* office, refreshed, and reinvigorated, ready to take on his new challenge. Maybe if he hurried and finished this project, he could save his marriage. But there was a problem. He did not want to return to Chicago. He was married to be a part of the history happening in Harlem. It was evolving as the cultural capital of Negro America and that was what he believed it should be.

Randolph was at his desk when Marcus walked in. Randolph waved at him. He hurried inside and sat in the chair in front of the desk.

"I understand you've been making your rounds, meeting and talking with practically anyone of any importance in Harlem," Randolph said.

"Yes, and I want to thank you for letting me work out of your office. George Schuyler has been very cooperative in sharing his space and also assisting me in meeting many of the leaders of this new movement."

"Can you share your findings with me, or do I have to wait for the story to come out?"

"I can share them with you, but I'm sure there's nothing you don't already know."

Randolph reared back in his chair. "You'd be surprised at what I do not know. I'm really not tied in with that crowd."

Randolph was not part of the new Negro movement. Marcus had to explore. "You're in Harlem and you have a leading newspaper. How can you not be tied in with them?"

"I'm more proletarian than elitist."

Marcus scooted up right to the front of his chair. He took a writing pad and a pencil from inside the pocket of his coat. "Do you mind?"

"Not at all. I'll stand behind everything I have to say."

"So, what makes you different?"

"The most important distinction is their efforts to be a part of this system. They believe that by producing good literature, they will achieve equality in this country. I respect Charles Johnson over at the Urban League, but that's why he has launched *Opportunity Magazine* to feature writers and poets with great ability and will be acceptable in the white literary world." He paused while Marcus took notes. "My efforts are to change the system totally."

"How do you think it should change?"

"Harlem is becoming a slum with all our people coming up here from the South thinking this is some kind of promised land. They get up here and they can't find a job or if they do, the pay is so low, they can't pay their rent. Just walk down Fifth Avenue above 131st Street and you will see what I am talking about. Our people are living in conditions unfit for animals, let alone human beings. My emphasis is on economics and not novels and poetry."

"How do you think the system should change?"

Randolph adjusted his body and leaned forward. "The capitalist system has to change, and this country needs to adopt a much fairer distribution of money."

"That sounds like socialism."

"And you look upon that as a bad thing?"

"No, as a matter of fact, I don't. I look at it as an impossibility in this country."

"You asked me how I think it needs to change, not how it will change."

"I understand, but how does that relate to what is happening here in Harlem?"

"We are all one, the artists performing over at the 135th Street Library, the dicties living on Strivers Row the poor and struggling on Fifth Avenue is Harlem, As a collective body we are in search of the same thing and that is an end to the deplorable manner that we are treated in this country."

His words, a collective body, captured Marcus and got his creative juices flowing. He had originally come to Harlem to write about the artistic movement but had expanded it to include the other side of Harlem, and now he thought about all the separate entities as one.

"How do you bring this collective body to recognize each of the parts?"

"I think they do know because they share a collective outcome. Right now, I'm working on organizing the Pullman workers into a union, to improve their conditions working on those trains. They know they have a collective interest and also know it is going to be one hell of a fight against the economic forces who see that as a threat to their profits. What I am doing with the workers is what has to be done in every corner of America for Negroes." Randolph pulled out his pocket watch and checked the time. "I have to go and meet my men, helping to organize the big rally of the railroad porters for this evening. In fact, it's something you might want to attend to get a feel as to how this works."

"I would be honored to attend. What time and where?"

"Seven this evening at the Elks Lodge on 129th Street

between Lenox and Seventh Avenue."

Randolph got up. "There will be five hundred railroad porters, hotel workers, and dining car attendants there, anxious to make a difference. You will see exactly what I'm talking about has to happen in this country."

Marcus also got up. "I will be there. I wouldn't miss it." His story had just taken on another challenge and, at that moment, Helen and divorce were not on his mind.

Mary froze up when she and Sam Arthur walked into Craig Restaurant. He took her by the arm and gently pulled her forward toward a table where Marcus was sitting. He did it also for his insecurities as well as hers. This was a part of Harlem that he never frequented. The people inside, well-dressed, were not the Negroes he was used to being around. He detected Mary felt the same way, so they supported each other.

Sam Arthur, still arm and arm with Mary, walked toward the table, but suddenly Mary forced him to stop. He looked at her.

"I don't belong here, Sam Arthur. Take me back to my place."

Sam Arthur jerked her forward. "No. You gonna do this 'cause you promised me."

"Damn you, Sam Arthur," she scowled, but moved along with him.

"Thank you for coming," Marcus said as Sam Arthur and Mary approached the table. He pointed to the two other chairs. "Please have a seat."

They took seats at the table.

Sam Arthur placed his hand on Mary's shoulder. "Mr. Williams, it is Mr. Williams, ain't it?"

"Yes, but please just call me Marcus."

"Okay, Marcus, this here is Mary."

Marcus looked directly at Mary. "Thank you, Mary, for coming."

The waitress sauntered up to the table and handed each of them a menu. "I'll be back to take your orders," she said, and walked away.

Marcus smiled as he watched both Sam Arthur and Mary pick up the menus. Obviously, they were nervous. He had to break the ice and make them feel comfortable.

"You two make a good-looking couple."

Sam Arthur and Mary looked at each other but did not respond.

He had to initiate the conversation. He looked at Mary. "Sam Arthur told me that you can help me."

Mary put the menu down. "I don't know nothing about that."

Marcus looked at Sam Arthur. "You didn't tell her how she can help me out?"

"No, I didn't. Just told her you write for a newspaper and you're writing a story where she can help out."

"Mary, I'm writing a story for my newspaper, the *Chicago Defender*, about all of Harlem."

"Why you doing that?" she asked.

"Because Harlem is the most important Negro city in the country."

She touched Sam Arthur on the shoulder. "I owe him, so I'll do my best to help."

"That's perfect." Marcus smiled. "I can start by interviewing you. Not today, but maybe tomorrow."

Mary grabbed Sam Arthur's hand. "I don't know about that. I ain't got nothing to say about Harlem."

"Weren't you born and raised in Harlem?" he asked in a very soft tone.

"Yeah, I was, right over on 138th Street between Fifth Avenue and Lenox."

"Well, I guess you been here all your life."

"Ain't ever been outside Harlem."

Marcus was making progress, but he didn't want to push too fast. "See, you've already been helpful. Why don't we have lunch and afterward, we can set a time tomorrow when we can talk some more? Is that okay with you?"

Mary looked at Sam Arthur, and he nodded his approval. "I guess that's okay, as long as Sam Arthur gonna be with me."

Marcus looked at Sam Arthur. "What do you say?"

"I'll be there."

"Good, I'll come to your apartment. What's the address?"

"It ain't quite an apartment," Mary said. "But the address is 215 West 141st Street."

Marcus waved to the waiter.

Nina woke up feeling confused. Not only was she concealing her identity, but she had been kissed by an older white man. She was still a virgin from a town not quite as sophisticated as New York. But she knew what came after the kiss and wasn't sure she was quite ready for that. She was no longer living in her world, but in a world totally foreign to her. Was her beauty and talent as a dancer taking her places?

She wasn't sure she could handle it.

She was living in a palatial apartment in the most sought-after part of New York that only those with money could afford. She wasn't making that kind of money and the question of rent was never discussed. She could only assume that Larry was paying her share. She needed to talk with Addie, who was much more mature and sophisticated about such matters.

After bathing in her separate bathroom, she dressed and hurried out of the bedroom and into the kitchen, where Myra and Lucille were sitting at the table.

"Morning." She opened the refrigerator and poured a glass of orange juice.

"Good morning," Lucille said. "You really got in late last night. What time did you leave the theater?"

"After the final routine."

"We were told we could leave after the stair-step routine," Myra added. "It felt good to get home and to bed a little earlier than usual."

"It certainly did," Lucille added. "Weren't you a little frightened having to walk here from the theater by yourself? I know you're not used to this part of town."

Nina wasn't sure she should answer. Lucille was probing, and she didn't want to give her the satisfaction of answering. She finished the orange juice and put the glass in the sink. "I got to run. I'll be back early enough to get ready for the show tonight."

"Wait," Lucille blurted. "You're not eating any breakfast? And where you off to this early in the morning?"

"Just got to make a run," she said, determined not to provide Lucille with any particulars. She turned and briskly walked to the door and out of the apartment.

She walked outside, waved down a cab, and climbed into the backseat.

"Where to?" the cab driver asked.

"139th and Lenox."

"Are you sure? That's no place for a young white girl to be going this time of the morning."

Nina wanted to scream, "I am not white," but she held back. This was the price she had to pay for all the benefits she was enjoying.

"Yes, I'm sure," she simply said.

Addie smiled as she opened the door and looked at Nina, who also smiled and walked into the apartment. Addie closed the door.

"It didn't take long for you to come back home," Addie said, as she and Nina sat at the kitchen table. "Is this a permanent or just a visit?"

"You're the only friend I got and the only person I can talk to."

"Okay, this is just a visit. What's going on?"

"They think I'm white."

"Did you tell them you're not?"

"No, I didn't, and it's bothering me."

Addie got up, took two cups from the cupboard, and dropped tea bags with hot water. Came back and sat down, giving one cup to Nina.

"Are you passing for white?"

"Well, no." She could tell from Addie's tone that if she said yes, her friend probably would put her out and never talk to her again. She couldn't have that.

Addie took a sip from her cup. "But you haven't told them you're a Negro. Nina, that's a dangerous game to play."

Nina took a sip. "I'm not doing that, I'm—"

"Has that white man told you not to tell anyone over on that side of town that you're a Negro?"

She knew Addie was reading her like a book. She had to lie again. "No." Nina's emotions got the best of her. She started crying. "All I want to do is dance. It's like my beauty and dancing is becoming a weapon against me."

"No, Nina, it's you and not your beauty."

Nina stopped crying. "What do you mean?"

"That man is flooding you with the very best New York has to offer. but the price you have to pay is rejecting your race, which includes your mother, all your friends and relatives, and me."

Nina thought of Claude and how badly she treated him when he showed up at the apartment on St. Nicholas. Was that the beginning of a transition in her life? She had rejected him, and now Addie suggested that her rejection of people close to her was nearly complete.

"Nina, I must be reaching you. I'm hitting home with you. Does it make sense?"

Nina frowned. "I don't know. I just don't know."

Addie refused to back off. "You do know, and hopefully you're having a difficult time dealing with the truth. That means there is still time to save you from a serious mistake."

Nina finished off her cup of tea. "I have a lot to think about." She got up.

"While you're thinking about it, just know you belong with your people and because you do, you'll never be happy over there. Most of the Negroes that pass is because they don't like being a Negro. That's not you."

Nina hurried over to Addie and hugged her. "I love you and thank you."

She walked to the door and opened it. Addie followed close behind.

"You don't just love me. You also love your race. Keep that in mind as you go back on that side of town that is not you at all."

Nina walked out wondering how Addie knew her so well in such a short period of time.

"You can come back here tonight after you finish at the club," Mary said to Sam Arthur as they both sat at the table in her tenement apartment. "Then you can already be here in the morning when that man shows up."

Sam Arthur peered into the bedroom at Henry asleep in the bed. "I can't do that. Ain't no room."

"No need to worry 'bout that. He'll be all right with my friend just for tonight."

Sam Arthur knew the temptation he felt the two nights he spent with her, one at the cheap hotel, and the other her bed, it took all he had within to stop from rolling on top of her and doing what was natural for a young man. But he still hadn't given up on Willa Mae and knew someday she would show up in Harlem. He had to remain clean and pure for her.

"No, I can't do that, it's not fair to—"

"No, then I can't do this with this man in the morning 'cause I won't be able to sleep tonight worrying if you really going to show up."

"I promised that I would."

"Yeah, remember, I know how reliable your promises are."

"That's not fair. You know why I said you could work with me but had to back off. I would've gotten in a lot of trouble and probably lost my job."

Mary frowned. "What is wrong with you, Sam Arthur? You don't have to worry. I'm not trying to steal you from your precious Willa Mae. You probably wouldn't know where to put it, anyway. And if she's as self-righteous as you are, then the two of you deserve each other."

"Okay, okay, I'll come back here tonight. Just don't get upset."

"Then I got some pig feet in the icebox. I'll cook them up and have them ready for you tonight."

Sam Arthur got up. "I got to get to the Y, shower and change, and get back to the club by ten."

He walked to the door and looked back at Mary sitting at the table, smiling. He opened the door and walked out.

Marcus sauntered into a packed Elks Club building right at seven o'clock. He spotted an empty seat in the middle of a row. He worked his way by men who were already seated until he made it to the seat.

The man sitting to his right faced him. "You a Pullman porter?"

Marcus hesitated in answering. He was not sure he wanted to tell this man, whom he assumed was a Pullman porter, that he was a reporter. But on second thought, these men did respect the *Chicago Defender*. The porters regularly picked up the paper on their stops in Chicago and delivered it throughout the South with a message to come North for a better life. He felt comfortable.

"I'm a reporter with the *Chicago Defender*."

With a surprised expression, the man blurted, "What? Are you serious?"

Marcus figured he could exaggerate his answer and really not be dishonest. Randolph had invited him and knew he was a reporter.

"I'm here covering this momentous movement that Mr. Randolph has started."

The man patted another man sitting to his left. "This man is a reporter from the *Chicago Defender* and he's here covering our organizing." He then turned back to Marcus. "My name is Rufus Jones and I live here in Harlem."

"Well, Rufus, you should know we at the *Chicago Defender* strongly support what Mr. Randolph is doing."

The man parted his lips to speak but stopped when Randolph walked on the stage.

"Good evening, fellow members of our newly formed Brotherhood of Sleeping Car Porters. This is a very special gathering, and you are very special people. We are all gathered here to make a difference. Pullman believes they can outwait us, and we'll give up on our determination to get better working conditions and fairer wages. But we won't ever give up and the five hundred of you gathered here tonight is proof of our determination." Randolph paused for the rousing applause from the audience.

"He's a great leader," the porter said to Marcus loudly over the noise.

Marcus did not respond. His concentration was on

Randolph—a Negro in the year 1925, willing to challenge the power of the white capitalist system. By sheer accident, he was now exposed to another compelling story taking place in Harlem. It couldn't get much better than all of this.

Nina, wearing another one of Erté's fashionable designed outfits, posed with eleven elite Ziegfeld girls, behind a singer that she knew nothing about, to a packed audience in the Roof Top Theater. Ziegfeld had again chosen her to perform with the specially chosen out of the two hundred. She knew it was special to be selected for these kinds of performances. But when Larry first introduced her to Ziegfeld, who had hired her on the spot, she assumed it would be to dance and perform as she had done at Connie's Inn. But for the past two nights, she was posing and not dancing. The music ended, and she strolled in rhythm off the stage with the other girls.

Nina sat in the dressing room, relieved the last performance was over. She wanted to get to the apartment and sleep. These shows were taking a toll on her mental and physical well-being. Ziegfeld was extremely demanding and had no problem attacking a girl if she failed to perform to his expectations. He hadn't attacked her yet, but the anticipation that it would happen was extremely draining.

She finished dressing and got up just as Lucille and Myra walked up to her.

"Hey, girl, it's only midnight and we're heading over to Harlem. You want to join us?" Lucille asked.

Perplexed, Nina asked, "What? You're going where? Why are you going over there?"

"Sometimes, when our show ends early, a few of us girls

go over to either the Cotton Club or Connie's Inn and check out their chorus line. We pick up ideas for new routines from their dancers and share them with Flo," Myra said.

"You haven't been here in New York long," Lucille said. "So, you probably haven't been over in Harlem yet. You have to go with us tonight and see how those girls really dance. They can't do much else, but niggers really have rhythm. Much like you, Nina."

Her first instinct was to slap Lucille. Just haul off and slap the white off her smug face. But to do that would give her what she wanted. Instead, Nina remained reserved. "I don't think so. I'm not interested in, as you put it, seeing how niggers dance." Nina felt guilty for using that word. Her mother had stressed all her life not to use that word, and she never did…until tonight. In this case, it was an appropriate response to an inappropriate person.

Myra intervened. "Come on, Nina, go with us. You'll have a lot of fun watching other girls dance instead of having to dance yourself."

"Exactly where do you plan to go?" Nina looked at Myra and ignored Lucille.

"Does it matter?" Lucille said.

"I guess it doesn't." She felt trapped. She didn't want to go, but if she didn't, that would only increase suspicions about her Negro blood.

"Good, then let's go have a girl's night out," Myra said. "Either of those clubs have a lot of rich white men, and who knows, we might get lucky."

"I don't think that will interest Nina," Lucille said. "Seems as though she's already been lucky with Larry."

Again, Nina ignored Lucille's remark. She had a more

pressing concern. Larry had instructed the chauffeur to pick her up every night after the show. He would be waiting when she walked out and would insist that he chauffeur the girls. He was very familiar with the secret she was hiding. If she asked him to drive them to Harlem, would he slip up and say something, exposing that secret? But at this point, she had no choice. She had to take the chance.

Nina walked out of the Amsterdam Theater, along with Myra and Lucille. She saw the chauffeur leaning against the limousine. He stood straight up as Nina walked toward him. Myra and Lucille were right along with her.

"Is this for you?" Lucille asked, looking at the chauffeur.

Nina did not answer. Instead, she kept walking.

"I asked you if this is you?" Lucille now asked with sarcasm in her voice.

The chauffeur opened the back door. Nina waved Myra and Lucille inside and she followed them in.

"How did you pull this off?" Lucille turned and looked at Nina. "I guess I know."

Nina did not bother to reply. Her concern was not with Lucille's sarcasm, but just what the chauffeur might say when she told him to take them to Harlem.

The chauffeur got in the car and pulled off toward the apartment.

Myra spoke up. "Excuse me, we are not going to the apartment." She looked at Nina. "Tell him we're not going to the apartment."

The chauffeur pulled over to the curb and stopped the limousine. He turned and looked at Nina. "Mr. Madison told me to make sure you got home safely every night."

"Oh, so that's what this is all about," Lucille said, again

sarcastically.

Nina again ignored her comment. "The girls wanted to go over to Harlem, preferably to the Cotton Club, to pick up on some new dance routines."

"But Mr. Madison insisted that I take you to your apartment every night. You gonna get me in trouble if I take you up to Harlem."

"I'll take the blame, so please, just take us to the Cotton Club."

"Why the Cotton Club? You're more familiar with—"

"The Cotton Club, please." Nina had to cut him off before he said Connie's Inn.

"You got it, but what time you want me to pick you up?"

"In an hour."

"What?" Lucille scowled.

Nina's nerves were wrenched. "Yes," she shrieked. "And if you want to stay longer, you can get your own ride home. Maybe, as you said before, you'll be lucky."

Walking into the Cotton Club, Duke Ellington's music had the dance floor filled with dancers. The host led the three girls to an empty table far back in the club. That suited Nina just fine.

The waiter approached the table. "The gentleman over at the table," he pointed to the table, "wants to buy you ladies a drink."

"Nothing for me," Nina quickly said.

"Speak for yourself," Lucille said. "I'll have champagne."

"The same for me," Myra added.

The waiter looked at Nina. "You sure you don't want a drink?"

"I'm sure."

The waiter walked away.

Lucille glared at Nina. "What's your problem?"

Nina glared back. "Why are you always picking at me? If you have a problem with me, take it up with Larry when he gets back. He's the one who insisted that I live with you."

"Oh, he had to insist that you live with us," Lucille shot back.

Myra intervened. "Girls, this is not the place. We have an hour before the chauffeur comes back, so let's make the best of it."

"You have an hour." Lucille now looked at Myra. "I can find my way back to the apartment if I decide this gentleman who is buying us drinks is worth hanging around to get to know."

The music stopped and the dance floor emptied. The waiter brought the drinks and set them on the table.

Lucille looked over at the man and blew him a kiss. Now all she needed was to make her move on the man who bought the drinks and go over to his table.

Nina wasn't sure what Myra was going to do, but she knew in just another half an hour, the chauffeur would be outside to pick her up. This had been a very long night, and all she wanted to do was sleep.

The smell of pig feet excited Sam Arthur's taste buds when Mary opened the door.

"That sure smells good." He walked into the apartment.

Mary closed the door and walked over to the counter and grabbed the pot with the pigs feet. Sam Arthur sat at the table.

"I cooked them with onions, celery, and a little vinegar. I know you a country boy and just love pig feet cooked right."

"Well, you a city girl. How you know so much 'bout cooking pig feet?"

Mary put the pig feet on a plate and placed them on the table in front of Sam Arthur.

"I'm from here, but my granny come here from Georgia about 1905. My mama was thirteen. I was born in 1905 and lived with my granny most of the time. She taught me how to cook. She died when I was fifteen."

Sam Arthur was chewing pig feet but also listening to Mary. He never considered there was a family life associated with her. He only viewed her as existing with no background. That was due to how he met her and what she was doing. Girls like her did not come from a structured family. In a way, that put her somewhat in the same category as Willa Mae.

"Sam Arthur, you hear me talking to you?"

"Yes, woman, I hear you," he answered with a mouthful of pig feet.

A banging on the door caught them by surprise. They both looked at the door as the banging continued.

"You expecting someone?" Sam Arthur asked.

"No, I ain't expecting someone. Would I be expecting someone knowing you was coming over?"

"Open this goddamn door, Mary!"

Sam Arthur looked at Mary. "Who is that?"

Mary frowned. "That's my baby's daddy, Oscar. He gets drunk and tries to get in here. I never let him in and he goes away."

"Why he be coming around here this time a night?"

Mary sighed. "Oh, Sam Arthur, don't be so dumb. He

wants to get at me, but I never open the door."

Sam Arthur felt a tinge of jealousy. "You never let him in?"

"I said I didn't, and why you care, anyway?"

He didn't know how to answer that because he wasn't sure why he cared. He was not developing feelings for her. At least, he didn't want to.

"No. I don't care," Sam Arthur lied.

"I'll get rid of him." Mary got up and walked toward the door.

Sam Arthur jumped up and took her by the arm. "No, let me do this."

Mary tried to break from his grip. "No, Sam Arthur, you can't do this. He'll kill you."

"Well, we'll be two dead Negroes." He swung the door open.

"Who is you?" Oscar asked.

"No matter who I am. You need to get on away from this door."

"I'll be goddamn." Oscar lunged and he couldn't get around Sam Arthur.

"Mary, who is this nigger?" Oscar shouted. "Is he fucking you now?"

Mary moved a couple of steps back from the door and did not respond.

"You fucking bitch, I'll get your ass for this." Oscar tried to get around Sam Arthur but couldn't.

"Watch your filthy mouth!" Sam Arthur barked. "And get on away from here."

"Fuck you, nigger." Oscar swung at Sam Arthur, but he blocked his blow, hitting Oscar in the jaw. The man fell back across the hall. Sam Arthur was on him, ready to hit him again, but the man held his arm up in surrender.

Sam Arthur moved back away from him. Oscar got up.

"I'll get your ass for this!" He looked back into the apartment at Mary.

"You get the hell out of here." Sam Arthur pushed the man away from the door. "And if you come around here bothering Mary again, I'll find you and beat you some more."

Oscar gave one final stare into the apartment, turned, and stumbled away.

Sam Arthur walked back in and closed the door. Mary stood in the middle of the room with a frightened look. Sam Arthur sat at the table and continued chewing on the pig's feet. Mary walked over and sat across from him.

"Thank you."

Sam Arthur stopped chewing and put the pig feet back on the plate. "Somebody got to protect you from yourself, and I guess that's my job now."

"I ain't never had nobody care about me the way you do."

"Somebody got to. You a good person, Mary, and I'm gonna help you best I can." He finished the pig feet and pushed the plate away from him.

Mary picked it up, got up, and placed it in the sink. "I'll wash it tomorrow. Right now, I want to go to bed. You coming?"

Sam Arthur got up and took Mary's hand. "We got an important day tomorrow, and I told you I'd be here for you and I am."

"Thank you. Seems, though, all I'm doing lately is thanking you."

"Right now, that's all I need."

"Well, I'm praying real hard that someday soon you'll need more than just that, and I want to be the woman to give it to you."

15.

MARCUS EXITED THE CAB, HURRIED up the steps and into the tenement house. He knocked on the door, holding his breath that it was the right one, and that they had been honest with him.

The door swung open, and Mary smiled. "It ain't much but welcome to our home." She waved him inside.

Marcus thought back on Randolph's comments in his office that night when he said Harlem was becoming a slum. The condition of the inside of this apartment supported Randolph's statement.

Sitting at the table, Sam Arthur stood up and extended his hand. Marcus vigorously shook it.

"Good morning," Marcus said. "Thank you for being here."

Sam Arthur pointed to the chair at the front of the table. "Please have a seat."

"All I got is some juice and water," Mary said.

"I'm fine, thank you," Marcus replied.

Mary took a seat on the other side of the table and placed her hands folded on the table.

Marcus leaned forward in his chair. "Let me begin by thanking the two of you for talking with me. Your comments will help me in writing what I am calling 'The Other Side of Harlem.'"

"We're happy to participate. So, what do you want to know?" Mary asked.

"I assume you work. What kind of work do you do?"

211

"I—"

"She helps me," Sam Arthur interjected.

"She's in the numbers game?"

"Well, not quite."

Marcus looked at Sam Arthur, and then Mary, with a confused expression. "I don't understand."

"She's helping me. Let's just leave it at that."

"Okay, if that's the way you want it," Marcus concurred, eager to get off that subject and not irritate the two.

"You know how hard it is to get a job here in Harlem?" Mary spoke up.

That was a good change of subject, Marcus thought, and he hadn't lost her. "No, can you explain to me?"

"You got all these Negroes coming up from the South and looking for jobs. They can play us off from one another and hire the cheapest person. And they prefer to hire the Negroes from the South 'cause they believe they more passive and been trained by the white folks in the South to keep them in their place."

Sam Arthur shot a look at Mary. He didn't like the way she described Negroes from the South because he was one of them.

"And I got a baby, so it's even harder for me. Don't nobody want to hire no girl with no baby, especially if she ain't married."

"You have a child. Where is the father?" Marcus asked, but really knew the answer.

"He ain't nowhere around and sure don't help with raising my baby."

"That sounds a lot like what is happening in Chicago," Marcus said.

"But someday I'm gonna to get married and have someone to help me," Mary said and looked at Sam Arthur.

Marcus also looked at Sam Arthur. "You up here from the South, aren't you?"

"From Gaffney, South Carolina."

"What brought you up here?"

"Needed to get away from an ugly situation." Sam Arthur didn't care to go into a lot of details, especially with Mary sitting there.

"So, are you two living together here?"

"No. I live at the Y right now, but gonna start looking for an apartment."

"I'm sorry, I didn't mean to pry." Marcus decided to move away from that subject. "Well, Mary, where do you think I can start to find out what is happening with the people down here in this part of Harlem?"

"Go to a rent party."

"A rent party?"

"Yeah, that's what poor people put on to raise enough money to pay their rent," Sam Arthur answered.

"I have in the past, but ain't been to one in a long time," Mary added.

"I went to one just to catch some number players, but haven't been back," Sam Arthur said.

"Is it possible you all could take me to one? I'm willing to pay for your time?"

"I can't 'cause I work every night and got to make up for some money I spent. Maybe Mary can take you to one."

Mary shot a stern look at Sam Arthur, then turned and smiled. "I guess I can do that. How much you gonna pay me?"

"How about ten dollars? Will that work for you?"

Sam Arthur spoke up and looked at Mary. "You know our deal."

Having no idea what Sam Arthur meant by that remark, Marcus moved on. "What's the best night?"

"Any night," Mary said.

"How about tonight?"

Mary again looked at Sam Arthur, who nodded to her. "Can you meet me at the Sugar Cane Club at ten? There is always rent parties up the street from the club. We can go from there, and don't be all dressed up, they ain't that kind of party."

Sam Arthur got up. "If we're finished here, I got to get back over to the Y and get ready for work."

Marcus also got up. "Thank you all for helping me out." He pulled out a dollar bill and handed it to Sam Arthur. "This is on tomorrow's number." He turned and looked at Mary. "You pick the numbers."

Sam Arthur took out a slip and a pencil, his tools of work he always carried with him, on the possibility that someone who knew him would approach him with numbers. He looked at Mary.

"Give me the three numbers you think are winners."

A smile spread across Mary's face. "705."

Sam Arthur wrote down the numbers and tried to hand the slip to Marcus. He refused to take it.

"Give it to Mary. It's hers if there is a winning."

He handed the slip to Mary, and they walked to the door. Sam Arthur opened it and Marcus walked out.

Sam Arthur closed the door and stood there. "You gonna be all right to go with that man tonight?"

Mary smiled. "I guess I can handle myself. Why, you jealous?"

"No, just always concerned for you."

"Why don't you come and go with us?"

"I can't do that 'cause last week I missed two days."

Mary moved in a little closer to him. "You did? Where were you?"

Sam Arthur stood his ground. "Can't tell you that, not right now. Maybe later."

"We got our little secrets."

Sam Arthur didn't want to respond to her comment. "I got to get going so I can get ready for tonight."

"Are you coming back over after you finish at the club?"

"Won't Henry be here?"

"Yeah, but I can make enough room for all of us."

"No, that just don't sound right."

"What's wrong with you? Henry just a little baby."

"I know, but it just don't sound right."

Mary pushed Sam Arthur to the side and opened the door. "Well, just leave and go on back to your room at the Y. Must have a woman there. Don't want to be here."

"Okay, I don't want you to get mad. Just come on back to the club after you finish with Marcus and we'll go together to pick up Henry."

Mary reached up and kissed Sam Arthur on the lips, but the kiss was a little longer than before. He kissed her back.

"I'll see you tonight," she said.

Sam Arthur walked out and closed the door.

As soon as Sam Arthur walked into the YMCA, the clerk behind the registration desk waved him over. He pointed to a man sitting in the chair on the other side of the lobby.

"The man over there been asking for you," the clerk said. "Sounds like he just up here from the South the way he talks. Been here since 'bout four in the morning."

Sam Arthur ignored the clerk's comment, turned, and walked over to the man, who got up from the chair.

"You Sam Arthur?"

"Who are you?"

"Name's Sonny and I'm the man Sadie hired to find the woman named Willa Mae in Charleston."

The mention of Willa Mae gave Sam Arthur's tired body a charge. "You found Willa Mae?"

"I found her, but—"

"Why she ain't here? I gave you fifty dollars for her to come up here. And how'd you know to come here, anyway?"

"What I'm trying to tell you is I found her all right, but she didn't believe me. Told me ain't no way you got that kind of money and ain't no way she just gonna up and leave her home and come up here alone."

"You give her the money?"

"No, she wouldn't take it, 'cause she didn't believe it come from you." Sonny pulled out thirty dollars and handed it to Sam Arthur.

"I gave Sadie fifty dollars." Sam Arthur's voice level rose.

"It was Ms. Sadie's idea that I take twenty to come up here and tell you 'bout Willa Mae. She told me where you was staying. So, I took a chance."

"What else Willa Mae say to you?"

"She say you ought to come down there yourself if it was really you what sent me with all that money." A smile crossed Sonny's face. "How you make all that money, anyway?"

"No matter how I made it. Did you get Willa Mae's address in Charleston?"

Sonny pulled out a piece of paper from his pocket and handed it to Sam Arthur. "That's the address in Charleston."

Sam Arthur stuffed the paper in his pant pocket. "Guess I should thank you for coming up here," he said as he took a ten-dollar bill and stretched his hand toward Henry. "Take this and you better get on back to Gaffney."

Sonny took the ten-dollar bill. "Don't know 'bout that. I kind of like what I done seen up here. Might decide to stay for a while."

"You can't do that. You ain't got enough money to stay up here, and how long you thinking about staying?"

"Don't know. I ain't got nobody back home but myself. Both my momma and daddy passed over. I'm tired of working in the fields for that white man, making no money at all. And look at you, seems you doing all right for yourself, throwing money around like its nothing."

Suddenly, it occurred to Sam Arthur that if he had to go to Charleston, he could have Sonny cover him while he was gone. He'd have to introduce him to Holstein and have him work at the Sugar Cane Club so his customers would know placing numbers with Sonny would be just like placing them with him.

"I might have something you can do while I'm in Charleston."

A broad smile covered Sonny's face. "What's that? I'm ready."

"You'll see tonight, but you got to be tired and need some rest."

"Naw, I slept from Gaffney all the way up here. Didn't leave until six yesterday evening and had to make stops in Richmond, Virginia, and then on to here."

"I works nights, so you got to be good and rested this evening." He took Sonny by the shoulder, and they walked back over to the registration desk.

"I need a room for this man," he said to the clerk. "You got one close to me?"

The clerk looked Henry up and down, then checked his registration book. "Yeah, I got one right next to yours. Be five dollars a night and for how many nights?"

Sam Arthur took the money that Sonny had just given him and handed it to the clerk. "Least six nights."

Sonny stood there smiling.

The clerk handed him a key. "This your key to the room."

"Thank you."

"Don't thank me." The clerk pointed to Sam Arthur. "Thank him."

Sonny turned and looked at Sam Arthur. "Thank you, brother."

Sam Arthur didn't respond to Sonny's expression of gratitude. Instead, he turned and started walking toward the elevator. "Come on, you got to rest 'cause you got a lot to learn in a very short time."

❧

Marcus sat in Craig's Restaurant with a plate of pancakes and bacon in front of him. Schuyler sat on the other side of the table with eggs, sausage, and toast. They both had a cup of coffee.

"From what I can gather, you been a pretty busy man," Schuyler said as he tossed eggs and sausage into his mouth.

Marcus was busy cutting his pancakes into eatable portions. He looked up at Schuyler while cutting.

"Lately, I been taking a different look at Harlem."

"What you mean 'a different look?'"

"I guess you can call it the other side or above 145th Street and Fifth Avenue."

"That is definitely a different side." Schuyler smiled. "What you looking for over there that's worth writing about?"

"Well. You see, everybody got this idea about Harlem as being the new living mecca for Negroes. They've heard about all the clubs, the music, and everything, and they want to be a part of it. But from what I'm learning, a lot of the Negroes coming here from the South never been to a restaurant like this and never been inside the library where so much is happening."

"That's probably true. Most of those folks didn't come here for the music and the writings. They came here seeking work and when they got here, they find out there isn't that much work for Negroes. The rents are sky high, and they have to give these things called rent parties to make their rent."

"You know anything about them?"

"Do I ever. You go to one of those parties after eleven at night and you going to get some loud music, some well-cooked chitterlings, some cheap alcohol that'll make you drunk and you going to see men and women dancing so close and all they do is scrunch their bodies until the man gets an erection and the girl's panties are wet. At the end of the night, they going to one of those cheap hotels and have wild sex."

"That's quite a visual." What else could he say to such a description? "There has to be more to it than just that."

"I guess there is. Those folks aren't thinking about poetry and novels. They can't go to the better clubs because it's too expensive, and some of them, like the Cotton Club and

Connie's Inn, couldn't go if they could afford it. They work all week when they have a job and need to unwind, if possible, with one of the single women who come into the party. In fact, women are usually not charged to come in." Schuyler took his fork and tossed more eggs into his mouth, followed by some coffee.

Marcus began to doubt what he had gotten himself into for the evening with Mary. "Well, I'm going to one tonight."

"You're doing what?" Again, Schuyler had to put his fork down and glared over at Marcus.

"You remember the man at the club who we talked to a couple weeks ago?"

"Sure do, when you hit big."

"Yeah, that's him. I visited him at the club the other night and he set me up to meet with who I think is his girlfriend. They both told me if I want to get to know the real people of Harlem to go to one of the rent parties, so his girlfriend is taking me tonight to one of them."

"You losing your direction?"

"What do you mean?"

"I mean, you're here to write about the growing literary movement taking place for the first time in the Negro race, and that has nothing to do with it."

Marcus took a drink from his coffee cup before responding. He had to make this right. "Someday, when this is all over, Negroes going to look back and study us. I don't think it's fair to give them only one side of Harlem during its heyday. I've heard that only about ten percent of the Negro population is involved in this new arts movement." He paused to place a fork full of pancakes in his mouth, followed by more coffee.

"I don't think you have to come all the way to Harlem to see those folks. Our people struggling are in Chicago, where you come from, in Philadelphia right down the road from here, and in Detroit and every other large city where we have a presence. There is nothing unique about that story. What is unique is what is happening among that other ten percent."

Marcus had to defend his position. "I agree with you, but what makes this so unique is that all these wonderful things are happening and way over fifty percent of our people are not involved. When historians look back at these times, the story needs to be complete."

"Is Abbott aware of the change?"

"Talked to him when I was back in Chicago for a day, and he agrees."

"You been back home? I didn't know you'd left."

"Had to take that five hundred dollars back home and give it to my wife."

"Is she on her way to join you in this adventure?"

"Not yet, but she'll be here soon." Marcus knew that wasn't the case, but by putting it in those terms, it might come true. At least that was what he wanted to happen. He watched as Cullen strolled into Craig Restaurant with his friend Jackman.

Cullen walked over to the table and looked at Schuyler. "How are you?"

"Being myself."

Cullen then looked at Marcus. "I believe you asked me about how I can reject being a Negro poet and then write my two poems on 'Heritage' and 'To Make A Poet Black.'"

"I'm impressed with your memory," Marcus responded. "It's good to know I had that much of an influence on the subject."

"Not that you did. It's the question I constantly get from Negroes that insists that I identify myself as a Negro poet."

Somewhat irritated with Cullen's smug response, Marcus asked, "How do you answer it?"

"I am simply a poet, and that is all. I do not want to be identified as a Negro poet because you don't identify Robert Frost or other white poets by the color of their skin. We need to refrain from being identified as racial artists as is happening all over Harlem, and I imagine you will write your story from that perspective."

"You differ from the way that your friend Langston feels. He thinks you should be proud to identify as a Negro poet," Schuyler interjected.

"I don't know." Cullen frowned. "Maybe it's because Langston is so light-skinned. He needs to always stress that he is a Negro. I don't have that problem. You look at me and you know what race I belong to."

"Can I quote you?" Marcus asked.

"Most certainly. I do not need to stress my race in my art because it stands alone."

Marcus watched as Cullen and Jackman turned and walked over to an empty table. He then tossed another forkful of pancakes into his mouth, followed by the coffee.

"I think you need to know the truth about this so-called new Negro movement in arts and letters," Schuyler said, bringing Marcus back around.

Marcus put his fork down. "And how do I find what the truth is if it isn't what I've experienced so far?"

"The situation is the same as it was ten years ago when Paul Laurence Dunbar and Charles Chestnut were writing."

"What do you mean?"

"They had to take their works to the white publishers, and that hasn't changed." Schuyler pointed over to where Cullen and Jackman sat. "That boy over there wants to keep his publishers happy, so they will continue to publish his poetry. The same is true for Langston and all the other young writers. White publishers have to approve their works, or they won't get published. That was the same for Dunbar and Chestnut." Schuyler ate some more of his eggs. He finished his plate and also swallowed the last of his coffee. "One other important fact for you to consider."

Marcus had also finished his breakfast and swallowed the last of his coffee. "What is that?"

"Their readers are not Negroes." Schuyler's voice held some contempt. "They are the white folks over there in Lower Manhattan and Greenwich Village and every other place in this country except, of course, not in the South. That means the sales have to be in the white world and the publishers want to make sure those folks approve."

"Are you suggesting that Booker T. Washington was right when he argued against Negroes reaching out to where they weren't ready to go?"

"After tonight, after your sojourn into one of these house parties, then you decide. I have an article I need to finish this morning." He got up.

"The story gets more complicated as every day goes by." Marcus also got up.

"Harlem is a very complicated place." They walked out of Craig Restaurant.

⁂

Nina wasn't sure just how many times she could be awestruck by the amazing surprises she continued to encounter in her new reality. The entire two hundred show girls strolled onto the two-hundred-and-ten-foot yacht owned by William Randolph Hearst. They were all surprised when they showed up at noon for rehearsal for tonight's show. Florenz had a fleet of limousines in front of the Amsterdam Theater to take them out to the harbor. It was to be a special lunch on the yacht as it cruised around the city along New York harbor.

Nina stayed close to Myra, and they all stood along the railing on deck as the yacht steamed out into the water. As confident as she had become because of her success on stage, she still felt insecure. She knew in this world Myra was her security, just as Addie had been in the other world in Harlem.

"Isn't this a beautiful view of the city?" Myra said. "Every time Flo surprises us with this special luncheon, I'm always amazed at this view."

"You've done this before?" Nina stared at the Statue of Liberty.

"She stands magnificent, doesn't she?" Myra momentarily ignored Nina's question. "She was a gift to the United States from France in 1886."

Perplexed, Nina asked. "What are you talking about?"

"The Statute of Liberty, of course." Myra turned and looked at Nina. "And yes, I have done this before. Flo surprises us with this very extravagant luncheon every six months. But it's no longer a surprise. We count the months and wait for the surprise."

"This must cost a small fortune."

"Well, we make him a small fortune," Myra responded with slight sarcasm.

Lucille walked up and stood next to Nina. "This is a pretty nice 'thank you' from him for the millions we are making Flo. I've been one of his girls since 1923, and this is my fifth time."

Nina turned to face Lucille. "Do you ever get used to it?"

"No, it's always special. It just seems to get better every time."

A man positioned himself at the entrance of the yacht. "Ladies, it's time. Lunch will be served so we would like for you all to come on inside."

Nina, staying close to Myra, walked inside the yacht and into an elaborate room with gold hanging chandeliers and paintings perfectly placed on the walls on both sides of the room. Nina sat between Myra and Lucille at one of the twenty tables with white-laced tablecloths and Chinese-decorated plates and cups. She watched as Ziegfeld walked at a fast pace to the front of the room.

"This year, this lunch is a celebration for an outstanding six-month performance by all you ladies. We are taking New York over and have been recognized by *New York Entertainment Magazine* as the number-one Broadway show. You all should be proud and it's only going to get better." He paused for a moment while the girls applauded. "And I am especially pleased with the new addition of Nina Jackson to the team. Stand up, Nina."

She was frozen in place and couldn't move.

Myra nudged her. "Get up, girl."

Nina slowly rose from her chair, totally nervous, as she knew all eyes were looking at her. Some were admiring and others were jealous of her recognition.

"Since you have joined the Ziegfeld girls, I have gotten praise for your performance from some of my most loyal followers. I want to thank you for bringing such talent, grace, and charm to our show."

There was applause resonating throughout the room. However, without having to look at her, she knew Lucille was one of the few not applauding.

Holstein glared sternly across the desk at Sam Arthur as he sat there with Sonny in the other chair. Jonas stood at his usual place, back against the wall, with arms crossed. Holstein pointed to Sonny.

"What is it you want him to do?" he asked now, looking at Sam Arthur.

"He's gonna stand in for me while I go home and take care of some business," Sam Arthur answered.

Jonas laughed. Sam Arthur shot him a menacing glare but did not say a thing to him. He didn't want a repeat of what happened the last time he was in Holstein's office.

"What the hell you talking about?" Holstein said. "Look at him, he looks like he just out of the field somewhere in the South."

Sonny, who had been smiling, stopped. He started to get up. Sam Arthur grabbed him by the arm and forced him back down into the seat. He looked over at Jonas, who had unfolded his arms.

"I'll cover him for some slacks, sport coat, and shirt from the hot man. Make him more presentable," Sam Arthur said. "He'll be with me tonight and he'll know what to do."

"How long you going to be gone?" Holstein asked.

"Less than two days. I got to go check on my Willa Mae, who moved up to Charleston."

Holstein looked over at Jonas, and they both laughed. "Your Willa Mae? Who is that?"

"It's my fiancé from back home. Why I been working so hard was to get enough money to get her up here and get married."

Holstein again looked over at Jonas, this time not smiling or laughing. "Jonas told me you been seeing Mary, the woman we set you up with a few weeks ago. You finished with her already?"

Sam Arthur shot a glance over at Jonas, then back at Holstein. He had to be careful with his response. He couldn't tell them he'd never had sex with Mary because that would reveal their little secret the first time they were together. He'd rubbed Holstein the wrong way one time when he didn't show up that night with the money. He didn't want to do it again. He liked the money he was making.

"She's a nice girl, but I got to find out about my Willa Mae," Sam Arthur said.

"Nice," Jonas shouted. "Mary is a fucking whore."

Sam Arthur couldn't control himself. "Don't call her that name!"

"Don't you two get started again," Holstein intervened, looking at Jonas and then at Sam Arthur. "I don't know about this setup. If things go wrong, I'm going to hold you accountable, Sam Arthur."

"Nothing gonna happen. I'll just be gone a couple days and be back on the job."

"Let me ask you, if you bring this Willa Mae up here, what you going to do with Mary?" Jonas asked.

Holstein ignored Jonas's question. "You took a couple nights off before and we lost that money. I don't want to lose it again. And if my competition finds out you have been ignoring that spot, they'll move in there. And Big Max will welcome them because he loses money when we're not down there. Sugar Cane's a big money winner for me and I don't want to lose it."

"You won't, Mr. Holstein, and I'll be back in no time. I just got to go get my business straight with Willa Mae."

Again, Jonas shouted, "What you going to do with Mary?"

"That's my business! Let me take care of my business."

"All right, don't the two of you get started. I'm going to let you do this, but if he messes up, it's on you, Sam Arthur. You understand?"

"Sure do, Mr. Holstein." Sam Arthur smiled.

"Now get out of here and get that boy some decent clothes."

Again, Sonny started to rise, but Sam Arthur stopped him. "I'll take care of it before we go to the club this evening."

Sam Arthur got up, as did Sonny. He shot a glance over at Jonas, and the two of them walked out of the office.

✺◈✺

A long line of girls came over to Nina's table and congratulated her for the acknowledgment she received from Ziegfeld. It made her nervous. She just did not like all this attention. Why couldn't they just leave her alone and really forget about the compliment she received?

"I'll say, you're getting awfully popular all of a sudden," Lucille said to Nina, sitting next to her at the table.

Myra leaned across Nina. "Don't get started today," she said to Lucille. "This is going to be an enjoyable afternoon before we report to work this evening."

Nina momentarily closed her eyes and sighed. She did not want a confrontation with Lucille, but she wasn't sure how much more of her bugging she could take. Evidently, Myra must have felt her and put an end to it right away.

The same man who had called out to the girls to come inside walked to the front and stood next to Ziegfeld. "Lunch is now served," he said, and doors opened in the back of the room as waiters in tuxedoes brought out plates of food and placed them on the tables.

Nina tried her best to relax and act like she was used to this special treatment, with tuxedoed waiters, bringing her a plate and setting it right in front of her. But she was nervous, aware that she might do something to expose who she really was, just an eighteen-year-old Negro girl from St. Louis. She sat there, staring at her plate of steak, roasted potatoes, and green beans.

"You okay?" Myra asked.

"Yeah, I'm okay." Nina picked up her fork and ate, taking the attention off her.

"I have a question." Lucille looked at Nina. "Has anyone at this table ever kissed a nigger man?" She laughed.

Nina kept eating and tried her best not to give any response.

A girl, whom Nina did not know was sitting at the other end of the table, dropped her fork. "Oh, hell no. How nasty."

Another girl also stopped eating. "You made me lose my appetite. They have to be the dirtiest people on Earth. Why you ask a question like that when you know we're eating?"

"But I hear they got really big…well, you know what I mean. And nigger girls got bigger holes than we have, so they can take it all in."

The other girls at the table broke out laughing. Nina did not.

Lucille looked at Nina. "You don't find that funny?"

Nina couldn't restrain herself. "No, I don't find it funny at all. What a disgusting subject to have while we're eating. You are just a disgusting person."

The others at the table became quiet. They looked at Lucille.

"How dare you?" Lucille's voice rose.

"It sounds to me that you might want one," Nina shot back.

The girls broke out laughing and kept looking at Lucille, who had turned red in the face.

Lucille looked away from Nina and across the table at the other girls. "Have you all ever noticed that Nina has a very unique and different rhythm to her dance than we do, and why is that?"

Another girl sitting at the table spoke up. "I don't know why it is, but I sure would like some of her rhythm myself."

"You got that right," another girl said.

Not to be distracted, Lucille continued. "We were all over at the Cotton Club in Harlem the other night and all those girls are Negroes, and they had the same kind of rhythm as Nina."

Nina remained silent, although she really wanted to scream as loudly as possible, "Because I am one of them and proud of it," but again, she considered what Larry had told her. No privilege comes to being a Negro. And the privileges were coming at a fast pace for her. One thing she knew was she could not continue living with Lucille and would have to make that point to Larry when he got back from Paris.

Myra finally intervened. "Now that's enough, Lucille, just leave it alone. Nina has told us, even though she didn't have to, that she is white like we are. So let it rest. This is not a time for that kind of talk. This is a time for sheer enjoyment. So, let's eat and get ready for tonight."

Myra's authoritarian tone had an effect, and the girls all returned to eating. Nina was steaming inside and knew a change had to come real soon.

***

At eleven o'clock, Marcus followed Mary up the stairs of an older apartment building on 146th Street between Fifth and Lenox Avenues. He felt like the walls were caving in on him; the stairwell was so narrow. He could smell the chitterlings, and fried chicken mixed with the smell of cigarette smoke as they reached the top of the stairs on the second floor. The music was blaring out of a room. Men and women filled the hallway, locked together in a slow dance, with the only motion coming from the movement of their hips.

A heavy-set, gray-haired woman and a large bald man sat in chairs at the front of the hallway. Marcus and Mary approached them.

"Twenty-five cents for you to get in," Mary said. "They won't charge me 'cause this woman's night. We get in free."

The woman smiled at Mary. "It's been a while. Guess you been working another rent party. You always did well here."

Not aware of what that woman was talking about, Marcus ignored her comment and handed her the twenty-five cents.

Mary did not respond to the woman, and she and Marcus walked past the two and started down the hall.

"Don't be acting all funny 'cause you already got your man for the night!" the woman shouted. "Better be careful. One of these other girls be done took him from you."

They stood at the entrance to the main room but could not get in because of the dancers occupying all the space. Marcus was able to look to the far corner of the room and saw a piano player pounding on the keys, a drummer beating on the drums, and a saxophone player blowing. They stood locked in place for the next three minutes, not saying a word, but just listening to the musical sounds coming from the corner of the room and staring at the dancers locked in an embrace and not moving their bodies at all. Finally, the music stopped, and the dancers walked back to rows of chairs lined up along the walls.

They strolled along in front of the dancers, now sitting, some wiping sweat from their faces and a couple locked in a kiss until they got to a room. Marcus looked into the room he assumed was a bedroom. It was void of furniture and at least ten men were bent over, making a semi-circle. One man shook his hands together, then tossed the dice down the center between the men. The dice stopped rolling, and half the men cheered, and the other half jeered.

Marcus and Mary kept strolling along until they reached the kitchen. Mary stopped.

"You want something to eat?"

"I don't think so," he answered. "How about you?"

"I could, yes, I'm kinda hungry."

The musicians returned to their positions and struck up another musical number. Dancers filled up the middle of the room. Marcus and Mary walked into the kitchen.

"Get what you want," Marcus said.

Mary looked at the woman standing next to the stove. "Bowl of chitterlings," she said.

The woman took the top off a large cast-iron pot, scooped some of the chitterlings, put them in a small bowl, and handed it to Mary.

"Fifty cents," the woman said, holding her hand out to Marcus.

"Fifty cents for that small portion?" Marcus sighed.

"You got to pay to play," the woman replied with no hesitation.

He gave the woman fifty cents, and just as they walked out of the kitchen, the woman said, "Got some real good gin if you want something to go with them chitterlings and mister, don't you want a good drink to get you hot and ready?"

Marcus did not respond. Instead, they walked back into the living room.

"Don't walk off with that bowl!" the woman shouted. "You know how you nigguhs can get. Steal anything."

Mary looked around and saw two chairs at the end of the room. They hurried over to them and sat down. Marcus sat there, not saying a word. He was so enthralled watching the dancers who really weren't dancing. Just standing still, moving their lower bodies like they were having sex.

Mary turned and looked at him and smiled. "You never been to no party like this back in Chicago?" she asked while chewing on a portion of chitterlings.

"I can't say that I have." Marcus kept his eyes on a particular couple right in front of him. The man's hands grasped the woman's buttocks, rubbing it and pulling her bottom in tighter to his lower portion. He began questioning why he was there. This was not a place for any decent conversation.

The music stopped and the dancers again returned to their chairs, while some made their way into the kitchen and a few couples headed for the exit.

Marcus looked at Mary. "I don't understand why you and Sam Arthur suggested I come here. The music is loud, and these people are in no mood to talk about anything at all, other than booze and sex."

"You said you wanted to see the other side of Harlem. Well, this is it."

"I think I've seen enough," Marcus said as he watched a man walk up to them and look at Mary.

"Hey, girl, you up for a dance?"

"Not this time," Mary answered, without looking up at the man.

He looked at Marcus and back at Mary. "Oh, I see. You going after the older niggers now. She's good and you in for a good time tonight." He turned and walked away.

That was it for Marcus. He'd had enough. He got up. "I've seen enough of what you call the other side of Harlem. I'm ready to get out of here."

Mary swallowed the last of the chitterlings and got up. "Where we going to go?"

"I'm going to my apartment and take a long, hot bath."

"You ain't going to the Sugar Cane Club to meet with Sam Arthur?" she asked as they walked out of the room and into the hall. She placed the bowl on a table against the wall filled with other dirty dishes.

"I don't think so. This was enough for one night."

They walked to the top of the steps, where the woman and man were sitting.

"Y'all leaving early?" the woman commented. "Mary, you can come on back when you finished with him. The night is still young."

Mary did not respond as she followed Marcus down the stairs and out of the apartment.

"Man, look at all these fine-ass women in this club," Sonny said, standing next to Sam Arthur in the Sugar Cane Club.

"That ain't why you're here. Let me make it clear to you. You can't drink, and you can't mess with any of these women while you working." He paused to let his words register with Sonny. "You understand what I'm telling you?"

"Yeah, I understand. You getting all wound up for nothing."

"Good, if I can't trust you, I can't use you."

"Seems to me you been doing more than just taking numbers."

"What you mean?"

"You got a woman here, according to Mr. Holstein."

"I ain't got no woman here and they don't know what they talking about. I got a friend, and that's all she is, a friend."

"You telling me you been up here all this time and you ain't been with nobody?"

"That's the truth 'cause I ain't gonna cheat on my Willa Mae." Sam Arthur watched Mary walk into the club alone.

"Who is that?" Sonny asked, also looking at Mary. "She sure is fine."

Sam Arthur gave Sonny a hard look. Mary walked up and stood next to Sam Arthur.

Sonny stared at her and smiled. "This the one they said was your woman?" He kept staring at Mary.

Sam Arthur ignored Sonny's question, even though it irritated him. "What happened? You back here so early." he asked Mary.

Mary frowned, looking at Sonny. "Who is this?"

"Never mind who he is. What happened? You back here so early. And where is Mr. Williams?"

"He didn't want to stay." She looked at Sam Arthur. "He wasn't comfortable there at all. He didn't belong."

"What you mean he didn't belong?" Sam Arthur asked.

"He's more like the dicties than them people."

"The dicties, what in hell is that?"

"That's right, I keep forgetting you ain't from here." Mary looked at Sonny. "You from here and know who the dicties are?"

A smile spread across Sonny's face. "Naw, I ain't from here, but fine as you is, I wish I was."

"Well, where you from?" Mary asked in a softer tone.

"Never mind all that," Sam Arthur intervened in a harsher tone. Mary and Sonny were flirting, and he was having no part of it. "I asked you what is a dictie?"

"They the better off Negroes, live up on St. Nicholas and on what's called Strivers Row."

Sam Arthur's attempt to keep Mary off the street by having her work with Marcus appeared to be failing. He couldn't let that happen. She needed to earn a little money from him so she wouldn't turn back to the street, and he couldn't keep giving her the money he made. And working with Marcus would keep her from hustling while he was gone to Charlotte. He had to get his plan back on track.

"He tell you how to contact him?" he asked.

"No, he didn't," she shot back. "Why you so interested in helping out that dictie?"

"You know why," Sam Arthur answered just as abruptly.

"What's going on with y'all?" Sonny asked.

"None of your business," Sam Arthur practically shouted.

The dancers turned, while dancing, and looked over at Sam Arthur.

Mary again looked at Sam Arthur. "Who is this man?"

"Don't matter who he is and ain't nothing for you to bother with."

"Well, can you come over tonight? Henry won't be home 'til tomorrow morning."

Sam Arthur looked at Sonny, who was smiling and taking it all in.

"Can't do it tonight. Got to get this boy all set up at the YMCA," he lied, and Sonny smiled.

"I can't do nothing more with that man if you ain't gonna cooperate. I still got a debt to pay to you and you have to help me."

Again, Sam Arthur looked at Sonny whose smile had spread across his face.

"I'll get with you tomorrow and get it all worked out," he said. "We'll walk you home then we got to get back over to the YMCA."

The music stopped, and the crowd headed for the exit of the club. A man ran up to Sam Arthur and placed a bet, then ran up the stairs. The final member of the band also headed out of the club.

"Let's get out of here," Sam Arthur said to Mary and Sonny.

It had been quite a day and night and Sam Arthur hadn't felt that exhausted since the time he spent in the fields back in Gaffney.

16.

"THERE REALLY ARE TWO HARLEMS," Marcus said on the phone in Schuyler's office with Abbott. "I got a portion of the other side last night at what is called a rent party."

"You went to a rent party? Who took you there?"

"The young man who sold me the winning numbers. It was his girlfriend. At least I think it's his girlfriend."

"You're really getting deep into your study."

"I'm starting to get the feeling that we have been somewhat misled about the fabulous things happening here."

"What do you mean, somewhat misled?"

"Well, there are some outstanding artists that have made this their home and are putting out good works, but that is only a piece of the story. Harlem is just like any other big city in the North—plenty of poverty and suffering."

"The question confronting you when you get around to writing your story is which of the two is most important for history?"

"As writers, we have an obligation to tell the entire story and let historians in the future make that decision."

"You're getting kind of philosophical on me." Abbott chuckled.

From Abbott's chuckle, Marcus knew his boss was satisfied with the work he was doing. "We're doing a great service for history."

"Okay, great service, I have a newspaper I have to get out today, so let me get off this phone and let you get on with the work you're doing for the future historians."

It had been two weeks since he talked with Helen and that was the day he left to come back to Harlem. Hopefully, she had cooled off from that day. He dialed their number.

"It's about time you called me," Helen said on the other end.

"How did you know it was me?"

"Because no one calls me this early in the morning?"

"Have you forgiven me for taking on the additional work here?"

"No, but what difference does it make? You're going to do what you want to, no matter how I feel."

"Helen, that's not true. When are you going to realize that I am doing this for us and not just for me?" He had to make her realize that fact.

"I had to spend some of that money you gave me." She changed the subject, and he knew why. He just needed to go along with her.

"Why? What happened?"

"Are you suggesting that I shouldn't have spent the money?"

"No, not at all, Helen, and please stop it."

"I'm sorry, Marcus, but I had to deal with this problem in the kitchen with the plumbing, and you weren't here. Little things around the house go bad and it becomes nerve-racking after a while. I don't mean to take it out on you."

Yes, you do, Marcus thought, but did not say. He needed to keep peace with his wife as best he could. That meant bending over and being quite submissive. After all, he had left her there alone to take care of the home while he had none of those worries.

"Marcus, you still there?"

"Sure am, and I'm sorry that you're having these problems. But if you came here, you wouldn't have to worry about those things."

"If you came home, I wouldn't have to worry about them."

"Why are you being so stubborn, woman?"

"Because I have my art here with my poetry and we have a very nice group of artists ourselves. Harlem isn't the only place where Negroes are doing things."

"I know what's happening there. Remember, I was a part of the artistic movement when it first began there, but you can be part of both movements: the one in Harlem and the one there in Chicago."

"I'll think about it, Marcus. I really will. Because, quite honestly, I do miss you."

"That's good to hear because I'd be in big trouble if you stopped missing me." He laughed, and Helen laughed on the other end.

"I love you, Marcus, and I want us to always be together. And hopefully, what you are doing there will soon end because we need you doing the same kind of reporting here."

"I love you and we can talk about it, but I do want you to at least come here and visit, maybe for a weekend."

"I'll think about it."

"That's a good start." They both hung up.

Marcus looked up to see Sam Arthur and Sonny walk into the outer office. Surprised, he got up and hurried out to greet them.

"What are you doing here and how'd you know where to find me?"

"I'm here 'cause I want you to keep your word to Mary, and Mr. Holstein told me where I could find you. I just took a chance that you'd be here, and it paid off."

Marcus looked at Sonny. "Who is this with you?"

"This is a homeboy from Gaffney. He just come up here for a short visit. Now can we talk?"

Marcus waved them back into Schuyler's office. Sam Arthur and Sonny sat in front of the desk.

Sitting behind the desk, Marcus leaned forward. "What do you mean, keep my word with Mary?"

Sam Arthur leaned forward in his chair. "You said you could use her to help talk with people on that side of Harlem. She took you to a rent party as a start and you ran out."

"I wouldn't quite put it that way. There was no way I could talk to anyone there. The music was loud, and everyone was getting drunk, and the dancing was outrageous."

"Okay, that might not have been the right place to start out, but at least you got a feel for what was happening up in those apartments every night."

"Yeah, you're right. I got a feeling, but I'm not so sure it was a good one."

"Let me get you back with Mary and you can talk to some of the people living in her tenement."

"What is your interest in that girl? I mean, is she your girlfriend or what?"

"No, that's not his girlfriend," Sonny intervened. "His girlfriend is in Charleston, South Carolina, and he got to go get her."

Marcus stared at Sonny for a moment and then at Sam Arthur. "You seem to have a pretty complicated life."

"Never mind my life. You gonna let Mary help you out?"

"Okay, but is there somewhere else she can take me so that it'll be worth my time and my dime to pay her?"

"I told you, she'll let you talk to some of the people where she lives and maybe if you're interested, she can take you to Abyssinian Baptist Church on Sunday. Them's more your kinda people."

"Can you tell her that tomorrow, about noon? I'll come by her place and hopefully, she can have some of her friends to talk with me. And I'll have to think about the church."

"I'll set it up today. And she'll be expecting you tomorrow about noon."

Marcus got up and walked around the desk. "Good, now I need you all to leave so I can get some work done."

"Nice meeting you, Mr. Williams," Sonny said.

"Yeah, nice meeting you, too." Marcus walked them back to the outer room, and they left out of the office.

<hr>

"What is he doing with you?" Mary pointed at Sonny, standing with her door halfway open.

Sam Arthur didn't appreciate her tone or her question. Evidently, she still had an attitude from last night. He had to be careful with his response. He had to convince her to keep working with Marcus. He also had to be stern, too.

"Never mind why he's with me. He just is, so can we come in?"

Mary held the door open, and Sam Arthur and Sonny walked in. They sat in the only two chairs at the table. Mary tapped Sonny on his shoulder.

"Oh, sorry," he said and got up.

"Thank you," Mary sarcastically said and sat down.

"I'm surprised you showed up. Even if it was with company."

Sam Arthur had to soften the conversation. "Where is Henry?"

"He went with my friend and her daughter over to the park."

Sam Arthur looked at Sonny standing next to Mary. "She got the cutest little boy."

"I know what you trying to do, Sam Arthur, and it's not gonna work."

"Do y'all want me to wait outside?" Sonny asked.

Mary spoke up. "No, not at all. This is just how we get along. We don't mean no harm."

She'd softened, Sam Arthur thought. Now was the time. "I was able to track down Mr. Williams, and he wants you to still help him with his project."

"What? Ain't nothing I can do for that man. He's a dictie."

"He ain't no dictie. He's just writing a story for a major Negro people's newspaper, and he wants you to help him. And it gets you off the—" Sam Arthur caught himself before he said streets. He had gotten to a place where he wanted to protect her from the past.

"You all sure got a funny kind of thing going on," Sonny intervened.

Sam Arthur ignored Sonny's comment. He didn't want him in the discussion. "You might even get wrote up in his story," he said, looking at Mary.

"Is he gonna pay me this time?"

"You still working off that one hundred dollars I gave you? That was our deal," Sam Arthur reminded her.

"You going to be with me this time?"

"No, I can't, but it'll about noon."

"Why? If it's going to be at noon, why you can't come along?"

"'Cause he got some business out of town," Sonny blurted. "I'm gonna work for him at the club while he's gone."

Sam Arthur could get up and smack Sonny because of his big mouth. He was having second thoughts about having him cover at the club for a couple of nights.

"It's your Willa Mae, ain't it?"

"It might be." Sam Arthur held back. Why he didn't emphatically say yes, but a weak answer bothered him. He didn't want to anger Mary. But thanks to Sonny, it was out.

"So, it's really about to happen," Mary said.

"Yeah, he's going to Charleston, South Carolina, to get her."

"Shaddup!" Sam Arthur shouted. "Don't say another damn word or you're out of here."

Sonny took a couple of steps back. "Sorry, Sam Arthur."

Mary ignored Sonny but stared at Sam Arthur. "I know what you're doing."

"What's that?"

"You want to make sure I don't go back to the streets if you bring your Willa Mae up here."

"You don't have to do that no more," Sam Arthur said, slightly pleading.

"Don't worry." Mary smiled. "I don't plan to. Remember when I needed to borrow that money?"

"Yeah, you never told me what it was for."

"I didn't 'cause you got me to working with Mr. Williams. Well, if this thing don't work out with him, I'm going back to what I planned to do. I still got the money to do it."

"What is that?" Sam Arthur leaned across the table.

"I'm not ready to tell you that right now."

"When you gonna tell me?"

"If you come back here with Willa Mae, you got no reason to know, 'cause I won't see you no more. If you don't, then I'll tell you."

Sam Arthur didn't want to respond to her trap. He stood up. "I got to get going."

"You leaving today?" Mary also got up, too.

"Yes."

They all walked to the door, and Mary opened it. As Sam Arthur started to walk out, Mary grabbed him by the arm.

"Remember what I said to you the other night?"

"What was that?"

"When you need more, I want to be the woman to give it to you."

Sam Arthur looked at Sonny, who was standing in the hallway, then back at Mary. He walked out of the apartment and Sonny followed him out of the building.

Nina couldn't believe it as she opened the package delivered to her at the apartment and saw the full-length Sapphire Mink Fur Coat with a note from Larry reading, "For someone very special. It will soon be getting cold in New York, and I want you to be warm."

"Myra!" she screamed. "Come here, you got to see this."

Myra ran out of her bedroom, followed by Lucille. When they reached the living room area, they stopped cold, looking at the fur coat Nina held high for them to see.

"Oh, my God, girl!" Myra shrieked. "Who sent that to you?"

"It's from Larry, all the way from Paris."

Lucille walked closer to Nina and ran her hand over the coat. "What did you do to that man?"

At that moment, Nina forgot she was still angry with Lucille. "I don't know. I don't know."

"You had to do something," Lucille said. "Man don't just up and buy an expensive fur coat for a woman unless they have fucked them."

Nina jerked her coat back from Lucille and moved away.

Myra saw what was about to happen and intervened again. "Lucille, don't be so crude." She walked over next to Nina.

"I don't know what to do with it."

"What do you mean, you don't know what to do with it?" Lucille said with sarcasm. "You're going to wear it wherever and whenever you can."

Myra detected Nina's concern. "Nina, I don't mean to get in your business, but I have to ask you, have you slept with Larry?"

"Of course, she has," Lucille said.

"I didn't ask you," Myra said sternly and looked at Lucille.

"No, I haven't. I haven't ever slept with anybody."

"What?" Lucille blurted. "You're telling us you're a virgin?"

"Yes, I'm telling you I'm a virgin."

Myra wrapped her arms around Nina to calm her. "How old are you?"

"Eighteen and I'll be nineteen in a couple months."

"Eighteen!" Lucille practically screamed. "How did you learn to dance so well and only eighteen?"

"You're just out of high school, or did you graduate from high school?" Myra asked, still with her arm around Nina.

"Yes, I did in June and came right to New York."

"You know, something is not right with this picture," Lucille said. "Where did Larry meet you, and how did the two of you get together?"

No way Nina was going to tell her how she and Larry got together because that would just provide her with more ammunition to attack her as possibly being a Negro.

"Does it matter?" she replied.

"Stop." Myra again came to her defense. "What's most important, are you going to keep this coat? Because if you do, you know you're going to have to give him what he wants."

Nina thought back on the two kisses before he left for Paris. She was aware of what comes after the kiss, and she enjoyed the second one. But she wasn't sure she was ready to take the relationship to its consummation with sex. He was white and her mother had always told her the biggest enemy to the Negro woman was the white man because he assumed he had a right to her body. But again, all the amenities and now the fur coat.

"Nina, what are you thinking?" Myra nudged her. "Are you ready for that kind of relationship with him? If not, you have to say thanks, but no thanks about the coat."

"Hell, give it to me," Lucille said. "I would have no problem giving him what he expects and probably could be better at doing it than a virgin."

Again, ignoring Lucille, Nina said, "I don't know. I just don't know, but I have a week to decide."

"He gets back next week?" Myra asked.

"Yes," Nina replied.

"Well, you got a whole week. In the meantime, I suggest you put it in the closet and don't wear it until you're sure what you want to do," Myra said.

Nina broke from Myra's hug. "I'll do that. Yes, I'll do that," she said and walked back down the hall to her room.

17.

"SAM ARTHUR!" WILLA MAE SHRIEKED when she opened the door to her house. "I didn't think you were going to come."

They broke from the embrace. "When the boy told me you'd left Gaffney and moved here, I had to come and get you."

She waved Sam Arthur inside. "Come on in. Mama will be glad to see you."

He followed Willa Mae inside. He looked around and frowned at the size of the house. There was only one bedroom, a small living room, and a kitchen. It was not much larger than Mary's small apartment in the tenement building.

Sam Arthur smiled as an older woman walked out of the bedroom. It was Ethel, Willa Mae's mother. She walked up to him, and they hugged.

Willa Mae pointed to a rough-looking couch. "Please sit down."

He plopped down on the couch. Willa Mae sat next to him, and Ethel sat in the only chair in the living room.

"When did you get here?" Willa Mae asked.

"Left New York yesterday and just got in here about an hour ago. Showed the first Negro I saw after I got off the train your address and he told me how to get here."

"You didn't bring no bag with your clothes?" Ethel said.

"I didn't 'cause I got to get back up to Harlem. I can't be away from my job no more than two nights."

249

"Back to Harlem?" Willa Mae questioned.

"Yes, 'cause I got a really good job up there making really good money."

"I was going to ask you where you got all that money you sent here with that man from Gaffney," Willa Mae said.

Sam Arthur turned toward Willa Mae and took her hand in his. "I got the money working all the time. I was lucky to get a job when I first got up there and went to work to make enough money to send for you."

"How much money you got Sam Arthur?" Willa Mae asked.

"I got close to a thousand dollars saved up and—"

"A thousand dollars?" Ethel interrupted. "Boy, you make that much money in that little bit of time you been gone?"

Willa Mae pulled her hand away from Sam Arthur. "That is a lot of money. What you been doing up there?"

Sam Arthur didn't like the questioning. Although his bigger problem was that he wasn't ready to tell them he made his money illegally. He hadn't really given much thought that Willa Mae wouldn't approve of his new lifestyle, which was very different from that in Gaffney. He had to be careful and wasn't sure how to answer.

"I made it working long hours," he finally stammered out an answer.

"Boy, you been gambling up there in Harlem?" Ethel asked.

"No, ma'am." He felt slightly guilty. The fact was that he didn't gamble, but he definitely was involved in the gambling business. Now he had to consider just how Willa Mae would respond to him being out every night of the week running numbers.

"You must have some kind of job, sending that man here with all that money, trying to get Willa Mae to come up there," Ethel said.

Willa Mae scooted over closer to Sam Arthur and locked her arm within his. "I got a great idea." She looked directly into Sam Arthur's eyes and smiled. "Why don't you come back here? We're not ever going back to Gaffney, and you don't have to worry about that white man coming here and they always looking for good, strong workers for the fields in Charleston."

He didn't see that coming. There was no way he would ever consider returning to the South after experiencing Harlem and especially returning to the fields.

"I thought you wanted to come up to Harlem."

"I thought I did when we were living in Gaffney, but Charleston's so much nicer and Negroes got better opportunity here. Soon as I got here, I got a job as a teacher's assistant at the Negro school." She paused and looked over at her mother, and then continued. "And I got to think about Mama. I'm all she got."

Sam Arthur pulled away from Willa Mae's grip on in his arm. He wasn't going back there. "But I thought you were looking forward to joining me up there."

She wasn't going to back down either. "I never told you that and we never got a chance to talk about my actually leaving 'cause you had to get out of Gaffney that night. We haven't talked since then."

His thoughts momentarily shifted to Mary and the last words she said the other morning before he left.

"To be fair." Willa Mae interrupted his thoughts. "Maybe I can come up there for a weekend when school is out."

"When will that be?" Sam Arthur asked with excitement in his tone.

"In a couple of weeks."

"Will you at least give it a fair chance?"

Willa Mae looked at Ethel.

"That's all right, honey. I'll be just fine," Ethel said.

"You'll love it up there," Sam Arthur added before Willa Mae could answer.

"How can I contact you?"

"Send a telegram to the Harlem YMCA. Let me know when you leave, so I'll know when you'll get here, and I'll meet you at the train station."

"Sam Arthur, I'll need money for all that?"

Sam Arthur pulled out fifty dollars and handed it to Willa Mae. "Here's enough money for the telegram and enough for the train ride up to New York."

Willa Mae again looked at her mother.

"Go on, girl. I told you I'll be all right."

She looked back at Sam Arthur. "I'm not making any promises."

"That's all right 'cause I know when you get there, you'll love it."

"Can you stay for supper?" Willa Mae asked, obviously wanting to move on from that particular conclusion from Sam Arthur.

"How about lunch? I got to be on the train back to New York, leaving here at five. I got to be back early tomorrow for work."

"That must be a real important job you got up there," Ethel said.

"It's important to a lot of people," Sam Arthur proudly replied.

"I'm kind of anxious now and interested in meeting some of those important people you're working with up there," Willa Mae said.

A reluctant Sam Arthur said, "You will." But the thought of Willa Mae meeting Holstein, Jonas, and Big Max caused him some trepidation within.

✻❀✻

Harlem

MARCUS WASN'T SURE HOW THIS would work out as he got out of the cab in front of Mary's tenement apartment. After the rent party experience with her, hopefully, this would not be a repeat performance.

Just as he reached the top step, the front door swung open, and a slovenly dressed man stumbled out, practically falling on Marcus. He pushed the man aside, and he fell down the steps, crashing face down on the pavement.

Marcus ran down the steps and turned the man onto his back. He was bleeding from the mouth but was conscious, with his eyes open.

"Are you all right?"

The man murmured some sounds, but Marcus couldn't understand him. He didn't want to leave the him on the ground, bleeding.

"Can you get up?"

The man again murmured something and again Marcus couldn't understand him. He looked up as Mary came out of the building. She stopped at the top of the steps.

"Don't bother with him. He's the neighborhood drunk."

"We can't just leave him here in the middle of the sidewalk and I'm responsible for his fall. Does he live here?"

Mary stood at the top of the stairs. "No, he don't live nowhere. Sleeps in the hallway on the second or third floor, depending on which he falls out on when he gets back here real late at night."

Marcus reached down and grabbed the man under his arms, but he was too heavy to lift. Instead, he dragged him toward the steps.

"What are you doing?"

"We have to get him inside and call an ambulance." Marcus kept dragging the man until he had him at the bottom of the steps.

"Stop, Mr. Williams!" Mary's voice rose.

Marcus, surprised by her response, stopped, and looked up at her.

"How do you plan to call an ambulance?" Mary's tone had softened.

"Someone has to have a telephone in this building."

"Do you know where you are? This is not St. Nicholas Street or Striver's Row. We don't have the luxury of a telephone."

"Well, still help me get him up and at least into the building."

"Why are you bothering with him? He does this every night."

Dismayed by Mary's nonchalant attitude about a man who desperately needed help, Marcus looked up at Mary. "You're not going to help me get him into the building?"

"Mr. Williams, I have my friend sitting at my table, waiting to answer whatever questions you have. I thought that's why you're here, not to help some drunkard who, if given the opportunity, would steal every penny in your pocket."

Having recovered from the fall, the drunkard pushed Marcus's hand away from him and started to get up. Marcus moved away, and the man forced himself up and stumbled down the street. Marcus momentarily watched the drunkard, then turned and looked at Mary.

"I guess you were right."

"Are you ready to come inside?"

Marcus walked up the steps and followed Mary into the apartment. He saw a young girl sitting at the table who didn't look any older than Mary.

"Mr. Williams, this is my friend Henrietta. She lives up on the second floor."

Marcus sat in the other chair at the table. Mary walked over and stood behind Henrietta, placing her hands on the back of the chair.

Looking at Henrietta, Marcus asked, "Do you know why I'm here?"

"Mary told me you wanted to talk to people living in Harlem. She told me you might pay me for answering your questions."

Marcus shot a sharp glance and Mary, who did not respond.

"Can I get paid first?"

Marcus pulled out a dollar bill and held it out to her.

She looked at it and frowned. "That's all?"

"That's all," Marcus scowled. She was irritating him. "I don't know how you can expect more than that when I don't have any idea how helpful you can be, so take it or leave it."

"Take it," Mary intervened.

Henrietta took the dollar and stuffed it in her pocket. "What is it you want to know?"

Marcus leaned forward. "Do you know who Langston Hughes and Countee Cullen are?"

"Never heard of them. Do they live in Harlem?"

Marcus didn't answer. "Have you ever been to the 135th Street Library?"

"Where is it at on 135th Street?"

"Right on the corner of 135th Street and Lenox Avenue."

"No, I don't ever get up in that area."

Marcus looked up at Mary. How could it be that she hadn't been to the library and not even to that section of Harlem?

"Are you from Harlem?"

"Born right in the Harlem Hospital." Henrietta turned and looked at Mary. Then adjusted her position in the chair.

Marcus watched as she went through those motions. He knew she was getting uncomfortable. Her inability to answer his questions in the affirmative had to be embarrassing to her, but her answers were exactly what he was seeking to find. She was a perfect example of the other Harlem. He had to continue.

"Do you work, Henrietta?" He deliberately called her name so she would feel more comfortable with the personal touch.

"Every once in a while, when I get maid work down on Lower Manhattan with the rich white folks."

"How do you manage to pay your rent?"

"I did have two girls who lived with me, but they just moved out, going back to Alabama, so I'm struggling right now. I would try to have a rent party, but the rats would scare everybody away."

Marcus frowned. "Rats? They're a problem in this place?"

This time, Mary answered. "Not only in this place but all up and down the street and on Fifth Avenue."

Marcus looked at Mary. "Do you have them in here?"

"Not too often, but if they get hungry, they'll come in here and I just shoo them away. They're part of the territory, but don't worry, they won't be coming in here right now."

Satisfied that a pack of rats wouldn't attack him, Marcus turned back to Henrietta. "Do you have children?"

"Yes, I have a little girl. Oh, and I take care of Mary's little boy when she's out working. She gives me money for watching him. They all upstairs with the girl who lives in the apartment next to mine, now."

"Is your apartment any larger than this one?"

Henrietta looked up at Mary and they both laughed. "No, they all the same size."

Marcus knew they were laughing at what they considered very obvious, not knowing that it wasn't obvious to him.

"How do you all live in such a small apartment?"

Mary was no longer laughing. "We have no choice but to figure out how to survive, and we do. We're a family and have to look out for each other."

Marcus knew he had exhausted all the possible information from Henrietta. He looked at her. "I think I've gotten the information I need."

"Are we finished?" Henrietta asked.

"Yes, we are for now," he answered.

"Do I get any more money"? she asked.

When she first asked for money, it irritated Marcus. But now that he knew more about her pathetic living conditions, he felt compelled to give her just a little more. He took out a five-dollar bill and handed it to her.

"Yes, you deserve a little more."

"Are you going to want to do some more interviews?" Mary asked.

"Yes, but not today." Marcus had to let all this settle in before he could continue. He knew it was going to be bad, but not this bad.

"Not today, but when?" Mary was insistent.

"I'll contact Sam Arthur and let him know when." Marcus got up and looked at Henrietta. "This was good, and I thank you."

Henrietta nodded in approval.

He walked to the door. Mary was right next to him.

"Was it really good?" she whispered and opened the door.

"Yes, it really was. This is the real world of Harlem, and you all are living it. I'll be in touch with you real soon." He walked out of the apartment.

The banging on her bedroom door woke up Nina.

"Nina, get up and get yourself together!" Lucille shouted. "The men will be here in an hour to take all of us to lunch."

Nina got up, hurried over, and opened the door. "What are you talking about? What men and what lunch?"

"You remember the night at the Cotton Club? Well after you left, the man who bought us the drinks came over and sat with me."

Nina did not like the way this was going. "What does that have to do with me?"

"After a few drinks and friendly conversation, he said he had a couple friends, really good guys, and he'd get with them and we'd all go to lunch, you, me, and Myra."

"And you're just now telling me this?"

"I didn't know it was going to be today until he called an hour ago."

"I just got up and I'm not dressed and most important, I don't feel like going out. This is our night off from the show, so I just want to stay in and relax."

"Come on, Nina, we don't have to work tonight. Don't spoil it by being a spoiled sport. It'll be fun and you don't have to worry. Larry will know nothing about it."

"I'm not concerned about what Larry knows. We're only friends."

"Yeah, but that's about to come to an end."

Myra walked out of her room from across the hall dressed in a slick matching dress and shoes. Nina wondered how she happened to be fully dressed and ready to go. Evidently, she knew about the plans.

Lucille turned to Myra. "Talk to Nina, please. She doesn't want to go and that will end the fun we all plan to have."

"Why are you just now telling me this? It appears that Myra already knew."

Lucille didn't respond to Nina, instead turned to Myra. "Please talk to her. She'll listen to you."

Myra walked past Lucille and closer to Nina. "Come on, girl, it'll be fun, and you won't be obligated to nothing more than a luncheon."

"Don't do this again," Nina said, looking at Lucille. She then turned to Myra. "Give me a half hour and I'll be ready."

"Thank you," Lucille said.

Nina closed her bedroom door.

Nina sat at the table next to her supposed date, Victor Hearst, a supposed distant relative of the newspaper mogul William Randolph Hearst at the Sleepy Hollow Country Club in Scarborough On Hudson outside New York City. She stared at Lucille sitting across from her next to Mitchell O'Leary. Myra sat to the right of Nina next to her date, Richard Marshall. They had arrived at the Country Club in a stretch limousine.

The waiter approached the table. "May I take your orders for cocktails?"

"Bring a pitcher of martinis and six martini glasses," Mitchell said.

"Not for me," Nina spoke up. "I'll just have water."

Lucille shot an evil eye glance at Nina as if to say, *Don't you dare spoil this.*

"Five martini glasses and one glass of water," Mitchell said with slight sarcasm.

Victor looked at Nina. "Are you all right?"

"I'm fine," Nina replied brusquely.

Myra came to Nina's defense. "She's just not much of a drinker."

"I remember when I first met you all. She had no problems drinking at the Cotton Club," Mitchell said.

"The Cotton Club," Richard said with enthusiasm. "Now those girls sure can dance."

"Oh, you think they're better than us white girls?" Lucille asked.

Victor spoke up. "I think it's a different kind of dancing. They have a kind of African rhythm different from you ladies who have a European rhythm."

Nina couldn't miss the smirk on Lucille's face. "Some of us girls call it the nigger rhythm. Isn't that right, Nina?"

"I don't know." Nina was not about to back down. She was not feeling good about this entire situation and was not in the mood to deal with Lucille. "I don't use that word." She couldn't wait for Larry to get back so she could move out of living with her.

The waiter placed the pitcher of martinis on the table with the glasses and placed the glass of water in front of Nina.

"Are you ready to order?" he asked, looking at Mitchell.

"Yes, the house special for everyone and a bottle of your best wine."

A pitcher of martinis and now a bottle of wine, Nina thought. They were trying to get them drunk. She really didn't know where she was and totally dependent on these men who she was beginning to dislike.

"You do drink wine, don't you?" Victor asked Nina as he placed his hand on her thigh.

With an instant reflex, Nina slapped his hand off her thigh. "I do, but not today."

"No problem," Victor replied. "We just want you ladies to enjoy yourselves."

The ambiance was outstanding, but the company was less enjoyable for Nina. And the discussion of nigger rhythm was outlandish and if she could just get through this afternoon, she would never accommodate Lucille or Mya again, for what they considered would be a fun afternoon.

"Man, I sure likes this number game," Sonny said as he sat on the side of the bed in Sam Arthur's room at the YMCA.

Sam Arthur sat in the chair next to a small dresser. He'd just gotten back from Charleston.

"Shit, I made fifty dollars in the two nights you were gone."

"Just understand it was for those two nights. You'd better be getting back to Gaffney."

"I don't think so. I ain't going back after I done saw Harlem. Hell, this is paradise for a Negro with all the money to be made."

That was not what Sam Arthur wanted to hear. He didn't want Sonny hanging around like a loose cannon. He hadn't forgotten his running off at the mouth with Mary, and he wasn't sure he trusted him.

"Can't you set me up with Mr. Holstein for a job?"

"What? I don't have that kind of pull with the man."

Sonny jumped off the bed. "Hell, I don't need you. I know where he lives."

"Don't do that, Sonny. I don't think this is the right place for you."

"How do you know what's right for me? You're making it here and for the kind of money you been flashing around, you're doing damn well. I want some of the same."

"You're right. I don't know what's good for you. If you wanna get into this game and see if you can make some money, go on over and talk to Mr. Holstein."

"Sam Arthur, will you go with me? He thinks a lot about you, 'cause you been making him a damn lot of money."

Sam Arthur did have his doubts about Sonny, but he was a homeboy from Gaffney, and it would be the right thing to help him out.

"We can go after the club closes. But right now, I need to get some rest 'cause I been on a train all night."

A broad smile covered Sonny's face. "Yeah, yeah, I need to get out of here and get some rest." He reached out and grabbed Sam Arthur's hand, vigorously shaking it. "I'll pay you back for this. I really will."

Sam Arthur broke from Sonny's grip. "Okay, now will you get out of here so I can get some rest?"

Sonny grabbed the handle to the door, opened it, and, bowing to Sam Arthur, left the room.

Marcus sat in Schuyler's work area in the *Messenger's* office, reflecting on the past two days and what a learning experience they had been. The rent party where the dancers were doing everything but having sex on the dance floor, then that morning and Mary's attitude toward the drunk man who needed help, and finally the interview with Henrietta left him feeling somewhat guilty and depressed. His guilt was because of his lifestyle. He and other Negroes in the more successful class went about their business of living a comfortable life while young Negro girls were living in the worst conditions of run-down tenement apartments, hardly fit for two, but accommodating four. And all the time having to fight the rats.

He had now collected quite a bit of information and it was time for him to organize his notes, so they made some kind of sense. After leaving Mary's apartment, he came straight into the office with that task on his mind, but his thoughts were not on the task. He reflected on all the *Chicago Defender* newspapers they had sent into the South with the Pullman Porters encouraging Negroes to come North, where their opportunities were plenty. Maybe Abbott was doing them a disservice because many of the problems they confronted in the South were waiting for them when they arrived in the big cities of the North. It was simply more controlled racism that existed there. How could he possibly have missed this identical situation in Chicago? No matter what city—Detroit, Milwaukee, or Philadelphia—Negroes were flocking to, the same dilemma awaited them.

"Seems as though every day I come into this office, you beat me here," Schuyler said as he walked in, accompanied by Wallace Thurman. "Do you sleep here?" He smiled.

He ignored Schuyler's friendly dig but wanted to share what he experienced that morning and the night of the rent party.

"I had quite an awakening this morning, interviewing a young girl who is a friend of Mary, the number runner's girlfriend."

"So, you been hanging around in Harlem's ghetto," Schuyler said as he and Thurman sat in chairs in front of the desk.

Again, ignoring Schuyler's comment, Marcus leaned halfway across the desk. "I don't know if we've been doing these poor folks a favor, encouraging them to come North from the South."

Thurman leaned forward in his chair. "Why do you think that?"

"From what I observed this morning, their living conditions can be absolutely deplorable."

"I can assure you they are worst in the South," Thurman countered.

"Wallie's right," Schuyler said. "At least they don't have to be worried that a lynch mob is going to show up at their door in the middle of the night because they offended some white woman."

"This story gets more complicated by the day," Marcus said.

"That's because Harlem is a complicated place," Schuyler said.

"And it's becoming the Negro capital just like Washington, DC, is the white folk's capital," Thurman said.

This time Schuyler leaned forward in his chair, reached out, and put his arms on the back of the desk. "So, are you going to confront the challenge and complete the study that has expanded from the very select artists to the poor folks who don't know how they're going to make it from day to day?"

"As depressing as it is, I'm going back over to the number runner's girlfriend's apartment and do a few more interviews."

"It appears that you've gone from one extreme to another, and you might be missing the middle where most of the people are," Thurman suggested.

"What do you mean?"

"I mean, there is a whole class of Negroes who are not a part of the artistic class or the extremely poor. They are the ones that have jobs on the docks or as chauffeurs and other occupations that pay them well."

"Please do not add to my burden." Marcus sighed. "I've stretched my capability in this one story to its limits. That will have to wait for another day and another story."

"Well, if you don't mind, Wallie and I need to get started working on stories for this week's edition or we'll miss the deadline and not get paid," Schuyler said.

"Of course." Marcus got up.

"Before you leave," Thurman said and also got up. "I'm working on what will be a special magazine featuring articles from young artists. I'd like to share with you exactly what we are planning for next year. I think you'll find it interesting."

"I already do. When and where?"

"How about tomorrow morning at about ten? The address where I sleep and work when I'm not here is 267 West 136th Street."

Marcus wrote the address on a pad and walked out of the office.

❀

Nina was nervously sitting in the apartment with some distance between her and Victor. Lucille and Mitchell were cuddled up on the loveseat and Myra was sitting close on the couch with Robert. Nina made sure there would be some distance between Victor and her by sitting in one of the overstuffed chairs. Victor was in the other overstuffed chair near the fireplace. They had just gotten back from the Sleepy Hollow Country Club. The other five had drank the pitcher of martinis and the bottle of wine with their dinner and they were feeling good. Nina did not feel the same way.

"Ladies, you sure have a nice place here," Mitchell said after they all were sitting. "Mr. Ziegfeld must be paying you really good money."

"We manage," Myra said.

Robert moved in closer to Myra and whispered in her ear. Mitchell leaned into Lucille, and they kissed.

Victor looked over at Nina and smiled. She deliberately looked away.

"What's wrong with you two?" Mitchell said between kisses.

Nina shifted positions in the chair and did not respond.

Mitchell and Lucille got up from the loveseat. He looked at Victor. "The two of you can have the loveseat." He took Lucille by the arm and walked down the hallway.

Robert and Myra also got up from the couch and followed Lucille and Mitchell down the hallway.

Smiling, Victor looked at Nina, who continued to look away.

"How much?"

Nina looked at him. "What do you mean, how much?" How much what?"

"How much is it going to cost me to get you into your bedroom?"

"How dare you! What kind of girl do you think I am?"

"A girl who would do anything for the right price. And I'm able to pay that price." Victor got up, walked over, and stood right in front of Nina. "Now, how much?" He pulled out a wad of money and flashed it in her face.

"I have a boyfriend."

"I don't give a damn about a boyfriend. We haven't spent all this money on you dames not to get a treat. And you're my treat." He reached down and grabbed Nina by her arms and jerked her up from the chair. He tried to drag her down the hallway.

Nina swung her arm around and slapped him, knocking him back against the wall.

"Why, you little tramp!" Victor started toward her.

She ducked him, ran to the door, and outside the apartment. She ran to the elevator, but stopped as she heard Victor right behind her. She saw the "Exit" sign, ran to it, opened the door, and ran down the stairs. Got to the front door and ran out.

When Addie opened the door, Nina practically jumped into her arms, crying.

"Girl, what happened?" Addie asked as she broke from Nina's embrace, took her arm, and led her into the apartment. "How'd you get here?"

"I walked—no, I practically ran all the way." Nina stammered as she sat on the couch.

"You look a mess. What have they done to you?" Addie went into the kitchen, got a towel, and wiped the sweat off Nina's face. "Now tell me what happened?" Addie tossed the towel to the other side of the couch and sat close to Nina with her arm around her.

Nina relaxed and felt secure with her friend. But she couldn't control the tears.

"Okay, take a deep breath, release it, and relax."

Nina did what Addie told her, then laid her head back on the couch. "He tried to rape me," she said as calmly as possible.

"Oh my God, who tried to rape you? Was it that white man that took you out of where you belonged?"

"No, it wasn't him," Nina said in a choking voice. "He's in Paris."

"Who was it? Get a hold of yourself and tell me what happened?"

"We'd gone to lunch at the fancy restaurant and came back to the apartment. My roommates took their dates to their rooms to do whatever they were going to do. Then this man tried to force me into my room, and I slapped him and ran out of the apartment." Nina got it out and felt relieved.

"So, he didn't rape you?"

"No, but he would've if I hadn't fought back."

"Well, you're here in one piece, so what are you going to do?"

"What do you mean?"

"I mean, are you going back over there?"

Nina thought about the fur coat hanging in the closet as well as the rest of her clothes and other belongings. "I don't want to, but I have all my things still there."

"What about Ziegfeld? Are you going to keep performing?"

"I don't know." Nina gasped. "I don't know. I just don't know what to do."

"Okay, calm down." Addie grabbed a church-style fan from the table next to the couch and began fanning Nina. "Do you have to perform tonight?"

"No, that's why we were all able to go to lunch with those nasty men."

"If those girls took their dates back to their rooms, they'll probably be there all night. I don't think you want to go back there tonight."

Again, Nina's voice shrieked. "I don't ever want to go back there!"

"You just said you have to get your belongings, so you're going to have to go back."

Nina, in a jerking motion, turned and looked directly at Addie. "Can you go and help me? Will you go with me?"

"What am I going to be, your bodyguard, and I'm smaller than you?" Addie laughed and for the first time in a very long time, Nina managed to laugh. "I'll be happy to go with you tomorrow if you still want out of there."

Nina hugged Addie. "You're right. I can't burden you with my problem over there."

Addie broke from the hug and patted Nina softly on her shoulders. "In the meantime, I do have to perform tonight and need to get ready. Your room is still empty because I had a hunch you might need it again. It's not as luxurious as what you had, but one thing I guarantee you, it's more peaceful."

Addie got up, but Nina continued sitting on the couch. She wasn't sure she could move. She felt exhausted.

"Nina, you need to go lay down. You're safe here. I'll be back about four-thirty and if you're awake, we can talk some more."

"Can I just sit here until you leave, then I'll go to bed?"

"You can do whatever you want to because you are back where you belong. The only thing that you have to decide is, is it going to be permanent?" Addie finished and walked back toward her room.

The Sugar Cane Club was overflowing with partiers. The band was blaring out music, and the dancers crowded the floor. It had been a busy night for Sam Arthur. His regulars were coming up to him all night and playing their numbers when they weren't dancing. Sonny couldn't stand still. He was so excited as every bettor came up to Sam Arthur.

"Man, you sure as hell making some money tonight," he said as there was a break in the music. "I sure didn't do as good as you in two nights and what you're doing tonight."

"Probably some of these people were holding back until I got back."

"I can't wait to get started on my own."

"You just got to wait and see what Mr. Holstein wants to do."

"I ain't worry. He'll listen to you."

"I don't know about that. We'll see tonight." Sam Arthur watched Jonas come down the stairs into the club. With the dancers all over the dance floor, Jonas had to walk around the side up to Sam Arthur. He looked at Sonny.

"What's he still doing here?"

"He wants to get in the business. We're going to see Mr. Holstein when the club closes and ask him to hire Sonny."

"I don't think so, at least not tonight."

"What you mean, not tonight?" Sonny asked.

"'Cause Mr. Holstein got to go down to Atlantic City tonight. Won't be back until tomorrow afternoon. That's why I'm down here early to pick up the cash and the slips and get them to him before he leaves."

"Oh, hell no, he can't do that," Sonny blurted out.

Jonas gave him a hard look and then turned back to Sam Arthur. "What the hell's wrong with him?"

"He just wants to get work," Sam Arthur said in defense of Sonny, who just didn't know when to shut up. He handed the bag with the money and the slips to Jonas.

Jonas took them. "Well, he just might be in luck. He lost a runner over in the jungle."

"The jungle. Where's that?" Sonny asked.

"If Mr. Holstein hires you, then you'll find out. I'll let him know." Jonas turned and walked along the side and up the stairs.

"What we gonna do now?" Sonny asked.

The music ended, and the dancers returned to their tables, grabbed their belongings, and headed up the stairs. It was three o'clock, and the club was closing.

Sam Arthur gathered his belongings. "Guess we just go back to the Y and wait until tomorrow to go see Mr. Holstein."

They walked up the stairs and Sam Arthur nodded to Big Max, opened the steel door, and stopped as he looked at Mary standing there.

"Mary, what you doing here?"

"He came back Sam Arthur, beating on the door and I wouldn't let him in," she said in a very excited voice.

"Who came back?"

"My baby's daddy. Hollered through the door that he'd be back and if you was there, he'd cut you up."

"Who is this nigguh," Sonny blurted out. "Ain't no way he gonna cut nobody, especially my homeboy. Let's go see him."

"Got any more of them pig feet?" Sam Arthur asked.

"No, but I can get them at the all-night market down the street."

"Why you ask about some pig feet?" Sonny asked.

"'Cause I'm hungry, and Mary fixes some good pig feet. Let's get some and go over there and wait for this fool."

Mary smiled, grabbed Sam Arthur by the arm, and they started walking up Fifth Avenue. Sonny followed next to them.

The aroma of cooked pig feet filled Mary's small apartment. Sam Arthur and Sonny sat in the two chairs at the table in the kitchen. Mary had just come back into the room with the pot of pig feet.

"That sure smells good," Sonny said.

"They gonna taste just as good," Sam Arthur added.

A knock on the door caused Mary to jump. Sam Arthur got up and started to the door. Sonny was right behind him.

When he reached the door, Sam Arthur looked back at Mary, who was standing frozen in place, next to the shelf where she had put the pot of pig feet. Sonny had his fist balled and was ready to strike.

Sam Arthur unlocked the door and swung it open. They all relaxed as Henrietta, with little Henry and her baby in her arms, walked inside.

"Hey, Mary, didn't know you had so much company this time of night."

Henry ran over and hugged Mary around her legs, clinging tightly.

"Which one of you fine men is Sam Arthur?" Henrietta looked at both of the men.

Sam Arthur closed the door but didn't lock it and took a step forward. "That's me," he said and pointed at Sonny. "This is my friend, Sonny."

Henrietta looked over at Mary, who was still standing next to the shelf. "Mary, you didn't tell me you were gonna have all these fine men at your place or I would have dressed up."

Sonny took a step toward Henrietta. "I couldn't tell you ain't all dressed up, 'cause you look so good," he said with a broad smile.

Henrietta smiled. "We got a fresh one."

"You two behave—"

The door swung open, and Oscar charged at Sam Arthur.

Mary grabbed Henry, putting her hands over his eyes. "Look out!" she screamed.

Sonny saw Oscar and moved quickly toward him.

Oscar took his knife and caught Sam Arthur on his arm, slashing it open.

"You mothafucka!" Sonny shouted and hit Oscar with his balled fist, knocking him back against the wall. Oscar recovered and started toward Sonny, but Sam Arthur hit his right hand and knocked the knife to the floor.

"Now your ass is mine!" Sonny shouted as he moved in close to Oscar and began punching him in the head, the stomach, and between his legs. Oscar ran out of the apartment and Sam Arthur closed and locked the door.

Mary released her grip on Henry, grabbed a towel, and ran over to Sam Arthur. "Sit in the chair!" she screamed.

Sam Arthur followed her instructions and Mary pressed the towel against the cut to stop the bleeding, soaking the towel with blood.

"We got to get you to the Harlem Hospital," Mary said in a calmer voice.

"How you gonna get him there?" Henrietta asked.

"I'll carry him if I have to," Sonny said.

"I can walk," Sam Arthur said. "Just got to keep this towel to stop the bleeding."

"I'm going with you," Mary said.

"We both going, 'cause if he falls, I'll have to pick him up and carry him." Sonny added.

"I'll stay here with Henry." Henrietta picked up the boy.

"We need to go." Mary pulled Sam Arthur out of the chair.

Sonny took him by the arm and helped him to the door. Mary opened it and they left with Sam Arthur still bleeding.

Sam Arthur sat on the side of the bed in the hospital with his arm well bandaged up. Mary stood next to him, and Sonny sat in the one chair in the room.

The nurse came in with a roll of gauze and a bottle of solution. "That was a pretty bad cut. Did you report it to the police?"

"No, I didn't think it was necessary," Sam Arthur said.

The nurse looked at Mary, then at Sonny. "When you get a deep cut like that, it should be reported," she said, now looking at Sam Arthur.

"He was protecting me," Mary said. "It was just one of those unfortunate incidents, but the person who tried to attack me, he's gone now and so there's no threat." She lied.

"Have it your way," the nurse said. "Just make sure you change the dressing tomorrow and rub some of that solution on the cut. You all are okay to leave." She walked out of the room.

"Thank you for covering for me," Sam Arthur said, looking at Mary.

Sonny got up from the chair. "We'd better get out of here before she changes her mind and calls the police."

"I need to get home," Mary said.

Sam Arthur took Mary's hand. "You're not finished yet."

"What do you mean?"

"Didn't the nurse say this cut needs to be changed in the morning?"

Mary smiled. "What's that got to do with me?"

"You got to be with me in the morning to change the wrappings, then your job will be done."

"Is it going to be like it's always been? If it is, I don't want to do that no more."

"I don't know what you all are talking about, but we got to get out of here," Sonny said.

"You can stay with me tonight or better still, this morning. It's already six o'clock," Sam Arthur said, ignoring Sonny's encouraging them to leave. "We all can get a little sleep, then go back over and finish eating them pig feet. Henry will be all right with Henrietta."

"You heard what I said, Sam Arthur. I ain't doing it that way no more."

"It won't be."

The three walked out of the Harlem Hospital.

18.

WHEN NINA FIRST WOKE UP, she was confused. This room was not the eloquent one she had at her apartment in Lower Manhattan, but it became all clear. She was back in Harlem in her old apartment, and the disgusting white man was the reason for her being there. She didn't wake up when Addie got in from Connie's Inn. She hadn't felt this relaxed since she left to live with Myra and Lucille.

Just the thought of Lucille caused her to tense up. She was responsible for yesterday's debacle. Lucille was responsible for all her irritating experiences over there. Now she knew it was necessary to go back over to the apartment and confront Lucille. The Ziegfeld schedule had her performing in every routine that night. She just didn't feel it and wasn't sure that it would not affect her performance.

Nina didn't want to go back to that apartment. She preferred to stay in Harlem, as she was gradually realizing that it was where she belonged. Laying there, putting it off, didn't make it go away. She needed to get up and confront the inevitable.

Dressed, Nina walked out of the bedroom and smiled as she saw Addie dressed and sitting at the kitchen table.

"You're already up." She sat on the other side of the table.

"Already? It's already eleven."

"What? Oh my God." Nina sighed. "I have to be at the theater by two for rehearsal and I have to go back to the apartment and change clothes and clean up. I don't want to bother you any more than I have. I can do it. I guess you can say I don't need a bodyguard."

They both laughed.

"There are cabs up and down Lenox Avenue this time of day. As soon as you get out there, they'll stop and pick you up."

"Problem is, when I ran out of the apartment yesterday, I didn't take anything, so I don't have any money."

Addie took a sip from her cup. "Like I said, relax. I got you covered. A couple of dollars should easily cover your fare."

"Thanks. I just keep getting deeper in debt to you."

"Don't worry about that." Addie got up. "You have enough to worry about already."

Nina watched as Addie went back to her room to get the two dollars. From the very beginning of her moving into this strange world that she did not know and was beginning to not like, it just kept getting more troubling. The worst of it all was hiding her identity, while all the time listening to demeaning insults constantly coming out of the mouths of race haters. Maybe it all would change when Larry got back in a couple of days. Maybe it wouldn't. She just wasn't sure.

Nina breathed in and slowly released it as she unlocked the apartment door and walked in. Addie had been right when she walked out on Lenox Avenue. It took only a couple of minutes to flag down a cab and she was back at the apartment by noon. That gave her plenty of time to get ready for rehearsal at two.

She hurried through the living room and before she reached her bedroom, Lucille's door swung open, and she stood in front of Nina.

"What the hell happened yesterday?" she asked in a sharp tone. "You almost messed it up for everyone. And where have you been?"

In just as sharp a tone Nina shot back, "Did you really think I was going to accommodate that man just because he took us to lunch at some fancy restaurant? And where I've been is none of your damn business. Now get out of my way before I slap you, just like I did to him."

She pushed Lucille aside, went into her bedroom, and slammed the door closed.

✕

Sam Arthur lay naked in the bed next to Mary, who was naked also. He was no longer what he had considered pure. The many times he'd been tempted by Mary he believed if he gave in, afterwards he would feel guilty. Now that it had happened, he felt nothing but pleasure. Mary navigated him through it all and made it so good, there was no way he couldn't feel satisfied. He was ready to do it again but refrained because they needed to get back over to her apartment and get Henry. He also had to take care of Sonny. He owed him big because the man actually saved his life. They needed to have that meeting with Mr. Holstein.

The bed was so small, his movement awakened Mary. She turned toward him, and they kissed.

"How do you feel?" she asked.

"Really good."

"Not great?"

"Okay, yes, great and I have no regrets."

"I'm glad to hear that. I'd be disappointed if you did."

Sam Arthur broke from their embrace and sat up in the bed. "I'd better get you home 'cause I know little Henry's missing you."

"He's fine with Henrietta and the baby. But you're right, I need to stop by the market and get him some food."

"Speaking of food, them pig feet should still be good."

"I'm sure Henrietta put them in the icebox. I can heat them up if you're coming with me."

"I owe Sonny."

"What's that got to do with me heating up the pig feet?"

"He wants to get in the business, and I promised him I'd talk with Mr. Holstein for him."

She twisted her body close to Sam Arthur and kissed him again. "You really liked what you got last night?"

"It sure was better than what I thought it would be."

"You want some more?" She rubbed her body against him.

"I sure do."

Right now?"

Right now."

"Let me satisfy you one more time this morning. Then I'll go home. You do what you got to do with Sonny, then come over and I'll feed you."

They slid back into the bed and Mary did exactly what she said she would do—satisfy him one more time.

"Mr. Holstein, Sonny would like a job working for you as a number runner," Sam Arthur said as he and Sonny sat in the two chairs in front of the desk in Holsten's office at the Turf Club.

Holstein shot a glance over at Jonas standing in his usual spot in the office. He then looked at Sonny.

"Why you think you want to work for me?"

"'Cause you treating my homeboy real good and I wanna be part of that."

Holstein turned and looked at Sam Arthur. "If he cheats on me, it'll be your ass. Remember when I told you there is not a second chance with me?"

Sam Arthur momentarily considered Holstein's warning. He also considered that he really didn't know Sonny that well. But he also had to consider that the man had saved his life and, in doing so, risked his own. He owed him so he had to take the chance but would watch over him like a hawk.

"What you say, Sam Arthur?" Holstein brought him back from his private thoughts. "You willing to take on that kind of responsibility?"

"Sonny gonna do right," Sam Arthur answered.

"That's not what I asked you," Holstein shot back in a crisp tone.

"Yeah, I'm willing."

Holstein opened his desk drawer and pulled out some bills. "Get this boy some more proper clothes." He handed the money to Sam Arthur. "I'll take it back out of his first commissions. He's going to work with you tonight and tomorrow night and then Jonas will take him over to the jungle and get him all set up."

Sonny started to say something, but Sam Arthur nudged him.

"If we're finished, you all can leave now," Holstein said. "Jonas can drive you where you need to go."

"That won't be necessary," Sam Arthur said. He did not want Jonas to know that he was still hanging around Mary after he told them he had to go to Charleston to check on Willa Mae.

"Suit yourself," Holstein said. "But I have another meeting in just fifteen minutes."

Sam Arthur knew that meant for them to leave. He got up, but Sonny did not.

"I want to thank you, Mr. Holstein, and I won't let you down," Sonny said.

"Just do not fuck up and we'll get along just fine."

Sonny finally got up. Sam Arthur looked over at Jonas, who was smiling. He knew Jonas was thinking that Sonny would fuck up and that would be the end of his rather successful career with Holstein. He smiled back at Jonas as if to say no way. He and Sonny walked out of the office.

Marcus walked up the steps at 237 West 136th Street, knocked on the door, and looked into the face of a handsome young man. "Wallie's waiting for you in the living room." The man opened the door so Marcus could pass by.

"Come on in." Thurman waved him into the living room. "I thought some others involved in this project would be here this morning, but Zora got an assignment driving Fannie Hurst somewhere this morning." He pointed to an overstuffed chair. Marcus sat down in the chair.

The man who had opened the door strolled into the living room and sat in the chair next to Thurman.

"This handsome young man is Richard Nugent just up here from Washington, DC. He is one of the most outlandish bohemians in Harlem, assisting me in gathering information for the magazine I mentioned to you yesterday."

Marcus nodded at Nugent and also noticed that he wasn't wearing socks. Not that it was a really big thing, but he found it different.

"Bruce is also a proud homosexual and doesn't hide his preference in lovers," Thurman added.

Sharing Nugent's sexual preference was irrelevant and of very little importance unless Thurman was testing his tolerance. He wanted to get right to the interview and away from this small talk.

"You mentioned yesterday that you're working on a publication. Is it going to be different from the *Crisis* and *Opportunity* magazines?" he asked.

Thurman nodded. "Absolutely. They are not really literary magazines. They are just house organs for the NAACP and Urban League. Their published works for writers are not their primary function. We need a purely literary publication, free of the propaganda works that Du Bois believes in at the NAACP."

"What about Johnson at the Urban League?" Marcus asked.

"He's a sociologist, not a literary man. Literature should not be a study in sociology." Thurman leaned forward in his chair. "Charles Johnson believes that through literary arts, Negroes will achieve equality in this country. Again, that is not the purpose of literature."

Marcus also leaned forward. "Why is that a bad idea and a goal to work toward through literature if it works?"

"Because if you make that the goal of your literature you will be constrained from expressing your art in the manner you feel it and art is feelings from the heart."

Marcus looked over at Nugent, then back at Thurman. "You referred to him as a bohemian. Is that how you describe yourself also?"

"That's how we describe ourselves and that is how the elitist class of Negroes describe us, so we adopted it as a positive."

"Why is that?" Marcus adjusted his position in the extremely uncomfortable chair.

"Because coming from the snobbish elites who like to act as though the everyday working-class Negro, but not educated and gets drunk every once in a while, does not exist. If they have their way, they would merge them out of the race."

Instantly, Marcus thought back on his last two encounters with Mary at the rent party and his interview with Henrietta. They were indeed a part of the Negro race. Not sophisticated like Jessie Fauset and Regina Anderson, but struggling young women caught up in the poverty trap of the North.

"The very Negroes that the elitists snub and ignore in their writings are the people we plan to bring to life in our magazine," Thurman continued.

"When do you plan to publish?" Marcus asked.

"Whenever we can raise the necessary capital to get it published," Nugent said, getting into the discussion.

Thurman ignored Nugent's answer to Marcus's question and continued in his line of thought. "We want to capture the lives of our people who have to live two or three families in a single apartment and constantly have to fight off the rats. Their story must be told just like the crowd living up on St. Nicholas Avenue and on Striver's Row. Those are the people that elitists like Dr. Du Bois feel are important to the history of our race. We disagree."

Listening to Thurman, Marcus knew he was on the right track when he expanded his study to include the very people Thurman was talking about. He needed just a little more information.

"Who are the other artists joining in this project?" he asked.

"Richard here is one and then there is Langston, Zora and the artistic design for the magazine will be done by an outstanding artist who recently arrived here from Kansas City, Aaron Douglas."

"So, you don't believe the older artists will like and enjoy your magazine?" he asked.

"We hope not," Thurman answered with no delay. "Because if we do, we will be just like them and that will not be how we want our works to be perceived."

Marcus thought back on his visit to Van Vechten's Fifth Avenue apartment in Lower Manhattan and his conversations with James Weldon Johnson and Alain Locke. The ambiance and the conversation with them were extremely different from the lack of ambiance and the interpretation of the literary obligation of Negro writers from Thurman. Then there were Mary and Henrietta, totally oblivious to either of these literary groups surrounding them.

"If you don't have any more questions..." Thurman brought Marcus to the discussion. "Then I can get back to writing my short story for the magazine."

He piqued Marcus's curiosity. "Want to share with me what it's about?"

"About a poor sixteen-year-old girl forced to move from South Carolina to Harlem with a rebellious spirit that leads her into a young life of prostitution. For the rest of the story, you have to wait and buy the magazine."

"If I am still here then, I'll definitely do just that." Marcus got up. "You've been very enlightening. Thank you."

Thurman also got up. "Hopefully, you'll be around next summer when we plan to release the magazine and observe the fireworks."

Thurman and Marcus walked to the door. Nugent, who followed, opened it.

"You believe you're going to upset the older generation?" Marcus asked.

"It won't be fireworks, it'll be an explosion," Nugent said.

"I believe I'll have to hang around or come back. That'll be a great story as a follow-up to the one I'm presently writing."

"You plan on doing that," Thurman said.

Marcus walked out smiling but anxious to get with Mary and some more interviews with the people that Thurman claimed the elite would like to eliminate from the race.

⁂

Sam Arthur and Sonny sat at the table sucking on pig feet. Mary sat on the bed in the bedroom, playing with Henry. The sudden banging on the door caused both Sam Arthur and Sonny to stop eating and look at each other. Mary ran out of the bedroom, holding Henry. She had a frightened expression on her face as she looked at Sam Arthur.

"He's not crazy enough to come back," she said.

Sam Arthur got up and hurried to the door. "We'll sure find out."

Sonny was right behind him. This time with a knife he grabbed off the table.

With a balled fist, Sam Arthur swung the door open, and Henrietta stood there holding her baby daughter.

"There's a rat in my apartment!" She ran past Sam Arthur and Sonny. "It almost got to my baby. I grabbed her and ran out of there."

"A rat out this time a day got to be hungry and dangerous," Sonny said. He went to the kitchen, looked around, saw a broom, and snatched it up. "Let's go." He looked at Henrietta.

"What are you gonna do with that broom?" Sam Arthur asked as Sonny hurried toward the door.

Sonny stopped long enough to respond. "Gonna knock him in the head to confuse him and he'll run out just like he came in." He looked at Henrietta. "Come on, girl, let's go."

"I got to go with you?"

"I don't know which one is your apartment. You just got to point it out to me, and you stand outside. Now let's go."

Henrietta handed the baby to Mary and followed Sonny out of the apartment.

Mary and Sam Arthur sat back down at the table. She had Henry and the baby in her arms.

"Does he know what he's doing?" she asked.

"Plenty of rats in Gaffney, especially where Negroes got to live."

"You ever have to fight rats?"

"All the time. It's part of living in the South."

"You ever have to fight off rats for Willa Mae?"

That was the first time Willa Mae's name had been mentioned since Sam Arthur got back from Charleston. He tried to keep her out of his thoughts, especially since last night. He figured Mary mentioned her in order to bring the subject out in the open now that their relationship had become intimate. But he wasn't ready to deal with it.

"No, I didn't," he said abruptly.

"Don't you feel different about me after last night and this morning?"

The door swung open. Sonny and Henrietta briskly walked back into the room, saving Sam Arthur from having to answer Mary's inquiry into his feelings.

"What happened?" Sam Arthur asked.

Mary got up so Sonny could sit back down. She handed the baby back to Henrietta.

"He ran off soon as I walked in the room," Sonny said as he grabbed the last pig's feet on his plate and sucked on it.

"Sonny was so brave. I mean, he went right after that rat and when he raised the broom to hit it, the little beast ran off," Henrietta said, looking and smiling at Sonny. "You're are real sweet man."

Sam Arthur ate the last of the pig's feet on his plate.

"You know that rat's going to come back," Mary said.

"Oh, lawdy, please don't say that," Henrietta said.

"Yeah, chances are you gonna have another visit from that creature once it's dark," Sonny added.

Sam Arthur looked at Mary. He knew what was coming.

"I think it's best that Henrietta stays down here with me while you all are working. When you leave the Sugar Cane Club, come back over here and Sonny can go back up there and make sure that rat is not back." She paused and looked at Henrietta. "Is that all right with you?"

"I like that," Henrietta said, looking at Sonny.

"How about you, Sam Arthur?" Mary asked.

Reluctantly, Sam Arthur replied, "Yeah, we can do that."

Henrietta put her free hand on Sonny's shoulder. "Is that all right with you?" She did not wait for an answer. "I'll really be afraid to go up there that late at night alone."

"You can count on it," Sonny said, with a wide smile across his face.

Sam Arthur pushed his empty plate to the center of the table. "We'd better get back over to the Y." He got up. "I need to rest before going to the club. I didn't get much sleep last night."

"I wonder why?" Sonny got up from the table.

"He got something better than sleep," Mary said.

Henrietta grabbed Sonny by the arm. "You sure you gonna come back?"

"Nothing could stop me," he said.

She reached up and kissed him on the cheek.

"We'll be looking for you men tonight," Mary said as Sam Arthur and Sonny walked out of the apartment.

It was the end of the show and throughout all four performances, Nina was not feeling it. She managed to dodge Ziegfeld's nasty attacks, but Lucille didn't. Nina figured Lucille hadn't totally recovered from her drinking and fling in the bed last night. Her rhythm was way off, and Florenz attacked her and dismissed her for the rest of the performances. She ran out of the dressing room crying. Myra managed to escape his wrath. Evidently, she did not drink as much and was not quite as active in bed as Lucille.

Sitting in the dressing room, changing out of the costume from the last routine, she watched as Myra walked up to her. She patted Nina on the shoulder.

"We need to talk. Are you coming to the apartment tonight?" she asked.

Nina did not look up. "Don't know, and why do we have to talk? And who is we?"

"Lucille told me you were going to slap her earlier today when you got home. Is that true?"

Nina got up, forcing Myra's hand off her shoulder. "She attacked me first, claiming that I practically ruined the party you all were having." She paused to take a deep breath and released it. "Well, I wasn't going to do what that nasty man tried to get me to do. I just wasn't going to do it." She pushed Myra aside. "Now get out of my way." Nina started to walk away.

"If you're not there and he finds out it's because of us, he'll put us out," Myra said as calmly as she could.

Nina stopped and turned back around." What are you talking about?"

"I'm talking about Larry. He owns the place and put us there to watch after you while he was gone and when he was not around."

"To watch after me? How long have you been there?"

"Two weeks before you moved in."

"He planned this all along?"

"Yes, he did, and I believe for longer than you think. We didn't know who he wanted us to look over until you showed up that day." Myra took a step closer to Nina. "We didn't know where he met you or anything about you. But we knew he frequented the clubs in Harlem, and that's why Lucille began questioning your race."

Myra had piqued Nina's curiosity. "Did he rent this apartment just for that reason?"

Myra momentarily chuckled. "Rent? You have to be kidding. He owns the building, and he buys whatever he wants."

This was all too much for Nina. She thought about the expensive fur coat, the limousine service and now to find out that he had put Myra and Lucille in that apartment, obviously not charging them to live there, but to watch after her. But why? She was beginning to feel this was a manipulative trap, and she did not want to go back to that apartment. She would no longer feel free there.

"What are you going to do?" Myra asked.

She didn't respond. She knew the chauffeur with the limousine was waiting for her in front of the theater and that was also part of this elaborate trap this man had sprung on her.

"Nina, we have to go," Myra said.

Nina looked around and the dressing room had emptied. "Sorry," she said and walked toward the exit.

"Please don't do this. I'll talk to Lucille and tell her to back off. You're doing great here with the show and you're living the life girls dream of. Don't walk away from it."

Nina stopped. "But at what price?"

"We all have to pay a price."

"You make sure Lucille stays out of my way."

"I will, I promise, just come back to the apartment."

They walked out of the empty theater together.

19.

AT NINE O'CLOCK IN THE morning, Marcus sauntered into the Urban League Building unannounced.

"Mr. Williams, we weren't expecting you this morning," Ethel Nance said. "I assume you're here to talk with Mr. Johnson."

Marcus stood in front of Ethel's desk but saw Johnson in his office, reading the morning *New York Times.* "I'm sorry to just show up like this without an appointment, but I just had to see him."

Johnson looked up from the newspaper. "Marcus, come on in. I have fifteen minutes before my first meeting."

Marcus looked at Ethel. "Thank you." He walked around her desk into Johnson's office and took the same seat he sat in before.

Johnson folded up the newspaper and set it aside. "It's good to see you. How's your study coming along?"

"It's coming along, but, I have to admit, with some surprising twists."

Johnson leaned forward. "And what are those twists?"

"You are aware of this new younger group of artists, led by this recent arrival from Los Angeles, Wallace Thurman?"

"Yes, we all are aware of him because of his homosexual activity at the train station when he first arrived in New York."

"He's also a homosexual?"

"What do you mean, 'also'?"

"I had a meeting yesterday and the young man there with him is a homosexual and does not try to hide it."

"Must have been the young man, Richard Nugent."

"Yes, that's him."

Johnson leaned back in his chair and chuckled. "Yes, I know him and all the others. They love to be referred to as the bohemians."

"Are they all homosexuals?"

"No, not all of them. Zora Hurston is not, and no one really knows that about Langston."

It was Marcus' turn to adjust his body in the chair. "That's the second time I've heard this about Langston, but no one seems to really know."

"We know there for a while, he was very close to Countee Cullen and Cullen had written a very intimate poem to him."

"But from what I can gather, Cullen is not a part of that bohemian crowd. Is that right?"

"And that's when he and Langston kind of parted company. Countee is much more traditional, meaning he does not want to be recognized as a Negro poet, whereas Langston takes great pride in his identification with the race."

Marcus now had another angle by which to pursue his story: the homosexual connection to the new Negro movement. However, he wasn't sure he wanted to delve into that story. Negroes all over the country admired what was happening with the new Negro in Harlem. If they were to know a segment of that movement were homosexuals, it would taint their admiration because Negroes, as a race, were quite homophobic.

"But you didn't come here to discuss that, I'm sure."

"No, as a matter of fact, I didn't. I had a meeting with Thurman yesterday and he informed me of his plans, along with the others, to launch a legitimate literary magazine next year." Marcus paused to catch his breath. "He claims the *Opportunity* and *Crisis* magazines are not designed to be literary, but more sociological. How do you respond to that?"

Johnson now leaned forward and placed his arms on the desk. "Before you arrived here, and as you well know, the Urban League conducted literary contests for this new group of young and gifted writers here in Harlem and all across the country. It was an overwhelming success. The *Crisis* has followed our lead and they are sponsoring literary contests also. I believe Langston has won prizes in both magazines. To suggest that our magazines are not literary is absurd."

"How do you plan to respond?"

"I don't. Why would I? Our approach is the correct one. We'll continue sponsoring literary contests and bringing our writers out to the world. Let those young folks do what they want. It won't affect me at all."

Ethel walked into the office. "Mr. Holstein is here."

Holstein walked past Ethel into the office and looked at Marcus. "I remember you. You were one of my big winners a month ago."

"You played the numbers?" Johnson asked Marcus.

"I got lucky the one time I played with a number runner I was interviewing for the story." Marcus got up. "I'll leave you, gentlemen, to your meeting." Marcus turned and faced Holstein. "Maybe I'll play again. That five hundred dollars made my wife very happy."

"You do that," Holstein said, as he sat down in the other chair in front of the desk.

Marcus said nothing more and walked out of the office, still curious about the connection of a criminal with a well-respected leader of this literary movement.

Sam Arthur came to an abrupt stop as he and Sonny walked into the YMCA. Willa Mae was sitting in the same place Sonny occupied when he first arrived in Harlem. She was stretched out in the chair, looking tired. She perked up as Sam Arthur hurried over to her.

"Willa Mae, what are you doing here?" he asked, obviously surprised to see her and feeling guilty, not knowing how long she'd been there while he was having sex with another woman.

Her smile disappeared. "I told you I'd come as soon as school was over, and they ended the school year early. Aren't you happy to see me?"

"He sure is." Sonny came to his defense. "All he's been talking about since I got here is you."

"Yes, you know I'm happy to see you."

Willa Mae moved in close to him. "Well, don't I get a kiss?"

Sam Arthur's guilty feelings shot up, knowing just a few hours ago he'd been kissing Mary. He put both arms around Willa Mae and they kissed, but not as passionately as with Mary.

She broke from their embrace and looked at Sonny. "You're here?" She said that more as a statement than a question. "I didn't know you were going to stay up here."

Sonny smiled. "I didn't either until I got here and saw the kind of money that can be made in Harlem."

"Sam Arthur's making a lot of money. Now you're staying here to make a lot of money. What you all got going to make all this money?" Willa Mae asked.

"Yeah, you're right. Sam Arthur got—"

Sam Arthur nudged Sonny, who turned and looked at him. "Well, we really ain't making all that much money."

Willa Mae looked at Sam Arthur and then at Sonny. "What you two got going on up here? And where you been? It's ten o'clock in the morning and you're just getting in. This is where you live, isn't it?"

"Calm down," Sam Arthur said. "Let me get you a place to stay and I'll explain everything to you."

"Why can't she stay with you?" Sonny blurted.

"How dare you? What kind of woman do you think I am?"

Sam Arthur looked sharply at Sonny. The man just didn't know how to shut up. He then looked back at Willa Mae. "Let me get you checked in at the YWCA. It's like this, but for women."

Still not smiling, Willa Mae said, "Yes, that would be good. I left yesterday afternoon and stayed on that train all night long and couldn't sleep. I need to rest and then tonight you can show me this city you've fallen in love with."

Sam Arthur looked at Sonny, who had a smirk across his face. "I'll be back as soon as I get Willa Mae into the Y and settled in."

Still, with a smirk, Sonny said, "I know you will."

Sam Arthur opened the door to the room at the YWCA at 137th and Lenox Avenue and Willa Mae hurried past him, looked all around, then turned and looked at Sam Arthur.

"This is wonderful." Willa Mae hugged Sam Arthur. "An inside toilet and a bath, that is, oh my God, just wonderful."

Sam Arthur was not smiling. He was thinking about Mary and the cheap motel he spent the first night with her and he was thinking about the place where she lived with the rats. He was not smiling because he was thinking about

Mary and not sharing in the joy Willa Mae was exuding. He was thinking about how complicated his life had just become.

✽✽✽

Nina awoke to the voices outside her room. One was Lucille and the other was a man. She sat straight up in the bed as she listened to them.

"I know I've seen her dancing at either Connie's Inn or the Cotton Club," the man said.

"I knew it, and they only have Negro girls over there, isn't that right?"

"No, that's not right. Sometimes they have some white girls if they got a good enough rhythm to match the Negro girls."

"Well, it's different with her."

"Why do you care so much about her?"

"Because if she is a Negro, she doesn't belong as a Ziegfeld girl. That should be only for white girls."

The voices faded. Nina climbed out of bed, put on a robe, and walked into the kitchen. Myra, fully dressed, sat at the table drinking a glass of orange juice. Lucille was not there.

"Did you hear them talking about me?" She sat in one of the three empty chairs.

"I sure did, but I didn't pay much attention to it."

"What's wrong with her? What is she trying to prove?"

"That you're lying about who you are." Myra took a drink from her glass. "That you're not white. Is it true?"

"Now it's you, too."

"I don't really care. What I care about is being able to stay here by doing what Larry asked me to do."

"If I'm going to stay here, Lucille has to go." Nina's tone was stern.

"That's why she's determined to prove that you are not white. She believes that if Larry knows you're a Negro, he'll put you out."

Nina had a strong urge to shout that Larry knew she was a Negro, and he was the one who told her to not reveal that to them, but she didn't.

"You didn't answer," Myra said.

"Answer what?"

"Do you have Negro blood?"

Nina glared at Myra for a second, got up, turned and walked back to her room, and closed her door. She sat on the side of the bed, staring at the fur coat hanging in the closet. Larry would be back tomorrow, and she knew what he expected from her. If she gave in to him, then she would be deeper into the lie she was living. Myra was now questioning her, and she couldn't lie to her. Lucille would never let up. She knew soon the other girls would also question her. It was time to act.

Nina got dressed, and tossed her clothes into a suitcase, without the fur coat. She walked out of the room and past Myra, who was still sitting at the kitchen table.

"Nina, where are going? What are you doing?"

Nina stopped, turned, and looked at her. "Lucille was right. I am a Negro and damn proud of it." She hurried out of the apartment.

"I'm never going back over there," Nina said as she hurried past Addie and into the apartment.

Addie closed the door and followed Nina into the kitchen. They both sat in chairs at the table. She briefly looked at the suitcase Nina placed on the empty chair.

"What happened this time?"

"When Larry told me to hide that I was—"

"A Negro."

"Yes."

"Go on."

"I never liked that idea, but I went along with it because of the life I could live. But I always felt guilty. It was like I was denying my mother and my grandmother."

"You were." Addie nodded.

"I can't do it anymore."

"What are you going to do now?"

"I was hoping I could stay here until I figured out what I can do. I've saved up some money and can pay you."

"That's fine. When you left out of here, I told you the welcome back door would be open for you. But what are you going to do about Ziegfeld?"

Nina leaned forward in the chair placing her arms on the table. "I can't go back there because Lucille is going to tell all of them who I am."

"What about Larry? When does he get back from Paris?"

"Today."

"He's going to come looking for you. He's not the kind to give up that easy."

"I don't want to see him. Oh, God, Addie, how'd I manage to mess up my life in such a short time I've been here?"

"Your problem is you wanted to be where your beauty would open doors for you."

"What do you mean?"

"You came to New York for the glamour of Harlem but didn't know there is an ugliness here."

"Do you think Mr. Immerman will let me come back to work there?"

"I don't know. He filled your spot right after you left. But you're a crowd-pleaser and a great dancer. He just might find a place for you."

"I can come up there with you tonight and ask him."

"You can do that, and he might take you back in, but if that white man gets to him and tells him not to let you back in, well, you know what that means."

"I'll take that chance."

Addie got up. "Why don't you get settled in and we'll just have to see what happens tonight? I know all the girls will welcome you back because you make all of us look better."

"I have only one additional interview and I'll be ready to begin writing my first draft for the series on Harlem for the paper," Marcus said on the phone with Abbott. It was early in the afternoon, and he'd just gotten back from his visit with Thurman. He was sitting at his favorite desk inside the *Messenger* office.

"That sounds good, so as soon as you finish that final interview, you can come back here to write the story. It's getting expensive for the newspaper to keep you there."

That was not what Marcus wanted to hear. He had to find an excuse to stay in Harlem. "I would prefer to stay here in case I need to talk with some of the people I interviewed to clarify my information in my notes. I am welcomed here at the *Messenger* and Mr. Randolph has been quite cooperative."

"You know this is quite expensive for the newspaper to cover your cost to stay there and also cover your regular salary." Abbott paused, and Marcus knew why. He wanted his words to register well with him. "How much more time do you need?"

"Maybe another month." He didn't really need that much time for the one interview he hoped to have with another of Mary's friends just to confirm the information Henrietta gave her. It would, however, give him enough time to decide his next move, either return home or seek new employment with one of the newspapers in Harlem.

"I'll give you two weeks. Take advantage of that time and wrap up your interviews and come into the office to write your story."

He thought about the five hundred dollars he'd won with the numbers runner. If half of it was left, he could have Helen wire it to him and that would give him sufficient funds to stay there and not need Abbott to cover his expenses.

"Are you listening to me?"

"Yes, I hear you, Mr. Abbott. I should be able to wrap up my work here and get back to Chicago. But let's not cheat the story. We're recording a historical time, and it deserves our very best effort."

"I'm sure you have given it your very best and will do so for the next two weeks. I have to go." He ended the conversation and hung up the phone.

Marcus respected Abbott and wanted to continue his work with the *Chicago Defender*, but he also respected the dynamics of Harlem with its different layers of Negroes. He knew this dynamic happening there would continue for a long while. If Abbott did cut him off financially after two weeks, he could use what was left of the five hundred dollars to keep doing his work. He needed to talk to Helen.

"Marcus, I'm so glad you called," she said before he could say hello. "We have finally gotten a movement started here in Chicago, just like the one in New York. It's all so exciting." She paused, and he knew why. She was waiting for some encouraging words from him. He didn't reply. "Now you can come home and help us to grow. Doesn't that sound like fun? The two of us working together to build our own Chicago renaissance." Again, there was a pause. "Marcus, are you there? What's wrong with you?"

Marcus wasn't sure how to respond or what to say, but he had to. "That's wonderful and sounds like you have been busy."

"I know and I want it to be you and me making history for Negroes in Chicago, but you called me, sweetheart."

"It wasn't anything important. I just wanted to talk to you and maybe find out when you planned to come here for a visit, like you said you would."

"Marcus, I can't possibly come there now. I have too much to do in organizing and inviting poets and novelists in the city to join up with us."

"But you promised," Marcus said in a sharp tone.

"I'm sorry, Marcus, but why are you so concerned with me coming there when you should be making plans to come home real soon? I just told you that I need you here."

"Helen, I appreciate what you're doing there, but my work is not complete and I'm not ready to come back there."

"Well, this is what I'm going to do, and will not have time to come up there."

Marcus knew there was no need to share with her his plan to use what was left of the five hundred dollars. Helen was set in her determination to stay there, and actually attempt to compete with Harlem. He wasn't interested in competing but continuing to be a part of what was happening there. He had a very difficult decision to make.

"Marcus, since you seemed to have gone silent, I need to go," she said in a harsh tone.

"I want you to seriously think about what you're doing and keep your word that you will at least visit Harlem sometime in the next few weeks. I'm sure you have enough money from the five hundred I left there to get here. I'll call you next week."

"You got to cover for me, at least until eleven tonight," Sam Arthur said, sitting on the side of Sonny's bed in his room. "I got to spend most of the evening with Willa Mae, then I can come over to the club."

"What about Mary? You going over there after the club closes? I'm sure going over to Henrietta's as good as she treats a man."

Sam Arthur sighed deeply. "I got to tell her Willa Mae's here and I won't be seeing her."

"You gonna tell her that before or after you sleep with her?"

"I guess I should tell her before I sleep with her and just go on to the Y."

Sonny gently slapped Sam Arthur on his shoulder. "Don't do it that way. You need to get you some good loving 'cause you sure ain't getting none from Willa Mae the way she acted when I said she could stay with you."

"I can't do that. That just ain't fair to Willa Mae. She sleeping in the Y, while I'm less than ten blocks away, sleeping with another woman."

"And it ain't fair to Mary. She done been in your corner since you been here in Harlem. What's not fair is that you're playing with her emotions. She likes you a whole lot."

"I know, I know. I don't want to hurt her, and I don't want to hurt Willa Mae."

"How long Willa Mae gonna be here?"

"Don't know for sure. Maybe two or three days, maybe longer." Sam Arthur balled up his right hand into a fist and hit his open hand. "Got to figure out what to do."

"What about Mr. Holstein?" Sonny changed the conversation. "You got to let him know I'm covering for you again."

"Why? He knows you gonna be there with me for the next two nights before you move on. Jonas won't come by before eleven and I'll be there by then."

"I think you playing a dangerous game, letting two women jeopardize your job."

Sam Arthur knew of the chance he was taking and didn't need to be told by Sonny. "Will you just do this one thing for me?"

"I can do it for two nights but after that, I got to go with Jonas and learn my location in the jungle. What you gonna do then?"

"Let me worry about that." He gave Sonny the slips and the pouch to put the bets and the money in. "I got two nights to figure this out and I'll get it done. I'm not about to lose my job."

Immerman sat at his desk in his office in Connie's Inn, looking at Nina in a chair in front of the desk. "What happened over at the Ziegfeld Follies?"

"It just wasn't right for me."

"Does Larry know what you're trying to do by coming back over here?"

"No, he doesn't. But he will today because he just got back from Paris."

"You know I can't pay you what you were making over there?"

Nina leaned forward in the chair. "I don't care. I just want to dance, but not there anymore."

"No doubt the girls will be happy you're back. The girl I hired to take your place doesn't really fit in with them."

"Does that mean I can come back?" Nina was excited about the chance to dance with Addie and the other girls again. For some reason, she was being given a second chance and this time she wouldn't foul it up.

"You can start back tomorrow night. The routine hasn't changed, so you should be able to fit in without any problems."

"Can I hang around in the dressing room tonight?"

"You can do that."

Nina got up. "Thank you." She turned and walked out of the office.

⁕⁂⁕

Sam Arthur had never been uncomfortable in the company of Willa Mae but sitting in the YWCA cafeteria in the basement of the building, waiting for the waitress to bring their dinner of smothered chicken, rice, and green beans, he struggled with the conversation.

"What's wrong with you, Sam Arthur? You acting awfully funny since I got here."

"Ain't nothing wrong with me, Willa Mae. Just got a lot on my mind."

"Well, why don't you just get those things, whatever they are, out of your mind and concentrate on me?" Willa Mae smiled. "We have important business we need to talk about."

"What do you mean, we got important business to talk about?" Sam Arthur leaned forward.

"We go to talk about us."

That was the very conversation he did not want to have. He needed time to work this out. When he first arrived in Harlem, there was no question about his intentions. Then Mary entered his life and pretty much dominated it. She was a prostitute who had been with many men for money. Willa Mae was the exact opposite. There should be no question Willa Mae was the right woman for him. For some reason, he wasn't feeling it.

"Sam Arthur." Willa Mae was no longer smiling. "Why do you keep drifting off?"

"You're right, we got to talk about us."

"Good." Willa Mae sat straight up in her chair. "Now, I don't know all you got going on up here other than you seem to be doing well with money, but I do know you're not a city man. You a country boy used to working in the fields."

"I don't know about that."

She ignored his comment. "Now, with the kind of money you say you saved up, we can buy a small plot of land and do our own farming. And in the fall, I can keep working as a teacher's assistant and we'll do really well when we get married."

"No, that was not our plan," Sam Arthur shot back with no hesitation. "The plan was for you to move up here when I got settled."

"Sam Arthur, that was your plan. I never agreed to move up here."

"Willa Mae, you just got here and already you done made up your mind about this place." He adjusted himself in the chair.

"I don't know nothing about this place, except for the men who approached me at the train station soon as I got out the train. Like to scared me to death."

"Them just hustlers, trying to catch a country girl, don't know no better. That ain't all Harlem."

Willa Mae frowned. "You sure know a lot about this city, and you have only been here a few months. How'd you do that?"

The waitress approached and placed the plates on the table. She walked away.

Sam Arthur grabbed his fork and took a piece of chicken. As he raised his fork, he looked at Willa Mae, who hadn't touched her food. She was staring at him.

"You don't bless your food anymore?"

He put the fork down and bowed his head.

"Well," Willa Mae tersely said.

Sam Arthur, somewhat confused, looked at her.

"Have you become a heathen, Sam Arthur?"

"What do you mean?"

"You are the man at this table, and you should bless the food for both of us. You probably haven't been to church since you been here and don't do those things we were taught as Christians to do according to the Bible and the Reverend George back home when we still lived in Gaffney."

For the first time in their relationship, he looked at Willa Mae as an irritant. He bowed his head. "God our Father, we thank you for this food. In Jesus' name, we pray." He began eating. He looked at Willa Mae, who was picking at her food. "You not hungry?"

She put the fork down. "Sam Arthur, what has happened to you?"

He also put his fork down. "Nothing has happened to me and why do you keep asking me all of these questions?"

"You've changed, and I don't know if I like the changes."

Sam Arthur felt the same about her but didn't want to say that. "Maybe it's because we've been away from each other for a while, but I ain't changed at all."

"If you say so, but I feel differently." Willa Mae picked up her fork and ate.

Sam Arthur knew he was losing her. A few months ago, he was willing to fight a white man over Willa Mae. Now he wasn't sure how he felt. Had the separation made a difference? If so, did he want to save their relationship? That also, he wasn't sure he wanted to do. What he did know was he would welcome Mary's company later that night after leaving the Sugar Cane Club. He was not confused about that anymore.

❧

Nina sat relaxed in the chair in the dressing room as she listened to the music inside the club. During each break, the girls huddled around her, filled with questions about how it had been downtown performing with the Ziegfeld Follies. When they asked her why she left, she looked at Addie, who knew, but told them she simply preferred dancing at Connie's

Inn more so than downtown at the Amsterdam Theater. She didn't know if they believed what she told them, but they didn't question her explanation. She could hardly wait for tomorrow night when she'd be back out there with Addie and the others. The music ended, and the girls made their way back into the dressing room.

Smiling, Addie walked up to Nina. "Are you ready to have a good time tonight?" She hesitated for a moment and before Nina could respond, she continued. "Yes, you are, and I am too. So, let's get out of here."

"It's late and aren't you tired?" Nina had no idea what Addie had in mind.

"I'm always tired at the end of the night and I always go right back to the apartment. But tonight, we have something to celebrate."

"What is that?"

"Your freedom, girl, your freedom. Yes indeed, your freedom to once again be you and not some contrived lie to satisfy white people."

"Where are we going this time of night?"

"We are going clubbing. Two young, beautiful, at least you are beautiful, Negro dancers who are always entertaining white men, going to entertain themselves for a change."

"Addie, you are beautiful, and where are we two beautiful dancers going?"

"To the Sugar Cane Club, right around the corner on Fifth Avenue from where we live. You ready?"

The Sugar Cane Club was packed, the music was jamming, and the dance floor was filled with dancers keeping beat to the music when Addie and Nina walked down the stairs and into the club. They walked along the side toward Sam Arthur and Sonny standing at the bar. They stopped at the bar, waiting to see if there were any empty tables once the dancers returned and claimed theirs.

Nina smiled as she felt the energy emanating from the synchronized movement of the dancers. She smiled because that rhythm and movement were unique to Negroes and Lucille was correct when she detected it early on in her. She was home where she belonged.

The music ended, and the dancers returned to their tables.

"Don't look like there's an empty table," Addie said. She saw two empty bar stools next to where Sam Arthur and Sonny stood.

Walking by them, they made it to the two empty bar stools and plopped down on them.

Looking at the line of people waiting to exchange money and in return get a slip from Sam Arthur, Nina turned to Addie.

"What are they doing?"

"They're playing the numbers," Addie said. "Girl, where have you been?"

The bartender approached them. "Can I get you ladies a drink?"

"Two rum and cokes," Addie said.

"No, I can't—"

Addie cut her off. "Stop, girl. We're celebrating." She looked back at the bartender. "Like I said, two rum and cokes."

The bartender hesitated for a moment, then walked to a place where the alcohol was located.

"What is numbers?" Nina was curious.

"It's a betting game where you choose three numbers that you think will be winners when the numbers come out and place a bet. If your numbers do come out, then you win a certain amount of money according to how much you bet."

The bartender placed the two drinks on the counter. Addie took out two dollars and gave it to him. She picked up her drink, held it high, and said, "Here's to you, Nina, and you coming home to where you belong."

Nina picked up her drink, and they touched glasses. They both took sips from the drinks. Nina put her glass down.

"I want to play a number." Nina took out a dime and walked over to Sam Arthur.

"What's your numbers and how much you betting?" Sam Arthur asked.

"How many numbers can I play?" Nina didn't know how many she could bet.

Sonny spoke up. "Three numbers per bet."

Nina handed Sam Arthur the dime. "How about 507, the month and year I was born?"

Sam Arthur took the dime, wrote the numbers on the slip, and handed it to Nina.

"Good luck," Sonny said.

Nina turned and walked back over to Addie. The music started, and the dancers returned to the dance floor.

"Finish your drink so I can order two more," Addie said.

Nina picked it up and drank the rest of the substance. "Ahh," she shrieked as she put the glass down.

"Two more," Addie called out to the bartender.

"How long are we going to stay here?"

"Until we know it's time to leave. We're going to stay here until you are totally relaxed. Tomorrow we can get serious, but for right now, we're going to be silly. You deserve it."

Nina picked up the refreshed drink the bartender had placed on the bar. She drank all the rum and coke in the glass. It was her second drink, and she was already feeling silly. She wanted to dance. She hadn't danced with another person since her high school prom night. That seemed like it was a very long time ago. She thought of Claude, who was so clumsy that night she forced him to dance with her.

Addie nudged her. "Do you want another?"

"Yes," Nina said with no hesitation.

"Two more," Addie said to the bartender.

"I want to dance," Nina said.

She jumped off the barstool and began dancing in place to the music. Two men rushed up and danced in front and back of her. As the music beat picked up, the men moved in closer, touching their bodies to hers.

Addie got off the barstool, pushed the man in front of Nina to the side, grabbed her by the arm, and back to the bar.

"You got to be careful," she said.

One man followed them back to the bar. He stood in front of Nina. "You're an excellent dancer. Can I get your name? Mine's Edward."

Nina felt a nervous twinge. "Thank you." She did not give him her name.

He moved in closer to her. "I gave you my name. Don't you have a name?"

"She does, but she's not interested in giving it to you," Addie spoke up.

The man continued staring at Nina but said to Addie, "Not talking to you."

Addie's voice rose. "Well, I was talking to you. Leave her alone. She's new to Harlem."

The man turned and faced Addie. "Bitch, mind your goddamn business."

Addie picked up the drink the bartender had just placed in front of her and threw the substance on the man.

Sonny was watching the growing confrontation. When the man made a move toward Addie with a balled fist, he ran to them and pushed the man. "I don't think these ladies want to be bothered with you."

"I'll cut your nigger ass." The man pulled out a razor. With his arm drawn back, he plunged toward Sonny. He swung at him, but Sonny dodged the strike. The man's motion carried him forward and Sonny hit him solidly in the jaw. The razor fell to the floor.

The dancers scattered back to their tables; the band struck up a louder tune. Big Max raced into the ballroom and over to the bar.

The man had gotten back up and pulled out a switchblade from inside his pocket. He started at Sonny. Big Max grabbed the man from behind, wrapping both arms around him.

"Calm down!" Big Max shouted. While still holding the man, he looked at Sonny. "Get back over by Sam Arthur."

Still looking at the man, Sonny walked backward to where Sam Arthur stood. Big Max dragged the man, still with both arms around him, toward the steps and walked up.

Addie turned and looked at Nina. "I think it's time."

Nina didn't respond. She just sat there, staring straight ahead.

"Nina! Let's go."

"What if he's waiting outside?"

"Then we'll deal with it. Let's go."

They walked up to Sonny and Sam Arthur. Addie stopped and looked at Sonny. "Thank you."

Sonny bowed toward them. "My pleasure."

"Will you walk us outside?" Nina asked, looking at Sonny.

He turned to Sam Arthur.

"Go ahead."

"Let's go, ladies." As the three of them walked toward the stairs, Sonny turned and looked at Sam Arthur. "I'll be right back."

The band had stopped playing, and the crowd was heading up the stairs when Marcus, dodging them, walked into the club and over to Sam Arthur.

"You remember me?" he asked

"Sure do. You down here pretty late, and we're about to leave. But I got time to take your bet." He opened up the pouch and took out the pencil and a slip.

"No, I'm not here to bet."

"Then, why you here?" Sonny asked.

Marcus ignored Sonny. "I need to talk to Mary."

"What the hell?" Sonny made a move toward Marcus.

Sam Arthur held him back. "It's not what you think."

Glaring at Marcus, Sonny took a couple of steps back.

"Why do you need to talk to Mary and why so late?" Sam Arthur asked Marcus.

"I have no way to communicate with her except through you. I just didn't want to show up at her apartment unannounced."

"She's expecting me. We can go over there after I give this money and bets to Jonas out front."

Sonny stuck his hand out. "I'm Sonny and a friend and business associate of Sam Arthur."

Marcus shook his hand. "Are you from here in Harlem?"

"No, up here from Gaffney, South Carolina, but I'm planning on staying in Harlem."

"Let's go," Sam Arthur said. He didn't want Sonny to say anything more for fear he would say the wrong thing. They walked up the stairs and out of the building.

Mary opened the door with a surprised look on her face. "Mr. Williams, what are you doing here this time of night?" She swung the door wide open as they all walked in.

Henrietta was sitting on one of the two chairs at the table. Sam Arthur moved aside to let Mary sit in the other one. Sonny stood behind Henrietta's chair with his arm looped over her neck. Henry and the baby were sleeping in the bedroom.

"No," she said and pushed Sam Arthur to the chair. "You been standing up half the night over at that club and I know you got to be tired."

Sam Arthur sat in the chair. "Mr. Williams came into the club just as it was closing and said he had to talk with you. Didn't think it proper to come over here unannounced."

Mary turned and looked at Marcus. "I didn't think I'd hear from you after we mentioned the rats."

Marcus ignored her comment. "I just need to talk with maybe two more people in the complex and I'll feel that I did a thorough job. Can you set me up?"

Mary looked at Henrietta. "Who can we have him talk to?"

"How about a man this time?" Marcus asked.

Both Henrietta and Mary laughed. "Ain't no men living in here but for an overnight visit with one of the girls and then they gone," Henrietta said.

Mary nodded. "Yeah, they just like the rats. They show up after eleven and gone when the sun comes up."

Marcus continued his questioning. "Why do you all put up with it?"

"Not you all," Mary quickly responded. "Don't no man come up in here at all." She looked at Sam Arthur. "He's the first man that ever spent the night in my place."

That caught Sam Arthur by surprise, but then it did make sense. Her sexual activity was for money, and she always said it was work. She didn't bring her work home. He was the only one, and that made him feel good.

"My baby's daddy used to come over and sometimes I'd let him spend the night," Henrietta said. "But when I finally recognized that bastard did not mean me or my baby any good that stopped. Ain't nobody been back but Sonny." She looked at him and smiled. "'Cause I got plans for that man."

"There's ten girls all with babies living in this rat hole and we have a pact. If we see one of the others getting weak for some no-good piece of a man, we get with her and remind her that we all stick together and don't let no man take advantage of any of us," Mary said.

Marcus had an idea. "Can you get all these young ladies together tomorrow and I can interview what you call the crew?"

Mary looked at Henrietta. "What you think?"

"If he got a little money, we can do it," Henrietta said.

"I'll cover the money," Sam Arthur spoke up. "If you got ten girls here tomorrow, I'll give each one ten dollars to participate."

Marcus looked at Sam Arthur. "Thank you."

"I ain't much of an educated man, but what you trying to do is important for our kids to know about after we all gone," Sam Arthur said. "I want to be a part of it."

"What time tomorrow?" Marcus asked.

"How about ten o'clock?" Mary suggested. "That's time enough before they all get out of here and do whatever they do during the day."

"That's a perfect time for me," Marcus said. "Let me get going. I have to go all the way to the other side of town."

"They'll still be some cabs up and down Fifth Avenue," Mary said. "You won't have any trouble. They run all night. Harlem never sleeps."

Mary walked Marcus to the door and opened it. "We'll be ready for you in the morning and be careful out there. This time of night, some of the rowdier Negroes be wandering the street, looking for a sucker."

"I'll be careful. I am from Chicago, and we have the same kind of rowdy Negroes there. They're everywhere." He walked out of the apartment and Mary closed the door.

Sam Arthur sat there staring at the two babies sleeping on the bed, thinking about Willa Mae. Things had gone badly with her earlier in the day. He needed to get with her in the morning and work out their differences, if that was possible. But he knew Mary would expect him to be with her in the morning when Marcus showed up.

Mary walked up behind him and put both hands on his shoulders. "I don't want you to leave in the morning. I need you here with me."

Henrietta reached back and put her hand on top of Sonny's. "I know Sonny going to be here, ain't that right, baby?"

"You right about that. I'm gonna be right here with you."

"What about it, Sam Arthur? You're not going to get up and leave before Mr. Williams gets here, are you?"

"I'll be here for you." Willa Mae would have to wait.

Henrietta got up. "We need to go because ten o'clock will be here in less than six hours. We all need to get some rest."

Sonny walked into the bedroom and picked up the baby.

"We have to gather all the girls by eight before they leave out," Henrietta said as she walked over to the door and opened it. Sonny was right behind her.

"Be down here by eight and we'll get started," Mary said and closed the door.

Sam Arthur did not get up. His mind was somewhere else. After tomorrow morning, he had to make a decision. Willa Mae wanted him to go with her back to Charleston. She still viewed him as a field hand, and he no longer agreed. Willa Mae had been in his life for a long time, and it would be a tough decision, but he had to make it. No more delay.

20.

MARY OPENED THE DOOR TO her apartment and Marcus walked into a room filled with young, good-looking women. The one exception was an elderly good-looking woman sitting in the chair at the table. He glanced at Sam Arthur on the bed in the bedroom holding Henry. Sonny sat on the other side of the bed. The women sent the two men to the bedroom so they could do their job with Marcus.

Mary hurried over and stood next to the older woman. She put her hand on her shoulder. "This is Mrs. Lucy. She's been living in Harlem as long as I been alive." She pointed to the empty chair. "Please sit, Mr. Williams."

Marcus sat down. "Thank you." He pulled out a pen and opened his tablet.

Mrs. Lucy initiated the discussion. "What you want to know?"

"Harlem is getting the reputation as the nation's capital for Negroes. Our people are trying to come here from the South because they believe it is their land of opportunity. What do you—"

"That's a lie," Mrs. Lucy shot back. "Ain't no paradise. People need to stop telling Negroes that it's so much better up here than down South."

"Have you ever lived in the South?" Marcus smiled. He was going to enjoy this interview.

"I was born in Hattiesburg, Mississippi, in 1870 right after we was freed as a race of people."

"So why did you come to Harlem?"

"Same reason all of us came here, looking for a better life and getting away from them racist rednecks."

"My mama came up here from Memphis in 1890," one young girl added to the conversation.

Marcus looked at the girl. "Why did your folks come up here?"

"Wasn't my folks, was just me and my mama. I ain't ever known my daddy."

"Why have you stayed up here?"

The young girl moved in closer to Marcus. "'Cause my mamma, bless her soul now in Heaven, thought that anything was better than Memphis."

Marcus turned his chair to face the girl. "So, you agree with Mrs. Lucy?"

The girl backed up while looking at Mrs. Lucy. "She's like a mama to all us girls and we don't ever go against her word."

Marcus turned his attention back to Mrs. Lucy. "If it's so bad here, why do you stay here?"

Mrs. Lucy pointed at the young girl who had spoken up. "Just like Gayle said, as bad as it is here, it's just a little better than down there."

A second young girl spoke up. "Our hope was with the Honorable Marcus Garvey. He had plans for all of us to return to Africa, where we'd all be queens."

"But the uppity Negroes was scared of him because he was organizing us poor folks, and ran him out of Harlem," a third girl added. "Now they done put him in prison."

"How many of you all were followers of Garvey?" Marcus asked.

Five of the girls raised their hands.

"So, none of you follow him any longer?"

Another girl stepped forward. "There's no one to follow anymore."

Marcus looked at Mrs. Lucy. She was frowning. Even though the girls did not like to go against her, it seemed she did not agree with the Garvey talk.

"He's gone now and like Margaret said," the girl pointed at the second one who had spoken, "the dicties ran him out. And the white folks put him in jail 'cause they was scared of him."

Marcus looked back at Mrs. Lucy. "You weren't a follower of—"

"No, not at all. Ain't no Negroes want to go back to no damn Africa. What the hell do we know about that place? We don't know nothing and don't want to know."

Marcus looked at Mary, who had remained quiet, then at Henrietta, who had also said nothing. Again, he looked at Mrs. Lucy.

"What do you think makes living here in Harlem so bad?" he asked her.

"We don't own nothing. All the businesses, the schools, and all those fancy nightclubs is owned by white people. And they don't even hire Negroes to work in their businesses. The Koch Department Store over on West 125th Street and others just come down here and take our money and leave."

Marcus again shifted his body in the chair. "Don't you think the NAACP and the Urban League are fighting to make things better for all Negroes?"

"Only for themselves. They're not interested in us poor folks. They just working for the dicties up on St. Nicholas and 139th Street."

Marcus was convinced now that there was a serious disconnect between the Negroes in Harlem. There was the good, with the growth of the literary movement in Harlem, the bad, with the poor, both young and old, who had to live in rat-infested tenement houses, and the ugly with the feeling of despair and hopelessness he detected among the ten young girls that could easily multiply to thousands, and even the elderly like Mrs. Lucy, who, a long time ago, had come there with high hopes but now those hopes had been destroyed.

He folded up his tablet, put his pen away, and looked at Mary. "I think I have what I need." He got up. "I want to thank you all for your time and information."

"When do we get paid?" Gayle, the first girl who had spoken up, asked.

"I'll take care of that," Mary said and looked in the bedroom at Sam Arthur.

Marcus walked to the front door. Henrietta hurried in front of him and opened the door.

He looked back. "Thank you, ladies, and especially thank you, Mrs. Lucy." He turned back and walked out of the apartment.

Sam Arthur and Sonny sauntered into the kitchen area from the bedroom, leaving the two babies asleep on the bed. The girls and Mrs. Lucy had left and were excited about the possibility that their words would appear in a publication.

He wanted to share in their excitement but knew he must now confront Willa Mae. It was afternoon, and he had no contact with her since their differences yesterday. He didn't want to sit down because that would indicate he meant to spend some time there with Mary. He glared at Sonny when he sat in the other chair.

"We need to get going?" he said to Sonny.

"What's your hurry? Oh, yeah, that's right. Willa Mae is here."

"What?" Mary shrieked. "Willa Mae is here. Where is she staying? In your room at the Y?"

Sonny had done it again, running his mouth. Sam Arthur fumed. He would deal with him later. Now he had to deal with an irate Mary.

"She got here yesterday," he said, looking at her. "No, she ain't staying at my place. She's over at the YWCA."

Sonny got up and took Henrietta by the arm. "I think it's time for us to leave."

"No, you all stay here," Mary insisted. "Don't you dare leave."

Sonny sat back down. He looked over at Sam Arthur, but quickly looked away.

"Mary, can't we discuss this some other time?" Sam Arthur didn't want to do this in front of others.

"I don't think so. You sleep in my bed while having another woman here in town to see you?"

"That don't mean nothing," Henrietta said." Most important, he was here with you and stayed like you asked him to."

Mary turned and looked at Henrietta with a scowl. "Whose side you on?"

"On your side, you know that." Henrietta hurried over and sat on Sonny's lap.

Sam Arthur couldn't help but stare at Mary. She was a woman who had sex with married men in the past and did not think much of it. That is why she always viewed sex as work and not as a sensual act. There was no feeling involved, but with him, that obviously had changed. There were feelings, and that's why she could show emotions toward him. She was angry because he had shared himself with another woman, even though they did not have sex. He just wasn't sure how to handle the situation, but he was sure he needed to get over to the YWCA. He owed that to Willa Mae just as he felt he owed staying with Mary that morning.

He looked at Sonny. "You coming?"

Mary got right up in his face. "You going to see her?"

"I have to, and you know that." He eased her back away from him.

"I need the money to pay the girls for coming down here this morning. Or are you going to back out of that also?" Her tone wreaked of sarcasm.

Sam Arthur took the money out of his pocket and handed it to her. He didn't respond to her anger.

Mary counted the money and then set it on the table. She looked at Sam Arthur. "Well, don't bother to come back here. Stay with your precious Willa Mae. After all, that's all you talked about since I met you. And don't worry, I'll get on with my life. I know how to take care of me and Henry." She walked into the bedroom.

He looked at Sonny. "I asked, are you coming?"

"Think I'll stay here and see if I can work things out for you."

"This is your last night working with me. Then you're on your own." He walked to the door and out of the apartment.

Nina woke up with a hangover. Her head was throbbing, and she felt nauseous, but there was something else bothering her more than the hangover. Even though it was the first time she had experienced having one. When they got to the apartment last night, she was pretty sure the Lincoln limousine parked down the street was Larry's. It had to be the chauffeur spying on her. Addie had told her Larry would never give up, but she had to be just as determined and never give in. She was not going to return to that life, no matter how glamorous it was. She would leave New York before she would let that happen. She briefly thought back on Claude's last words that he would be there in Washington, DC, for her if she needed him.

She got up, took her tired body into the bathroom, and poured bath water. She needed to wash everything from last night at the Sugar Cane Club off her body. She reclined in the tub with her eyes closed. All kinds of thoughts flashed through her mind. She knew the confrontation with Larry was going to happen. She recalled the last kiss with him and how it affected her. She didn't want that to happen again for fear she might get weak and return to that life she was determined to put behind her. Maybe she might even go down to Washington, DC, and visit Claude just to get away from all of this. She needed a change and maybe that could be just what she needed, at least for a weekend. But if she started dancing at Connie's Inn, there would be no time, especially on the weekends, the busiest time in the club. She sat up in the bathtub and bathed herself. She had to make the rehearsal in just a couple of hours.

Fully dressed and refreshed, Nina strolled into the kitchen where Addie was sitting. She took a seat across from her at the table.

Addie greeted her with a smile. "Welcome! Welcome to the world of the living. I didn't think you were ever going to get up. How you feel?"

"Fine, now that I've washed last night off my body."

A knock on the apartment door caused both Nina and Addie to jerk and look at each other.

Nina looked at Addie. "You expecting someone?"

"No." She got up and walked over to the door, and called out, "Who is it?"

"It's Larry. Is Nina here?"

Nina sat straight up in the chair and signaled for Addie to tell him no.

"I haven't seen Nina. She hasn't been here since she left to move over to her new place in Lower Manhattan."

"Don't lie to me, girl! If you want to keep your job, just don't lie to me. Now open this door right now."

Addie looked back at Nina but did not respond to Larry's threat.

"My chauffeur saw her come in here late last night. Now this is your last chance to open that door, or you can look for work somewhere else, maybe in one of the cheap nigger dives."

Nina got up, walked over, pushed Addie aside, and opened the door.

Relaxing his posture, Larry asked in a much softer tone, "What are you doing? Why are you back here and what happened? When I left to go to Paris, you were happy and three weeks later, Myra told me you had moved out and Florenz told me you did not show up for work. He was very upset and disappointed. Said he had great plans for you."

"I can't pretend to be somebody I am not." Nina stood with the door partially ajar, her arm extended from its end.

"That's fine. You don't have to, but please come back over to the apartment and we'll figure something out."

"I'm not going back there, and I don't want to dance anymore over there."

"How about us? I thought we were making some progress together."

Addie moved in a little closer to the door. "Nina, we have to get ready for rehearsal."

Larry gave Addie a scowled look. "Please stay out of this."

"This is my apartment, and I don't give a damn how much money you got or if you can get me fired. I'll not stand here and allow you to talk to me that way," Addie shot back, with fire in her words.

Nina was feeling guilty because she knew Larry could get Addie fired and it would be her fault. She had to put an end to this brewing confrontation. She did not really care about Larry but did for Addie. She was her only friend.

Nina looked a Larry. "Can you pick me up after the show tonight, and I'll explain it all to you?"

He smiled. "I'll do that." He gave Addie one final harsh look, turned, and walked away.

Addie closed the door and turned to Nina. "What do you think you're doing?"

"I didn't want to get you fired."

"Girl, what's wrong with you? You can't go with that man tonight."

"I'll be all right. He won't do anything to me."

"Nina, Nina, Nina, what is wrong with you? That man does not mean you any good. He did all those things to just get you in the bed and unless you're willing to do that, don't go with him tonight. I'm warning you."

For a quick moment, Nina thought back on what Lucille and Myra had also told her about Larry's intentions, but she could not allow him to get Addie fired. She wouldn't be able to live with that, knowing it was because of her. She'd take her chances that Larry would not force her to do what she didn't want to, and that he would accept her desire to no longer continue that growing relationship. And if he didn't, she would deal with the consequences.

"I'll be okay. I can't let him get you fired from the club. You been there a long time and it would just make me sick if that happened."

Addie hugged Nina. "You are a wonderful person, and I don't want to see you get hurt by that monster. Maybe he'll change his mind and not show up tonight. If he does, we'll deal with it."

"We better get ready to go to rehearsal."

"You're right."

The two walked back toward their rooms.

⁂

With his nerves practically shot when he walked into the YWCA after two o'clock in the afternoon, Sam Arthur knew Willa Mae would be upset, and he also knew she had a right to be angry. He walked by the registration desk.

"Sir, excuse me," the teller called out to him.

Sam Arthur stopped and walked up to the counter.

The teller picked up a letter-size paper and looked at the name on it. "Are you Sam Arthur?"

"Yes." Sam Arthur held his hand out, assuming the letter was for him.

"The lady in room 238 left this for you."

Sam Arthur took the letter. "Is she still in her room?"

"No, checked out about an hour ago."

He opened the letter, read it, and then ran out of the YWCA.

Outside, Sam Arthur flagged down a Checker Cab and got in. "Grand Central Station." He sat back as it headed down Lenox Avenue toward Lower Manhattan.

Since there was only one train going South, he knew it didn't leave until four-thirty. He had taken that same train when he went to Charleston to see Willa Mae. He had plenty of time to decide what he planned to say to her when he caught up with her at the train station.

When the cab pulled up in front of Grand Central Station, Sam Arthur gave the driver a dollar, jumped out, and ran inside, ducking around other people. He saw Willa Mae sitting in a row close to the passageway to the train. He ran up and sat in the empty seat next to her.

Willa Mae looked at him and jerked away. "Why are you here, Sam Arthur?"

"To be quite honest, I don't really know."

She looked straight ahead and not at him. "Did you read my letter I left at the front desk of the Y?"

Sam Arthur pulled the letter from his pocket. "I read it."

"Well, then you know my position about us." Still looking straight ahead, she refused to look at him.

"I am not returning to the South, Willa Mae, for no reason." He was adamant in his decision.

"I am." She turned and looked at Sam Arthur. "It may not be perfect, but it is home to me. And I know Mama would never agree to move up here. Now I'm catching this train and going home. If you decide to come to your senses and come back home, I'll be waiting for you. But I am not waiting forever."

Her final words struck hard on Sam Arthur, and he had nothing more to say. He loved Harlem, and it happened in just a short period of time. Willa Mae had made the decision for him. He leaned over, kissed her on the cheek, got up, and hurried out of the train station, without looking back.

※※

Holding the phone to his ear, Helen exuded excitement. "Marcus, Ida Wells Barnett has moved here to Chicago, and she is willing to help us get our literary movement going. You got to come home and help us."

Sitting in his usual space in the *Messenger* office building, Marcus had called Helen to make one final gesture to get her to come to Harlem, but before he could make the plea to her, she excitedly beat him to the punch.

"I had heard that Mrs. Barnett was moving to Chicago with her husband, who is a prominent attorney. That is good news. She can be very helpful to what you're doing." He paused to get the right words to share with her. "I'm proud of you, sweetheart, and I really do miss you."

"Well, then, why don't you just come on home? You told me in our last conversation that you'd pretty much finished your interviews. Please, Marcus, come home and write your series on Harlem here. Don't you want your marriage more than you want Harlem?"

"You know I do, but why can't I have both?"

"Marcus, over the years I have always sacrificed my career in order to support yours at the *Defender*. I did it because I was taught that a woman should be the support behind her husband, and I have accepted that responsibility with my love for you." She paused to catch her breath. "Can't you do it just this one time for me, for the very same reason?"

She drove a hard bargain because now she had introduced love into the conversation, he thought, listening to her. But he also knew Helen was telling the truth. For the years they had been married, she was always there for him, even when he came in late at night a little tipsy from covering an entertainer as he had done a few months ago with Louis Armstrong. This was the most magnificent story he had covered in all his years of writing as an investigative reporter. He had to make one final attempt to convince her to come to Harlem, and he knew she would feel the same as he did.

"Are you there, Marcus?"

"Yes, yes, I'm here. I'm thinking about what you just said. I know you have always been there for me. And I'm asking you one more time to be here for me and come to Harlem, just for a week. You'll love it."

"No. I have never asked you to do something for me. If that place is more important to you than what I am asking, then I guess that tells me all I need to know."

"What does that mean, Helen?"

"You figure it out. You're a real smart man. It shouldn't take you long. When you do, you call me." Helen hung up.

He sat there staring at the phone. She actually hung up on him. He wasn't sure if he should be angry or understanding. She laid her heart out to him and made it known that she did love him. She questioned his love for her, and he failed in his answer. It finally hit him. A story of any kind, no matter how important to the history of the country, shouldn't take precedence over what she had just shared with him. As he opened his tablet of notes from over the past four months, he couldn't concentrate on what he was doing for thinking about her.

Nina's first night back at Connie's Inn with the chorus girls was just as if she'd never been away. She did four routines and each time on the stage, she looked at the crowd and he didn't show up. Maybe that meant he wouldn't be there to pick her up. That was her thinking as she changed out of the outfit and into her clothes.

Addie walked up and stood next to Nina, who was still sitting. "Do you still plan to go with him if he is out front when we walk out?"

Nina looked up at her. "Maybe he won't show up. Maybe he changed his mind. After all, he wasn't in the club."

"Maybe he won't, but if he does, what do you plan to do?"

Nina got up and faced Addie. "I have to because if I don't, he's going to get you fired, and I'll feel guilty because I can stop that from happening."

"Girl, I really do think you should think about leaving Harlem. You're so naïve. Don't you know he's going to do that if you don't give in to all his demands? You can't be so naïve that you don't know what those demands are."

Nina took hold of Addie's arm and gently held it. "What will you do if I don't? You love dancing and you're so good at it."

Addie wriggled free from Nina's grasp on her arm and then placed both of her hands on Nina's arms. "Don't you dare give in to that monster because you're concerned about me. I've been in Harlem for ten years. I got here when I was your age and was as naïve as you are right now." She paused for a moment and smiled. "I took some lumps, but I've made it so far. If that happens, I'll find my way."

The bouncer stuck his head in the dressing room. "Let's go, ladies. You're the last two and we need to close up."

As Nina walked out of the club with Addie next to her, she looked directly at Larry, who was leaning against the limousine with the fur coat tucked under his arm. He stood straight up, held the fur coat out in front of him, and smiled.

"What are you going to do?" Addie whispered.

"I can't let him get you fired. You're my only friend, and I love you dearly. I'll be all right." She hugged Addie, turned, and strolled over to the limousine.

Larry opened the door to the limousine and as Nina walked past him, he tried to kiss her, but she turned her head and got in. He got in and closed the door. She moved to the end of the seat, leaning against the door. The limousine driver pulled out onto Seventh Avenue and headed toward Lower Manhattan.

Larry shoved the fur coat toward her. "I bought this for you, and I expect you to take it and wear it."

She didn't touch it, keeping her arms folded across her chest and looking straight ahead. "It comes with a price that I'm not willing to pay. Now please take me to my apartment."

"Why are you doing this?" His voice was extremely stern.

"Because I don't want to be what you expect me to be."

"And what is it you think I expect to be?"

"White," she shot back.

"What is wrong with you? Don't you realize there is nothing good for you as a Negro? You were given a gift of having white features and white beauty as a Negro and you want to throw that away?"

She finally turned and looked at him. "How dare you?" Anger rose in her voice.

He slid over toward her. She had nowhere to move. She was tempted but wasn't going to jump out of a moving vehicle into Seventh Avenue's traffic.

"You are one ungrateful little nigger bitch! I've given you what you never could have earned in a lifetime, and this is how you want to treat me? Well, you're not going to get away with it!"

He grabbed Nina and pulled her toward him and tried to kiss her. She turned her head to the side.

The sting across her face was excruciating. Her natural impulse was to strike back. She hit him with a fist that knocked him back.

He lunged forward and grabbed her by the throat and squeezed. She couldn't breathe, and as it worsened, she remembered her mother's advice from a long time ago. "If a white man ever attempts to rape you, grab him between his legs and squeeze with all the strength God has given you." She took her free hand, reached between his legs, and squeezed.

He shouted and released his grip around her throat. He wrapped both hands around the pain below his waist.

Nina sat back and rubbed her neck.

"Stop!" he shouted to the chauffeur.

The chauffeur pulled over to the curb and stopped the limousine.

Larry opened the door, snatched Nina, pulled her across his body, and threw her out of the car. She hit her head against the curb, and everything went dark.

The Sugar Cane Club was rocking with music and a floor full of dancers. It had been that way the entire night. When they weren't dancing, they made their way over to Sam Arthur and placed a bet. He was rolling in plenty of money, for some reason, everyone felt lucky, and he should have felt the same way, but didn't. He hadn't confronted Sonny about what he did over at Mary's apartment earlier in the day. He decided not to because that was just a country boy, being just that—a loudmouth country boy. He had lived that life for the first twenty-three years of his life, and there was no way he was going back. Willa Mae had made that decision quite easy. Now, he had to save his relationship with Mary. Just as that thought crossed his mind, she strolled into the club and walked on the other side, away from him.

The music ended, and the dancers returned to their tables. He could now clearly see her, but she didn't look his way. He noticed that her dress was not as provocative as in the past. She didn't appear to be her old seductive self.

"You need to go over there and talk to her," Sonny said, who had been quiet all evening and not his usual energetic self.

"She probably don't want to talk to me," he scowled. "You took care of that."

"Go on over there and talk to her. Tell her that you're no longer tied to the other woman."

Sam Arthur handed the money pouch to Sonny and hurried across the dance floor before the music began. Mary saw him coming and instantly walked further toward the bandstand. He caught up with her.

"Mary, stop. Listen to me. Willa Mae done gone back home and don't really want to be bothered with me."

Mary turned and looked at him. "How about you? You still want to be bothered with her?"

"I want to be bothered with you. Mary, you been good to me, and I want to be good to you other than giving money every once in a while."

"What you saying, Sam Arthur?"

"I'm saying there's no longer a Willa Mae in my life, and hopefully there's a Mary."

Mary's demeanor softened. "What happened? I thought you was over there with her all day?"

The music started, and the dancers flooded back onto the dance floor. Sam Arthur took Mary by the arm and moved away from the bandstand.

"Don't matter what happened. What matters is that I'm gonna make a commitment to you and Henry to get you out of that dump where you live and make you an honest woman if you'll have me."

"Sam Arthur don't play with me. You saying you going to marry me?"

"Ain't that the right thing to do?"

She jumped into his arms. The dancers all stopped and looked over at them. The band stopped playing momentarily. Sonny smiled from the other side of the room.

Mary shouted, while in his arms, "He's going to marry me!"

The dancers all clapped and shouted, "Way to go, Sam Arthur."

The music started up, and the dancers began dancing again.

21.

NINA WOKE UP IN A bed with pain rushing throughout her body. She tried to smile as she looked at Addie sitting in a chair next to the bed.

"Where am I?"

"Harlem Hospital. They brought you in here last night."

"I guess I was wrong." It was a struggle for her to speak.

"Don't try to talk. You took a pretty serious blow to your head."

She frowned. "Do I have a scar on my face?"

"No, you don't. You landed on the back of your head." Addie paused for a moment, then continued. "Do you recall what happened?"

Nina grimaced as she adjusted her body in the bed. "Can you believe that bastard hit me, and I hit him back? He choked me and when I grabbed his private parts, he threw me out of the car, and I don't remember nothing after that."

Addie broke out laughing and in between her laughter, she said, "You grabbed him by his balls and squeezed?"

Nina tried to laugh. "Yeah, just as tight as I could."

After a few more moments of laughter, Addie took on a more serious demeanor. "We both were fired. I went by the club this morning and Immerman gave me a check and a check for your one night and told me that was it. I didn't put up a fuss because I knew it was coming."

"Oh, no, Addie, I'm sorry." Nina sighed.

"Girl, don't worry about me. I know how to survive in this place." She reached over and touched Nina on the arm. "But what about you?"

"I don't know." Nina rubbed the side of her head. "I guess I have to figure it out."

"Are you in pain?"

"Just a little."

The nurse walked into the room. "How are you feeling?"

"Like I want to go home," Nina replied.

"You can do that, but if you develop headaches, come on back in here." The nurse walked to the door but stopped. "What happened to you? They picked you up off the street in Lower Manhattan."

"I have made all the wrong decisions in life and that was the result."

"Well, I pray you'll make better decisions going forward with your life." The nurse walked out of the room.

Nina struggled to put on her clothes. She concentrated on the nurse's words. All along, she had made the wrong decisions from the time she decided to come to Harlem to the time she snubbed Claude to the momentary decision to reject her race. As she finished dressing and followed Addie out of the room, she would not make those same mistakes going forward. Dancing was not the most important thing a person should strive for, happiness was.

Sam Arthur held Henry with one arm and Mary's hand with the other. They walked into the apartment building at 580 St. Nicholas and to the manager's office. As he reached for the door to open it, Mary pulled on his hand, stopping him.

"What's wrong?" he asked her.

"This is so fancy. You sure you can afford this place?"

Sam Arthur chuckled. "I'm sure."

"But are they going to rent to us? This is where the dicties live and they won't want us around."

"They don't own it. The white man does, and he'll rent to anybody can afford it."

"I don't know, Sam Arthur, this is way above me."

"You want to go back to your old apartment?" He smiled.

"Oh, no, never."

"Then let's go in here and get our new home."

"Thank you, Sam Arthur. I'm going to make a good wife and the mother of our babies."

"This is only the start of what I got planned for us."

Still standing at the door to the office, Mary asked, "What do you mean?"

"Just like I done saved all this money for us to move in here, I'm gonna save more so we can open our own business."

"What kind of business?"

"A restaurant so you can show off all your cooking skills you learned from your mama and your grandma."

"I love it and I love you, Sam Arthur."

Together, they walked into the manager's office, holding hands.

⁂

With all his notes in order, Marcus began writing, but stopped after only five lines. Helen's words flooded his thoughts and took over. He had all along been confident that she would come around and join him in Harlem. Once in the environment with the best Negro poets in the country, she would recognize the value of being there, but that didn't happen and, as much as he liked Harlem, he loved Helen. Maybe it was time to go home and write his story. He picked up the phone and dialed Abbott's number, who picked up on the first ring.

"Marcus, have you come to your senses and ready to come home?" He did not wait for an answer. "There is a lot happening in Chicago and I need you here to cover it."

Marcus smiled and thought that first he needed him to cover the hottest story in Negro America, and now he needed him to cover the hottest one in Chicago. What would be next, the West Coast? He didn't respond with those thoughts.

"I have given my best effort to at least get Helen to come here and see what Harlem has to offer, but that never worked."

"No, it didn't, and I'll tell you why. Are you listening?"

"You bet I am."

"Good, because not every Negro in this country is unhappy or miserable with where they live, so they see no need to up and relocate there." Abbott paused. Marcus said nothing, so he continued. "Most of the Negroes flocking to Harlem are running from something. But not everyone is running. They are staying and if there are problems where they live, they fight them. If there are changes that need to be made, they make them. But they stay home, and this is your wife. Helen."

"She is excited because the artists there are determined to create their own renaissance. And now that she has the help of Mrs. Barnett, she's almost beside herself."

"Don't you dare ask her to give that up. But I have to go. I'll look for you in the next week." Abbott hung up.

Marcus sat there, again in deep thought. Abbott's final words, "Don't you dare ask her to give that up," struck a nerve. He recalled the first day he asked her to support what he was going to do. She said she would, or he would probably never forgive her. Now it was his turn to make the sacrifice, and that was what he knew he must do, and he would do. He packed up his notes and walked out of the office and walked out of Harlem.

Washington, DC

NINA HAD LEFT HARLEM EARLY in the morning, taking a bus down to Washington, DC. The day after she left Harlem Hospital, she spent her time considering whether she still had a future there. Addie, the one friend she had in that city, was always truthful with her. She told Nina that her ambitions and her naivete about the vicious world of Harlem had led to her demise, even before she really got started.

Early on when she first arrived, Ethel and Regina had warned her about the danger for a young girl who just arrived there to take a job dancing in a club that didn't even allow Negroes inside. Addie warned her about getting involved with a white man who really meant her no good. Addie also advised her not to get involved with the Lower Manhattan white crowd—none of which cared about Negroes—and not to join the Ziegfeld Follies. And her final advice to her was to get down to Washington, DC, and try to save her relationship with the young man that Addie had never met, but knew he couldn't be any worse for her than what Nina had experienced there. Having rejected all of Addie's advice, this time she would heed it.

She got out of the cab in front of Howard University and walked onto the campus, having no idea where she was going. She recalled right before Claude left that Sunday morning, when she had been so rude to him, that he had a part-time job with Professor Woodson. She stopped a young girl wearing an AKA sweater.

"Can you help me?"

"What is it you want? If you want to find out about pledging Alpha, I can give you the name of our leader here on campus."

"No, I'm looking for Professor Woodson's office."

"Oh, that's easy." She pointed to a building. "That's it, over there."

"Thank you."

She slowly made her way into the building and stood in the lobby with no idea what room was the correct one.

A young student walked out of a room down the hall and came toward Nina. He stopped when he got to her. "Are you lost?"

"Oh, thank you. Can you help me find Professor Woodson's office?"

He pointed to the room. "It's the room I just came out of." He started walking away.

"Excuse me," Nina called out.

The boy stopped and turned around. "What is it?"

"Do you know a student, Claude Lee?"

"Absolutely." He smiled widely. "He's the president of our freshman class."

Nina pointed to the room the student had come out of. "Is he in there?"

"Sure is. Want me to get him for you?"

"No, thank you."

Nina walked over to the office, opened the door, and stepped inside.

Standing behind the counter, Claude looked up from a paper he was reading. He looked at Nina's suitcase in her hand.

They stood in place—Nina just inside the room and Claude behind the counter—staring at each other. He finally broke the silence.

"Nina, what are you doing here?"

She smiled. "I think that's what I asked you when you surprised me and showed up in Harlem. And I think you said, 'I had to see you.' Well, it's my turn. I had to see you."

Claude came from behind the counter. "Is this just a visit?"

"That's up to you."

"You're not planning on going back to Harlem?"

"Like I said, that's up to you."

Excitedly and with joy resonating in his voice, he asked, "I got my Nina back?"

"Again, that's up to you."

He hurried over and put both arms around her. "I have been taking dancing lessons and getting better than when we were in high school. You going to stick around so I can show how well I can now dance?"

She moved in close to him. "Once again, Claude Lee, that's up to you."

"If it's up to me, then I promise you that you'll never be sorry if you really do mean it."

"I do."

They kissed and held each other like they had never done before.

EPILOGUE

SAM ARTHUR KEPT HIS promise, saved enough money, and opened a restaurant on the corner of Eighth Avenue and 136th Street. He dedicated all his time to running the restaurant because Mary's secret regarding the fifty dollars was used to attend beauty college and become a beautician. When she graduated, she went to work at Madam C. J. Walker's Beauty Parlor at 108 West 136th Street, not far from the restaurant. They bought a brownstone home on Striver's Row on West 139th Street between Seventh and Eighth Avenues. Sam Arthur became involved in Reverend Adam Clayton Powell Jr.'s political campaigns as a contributor to his election as the first Negro Congressman from the state of New York.

⁂

CLAUDE AND NINA WERE MARRIED while he continued his studies at Howard University. He went on to law school there and accepted an appointment as a Professor of Constitutional Law after he completed his courses and passed the bar exam. He worked closely with Charles Hamilton Houston on civil rights cases and was an advisor to Thurgood Marshall. Nina opened a dance studio on 7th Street, four blocks from Howard. Her dance troupe performed several recitals at Constitution Hall with the assistance of First Lady Eleanor

Roosevelt. Her only return to New York came when her dance troupe performed at Carnegie Hall.

MARCUS'S FOUR-PART ARTICLE ON THE Harlem Renaissance appeared in the *Chicago Defender* and received several awards. Working closely with Helen, he assisted Vivian Gordon to establish the George Cleveland Hall Branch Library located at 4801 South Michigan Avenue as the intellectual center for Negroes. It was similar to 135th Street Library in Harlem. Helen became one of the many poets who performed their works there. Richard Wright and Gwendolyn Brooks did many readings at the library. Marcus conducted interviews with the artists who performed at the library just as he did in Harlem for the collection on Negro history and literature. He never returned to Harlem.

About the Author

Frederick Williams is one of the original founders of the Black Studies Minor at University of Texas at San Antonio, where he taught courses to include: Novelists of the Harlem Renaissance; African American Literature from Phyllis Wheatley to the Black Arts Movement; African American Political Thought; African American Politics; Politics of the Civil Rights Movement; and Introduction to African American Studies.

Among Mr. Williams five published novels are *The Nomination, Beyond Redemption,* and *Just Loving You,* and historical novels, *Fires of Greenwood: Tulsa Riot of 1921* and *Bayard and Martin: A Historical Novel About a Friendship and the Civil Rights Movement.* He is also the editor of two anthologies: *Black is the Color of Strength* and *Black is the Color of Love.*

In 2022, Mr. Williams completed the screenplay, *Heroes of Black Wall Street.*

Mr. Williams is the host of *Contemporary Black Voices* a Black Video Network show on YouTube. He lives right outside San Antonio, Texas, with his wife Venetta and grandson Jordan.